WANT SOME *REAL* EXCITEMENT? GET READY FOR THE *REAL* DEAL.

Here are Frank and Joe Hardy, full force and in your face—a triple-header of nonstop action and adventure!

THE HARDY BOYS CASEFILES™ COLLECTOR'S EDITION

It's a crime-busting blowout, packed with mystery, intrigue, and danger!

From the first page to the last, here are three supercharged stories in one super book!

Books in THE HARDY BOYS CASEFILES™ Series

Available from ARCHWAY Paperbacks

THE
HARDY
BOYS

CASEFILES™
COLLECTOR'S EDITION

FRANKLIN W. DIXON

AN ARCHWAY PAPERBACK
Published by POCKET BOOKS
New York London Toronto Sydney Tokyo Singapore

AN ARCHWAY PAPERBACK *Original*

An Archway Paperback published by
POCKET BOOKS, a division of Simon & Schuster Inc.
1230 Avenue of the Americas, New York, NY 10020

Diplomatic Deceit copyright © 1990 by Simon & Schuster Inc.
Flesh and Blood copyright © 1990 by Simon & Schuster Inc.
Fright Wave copyright © 1990 by Simon & Schuster Inc.
Produced by Mega-Books, Inc.

ISBN: 0-671-02033-1

First Archway Paperback printing May 1998

10 9 8 7 6 5 4 3 2 1

THE HARDY BOYS, AN ARCHWAY PAPERBACK and colophon are registered trademarks of Simon & Schuster Inc.

THE HARDY BOYS CASEFILES is a trademark of Simon & Schuster Inc.

Cover design by Jim Lebbad

Printed in the U.S.A.

IL 6+

DIPLOMATIC DECEIT

Chapter

1

"Do you think we should get out of the cab in case Callie explodes?" Joe Hardy's blue eyes danced with laughter as he leaned forward in his seat to see past Callie Shaw. He wanted to hear what his brother on the other side of the cab was going to say.

Frank Hardy gave his kid brother a grin and slipped an arm around his girlfriend, Callie, who was between them. "Oh, I don't think she's ready to explode," he said in a low, teasing voice. "Not yet, at least."

Callie threw out her arms, shaking her head so her blond hair flew around her head. "Okay, so I'm excited—why not? I've been thinking about nothing but this trip for three weeks now, ever

1

since Madeleine and her family came to America.''

"Tell me about it," Joe said sarcastically.

Callie ignored the remark. "When you've got a foreign pen pal, you don't expect to meet him or her. I knew from Maddy's letters that her father was a French diplomat, but I never expected him to come to Washington. Now I can actually meet my friend, after swapping letters all these years.''

Joe rolled his eyes. "So, Frank, did you know about this mysterious correspondence? Maybe Callie has other pen pals, like a handsome Swede or a soulful Slav with dark gypsy eyes.''

Frank Hardy stretched his six-foot-one frame. "Well, Callie? Have you been two-timing me through the international mail?" The twinkle in his dark eyes showed he was only kidding.

Callie batted her eyelashes playfully. "I'll never tell.''

The cab made its way along the parkway from National Airport to the city of Washington. As they passed the military cemetery at Arlington, Virginia, they admired the bright spring flowers planted in front of the white stone gateposts. The beautiful landmark meant they were close to the bridge that crossed the Potomac River, separating Virginia from the capital city.

"This is the way I always think of Washington—everything white and classical," Frank said as they pulled onto the bridge. Even the bridge's

2

safety rail was held up by little white concrete pillars. The joggers and bike riders who swarmed over the bridge, however, weren't dressed in white Roman togas.

Callie couldn't concentrate on the local scenery. She was much too excited. "I've been writing to Maddy Berot since I was thirteen. She's like a close friend and now I'm finally going to meet her."

"How are you going to recognize her?" Joe asked.

"I've got a recent picture in here." Callie began digging through her purse. "Maddy asked me to bring all her old letters. She's kept all of mine. We thought we'd go through them and have some laughs." She kept rummaging through a thick bundle of papers. "Here it is."

She held up a snapshot of a girl with short dark hair whose smile seemed to leap off the photograph.

Joe leaned forward for a better look. "Hey, she's pretty," he said. "I'm beginning to feel a lot better about this trip."

Frank shook his head. "You know, Callie, you could have saved us a whole lot of kicking and screaming from little brother here. All you had to do was show him that picture when you first asked him to come with us."

"You mean he didn't want to tag along?" Callie spoke with just a bit too much innocence in her voice. "I thought the world-famous Hardy Boys did everything together."

"Not exactly *everything*." Frank winked at her.

"Just when it comes to crime," Joe cut in. The Hardys actually did have a reputation for cracking mysteries and tackling tough crimes. But both Frank and Joe were happy for a rest after their last adventure, *Danger Zone*. Crime fighting had come a little too close to home when they'd had to rescue their own mother from kidnappers. They were determined that this trip should be just for fun.

Joe took the photo of Callie's pen pal and studied it. "If Maddy was a crook, I guess I could force myself to romance her to get the necessary information—"

"Yeah, yeah." Callie shook her head.

Joe put a hand on his chest. "Come on, Callie, *I'm* the one who's doing you a favor. I'm being a nice guy and going out with Maddy—"

"I'll tell you right now, Joe Hardy, I've warned Maddy about you." Callie waved a finger in his face.

Turning to his brother, Joe just raised his eyebrows. "Hear that, Frank? Callie wrote Maddy and warned her about me. I wonder what those letters say about you?"

Callie stuffed the photo and letters back in her purse. "You'll never find out," she told them.

"Maddy and I will go over these later—when we're *alone*."

She gave both the Hardys a suspicious look. "In fact, I'm going to leave these letters with Maddy—just so some people won't get the bright idea of snooping in my hotel room. I know how clever you guys are with locks and things."

Joe fell back against the seat with a pained expression on his face. "I'm shocked and hurt that you'd think Frank is capable of doing such a thing," he said, shaking his head.

"I wasn't thinking about Frank," Callie told him.

Pretending to be offended, Joe drew himself up. "Well, I hope Maddy will be nicer to me than you are, but I don't know if she will if you've been poisoning her mind against me."

"Well, we're here," Callie announced as they passed under the portico of the hotel. It was one of the glistening new brick-and-concrete buildings in the city's northwestern corner. She glanced at her watch. "We should have lots of time to check in and unpack before we head for Maddy's apartment."

"A brilliant young Frenchwoman," Joe said. "I can feel myself losing my heart already."

"Well, it may work out—as long as you don't open your mouth," Callie said, a serious note in her voice.

The doorman rescued Joe by opening the cab

5

door just then. "I'll take care of the bags," Joe said. "You guys go on in and register." Before he got out of the cab, he turned to Callie. "I don't suppose you have anything else you'd like to leave with me—those heavy letters, for instance?"

Callie laughed. "Keep dreaming."

A few minutes later the Hardys were in their room, checked in and unpacking their bags. "Another episode of the Joe and Callie Show," Frank said, shaking his head. "You know, you guys argue like an old married couple."

"I thought we were kidding around," Joe answered, dumping his socks and underwear into a drawer. "Jealous of all the attention Callie pays me?" He grinned. "No worries there. I've got a date with a beautiful French girl. What do you say we enjoy this visit to Washington? It should be a lot better than the last time we were down here."

Frank nodded. "Quieter, at least." The last time they'd been in Washington, they were attending a counterterrorism seminar. Callie had been involved in a hijacking and had nearly gotten killed before the boys figured out how to get onto the plane to rescue her.

"You're right, Joe," he said. "This time around, all we have to worry about is you—and whether you make a fool of yourself over Madeleine Berot." They headed out the door and down

6

the hall to the elevator. "I wonder if Monsieur Berot is here for the exhibit of the Lafayette sword."

"I didn't know he was into fencing," Joe said.

Frank couldn't believe Joe hadn't heard of the Lafayette sword. "It's an artifact that belongs to the French government. I read about it in the *Bayport Times*. At the lowest point in the American Revolutionary War, a young French nobleman, the Marquis de Lafayette, came here to help the Americans win. Grateful officers from the Continental Army presented him with a sword with a jeweled hilt or handle."

"Valuable, huh?" Joe said as they rode down in the elevator.

"Not just for the gold and jewels," Frank said. "The blade was personally inscribed by George Washington."

The elevator stopped, and they stepped out to find Callie waiting for them in the lobby.

"Ready to go?" She slid her purse strap up onto her shoulder and led the way to the door. "The Berots' place is close enough for us to walk."

Moving from the air-conditioned coolness of the lobby into the brilliant sunshine outside was like stepping into a warm, humid shower room. Frank paused for a second to catch his breath, but Callie plowed straight ahead, right past the doorman.

After she stepped from under the hotel portico, Callie turned back to the Hardys to tell them to hurry up. Just at that moment Frank saw a tall, pale man in black jeans, a tight black T-shirt, and sunglasses running behind Callie on the sidewalk. He was aimed right for her—his arm straight out.

He didn't bump into her. He ran up to her and shoved. Callie tottered for an instant before falling to her knees. The assailant swooped down and reached for her, but not to help her. He helped himself instead.

Callie's purse was in his hands as he took off.

Chapter
2

FOR A BRIEF SECOND everyone froze. It was like a scene from a bad dream. Callie was down on the ground, the doorman stood staring, and Frank and Joe were rooted in place. The only one moving was the man with Callie's purse—he was halfway down the block.

Joe broke out first and burst into motion, taking off after the purse snatcher. Frank hurtled forward next, joining the pursuit. Behind them, the doorman blew his whistle, trying to attract a police officer.

Frank grinned without humor as he heard the shrill blast and kept on running. In his experience, there was never a cop around when you needed one.

He broke stride as he reached Callie, who had

gotten to her hands and knees. His girlfriend waved him on. "Forget about me—get that creep."

Frank kept on pounding along the pavement, trying to catch up with Joe, who was far ahead now. The man in black, however, was outdistancing them both. He whipped around the first corner, and by the time Joe reached it, the short block to his right was empty.

Joe didn't slow down, however. He pushed down that street to the next corner, where a street cut across the one he was on. Glancing right then left, Frank caught just a fleeting impression of a figure in black tearing around the far corner.

"This way," Joe gasped, pointing the way for his brother, who had caught up to him.

Rounding the next corner, they faced a large boulevard, with a huge open traffic circle beyond. The purse snatcher in black was weaving in and out of the midafternoon crowd. No one said anything to him. He only got a couple of annoyed glances—that was all. The guy moved too quickly for people to focus on him.

Frank realized that if he yelled the traditional "Stop that man!" people would hesitate a second and the guy would get past. No, they had to continue to chase him—and get him, too.

There was no place for the thief to hide. Frank and his brother could see around them for about four square blocks.

"How does this guy think he can lose us here?" Joe said.

"Maybe he doesn't know the neighborhood either," Frank panted as he kept up the pace.

The man in black didn't slow down. He darted through unseen gaps in the crowd like a running back on the way to the end zone. Apparently, he did know the area. He zigzagged through the traffic passing around the traffic circle, extending his lead over the Hardys. As they got closer, Frank and Joe saw their quarry run straight for a large concrete structure that looked like a gigantic funnel leading deep into the ground.

Joe skidded to a halt and turned to a young man walking by. "What's that?" he asked, pointing.

"Metro station," the passerby answered.

Frank dashed up at that moment. "The Washington subway—remember?"

Ahead of them, the purse snatcher was already beginning a broken-field run down the escalator to the train station and platform.

Joe leaped into the street, paying no attention to the taxi hurtling toward him. The brakes screeched as the cab swerved to another lane. Leaning out the window, the cab driver shouted something in a foreign language.

Frank took a deep breath and plunged into the traffic, too. It was like playing "chicken"—without a car. He had to dodge around and sidestep a couple of times.

At last they were across the street and on the escalator. The thief was already at the bottom. Frank and Joe got lots of dirty looks as they jostled their way down to the station lobby.

"There he is—running through a turnstile," Frank said, pointing.

Joe jumped the last few yards of the escalator and landed ready to run full tilt for the turnstiles. There he stopped dead, fumbling in his pockets. "How much is the fare?"

"Hey, kid, you have to go back and get a fare card." One of the regular subway riders pointed over his shoulder to a bank of what looked like vending machines. People were stepping up to them, slipping in coins and bills, and coming away with little computerized cards. Then they slipped the cards through a groove in the turnstile machines to enter the subway system.

Joe yanked out a handful of change and headed for the machines, but Frank grabbed his arm to stop him. The guy they'd been chasing was heading down another escalator. Below, they could hear a train arriving. "Too late, Joe," Frank said. "We've lost him."

Frank thought the trip back to the hotel seemed a lot longer than the journey out. Maybe that was because he and Joe had run one way, but were dragging their feet coming back.

12

Callie was standing in front of the hotel, where she was talking to a young police officer. He nodded very seriously as he took down her statement in his notebook. From the look on her face, he hadn't given her very much hope. "Did you catch the guy?" she asked eagerly as Frank walked up.

He shook his head. "He got away into the Metro station a few blocks away."

The police officer just shook his head. "I'm sorry to say this, but I think your chances of ever seeing that bag—and its contents—are pretty slim."

Callie's shoulders sagged. Frank went over and put an arm around her. "Are you okay?"

"I've just got a couple of bruises, but, Frank, all my money for the trip was in that purse!" She shook her head. "I guess I'm lucky that I brought it in traveler's checks, but all of Madeleine's letters were in there, too. I was going to leave them in the hotel, but she called and insisted that I bring them."

"Speaking of calls, maybe you should get on the phone to the Berots," Frank suggested. "They're probably wondering where we are."

Callie called and arranged to visit the Berots after she spoke to the desk clerk about replacing her traveler's checks.

The Berot family had settled in an old-fashioned brick apartment house not far from the hotel. It was an easy walk—now that there were no interruptions. Callie found the name Henri Berot on the intercom, and after a few moments she and her friends were buzzed into the building.

They arrived on the fifth floor to find an apartment door open and a tall, slim man standing in the doorway. He had thin, sharp features—a hatchet face, Frank's father would have called it—and his graying hair receded at the temples, forming a dramatic widow's peak. "Mademoiselle Shaw?" he said, a brief smile passing across his face. "And these are your friends? I am Henri Berot. Please come in."

Mr. Berot's smile faded as Callie and the Hardys followed him inside. Joe noticed that he immediately double-locked the door. "I am sorry for your trouble," the diplomat said. "This is a very dangerous city." He frowned. "Such lawlessness. Snatching of purses would not be tolerated back home."

Frank's eyebrows rose. "Well, Mr. Berot, whole countries can't be judged by looking at one city—or one area. I wouldn't judge France by the fact that it has so many trained gangs of child pickpockets."

Mr. Berot stiffened, offended. "You are insulting, Mr. Hardy. Has your pocket been picked in France? Your friend was stolen from *here*. If you think your home is safer, perhaps you should go back there."

He went on for several moments, his voice rising in anger at the "offense" to his homeland.

"Some diplomat," Callie whispered.

"Nice work, Frank," Joe added in a low voice. "We haven't even made it into the living room and you start World War Three—with France."

They could hardly understand what Mr. Berot was saying, since as his tirade went on he spoke more and more French. Just as he reached the shouting stage, two women appeared from the living room. A blond, middle-aged woman in a plain black dress rubbed her hands together nervously, then took Callie's hands in hers. "I am Sylvie Berot," she said. "And this, of course, is Madeleine—"

Sailing out from behind Madame Berot came a slim girl in jeans and a black satin baseball jacket. She grabbed Callie by the hands, kissed her on both cheeks, then turned angrily to her father.

Joe squinted, surprised. Maddy in person was a lot less pretty than her picture. Her voice was also high and whiny as she began arguing with her dad. Joe couldn't understand what they were saying. Both Berots spoke very rapidly in French. He glanced at Callie, who had taken French in school.

"Maddy's saying something about being tired of staying cooped up in the apartment. She wants to go out with us," she whispered.

While Callie and the Hardys stood in embar-

15

rassment, listening to an obvious argument, Mr. Berot finally turned to Mrs. Berot. She shook her head helplessly. He shrugged and abruptly held out an arm to escort his wife from the room.

Madeleine watched them go, then turned with a bright smile. "We can go out!" she said. "Callie, you have not introduced your friends."

"Maddy"—Callie turned to Joe and Frank—"I'd like you to meet—"

"What is this *Maddy?*" The smile quickly disappeared from the girl's face. "My name is Madeleine."

Callie blinked in puzzlement. "But in your letters . . ." Her voice trailed off.

"Hey, Madeleine," Joe tried to fill in. "We're sorry if—"

The French girl cut him off. "Not Mad-duh-linn," she said, mimicking Joe's pronunciation, making him feel like a real idiot. "It is a beautiful French name." She said it for him. "Madh-lenn."

"Okay, Modd . . . uh, Mah-deh-lenn." Frank watched the color glow in Joe's face as he stumbled over the name. Usually Joe picked up foreign words easily. Frank knew it was the unfriendly audience that made him hesitate now. It didn't help him to like Madeleine any better.

Madeleine rolled her eyes. "Maybe it's better that you call me Maddy," she said.

"Great family," Joe muttered to Frank as they headed for the elevator.

16

Frank nodded. "Very friendly."

"So," Callie said as they got into the elevator. "Where would you like to go, Maddy?"

Madeleine immediately took Callie's arm. "Shopping," she said with another dazzling smile.

Callie glanced over at Frank. "That might not be much fun for the boys. I thought maybe we could grab a snack and talk—"

"We can do that, too," Madeleine said. "But first, we shop."

They headed down Connecticut Avenue, popping in and out of the expensive boutiques that lined the street. Frank and Joe sighed and rolled their eyes as Callie and Madeleine flitted from skirts to shorts, from blouses to silk scarves.

Maddy was like a little kid, grabbing Callie's arm to show her a special item, hugging her. That brilliant smile kept lighting up her face.

Callie smiled back, but Frank thought she looked a little embarrassed as Maddy got louder and more excited. It was almost as if she'd never seen really good clothes before. How could that be when she came from Paris, the world capital of fashion?

Frank and Joe finally stopped going into the stores when the girls entered. They just watched through the window as Maddy moved through shops like a whirlwind, throwing an arm around

17

Callie to point out a special bargain or a beautiful outfit.

They stopped by the door to check a display of scarves, Maddy giggling and hugging Callie again.

As the girls came out, Frank asked, "More stores? Or have you had enough yet?"

"I've think I've had enough," Callie said. "Everything we've seen here I couldn't afford. How about you, Maddy?"

"Oh, I don't know—" Madeleine suddenly broke off. "What have you got there?"

The French girl pointed to the pocket of Callie's jacket, where a tiny piece of brightly colored fabric stuck out. Maddy tugged on it, pulling out a silk scarf—just like the ones the girls had admired inside the store.

"Callie, I never guessed. You are a clever one!" Madeleine burst out, handing the scarf back.

"Not so clever," a cold voice came from behind them.

The kids turned to see a salesclerk standing in the doorway. Her blond hair was wrapped in a bun, and her icy gray eyes were staring hard at Callie.

She pointed at the scarf in Callie's hands. "Most shoplifters don't flaunt stolen goods right in front of the store they took them from."

Chapter

3

CALLIE'S FACE went from bright red to dead white. "W-what are you talking about?" she asked, staring at the blond woman in the doorway.

"I'm talking about that scarf you just stole." The saleswoman's face was grim as she gestured to the door. "Now come back inside and we'll see what other 'bargains' you and your friend picked up."

The woman's glare included the Hardys. "You guys, too. They may have passed something on to you."

The four teens stood in a huddle by a rear counter, getting sidelong glances from customers as the manager of the store demanded IDs from them. Callie appeared to be numb as the manager turned to her. "I—I don't have any," she stammered. "I just got into town, and my purse was stolen—"

The manager cut her off with a toss of her red curls. At any other time, Joe might have considered her pretty. He didn't right then, though—not with that superior sneer on her face. "Look, don't try some stupid sob story on me—I've heard them all. Now, how about some ID?"

Callie shrugged helplessly. "It's all been stolen. My friends will tell you what happened, and the police—"

"Oh, don't worry, honey, the police are coming, all right." The manager looked up as the saleswoman rejoined them. "You called the cops?" she asked.

The saleswoman nodded. "They're on their way."

"Police?" Callie repeated, still in a daze from the turn of events.

"That's what you usually do when you catch a thief," the salesclerk said.

"Take this one into the dressing room." The manager pointed to Callie. "I want her searched—thoroughly." The young woman moved to the Hardys. "You guys turn out your pockets on the counter, here."

Robotlike, Callie began to reach into her pockets, as well.

"Not you," the manager snapped. "I told you

20

already—you're going in the back for a full search.''

Callie recoiled from the angry face glaring at her. "This has never—I mean, I've never—" she began haltingly, but the other woman cut her off.

" 'Done this before in my life?' " The red-haired woman's voice mimicked Callie's. "Well, maybe you should have thought of that before you tried to take something that didn't belong to you."

The saleswoman took Callie's arm. She was shaking as she was led off a couple of steps. She glanced back at Frank, her tear-filled eyes begging him to do something to help.

"Let's just cut this nonsense right now." Frank's voice was angry as he stepped forward to protect his girlfriend. "You'll see from our ID that I'm Frank Hardy and this is my brother Joe."

"Hardy, huh?" The manager was definitely not impressed. "As far as I know, we don't have a Senator Hardy. So who are you? Some congressman's kids? Or maybe your dad is a big mucka-muck at the State Department?" She seemed rather amused by Frank's outburst. "We get all kinds here."

Frank sighed. This wasn't Bayport, where people knew the Hardys and their reputation. And from the look of things, claiming a famous detective for a father wasn't going to cut much ice with this woman.

Like it or not, Frank—and Callie—would have to put up with a lot of flak until the Washington police checked with Chief Collig back in Bayport. Frank tried to dig up the name of any of his dad's friends on the D.C. force. No luck.

"Let's just get on with it," the woman said. Callie was marched to the back.

Frank's mind had already leaped ahead to the next problem—the police. Callie had been caught with a stolen scarf in her pocket. That would be hard to explain—even if he got a sympathetic ear from one of his father's friends. He knew Callie hadn't shoplifted!

He said so to the manager, but she only shrugged.

"Kids think the world owes them everything—always coming in here trying to lift stuff. Rich kids, college kids, even tourists," the woman growled, checking out the Hardys' Bayport High IDs.

The manager whirled on Madeleine. "Don't you grin, girlie. You're the next one going back to be searched."

That got her a murderous glare from the French girl.

The saleswoman returned. "This one is clean—all she had was the scarf." Callie walked behind the woman, her clothes rumpled and her face a picture of humiliation. Tears began to spill out of her eyes. "I don't know how that scarf got in my jacket, but I didn't put it there," she insisted.

Neither the saleswoman nor the store manager listened to her. "This one goes next," the manager said, pointing to Madeleine.

The French girl looked ready to deck the two women. "No one touches me," she snarled.

Glancing out the store window, the manager shrugged. "I see the cops are here. They can take care of searching her at the station."

Two police officers entered. "These the kids?" they asked the manager, pointing to the Hardys and the girls.

The woman nodded. "Hold on a moment," she said, stepping into the back of the store. A moment later she reappeared, holding a videocassette. "Another piece of evidence. We tape everything that goes on in the store. You'll probably have a lovely shot of Blondie over there stealing the scarf." Without another glance at the kids, she turned to a customer.

The ride to the local police station was quiet and cramped. All four kids were squashed into the back of the police squad car. Callie cried quietly the entire way. Frank held her hand, his face stiff. When he found out who was responsible for getting Callie in trouble, he'd make the person pay—and pay hard.

Madeleine squirmed in her seat, then grabbed Callie's free hand. "Don't worry," she said. "Everything will turn out okay. I'll take care of it."

Callie stared at her for a second. "How?" she finally asked.

They arrived at the station and were unceremoniously led into a waiting room. After they'd spent almost an hour sitting on a wooden bench, a man in shirtsleeves and a shoulder holster came in.

"I'm Detective Cook," he said. "Follow me." They filed silently along to what looked like an interrogation room. This one, however, had a television set and a VCR. The policeman gestured to a group of wooden chairs spread out in front of the set. "We thought you might like to see this," he said, punching a button.

On the TV screen, the image of the boutique appeared. The angle of the shot was weird—it seemed to come from the ceiling. Of course, Frank realized, that's where the security cameras must be hidden.

In spite of the strange point of view, the picture was clear. There were Frank and Joe standing outside the window, pacing up and down as if they were bored out of their minds. And there, by the doorway, were Callie and Madeleine, looking at the scarves.

Maddy turned to Callie with a big grin, hugging

her. At the same time the French girl slipped the gaily colored silk scarf into Callie's pocket.

Callie jumped in her seat as if it were electrified. She turned to Madeleine, her eyes still red with tears. "*You* did this to me?" she finally managed to say.

"Oh, Callie," Madeleine said, grabbing her hands, "I am so, so sorry. It was only supposed to be a little *plaisanterie,* a joke. Then that fool of a salesgirl came out and made so much trouble. I . . . didn't know what to say."

She turned to the detective, giving him her 150-watt smile. "These are my American friends, you see," she said, her French accent becoming a bit more pronounced. "I met them today for the first time. What I did with the scarf, that was only a joke."

Maddy patted Callie's shoulder. "Poor Callie, here, she had her purse stolen. So I thought to make her laugh, you see? I would have paid for the scarf, but the woman wouldn't listen, and the manager was insulting to me. I will pay now, and then everything will be okay, yes?" Joe thought that Maddy looked downright cute as she looked up at Detective Cook.

The frowning police officer didn't seem to think so, however. He was shaking his head. "I'm afraid it isn't as easy as that," he said. "The manager of the store has sworn out a complaint for theft. You admit you took the scarf without paying for it. Under the law—"

Madeleine's face turned ugly as she glared at the man. "What do I care about the American law?" she burst out. "I am a French citizen."

"That doesn't—" Detective Cook started, but Maddy cut him off again.

With a contemptuous toss of her head, she said, "*And* I have diplomatic immunity."

Chapter

4

JOE HARDY FELT as if he were watching a very fast tennis game. His eyes moved back and forth from Maddy to Callie, to Frank, who looked as if he were going to burst a blood vessel when he heard Maddy was responsible for the whole mess. His eyes darted back to Maddy when she claimed diplomatic immunity.

She dug through her bag and came up with a small blue booklet, which she pressed into Detective Cook's hand.

He paged through it, sighed, and went to the door. "Our shoplifter has a French diplomatic passport. Better call Lieutenant Grant."

They had a much shorter wait for this investigator than for the station house detective. I guess international incidents get a lot faster service from the D.C. police, Joe thought.

Lieutenant Grant turned out to be a tall black man, dressed in a well-cut gray silk suit. Comparing his expensive clothes to the rumpled, cheap ones of Cook, Joe decided the Washington police *did* make a big deal out of possible international incidents.

The lieutenant held the gaily colored scarf that had turned up in Callie's pocket. Grant spoke for a minute with Detective Cook. As they conferred in whispers, the lieutenant kept shooting glances over at Madeleine—the way a person would check out a strange animal that could be dangerous.

The detective ran the videotape again while Grant watched. The lieutenant then rubbed his face with one hand and began speaking. "I've gone over the reports on this case and gotten the latest wrinkles from Detective Cook here." He nodded at the other man. "I'd like to get statements from all of you—"

A "harrumph" from the doorway interrupted Lieutenant Grant's flow. Everyone turned to see a short man standing just inside the door. His blue suit, elegantly cut, just called attention to his skinny frame and knobby knees. With his white shirt and red bow tie, Joe thought he looked like a cross between Jiminy Cricket and Uncle Sam.

The man cleared his throat again. "Ambrose Wilmer—State Department," he announced.

"Nice to see you again, Mr. Wilmer." From the tone of Lieutenant Grant's voice, Frank figured that was an out-and-out lie. "Been a long time."

"Approximately three weeks," Wilmer corrected him prissily. "You failed to inform me of this new case, Lieutenant. Luckily, I happened to be in contact with your office just now. I've taken the liberty of informing the young lady's father already. He assured me that he would be arriving momentarily."

Henri Berot appeared behind the State Department man just then. The look on his face reminded Frank of Joe's earlier joke—how Mr. Berot was ready to start World War Three. Right then, if Mr. Berot would have had anything to say about it, the French army would be on the march.

He spared one searing glance for his daughter, then turned on Lieutenant Grant. "This—this Wilmer person called me at my home to tell me that the police are holding my daughter," he said angrily. "He said something ridiculous about her stealing a scarf."

"Now, now, Mr. Berot." Wilmer's voice tried to sound soothing but came across more like a set of fingernails on a blackboard. "I'm sure the report is exaggerated."

"I'm afraid not, Mr. Wilmer," Lieutenant Grant said. He stepped over to the VCR and rewound the tape. As it started playing again, he said to Madeleine, "I guess you're getting pretty tired of seeing this."

She only shrugged. "Good practice in case I decide to become a movie star."

Fuming, Mr. Berot almost shouted the words, "Start it!"

He sat in absolute silence as the scene of Madeleine's slipping the scarf into Callie's pocket played. When Lieutenant Grant moved to stop the tape, he suddenly spoke up. "Bring it back— all the way back to when they entered the store."

Lieutenant Grant paused in midmotion to stare at Mr. Berot.

"I want to see *everything* that happened in that store," Berot said.

Grant's eyebrows rose. "You think we're hiding something here?"

"I know my daughter would not do something like this—unless she had been led into it." Berot glanced at the Hardys and Callie. "In the few weeks I've been here, I've found America to be a very dangerous country. People—especially young people—have no respect for the law."

Lieutenant Grant started the VCR again. They watched the girls' entire visit to the boutique— right up to the unfortunate ending.

"It appears that Miss Shaw did nothing suspicious," Lieutenant Grant said. "In fact, she seemed somewhat embarrassed even before the shoplifting incident."

Mr. Berot shook his head. "This videotape proves nothing. I think it is these wild American kids—*they* are responsible. Maybe they dared my Madeleine to steal something before they went in. Did you think of that?"

"In any event, Ms. Berot is indeed protected by diplomatic immunity," Mr. Wilmer said. The State Department man gave them all a rabbity smile. "We would prefer to end this incident with as little publicity as possible."

Berot nodded abruptly, pulling out a wallet. He quickly counted some bills onto the table beside the VCR. "This should cover the price of the scarf."

He snatched up the silk scarf that had started all the trouble and thrust it into Madeleine's hands.

Maddy, however, lagged behind her father. She pressed the scarf into Callie's hands. "Callie, you keep this. I'm very sorry for what happened. At least you aren't in trouble anymore. I'll call you tomorrow at your hotel. Maybe I can find some way to make this up to you." She ran from the interrogation room before Callie could say anything. Wilmer had already set off after Mr. Berot.

"Wilmer is usually more interested in soothing

a diplomat's ruffled feathers than dealing with American civilians," Lieutenant Grant said to Frank, Joe, and Callie. "He usually leaves that menial stuff to me."

The lieutenant gave them all a long look. "Officially, you are free to go. Unofficially, I have some advice for you." He raised his hand when he saw Callie jump from her seat and head for the door. "It's not a long lecture—just a quick line. When Madeleine Berot calls you tomorrow, don't answer the phone." Grant shook his head. "Trust an old cop's instincts—that kid is trouble."

A few minutes later Callie, Joe, and Frank were out of the police station and on the street. Callie made her exit on wobbly legs. "I feel like a dish towel that's been wrung out—about five times."

"It's a long walk back to the hotel," Frank said.

Joe nodded. "Yeah—I wish Lieutenant Grant had given us a lift back instead of his advice."

Callie shook her head. "No way. I've had enough cops today."

Joe dug a guide to Washington out of his back pocket. "There's a Metro station nearby. Feel up to a short ride, Callie?"

Callie glanced at her watch. "It's not rush hour yet. So far, this has been the worst day of my life."

They took the escalator down to the station

lobby, to find a rank of fare card vending machines. "I'll pay for each of us," Joe offered.

He slipped a dollar into the machine, hit a button, and out popped a fare card, which he handed to Callie. Another dollar went in, and out came another card. Joe handed it to Frank. But when he tried to slip his next bill in, the machine spat it out.

"Look at this thing," Joe said, holding it up. "This has to be the world's worst-looking dollar bill. It must have gone through a washing machine." The dollar was limp and worn, looking almost chewed on.

Digging another bill out of his jeans, Joe slipped it in, got his card, and headed for the turnstiles.

As they rode the escalator down to the platform, lights set into the concrete began to flash. "Hey, we're in luck," Frank said. "There's a train on the way."

They began to run down the escalator. The train still hadn't reached the station when they reached the platform.

Callie moved to the edge of the platform, peering down the tunnel to watch for moving lights.

Joe saw a thin man in sunglasses, tight black jeans, and a skimpy, European-cut shirt walk up behind her. As he came up to Callie, he didn't step around her. Instead, he purposely bumped into her, sending her staggering toward the edge of the platform.

"Callie!" Frank yelled, whipping around to grab his girlfriend's arm before she fell onto the tracks.

The thin guy sprinted away, cutting in and out of the crowd waiting on the platform.

"This one isn't getting away," Joe muttered to himself grimly as he took off after the guy along the platform.

His quarry raced ahead, but Joe was the Bayport football team's best broken-field runner. He closed in quickly.

The guy darted to the edge of the platform, trying to wriggle through the heart of the crowd to lose Joe.

It didn't work. In another minute Joe stretched out an arm and caught him by the shoulder.

"Don't be shy, buddy," Joe said. "Turn around. We have to go back and you can apologize to our friend. Then maybe you might explain why you almost knocked her onto the tracks."

The man did turn around, and Joe gawked. He knew him! Same sunglasses, same dark hair, and a black T-shirt showed at the neck of his European-cut shirt. This was the same person who'd snatched Callie's purse! The man's hand came out of his pocket, clenched in a fist. Joe moved, ready to block a blow, but this guy wasn't throwing a punch. His hand opened about a foot from Joe's face, releasing a cloud of reddish powder.

Joe blinked in surprise—until the powder hit

his face. He began coughing and sneezing as the orangy red particles got into his nose and throat. His eyes hurt the worst. They burned as if someone had thrown acid in them.

Suddenly blinded, Joe recoiled. His antagonist gave him a vicious shove, and Joe staggered backward, his arms flailing in large windmill patterns. His right foot stepped back and found only air under it.

He was going over the edge of the platform— just as the train was coming in!

Chapter

5

As HE FELL OFF the platform, Joe heard and felt a rumbling sound. The train was coming in! He landed hard in the track area and lay stunned for a moment, the air knocked out of him.

He had no time to stay there and catch his breath. He forced his tearing eyes open and got a blurry view of the track bed in front of him. All he could see was a pair of oncoming headlights. The train was nearly on top of him, with no time or space to brake. If Joe tried leaping for the edge of the platform, the train would probably hit him in midair. There was no way he could outrun it.

His thoughts fast-forwarded. If he couldn't outrun or go over the onrushing train, there was only one way to avoid being squashed like a bug. That was to go under it.

Joe lay in the center of the track bed, pressing his body flat between the rails. He was just in time. The carriages swooped over him with a swoosh of cold air. Joe pressed his face to the track bed. His entire body shook as the train screeched to a stop. A chill ran along his spine— partly from the breeze made by the stopping cars, but mostly from terror.

Wiggling his way to the closest opening between cars, Joe finally managed to scramble back onto the platform.

Callie and Frank came rushing up. "Joe! Joe! Are you okay?" Callie shouted.

"Just great," Joe said, rubbing a bruised shoulder. "The guy who almost nailed you had some nastiness left over. So he gave it to me—right down to the rails. Believe it or not, he blinded me with a handful of cayenne pepper." Joe blinked his still-bleary eyes. "Where did he go?"

"He disappeared into the crowd when you fell." Frank shook his head. "I was with Callie— and too far away."

"I'm sorry, Joe," Callie said. The train began to pull out of the station.

Joe laughed as he watched it disappear into the nearest tunnel. They had missed their train after all that. "I suggest a vote," he said. "Those in favor of a cab back to the hotel raise their hands."

His hand and Callie's immediately shot into the

air. Frank stared after the train for a second, thinking. Then in a distracted way he raised his hand as well.

They spent a gloomy evening in Callie's room, eating a room-service meal. Callie hardly touched her food. She just sat on the couch, looking blue. Frank sat beside her and held her hand. "You okay?"

Callie shrugged. "You know, I've been looking forward to this trip for weeks. It was all going to be perfect, like a dream, meeting a friend I'd never seen before." She shook her head. "Instead it's been a nightmare. Three times today, something awful has happened—or nearly happened—to me."

Joe laughed. "So what do you think, Callie? Is this a plot against you?" He pretended to pull out a notebook. "Tell us, Miss Shaw, do you have any enemies in the Washington area?" Then he turned to Frank. "Maybe we should round up the usual suspects."

"That's not funny, Joe," Frank said.

Callie took her hand out of his. "I got both you guys in trouble, and Joe nearly got killed." She sighed. "And let's face it, Madeleine Berot hasn't turned out to be the perfect friend."

"She ought to be arrested for false advertising, sending you a picture that made her look like a knockout," Joe complained. "But she'd probably get out of it by claiming diplomatic immunity."

Callie refused to be cheered up by Joe's joking around. "Guys, I'm thinking about cutting this vacation short. Maybe we can get a flight home tomorrow."

"Bayport's beginning to look better and better," Joe admitted. Before he could say anything more, the phone rang.

Callie picked up the receiver. "Yes?" she said, then her face froze. "Oh, hello, Maddy. No, I wasn't asleep. I was sitting here with the guys."

She beckoned the Hardys closer, holding up the phone so they could hear Madeleine's voice.

"My father was *furious* over what happened," Maddy said. "I thought he was going to—what do you call it—ground me. I'll probably have to stay around the house tomorrow and get him calmed down. But what are you doing tomorrow night?"

Callie stared at the receiver, speechless.

Maddy's voice rushed on. "I know you should be angry at me for that stupid joke. But I didn't mean for it to turn out the way it did. I was going to tell you to watch your pockets, then go back and pay for the scarf. Instead, that crazy woman came out and started making accusations."

"You still might have explained," Callie said stiffly.

"I should have," Maddy agreed, her voice contrite. "Things just moved so quickly—and those women were all ready to believe the worst about us. It is all my fault, and I'm very, very sorry."

The French girl's voice brightened. "Anyway, I want to make up for all of it. There's a new club that's opened not far from your hotel—the Quarter. It's supposed to be really hot. I hear that all the kids from diplomatic families hang out there."

Now Madeleine's voice grew pleading. "Would you, Joe, and Frank like to go there tomorrow night? It will be my treat."

Callie looked as if Maddy had just invited her out for a mud fight. "I don't know," she began hesitantly.

Apparently, Frank did. He tapped Callie's shoulder to get her attention, vigorously nodding his head up and down.

Joe was surprised by his brother's enthusiasm. Back at the police station, Joe had seen Frank's face when he realized that Maddy was responsible for Callie's trouble. Joe thought Frank had been ready to unscrew Maddy's head from her neck—without tools. Now he wanted to make a date for all of them to go out with her.

Joe was about to make a joke about it until he caught the serious expression on his brother's face. Frank seemed to have more than dancing on his mind. Unless Joe was badly mistaken, his brother had a case to think about.

"Okay," Callie said, scribbling down the address of the club. "The Quarter, at eight-thirty. See you then."

Callie hung up the phone, staring at Frank. "Lieutenant Grant said to stay away from Maddy—how come you want to go dancing with her?"

"Call it a hunch," Frank said.

Joe was startled and stared at his brother. He was the one with hunches in this investigating team.

"Somebody seems to be going out of his—or her—way to make our visit to Washington as unpleasant as possible," Frank said. "Somehow we may have wandered into someone's way. And that someone may be up to something big."

Now Callie was staring at Frank, too. "I don't think I'm ready to buy a conspiracy theory to ruin our vacation," she objected.

"Frank may not be as crazy as you think," Joe suddenly said. "I didn't mention it before, but I think the guy who tried to push you on the tracks was the same one who stole your purse."

Frank turned to him, eyes blazing. "Are you sure?"

Joe shrugged. "If I was, I wouldn't have said, 'I think.' He had the same shades on, and under his shirt was a black T-shirt."

"So we have a firm *maybe*." Frank looked over at Callie. "But you may have had a good idea before. You know, about heading back to Bayport, while we—"

"While you guys look into things? No way, François," Callie said emphatically. "Either we all stay and check this out, or we all go."

Frank and Joe exchanged a quick glance and a shrug. They knew they'd get nowhere when Callie used that tone of voice.

Joe yawned and stretched. "It's been a long day. I'm going to hit the sack." He headed for the door, then stopped. "I'll expect to see you soon—*after* you've said good night." He headed for his room, grinning because he'd been able to make both Frank and Callie blush.

The next morning at breakfast nobody mentioned the conspiracy theory. Frank, Joe, and Callie decided to act like typical tourists and explore the two-mile long Washington Mall, with all its famous museums.

They stopped moving back and forth on the gravel paths long enough to gaze at the red sandstone walls of the Smithsonian Castle. "It's so weird. It looks like somebody dropped a huge castle right in the middle of Washington," Callie said. "What do they keep in it, the National Armor Collection?"

"It used to be a museum, but now it's full of

offices and things like that," Frank said, consulting his guidebook. "The building next door has all sorts of great stuff, though."

"Great stuff" was just what they found next door in the Arts and Industries Building. The sprightly, bright-colored brick building contained everything from Indian totem poles to an old-fashioned train locomotive.

"That was pretty cool," Joe said as they walked back out into the sunshine forty-five minutes later.

"There's a modern art museum nearby," Callie said. "Want to check it out?"

Joe stared at the round bulk of the Hirshhorn Museum. "Looks like a giant concrete pillbox," he said.

"It's more like a doughnut," Frank said, his nose back in the guidebook.

They explored three floors of modern art, and enjoyed a great view of the Mall from the museum's balcony room.

"Going to become a painter now, Joe?" Callie teased as they went back.

"Only if Dad catches up with me and makes me do the garage," Joe said.

"An awful fate." Frank laughed. "Tell you what—you choose the next museum."

"I think we've seen enough art for a while. How about animals?"

They trudged across the central grassy space

of the Mall to the Natural History Museum. "Nice effect," Frank said as they stepped through the entrance to find themselves confronted with a gigantic stuffed elephant.

"Your turn," Callie said to Frank after they toured that museum for an hour.

"I bet High-tech Hardy picks something with machines," Joe said.

"You read my mind," Frank told him with a grin. "How about the National Air and Space Museum?"

Back across the Mall again, they headed for a huge glass, marble, and steel building. The first airplane from 1903 and the first American space capsule to orbit the earth were inside. Not only that, there were hundreds of other fascinating pieces of flight and space technology.

They started into the museum cafeteria for a late lunch at two-thirty. "So what do you think?" Frank asked.

"I just wish we could take longer in each museum. We barely skimmed the surface of each of them," Callie complained.

Joe, however, didn't answer. He threw a puzzled glance over his shoulder.

"What's the problem, Joe?" Callie asked.

For an answer Joe threw an arm around Frank and Callie and turned them around. He headed for the escalators. "Don't all look at once, but there's a guy behind us."

"Dark suit, straw hat?" Frank said, pretending to kid with Callie so he could steal a peek.

"That's the one. Have you seen him before?"

Callie angled for a quick look, then shook her head. "I've never seen him before."

"Well, I have," Joe said grimly. "We've been zipping back and forth between these museums at random. This guy has popped up at the last three places we've visited."

"He likes our taste in museums?" Callie tried to sound light about it, but she didn't succeed.

Joe picked up the pace. "Let's face it, guys," he said. "We're being followed."

Chapter

6

"LET'S GET OUT of here." Frank kept up the cheerful act by smiling, but his voice came out tight and strained. He steered them quickly through a couple of exhibits at the museum, not wanting to warn their shadow that he'd been spotted.

"What do we do now?" Callie asked.

"If we were alone, I'd suggest leading the guy tailing us to a quiet corner where we could ask him what he's doing," Joe answered Callie. "But the problem is, we're not alone—"

"Now wait a minute," Callie burst out. "We've been on enough cases together that you should know I can carry my weight."

"Let's quit arguing and just lose this clown." Frank felt his temper rising because of the squabbling. They had a job to do now. Maybe later, when they had a better shot at their tail, they could confront him. But this wasn't the time.

"How do we lose him?" Callie asked.

"Just look out there." Joe nodded toward the mass of tourists on the Mall. "Frank and I have lost tails in smaller crowds than that."

Frank led the way out of the museum, using the huge plate-glass windows around them as mirrors to check on their tail.

The man following them was hardly a character who blended into the crowd. He was a short, heavyset man wearing a dark suit, no tie, dark glasses, and a straw hat. He had at least a day's growth of beard on his round face. He was vaguely foreign looking, but he didn't look like a tourist. He looked like a well-dressed slob.

Well, they'd find out how sloppy he was in a minute. Once out of the museum Frank led his brother and Callie into a gap in the crowd. A mob of people soon filed in behind them, cutting them off from Shorty, as Frank had nicknamed their pursuer. He was a good tail, but following the Hardys and Callie now would be like swimming against the current.

Frank grinned as the man fell behind them. "That was simple enough," he said.

"Not as simple as you think." Joe jerked his head over his left shoulder.

Frank checked and spotted another man keeping pace with them.

This follower was tall and thin, with long, greasy black hair. His skinny frame was only emphasized by the loud Hawaiian shirt he wore. Three of him could have fit inside its billows. This guy, too, wore sunglasses. He was too far away for Frank to make out his face clearly, but he did resemble the purse snatcher and the guy at the Metro. Of course, it might just be that he looked like the other guy—a young, greasy punk.

Frank could tell his brother was thinking the same thoughts. All Joe said was, "He picked us up as soon as we left the museum."

"Great," Frank muttered. "Now we've got to peel this guy off, too. It won't be as easy. He's got to be suspicious."

Frank led the way, following one of the gravel paths. "There's a Metro station about two and a half blocks away, near the National Archives," he said. "Maybe we can jog down there and pull the same trick the purse snatcher pulled on us."

It could have been a good plan, but it didn't work. They hadn't gotten even halfway across the Mall when Frank picked up yet another man cutting across the grass to move in ahead of them. Unlike Shorty and Mr. Hawaii, as he decided to call the guy in the loud shirt, this follower looked dangerous.

He was tall and stocky, built like a bull, with a

head smaller than it should have been. He wore a garish sport coat and tight pants, and both appeared to be foreign cut. He was also wearing sunglasses.

Using the regulation sunglasses, Frank made out a big, puffy nose like a potato, sagging cheeks, and an oversize, jutting chin. The guy's yellowish, unhealthy-looking face was covered with pockmarks.

Joe caught sight of the new player in this scary game of tag. "That guy could be on a poster for the War Against Zits," he joked.

"Looks like Old Ugly's been sent in to cut us off," Frank said, changing course.

They abruptly turned and headed back the way they had come. "There's another Metro station beyond the Air and Space Museum—a big one, with lots of trains going through."

They could just see the two guys they'd left behind circling around to cut them off. And just then Frank thought he saw someone else in sunglasses moving their way.

"What do we do now?" Callie wanted to know. "These guys obviously know that we've seen them. They're not going to let us ditch them."

It was a ridiculous situation, Frank thought. Here they were, in one of the most heavily visited areas of the nation's capital, surrounded by tourists, being tailed by three or four men. The afternoon sun shone brightly down on the open green space, reflecting off the limestone, marble, glass, and steel fronts of the distinguished museums and offices that lined the Mall. It was crazy that this should be happening there in bright daylight.

Frank felt as if he were wearing a target on his head. He had been afraid that their followers would catch up to them in an isolated spot. Now, from the way these guys were moving in and cutting off every escape route, they could be planning to pull something right in the middle of the crowd.

"Frank," Joe said, "we've got to find a way out of here—*fast!*"

"Unless you can call down a helicopter or an air strike, I don't think we're getting out of here," Callie said.

"We'll have to settle for something a little more down-to-earth," Frank answered. He grabbed Callie's hand and sprinted forward, with Joe following close behind, as if heading for the open space between the two men who blocked the way back to the Air and Space Museum. The two thugs moved together, filling in the hole.

Frank then abruptly changed course, and they all climbed on board one of the Tourmobile buses that constantly circled the Mall. Frank paid all three fares to the driver. Just as the bus began pulling away, Old Ugly managed to get on. His partners, however, were too far away to catch up.

"Nice going, Frank. At least you cut down the

odds," Joe whispered with a glance at the large plug-ugly who stood by the front door.

"For the moment," Callie said, looking out the window. Far behind them, two of their shadows were running along behind the bus.

The kids sat quietly until the bus reached its next stop. At the last possible moment they burst out. Old Ugly was caught by surprise as they left the bus, but he managed to pry the doors open and get off, too.

Callie and the Hardys had a big lead and ran hard, passing the huge reflecting pool, before they stumbled up a set of marble stairs. Above them was a statue of General Grant sitting on his horse and looking grim. They ran past him, then past a statuary group of charging calvary troopers. That's just what we need right now, Frank thought—the cavalry to come charging to the rescue.

The bronze soldiers didn't leap into action, so Frank kept moving, keeping pace with Joe and Callie as they headed for Capitol Hill.

Ahead of them now rose the gleaming white marble of the Capitol Building, with its huge, soaring dome. From not far behind them, Frank could hear the pounding of footsteps up the marble steps of the Grant Monument. Taking a second to glance back, he saw that Old Ugly was pretty close on their tail. The pockmarked man moved fast for a man of his weight.

Frank's blood froze as he watched their tail reach under his loud sport coat, but the man suddenly stiffened, and his hand came away empty. Turning toward the Capitol, Frank saw an armed police officer stroll toward them. "Take it easy, kids," the guard told them. "The Capitol's been here almost two hundred years. It's not going to disappear before you get there."

Frank glanced nervously at Joe. Should he tell the police officer they were being followed? Would he believe it? Even Frank didn't know what was going on. "Okay, sir," he said, slowing down his pace.

Callie, who'd been about to spill everything, shut her mouth with an audible snap. Shrugging her shoulders, she walked quietly toward the entrance.

That lasted for about ten seconds. "Why didn't we get that cop to help us?" she whispered furiously to Frank.

"He wouldn't have believed me," Frank told her. "Besides, I've got a better plan."

They joined a line of tourists in the entranceway, walking through a small metal archway. As one of the people ahead of them stepped through, a loud buzzer went off. The man stepped back and started going through his pockets, removing coins and keys.

"A metal detector!" Joe said, grinning as he began to understand.

He glanced behind them. Old Ugly, seeing the metal detector, hung back at the entryway, his hand almost protectively going under his left arm.

"If he's carrying a gun—and it looks like he is—he can't come through the detector." Joe grinned. "Nice move, Frank."

"So, we could go straight through the Rotunda, out the other side, and lose him," Callie said.

"Or . . ." Frank's voice trailed off.

"Or?" Callie prompted.

"We could let them send a guy in after us—unarmed—and face him down in here," Joe said. "That's what you were thinking, right?"

Frank nodded, checking out the large round room, crowded with tourists. "I wonder, though, if Congress will lend us a committee room for a real, in-depth interview."

"We'll just have to see," Joe said, his eyes lighting up at the promise of action.

Back at the doorway, the rest of the pursuers had joined up with Old Ugly. They seemed to be arguing with him. Through a trick of acoustics, Frank caught two words from the man. *"Le coup."* Then, using the others to shield him, he slipped something to one of his accomplices and headed through the metal detector.

Callie, Frank, and Joe joined the end of a tour group that was just leaving, Old Ugly grimly trailing them. They saw officers' and committee rooms, then went underground to the subway system that ran between lawmakers' offices and the Capitol.

As they entered the underground area, the three kids held back as the main group boarded a train. Frank and Joe moved to confront Old Ugly.

The big thug paid no attention to them. Reaching into his coat, he whipped out what seemed to be a thin piece of paper. What was he going to do? Frank wondered. Give them a paper cut?

Frank suddenly realized that the white object in the man's hand wasn't paper—it was a five-inch knife blade. "Watch out!" he yelled.

Old Ugly was already on the move, knife extended—aiming straight for Callie Shaw.

Chapter

7

FRANK LEAPED FORWARD as the blade in the huge thug's hand went straight for Callie's throat. Joe was there first, though, knocking the knife off-course. It flashed inches from her face as she scrambled back.

Even as he struggled with Joe for the knife, Old Ugly swung out with his free hand. Frank winced as the thug's openhanded blow sent Joe flying into the wall, stunned.

That left only Frank between the killer and Callie. He stood his ground, raising his hands in an almost pleading gesture. "Now wait a minute, big fella. Can't we talk about this?"

The ugly face looming over him twisted into a nasty smile. Old Ugly shook his head no.

Frank shrugged. "Okay, then." His foot lashed

out to catch Old Ugly in the shin. The big guy leaped back one step with a roar. He instantly limped forward, though, brandishing his knife. Frank began to wonder if the confrontation in the temporarily empty area had been such a bright idea.

As soon as the thought came, the area was no longer empty. A man in a suit—maybe a senator, maybe a legislative aide—walked up, reading some papers. When he saw the guy with the knife, he threw up his hands, the papers went flying, and he ran back along the corridor, screaming. Frank just hoped help would come before he was sliced and diced.

Old Ugly was taking him a lot more seriously now, advancing slowly in a knife fighter's crouch. The blade was out, flicking slowly back and forth. Unarmed and unable to get past the knife, all Frank could do was retreat.

The area was still completely empty. Anyone who did come in ran screaming when they saw the knife-wielding Old Ugly. Frank hoped Callie had the sense to get out of there. He didn't dare turn around to look for her—not with that strange-looking white knife just inches from his heart.

Old Ugly feinted left, then right, then drove the knife straight at Frank's chest.

Frank's attention was riveted on the blade—he didn't see Joe launch off the wall in a wild leap.

The knife swung wildly as Joe plowed into Old Ugly, who struggled to stay upright. With a guy this big, they had to keep at him until he went down all the way.

Frank twisted the thug's knife arm fiercely, smashing it down on his knee. Old Ugly lost his grip, and the knife dropped to the tile floor.

As soon as the white blade hit the ground, it shattered.

"No wonder he got that thing through the metal detectors," Frank said. "It's made of ceramic!"

His momentary distraction nearly got him decked. Old Ugly had wrenched his arm free and was swinging at him. Frank ducked, and the big thug pulled away, moving fast despite his limp. Joe grabbed for him, but Old Ugly was free now, lumbering down the corridor. Passengers from a train that had just arrived hit the walls as he plowed through them.

Frank grabbed Joe's arm and led him in the opposite direction. Joe pulled against his lead. "Come on, Joe, you've got to know when to end a fight. We'll never catch him," Frank said.

Callie came running back to them. "Let's join up with that tour," she said, pointing. "Then we can get out of here," she said.

Frank shrugged. "Sounds good to me."

They blended in with the tourist group and headed back for the Rotunda. The whole Hill was

57

swarming with Capitol police—and there was no sign of Old Ugly or any of the other tails.

"I guess they got scared off," Callie said. "I don't know about you guys, but I think I've done enought sight-seeing for today."

"Yeah," Joe agreed. "I'm in the mood for a nice cab ride back to our hotel."

As they pulled up at the hotel entrance, Joe pulled out his wallet. He counted out the money for the fare and found that worn bill that wouldn't go into the fare card machine. For a second he grinned, almost tempted to use the Worst Dollar Bill in the World for the trip. But he was afraid the driver might run over his foot as he pulled away.

"I am ready to sleep till next Wednesday," Callie said as they rode up in the elevator.

"Well, you'll have to cram your rest into what's left of the afternoon," Frank said. "We're going to the Quarter tonight, remember?"

Callie stared at him. "You're kidding, right? We nearly got killed, and you still want to go out tonight?"

Joe's eyes narrowed as he looked at his brother. "Maybe that's how he expects to find out who's been trying to kill us."

The Quarter was in a new building on a small side street off Connecticut Avenue. It was pretty easy to find. The Hardys and Callie just had to look for a place with a lot of kids hanging around outside—and lots of expensive cars parked nearby. Joe stopped halfway down the block. "Check this one out, guys. A Porsche convertible."

"Right now, I want to check out Maddy," Frank said. "And her friends," he added hastily when he saw Callie's raised eyebrows.

Madeleine Berot was already in the club, dancing up a storm. Her partner was a tall, good-looking blond guy, dressed in a tapered raw linen shirt. The lights flickered and the music was loud, and Maddy's dancing was wild and abandoned.

"What do you think?" Frank shouted over the noise.

Joe shrugged. "Looks pretty good to me."

There was a break in the music, and Madeleine ran over to them. "You came! You came!" she shouted. "I'm so happy!"

Her blond friend strolled over with her. By the look on his face, he wasn't too glad to see the newcomers. "This is Ansel," Madeleine said, patting his shoulder. "His father works at the German embassy."

"What a surprise," Joe muttered.

"I met him and his friends here," Maddy went on. "They're all diplomats' kids."

"Dips and dip-ettes," Frank whispered to Callie, staring at the elaborately dressed guys and girls Madeleine was pointing toward.

"What is the story with you?" Ansel asked. "State Department? U.S. Information Service? I haven't seen you around before. Did your parents just move into the District?"

"We're just visiting," Callie said.

"Right," Frank added. "Just plain civilians from Bayport."

"Tourists?" Ansel's tone of voice made the word sound as if he'd said "pond scum."

Joe faced off against the German kid. "Callie and Madeleine are old friends," he said. "They had a chance to get together here in Washington, and Callie wanted us to come with her. Is that a problem?"

"No problem," Maddy said quickly, grabbing Joe's arm. "Come on, the music is starting again. You must dance with me." She gave him that 150-watt smile. "After all, Callie told me she brought you with her because you're such a great dancer."

Frank and Callie joined Maddy and Joe, leaving Ansel to stand alone.

They danced for half an hour, then Maddy led them all back to the table where the diplomatic brat-pack was sitting. She introduced them quickly, rattling off names and countries. There was Willem, a doughy-looking Dutch guy with lank brown hair, and Stephanie, a cool blond girl whose father was someone fairly important in the

British embassy. Indira was an Indian girl with beautiful dark hair that reached her waist. She wore jeans, an expensive sweater, and a caste mark on her forehead. Joe didn't hear what country Tomas came from. He was tall and elegantly thin, with handsome dark looks.

Obviously, Ansel had already reported on them. The diplomatic brats greeted the Americans as if they'd just crawled out from under a rock.

Maddy, however, stayed with her American friends. She seemed almost defiant about it, keeping an arm around Joe as they stood by the table. That got her dirty looks from Ansel, Willem, and Tomas.

"So, Madeleine," Ansel said. Joe noticed that he pronounced her name perfectly. "Do you think you could get us invitations for the costume ball at your embassy this weekend? The one in honor of the Lafayette sword. I heard that your father is in charge of the display—"

Frank turned to Maddy. "Your father is in charge of the Lafayette sword?" he asked.

Madeleine barely looked at him as she yanked on Joe's arm. "This is my favorite song!" she exclaimed with another brilliant smile. The next second they were on the dance floor again. Joe could almost feel Ansel's and Frank's eyes boring into the back of his head.

They danced for three more songs—all of them

her favorites, Madeleine assured Joe. He couldn't help noticing, though, that they only returned to the table after Frank and Callie and Ansel and Indira had gotten up to dance.

They sat down even though the remaining diplomatic brats didn't bother to greet them. No one talked to them. Madeleine was determined to have a good time, anyway. She ordered fresh sodas for everyone and appetizers for the table. Joe decided that money was no problem for her.

Maddy made bright conversation, even though the other kids at the table didn't join in with her and Joe. Joe tried to keep up his part of the conversation, but it wasn't easy with all those hostile eyes shooting icy glares at him. When Ansel and Indira returned to the table, Joe could barely put up with the bad vibrations.

He breathed a sigh of relief as Frank and Callie rejoined them. "What do you say we move along?" Joe asked.

"Oh, you can't leave yet!" Madeleine said. "I wanted you to have a good time. To make up for—well, you know."

"It has been a pretty full day," Joe said. "We were all over the Mall, looking at museums—"

"Tourists," he overheard Indira saying to Ansel.

"And then we got jumped by some guy with a knife," Joe said, finishing his sentence.

"Jumped?" Tomas said, showing interest for

the first time. "You have to be careful in this city, you know."

Maddy, however, turned pale. "With a knife?" she echoed.

"Where did it happen?" Indira asked.

"Would you believe Capitol Hill?" Joe told her.

"I don't believe you," Ansel said bluntly. "But if you want to go home, go."

He became nasty, however, when Maddy got up as well. "We just treated you to a round of sodas," he said.

Joe sighed. "Look, we don't want any trouble. Why don't I pay?" He reached for his wallet—and found nothing in his back pocket. His face became red as he checked his other pockets and turned up nothing. "My wallet—I've lost my wallet!"

"Sure," Ansel told him, rising to his feet. "If you want to sponge off us—"

"Hey, pal, I don't—"

Ansel cut off Joe's words with a sharp shove to his shoulder.

All of a sudden a bouncer appeared at Joe's side, and the manager of the club was beside Ansel. "I want no problems," the manager said, smiling through gritted teeth.

"I'll take care of it," Frank said, throwing some money on the table.

Ansel swept the bills away. "I've come here

for months with no problem. Now you have the manager after us."

"You do have a problem, champ," the manager told him. "I want you out of here—now. All of you. Pick up your money," he said to Frank, then turned back to Ansel. "As for you, I've had it with you and your friends. You're eighty-sixed."

"What is eighty-sixed?" Ansel demanded.

"You and your friends aren't welcome to come here anymore," the manager said.

Ansel's face turned a dull red. "Do you know who my father is?"

"I don't really care," the manager told him with a shrug. "There are lots more like you out there."

Ansel was about to swing at the manager when the bouncer took him by the shoulder. "This way," the big, beefy guy said. With that hand clamped onto him, there was nothing Ansel could do but let the bouncer march him off. Ansel's diplomatic brat friends trailed along.

The Hardys, Callie, and Madeleine left a minute later. "Maddy, I'm sorry how this turned out," Callie said. "I don't think your friends—"

"They weren't my friends," Madeleine told her. "I just met them tonight—real snobs, wouldn't you say?"

"Well, I'm glad we're out of there," Joe said. He was trying to cool down, but his angry feelings showed in his long strides. He was crossing the street in the middle of the block way ahead of the others. "That Ansel—"

His voice was cut off by the roar of a car engine. The Porsche convertible he'd admired earlier was speeding down the street.

Joe saw the blond hair and knew Ansel was behind the wheel. He had the car set on a collision course with Joe.

Chapter

8

THE STEAMY AIR softened the outlines of the
onrushing Porsche, making it seem almost
ghostly. Joe knew that it was no phantom heading
for him, though. If Ansel hit him, he'd be dead.

Joe swung his arms behind him, sending Madeleine, Callie, and Frank staggering backward.
Then Joe dove and rolled to the far side of the
street.

The Porsche missed him by inches.

Frank ran over to help Joe up. As he did, Ansel
was throwing his Porsche screaming into reverse,
not caring who got hit now. Joe and Frank were
on one side of the street, the girls on the other.

Ansel angled his car up onto the sidewalk
where Callie and Maddy were. Joe knew he had
to do something to turn Ansel away from the girls.

He ran back into the street, yelling, "Hey, stupid, over here."

Ansel obliged and began a three-point turn. Joe hopped back up onto the sidewalk for a few steps, then dashed into the street again. The Porsche's tires screamed as Ansel completed the turn and sent the car rocketing forward again.

Got to get him away from the others, Joe thought as he zigzagged down the street. The roaring of the engine and the squealing of the tires were deafening. But even over the noise, Joe could hear Ansel's diplomatic brat-pack friends yelling encouragement for their driver. Screaming for blood—really nice guys, he thought.

The block he was running down looked as if it hadn't been touched in the last century. Solid row houses built of dark bricks formed ranks on either side of the street. They appeared quietly elegant behind their cast-iron fences and gardens.

However, the screeching of the diplomatic brats plus the engine roar of the car were neither quiet nor elegant. Lights began appearing in windows and then silhouettes of people. With luck, someone will call the cops, Joe told himself. All I have to do is survive till then.

Of course, these kids would claim diplomatic immunity. Joe hoped Lieutenant Grant would find some way to give them a hard time.

He reached a corner and glanced at the street sign. Church Street, one way. If he crossed over and went up that block, Ansel couldn't follow him.

Joe took a deep breath and started up the one-way street.

Ansel was past caring about traffic laws. He whipped the Porsche in a tight turn and sent it fishtailing up the narrow street and after Joe. A car was coming down, and for a moment it looked as if they would crash head-on into each other. At the last second, the other car swerved and ended up with two wheels on the sidewalk.

Ansel had slowed down for a second, but the moment the obstruction was out of the way, he flew past.

Joe hopped up on the sidewalk, and suddenly the immediate area around him was brightly lit. He glanced over his shoulder—and nearly stopped in shock. Ansel had pulled his car onto the sidewalk.

The car kept coming. Joe looked forward and noticed the knot of pedestrians moving his way. They were teenage girls, busy talking among themselves. They hadn't noticed what lay ahead on the sidewalk.

Joe tore down the long block, legs aching, lungs burning, yelling, "Watch out! This guy is a maniac!"

The girls stopped, gawked, then ran for safety. Joe was amazed he wasn't dead yet.

Then he realized Ansel had only been playing

with him. He could have taken Joe out whenever he wanted. The Porsche roared with new power. Joe glanced to the side and took the only chance he had. Grabbing the top of a cast-iron fence, he swung himself up and over to land in a private garden.

Ansel screeched by as Joe landed—right on top of a rosebush. Joe winced as he pushed himself up on wobbly weak legs, totally worn out. His outfit was ruined, thanks to all the thorns that had cut into his clothes. Of course, he would have looked a lot worse if Ansel had nailed him.

Joe took a few long, shaky breaths and leaned against the cast-iron fence, checking down the block for the Porsche. Its brake lights had come on, and a moment later, Joe heard rapid footsteps moving toward him. He went to one knee, and tried to remain hidden in the shadows.

"Which house was it?" Tomas's voice floated out of the darkness. "I think it was this one," he said, scaling the fence.

He was actually standing over Joe before he realized it. "Hey! He's here! Over here!" Tomas yelled.

Joe lurched to his feet, bringing his fist straight up from the ground. He didn't have Ansel's Porsche to hit Tomas with, but he did have the advantage of surprise. Joe's punch took Tomas right on the chin. He reeled back, then sat down hard.

Before Tomas could say anything more, Joe was up and swinging over the fence. He dashed across the street.

This could work out, he thought. Maybe I can lose these clowns.

"He's crossed the street, doubling back!" a voice cried from behind him. Willem's voice.

Regretting only that he didn't have a chance to punch out the Dutch kid as well, Joe broke into a shambling run.

Before he'd reached the corner again, Ansel had turned the Porsche around. Willem was running along Joe's side of the street. Joe could hear the footsteps on the pavement behind him. Across the street, judging by the noise, Tomas had gotten back on his feet and had joined Willem in the pursuit.

This old-fashioned neighborhood had large trees. Their branches cut out a lot of light from the street lamps and the moon. Joe felt as if he were running down a long tunnel with nothing at the end. His heart was pounding, his lungs burned, and his legs felt as heavy as lead. To top it off, pricks from that stupid rosebush stung. He was trying his best, but there was no way he could outrun a Porsche.

Joe knew he was fading fast. He'd be dead soon.

However, as he made his way down the street,

he found his brother standing in the middle of the road.

"Hey, Ansel," the older Hardy called, "stop picking on my kid brother."

Joe had to smile at that.

Ansel's answer, however, was to stomp on the gas. Joe started in horror as the Porsche shot out, dead on target for Frank.

Hopping up and down curbs hadn't been good for the car. As it roared toward them, its muffler trailed along the pavement, sending out showers of sparks. The effect was like that of a rocket set to search and destroy.

Frank stood still and faced the onrushing car, a confident smile on his face. At the last possible second, he leaped aside, landing on his shoulder in a roll that brought him immediately back to his feet.

Ansel frantically hit the brakes. He'd been so interested in smearing Frank, he'd forgotten a very important fact.

They were on a dead-end street. The Porsche was heading straight for an old-fashioned, cast-iron light pole.

Ansel's yell was drowned out by the screech of brakes. Then came the sickening crunch of a fender crumpling on the light pole. Nobody in the car appeared to be hurt, but there would be a few thousand dollars' worth of damage to the Porsche. Willem and Tomas ran to help their friends.

Frank appeared at Joe's side, taking his elbow. "Let's get out of here while they're distracted," he said.

"I think they'll have more distractions in a minute," Joe said. From the distance came the sound of sirens. He laughed as he and Frank hustled off. "Even if they get away from the cops, they'll have to pay plenty to get that fender fixed. By the way, Frank, thanks for handling them so neatly."

Frank grinned back. "Hey, what are big brothers for?"

Callie and Madeleine were waiting around the corner and halfway down the next block. "You were wonderful—both of you!" Maddy said, throwing her arms around the Hardys. "But I feel so bad, making trouble for you again."

"You can't blame yourself for this, Maddy," Callie said. "Joe just happened to lose his wallet, that's all."

"If I hadn't insisted on taking you to the Quarter, there would have been no trouble at all." Madeleine looked at her friends. "I don't know about you, but all of a sudden, I'm starving. Why don't we stop for a snack." She grinned at them. "My treat, but *you* pick the place."

They finally found a burger restaurant and took over a back booth. After a soda and something to eat, Joe began to feel human again. Maddy ordered an extra glass of seltzer and dipped a napkin in it, dabbing at Joe's face. "You have scratches on your cheek," she said, concerned.

"Yeah, but you should see the rosebush I landed on," Joe said with a laugh.

"You didn't come out of this unscathed, either," Callie said to Frank, pointing at his shoulder. "Trust you to roll through the only oil patch on that street."

Frank looked at the greasy smear on his shoulder. "This is going to take more than some seltzer," he said unhappily. "I'll see what I can do in the men's room."

"I'll walk you partway," Callie said with a grin. "I'm heading for the ladies'." She asked Madeleine, "Do you want to come along?"

Maddy shook her head, looking at her watch. "It's getting late. Suppose I pay our bill. Then, when you come out, we can all leave."

"Sounds good to me," Frank said, leaving the table.

After Madeleine got the check, she carefully began to count out the money to pay for it. Joe smiled, watching her serious face as she left a small pile of singles for the tip.

Then his smile disappeared. He recognized one of those singles. It was an old friend—the Worst Bill in the World. The last time he'd seen it, the bill had been in his wallet.

So what was Madeleine doing with it now?

Chapter
9

JOE'S HAND SHOT OUT, catching Madeleine in midcount. He had to force himself not to grip the girl's wrist too hard, but he wanted a good look at that dollar bill.

Maddy froze, staring at him.

"So, tell me, Maddy," Joe said, his voice mild but ice-cold. "Did you hold on to my wallet as well? Or did you just throw it away and keep my money?"

"W-what?" she asked in total shock. The dollar in her hand dropped to the table.

"It's plain bad luck." Joe shook his head at Maddy, pretending to sympathize. "Most people wouldn't recognize a bill that had been in their hip pocket even if you waved it under their noses."

74

The words came out as if his chest were being slowly squeezed. "But I had a dollar in my wallet that was the crummiest thing I'd ever seen. I mean, that buck was worn and about as limp as toilet paper. It also had a coffee stain, right over George Washington's face. Made George look like he had a big, brown mustache."

His finger tapped the bill on top of the pile Madeleine had been counting out. It landed right on the ring over Washington's face. "In fact, it looked just like this one. How do you explain that, Maddy?"

Madeleine seemed to shrink into herself. When she looked up at Joe again, her eyes shone with tears. "It *is* my fault after all," she said, her voice quavering as she dug around in her bag. "Here."

She pulled out Joe's wallet, then handed over what was left of his cash. Then she grabbed his hand in both of hers. "Joe, please don't tell Frank and Callie. *Please!*"

"Why not?" Joe's face was set in a cold, hard stare.

"It was all a mistake—a stupid mistake," Maddy said feverishly, begging him to understand. "My father was very angry about what happened at the store. He didn't give me permission to go out tonight. I wasn't supposed to leave the house for a week."

"You were grounded?" Joe said.

Maddy nodded her head vigorously. "Yes. Grounded. I had to sneak out."

She looked at him as if that should explain everything. "There was no way I could get any money for the evening. I met Ansel and his friends outside, and they got me into the Quarter. Ansel started paying all sorts of attention to me. He ordered everything for me, telling me my money was no good with him around." Maddy shrugged her shoulders. "I—I let him, so I didn't have to worry about paying."

Her grip tightened on Joe's hand. "But I was supposed to be treating you, my friends. How was I going to do that without any money? Especially since I had invited you to make up for everything."

Madeleine used one hand to wipe a tear from her cheek. "Then I found the wallet under our table. It was the answer to a prayer. I thought all my problems were over. If I'd known it was yours, Joe—if I'd known how much trouble it would cause . . ."

Maddy's words ran down as Joe's gaze bored into her. His eyes were like chips of blue ice as he stared at her. It was the look a scientist would give to an unpleasant but interesting specimen.

"Nice try," Joe said, his voice mildly impressed. "You really should consider becoming an actress—that is, if you fail at your first career as a thief."

"But, Joe—I—you don't—" Madeleine floundered for words, thrown off balance by Joe's chilly response to her story.

"I should have figured it out before," Joe said. "It was obvious on the videotape from the store security camera. I ought to have spotted it back in the police station."

Maddy was staring at him now, her face pale. "S-seen what?"

"You used the same technique on me that you used with Callie. You jumped around and kept throwing your arm around me, getting me used to your touch—just like you did with Callie. Of course, with her, you used it to slip something into her pocket. With me, you slipped something out—my wallet."

He kept his gaze leveled on her. "You're a skilled dip, aren't you, Maddy—a professional pickpocket."

Her fingers left his hand as if it had turned red-hot.

"I can't imagine how a diplomat's daughter would pick up a skill like that. Picking pockets is something you're taught, not born with." He gave her a sour smile. "Besides, diplomats are usually better liars than thieves."

Madeleine sat huddled on the other side of the table. "I—I learned it from this girl I knew in Paris. She was—her name was Nadine—she was a street kid, working for a ring of pickpockets."

77

The words tumbled out of Madeleine now, like water that had been dammed up and suddenly broken loose. "We used to—I guess you'd say, hang out, sometimes. She had many crazy stories. Then she taught me how to do it."

She looked up at Joe with tear-filled eyes. "It started out as a joke, that's all. I was good at picking pockets. Very good. Nobody even knew when I did it—only Nadine."

"So, since you got away with it, you just kept it up." Joe's voice was cold.

"You don't understand!" Maddy's voice shook. "It's like a sickness. Sometimes I can't control it. I have this talent that I'm not supposed to use. Sometimes, when I'm happy or nervous, I forget."

Madeleine buried her face in her hands. "Oh, I wish I'd never learned it!" she whispered fiercely. "All it's done is get my friends into trouble."

She looked up pleadingly. "And if my father finds out—it will kill him. Papa works so hard at the foreign office. Any kind of scandal will wreck his career."

Madeleine's teary eyes begged Joe for help. "I think that's why he decided to bring us to America. He was afraid that I was hanging around with the wrong crowd back home."

She choked back a sob. "Poor Papa. He didn't know it was already too late."

78

Joe looked uncertainly at the French girl. Her tears seemed real, but he had a suspicion that they came as readily as her brilliant but phony smiles. "So what do you want from me?" he demanded.

"Don't tell your brother or Callie or my parents about—what I can do." Maddy shuddered with fear, then looked up at him with feverish eyes. "I'll make it up to you—I swear—I'll do anything."

Her fingers clutched at his hand again. But Joe shook her off. "Cool it. Frank and Callie are coming back."

"So," Frank said as he strolled up to the table. "Are we all set?"

"Maddy's just taking care of the tip," Joe said. "Guess what? We found my wallet. It must have fallen out of my pocket when we were at that club."

"Where did you find it?" Callie asked.

"Would you believe in Maddy's bag?" Joe answered with a grin.

That got a laugh from the other two. Maddy gazed at Joe with gratitude in her eyes.

They decided to walk back to Maddy's house and drop her off before heading for their hotel. As the foursome strolled down the street, it quickly broke into two couples—Frank and Callie in the lead, Joe and Madeleine bringing up the rear.

Maddy put an arm around Joe's waist and snuggled into his side as they walked along the quiet street.

"What are you going for now?" Joe asked. "My spare change?"

Madeleine leaped away from Joe as if he'd given her a megavolt electric shock. "I was—I just wanted to show how grateful I was." She stumbled over the words, her eyes going wide. "I thought you were being nice to me," she said in a small voice.

They stood for a long moment on the sidewalk looking at each other. "Maybe I'm being too nice to you," Joe finally said.

He was frowning, the troubled frown of a person who's not sure he's doing the right thing.

"I don't know if I can trust you, Maddy," Joe said slowly. "And once you lose somebody's trust, it's hard to earn back."

Madeleine sighed. "I'll just have to do my best," she finally said. "Come on, let's catch up with Frank and Callie."

It wasn't easy for Joe. Sore muscles in his legs screamed in protest when he picked up the pace. He was still aching from playing hide-and-seek with Ansel's Porsche.

As they headed down the street, Maddy took Joe's hand in hers. "At least you'll know where one of my hands is," she said with a ghost of a smile.

Joe knew he was supposed to laugh, but the laughter just wouldn't come.

They had cut the gap between themselves and the others to half a block when Madeleine suddenly froze, her fingernails digging into Joe's hand.

"That parked car we just passed," she whispered, her voice hoarse. "There's a man in it—with a gun!"

Chapter

10

As Joe Hardy turned back to see the car, he was momentarily blinded by the sudden glare of headlights. The car was moving now—it had pulled from the curb.

Up ahead of him were Frank and Callie, unaware that a car with an armed man inside might be following them.

Ignoring the stiffness in his aching legs, Joe forced himself into a shambling run down the nearly deserted street.

I'm probably overreacting. I never actually saw the gun, he thought. He couldn't stop himself from running to warn Callie and Frank, though. Must be a reaction to being chased by Ansel.

Luckily, the car was barely gliding along. As it pulled level with Joe, he could see the bulky outline of a guy leaning out the passenger-side window. Joe couldn't make him out clearly, but the MAC-10 submachine gun cradled in the guy's hands was impossible to miss.

The guy hadn't noticed Joe. He must have had all his attention on Frank and Callie. Unfortunately, the car had almost caught up with Callie and Frank by then.

"Watch out!" Joe yelled. "Get down!"

The guy in the car shot a look back at Joe, then took direct aim at him.

Joe dived for cover behind a parked van as half the MAC-10's clip whistled through the space where his chest had just been.

The muzzle flash from the gun lit up the gunman's face for an instant. Joe recognized the mismatched features of Old Ugly, the guy who'd tried to knife Callie in the Capitol.

Then the instant was past. Joe was behind the van, landing hard. He lay flat on the ground for a moment, the wind knocked out of him.

He heard another chattering burst of death from the MAC-10. Old Ugly must be emptying the gun's clip at Frank and Callie!

The sound of gunfire abruptly cut off and was replaced by the noise of an engine being revved and the squeal of tires as the car took off.

Joe forced himself to his feet and set off at a slow run for where he'd last seen Callie and

Frank. There they were, lying flat on the pavement. No blood—they were all right.

A second later they got shakily to their feet. Both were pale, but neither had been hit. They'd had a close call, but close doesn't count for hit men.

"Are you guys okay?" Joe asked.

"If we hadn't gotten your warning, we'd look like Swiss cheese," Callie said, shuddering. "Thanks, Joe."

"I was just carrying the message," Joe said. "Maddy's the one who spotted the guy in the car. Isn't that right, Maddy?"

He looked over his shoulder, but Madeleine wasn't standing there. In fact, she didn't appear to be on the block anymore.

Joe felt a cold chill run up his back. Had the gunmen gotten Maddy?

No, she wasn't on the sidewalk. She wasn't anywhere nearby. The car hadn't stopped to abduct her, either. No one else was around. Madeleine had just taken off after warning him. Joe shook his head. Should he thank her? Or was he trusting Madeleine too much?

Frank, Joe, and Callie took the fastest route back to their hotel. When they arrived on their floor, Frank took the key to Callie's room.

Motioning to the other two to stay away, he leaned against the wall, extending his arm to unlock the door while staying out of the doorway itself.

As the key clicked in the lock, he threw the door open, flattening himself against the wall again.

No shots rang out. In fact, nothing happened.

Frank went into a crouch and swung around the door to take a quick look inside the room. Then he shrugged and stood up. "Looks empty to me," he said.

Callie shook her head. "Don't you think you're taking things a little far?" she asked.

Joe shrugged. "You've never seen him when the family comes home from a long vacation."

"Hey, we were just shot at by a bozo who meant business," Frank said. He stepped back into Callie's room. "That reminds me—I'd better check for bombs or bugs."

A couple of minutes later Frank came back into the hall. "As far as I can see, the place is clean. Come on in, guys—we've got some stuff to talk about."

Joe took a quick trip down the hall to get some cans of soda, then they all settled down for a council of war.

"We've only been in this city for two days, and a lot of weird stuff has gone down," Frank said.

"That's putting it mildly," Joe said.

Callie nodded, ticking off the incidents on her fingers. "We've got a purse snatching, and the shoplifting accusation by the store manager. Then there's that pushing scene in the Metro— first me, then Joe—''

"Not to mention those guys following us at the Mall,'' Joe added.

"Ending with the guy and his knife in the Capitol,'' Callie went on. "Do we count Joe's fight at the club, that Ansel guy trying to run us down, and the Roaring Twenties–style rubout on the way home?''

She looked down at her fingers. "That's eight separate bits of trouble since we got here. Boy, time really flies when you're having a great time.''

Joe shook his head and looked at his brother. "Who told me this was going to be a nice, quiet vacation?''

Frank wasn't in a mood for joking. "We've walked into the middle of something here, something dangerous. The only way to get out of this alive is to find out what's going on. That was why I wanted to go to the Quarter tonight.''

"Well, I knew you had to have another reason,'' Joe said.

"Did it help?'' Callie asked.

Frank shook his head. "I'm not sure,'' he admitted. "But I have noticed something. We can break down all the incidents of the past couple of days into two categories. There's the purse snatching, the pushing on the platform, the tails, the guy with the knife—"

"And the guy with the gun," Joe cut in. "Did either of you notice that he was the same guy who followed us into the Capitol?"

Frank stared at his brother for a second. "Are you sure?" Then he shook his head. "That ties it up a little closer."

Callie and Joe looked at him in confusion.

"Don't you see?" Frank said. "Five incidents dealing with complete strangers—and all, it seems, aimed at Callie."

"*What?*" Callie sat up straighter on the couch.

"Sorry, Callie, but look at the facts." Frank's face wasn't happy as he tried to convince his girlfriend. "It was your purse that got snatched. You were the first guy's target on the Metro platform. Joe was attacked only when he took off after the guy."

"You can't blame those guys following us at the Mall on me," Callie said.

"We don't know who they were following," Frank admitted. "But when the guy with the knife finally attacked us, he went for you."

"And when he came back with a gun, he went for you and Frank, not me and Maddy." Joe frowned. "This is getting a little scary."

"You're telling *me,*" Callie said with a gulp. She looked at Frank. "Why is this happening?"

"I keep remembering Old Ugly talking to his

friends back at the Capitol,'' Frank said. "I caught two words—'le coup.' ''

"Sounds French," Joe said, frowning. "But I don't think these guys look like they're involved in a military coup."

"It means other things in French, too, you know," Callie said. "It could be a blow." She shuddered. "Like a knife blow. Or a shot."

"Or a criminal job," Frank added. "Maybe we've gotten in the way of a gang."

"Great." Callie rolled her eyes. "But you said there were two categories of incidents."

"You're not going to like this any better," Frank said. "We've got the shoplifting incident, where Maddy got you in trouble. Then there was the run-in at the club." He looked sharply at Joe. "Are you sure you simply lost that wallet?"

Joe stiffened. "What do you mean?"

"We all saw that videotape from the store. Maddy is pretty light with her fingers." Frank leaned over his brother. "Could she have gotten it out of your pocket?"

"No way," Joe told him. Even as he spoke, he wondered why he was protecting Maddy. Maybe it was a hunch, but he thought he'd get more out of her alone than siccing Frank and Callie on her as well.

Frank's gaze was still leveled on Joe, but he didn't keep up his questioning. "Well, anyway, Maddy was responsible in part for that whole scene—and involved in what came after," he finally said.

"So we've got five things that are strangers' faults and three that are Maddy's." Callie rubbed a hand over her face, suddenly looking very tired. "I just don't understand. We've been writing letters back and forth for years. I really thought I knew Maddy. Here was my chance to meet her, and I was so excited."

She flung herself back on the couch, scowling. "Some excitement. My friend gets me in trouble, and people are trying to kill me. It doesn't make any sense. The Madeleine Berot who wrote all those letters is nothing like the girl we've met. She's gone through a complete change of personality—it's like she's another person." Callie sighed. "She really had me fooled."

"She isn't all bad," Joe pointed out. "She really seemed sorry when she got you in trouble, and she did warn us about that guy with the gun."

Frank looked grim. "The only reason Callie's in this city is Madeleine Berot."

"It could be two separate cases, or two separate gangs," Frank continued, deep in thought. "The question is, what does anyone want?"

"Well, I know what I want," Callie spoke up suddenly. "That's the key to your room. All of a sudden I don't feel very safe sleeping in here."

Frank got out his key. "It's yours—just as soon as we check for any possible surprises."

The room next door was clean, too, and Callie moved in.

"You know what to do now?" Frank asked at the door.

Callie nodded, reciting Frank's instructions like a schoolchild who's memorized them. "Keep the door locked, and don't let people in unless they're accompanied by a Hardy." She grinned, staring hard at Frank and Joe. "Just memorizing your faces."

"Hilarious," Frank said sourly. "Please, Callie, be careful."

"Okay."

Frank stood outside the door as Callie double-locked it, then put on the bolt. Then he headed for Callie's room, where he and Joe would stay.

"Think we'll have any unfriendly visitors tonight?" Joe asked.

Frank growled in response as he settled down for sleep.

Joe lay under the covers but couldn't drift off.

Neither, it seemed, could Frank. He quietly slipped out of bed, picked up a chair in the darkness, and brought it over to the door, where he jammed it under the knob and sat on it. He had scoffed at Joe's suggestion earlier.

But now Frank Hardy was taking no chances.

Chapter

11

A HEAVY HAND landed on Frank Hardy's shoulder, brutally shaking him out of his uneasy sleep.

Instantly, Frank was awake—if not very aware. He took a wild swing at the fuzzy figure in the murk in front of him, nearly falling to the floor. The shaker jumped back as if he'd just awakened a wild man.

Maybe he had.

"Wha-whazzat?" Frank said, trying to figure out why he was sitting in a chair. This wasn't his room at home. It was a hotel room. Callie was next door—maybe in danger!

"You sure you're awake?" Joe asked a little skeptically.

Frank calmed down. "Yeah. I'm awake and hurting." He stretched, rubbing his back.

"Chairs are not constructed for sleeping in. But I'm sure you didn't shake me to get a furniture report. What's up?"

"I was lying here, wide awake, and I had an idea," Joe explained.

Frank fixed him with the evil eye. "You woke me after I'd finally fallen asleep to tell me you had an idea?"

"It's early morning," Joe said. "And that ties in with my idea." He explained what he had in mind while Frank went into the bathroom and threw some cold water on his face.

Awake at last, Frank studied his brother. "That actually does make sense," he finally admitted. "But I'm going to make *you* go over and wake up Callie and explain it to her." He looked around for a clock. "What horrible hour is it, anyway?"

"Six-thirty," Joe said. "We'll have to move if we really want to catch them. You get Callie, and I'll try to wash the sleep out of my head," Frank said as a yawn popped his jaw open, startling him. "I think this is no time to get up during vacation."

Forty minutes after Joe had awakened Frank, he, Joe, and Callie were standing under the awning of an apartment house. The three of them were across the street and down the block from where the Berots lived.

Callie hid a yawn behind her hand as they stood

watching the Berots' door. "You want to explain this to me one more time?" she said.

"Frank started me thinking last night," Joe began.

Callie gave him a look. "I'm glad something started you," she said.

Joe ignored her, going on. "Frank blamed one set of awful stuff on strangers, and the other on Madeleine Berot. We can't check up on the mystery men, but we can check up on the Berots. There are three of them, and three of us."

"So we're hanging around here at this ungodly hour so we can follow them when they come out," Callie finished. "What do you think we'll find out?"

Joe shrugged. "I don't know, but it's better than being sitting ducks."

"You got me there," Callie admitted. "Okay, who gets which Berot?"

"I'm following Maddy," Joe quickly announced, getting a shake of the head from Callie.

"Trust you to follow the girl," she told him. "Are you sure you aren't falling for her?"

"Falling? No way," Joe answered. But there are things I want to talk to her about, he said to himself.

"I'd like to tail Mr. Berot," Frank said, "if that's okay with you, Callie."

"Sure," Callie said. "That leaves Mrs. Berot for me—or should I call her Madame?" She grinned. "I think you guys are sticking me with the easiest tail job because I have the least experience in following people."

Frank and Joe both held their breaths, expecting an explosion.

"Actually, that's probably a good idea. Thanks for thinking ahead, guys."

The Hardys remained in astonished silence for a good half-hour before Mr. Berot emerged from the building, dressed in a suit.

"Here's my guy," Frank said. "Wish me luck." He waited until Mr. Berot had half a block on him, then started strolling after him.

Joe glanced at his watch. "Frank may have a more boring job than he thinks. Mr. Berot's probably on his way to work."

"Well, then, I guess he'll have to plant himself in front of the French embassy," Callie said. "You can never tell when Mr. Berot might pop out for some sort of funny business." She grinned. "I expect he gets a lunch hour and a couple of coffee breaks."

How much longer would they have to wait there? Joe wondered.

Not much, as it turned out.

"Joe," Callie whispered, grabbing his arm. "Look."

A blond woman stepped out of the building, wearing a navy blazer and a gray skirt.

"That's Mrs. Berot—my turn," Callie said.

As Joe turned to look, the woman across the street glanced at her watch, then rubbed her hands together in a nervous gesture. He remembered that from his introduction to the woman. She'd rubbed her hands the same way when Frank and her husband got into that very undiplomatic argument.

Callie let the woman pass, then set off after her. "Wish me luck, Joe."

"Good luck," Joe said dutifully. You'll probably need it, he added silently.

Joe settled back to wait for Madeleine. She didn't show—apparently taking a nice, long rest after the night's dancing and running around.

Joe looked at his watch for the hundredth time and shook his head. I could have slept for another two hours, he told himself, shifting his weight from one foot to the other.

At last, however, his waiting was rewarded. The apartment house door swung open, and there was Maddy. Joe stepped back into the shadows of the awning, allowing her to get a lead on him.

He let Maddy get well ahead—no use taking a chance that she'd see him tailing her. And he certainly didn't have to run to keep up. Wherever Madeleine was going, she was heading there at a very easy pace.

Joe followed as Maddy strolled down to M Street. He remembered there was a bridge over the gorge between Washington proper and

Georgetown up there. Sure enough, that's where Madeleine was heading.

Time to close up the gap, Joe told himself. There are lots of winding little streets in Georgetown. We had a case where someone almost lost us there.

At least the streets weren't jammed. Maddy stayed to the main shopping areas on M Street.

Joe sighed as she started hitting the boutiques. Hope she doesn't get popped for shoplifting again, he thought. I don't know how the cops would react to my staking out the station house.

For the next hour and a half, Madeleine went from shop to shop, trying things on and checking things out. Generally, she spent about twenty minutes per store. So, when she was in one for half an hour, Joe began to get a little concerned.

What if there's a back entrance I don't know about? he wondered.

Finally he abandoned the observation post he'd taken up across the street by a stationery store and went to look in the window.

There was Maddy—standing right in front of him at the checkout counter.

Joe ducked down and headed across the street to hide in the entrance of an old-fashioned pharmacy. Just my luck to peek into the first store where she buys something, he groused. Hope she didn't see me.

Madeleine came out of the boutique and set off down the street without checking for any tails—and without a glance in Joe's direction.

He stayed on the opposite side of the street from her and nearly a block behind. Maddy didn't seem suspicious at all. She was just walking along, obviously very pleased with herself and her window-shopping.

She walked up to a pay phone, put in some coins, and started punching in a number. Taking advantage of the distraction, Joe moved closer. He slipped into a candy store on her side of the street and watched Madeleine through the panes of the front window. She seemed to be making notes on a copy of a guidebook.

"Get you something, son?" the elderly owner asked.

A few minutes later, armed with a small bag of peppermint sticks, Joe took off after Maddy as she walked along Wisconsin Avenue.

He sighed through another boring round of window-shopping. Then Maddy suddenly left the main street, turning right on Q Street.

Joe remembered that there was another bridge back into Washington proper up ahead—as well as a bunch of embassies.

Maddy had reached the pair of massive buffalo statues that flanked the end of the bridge. There was a sharp curve, and for a moment Joe lost sight of her. He picked up his pace.

Out of the corner of his eye, Joe saw a car move up. He didn't think about it because he was so interested in seeing where Madeleine had gone.

Before he got four more steps, though, the car suddenly swerved off the road to block the sidewalk right in front of him.

Joe took a step back as three guys burst out of the car. He recognized two of them. One was the short, stocky guy who'd followed them around the Mall. The other was the tall, thin one who'd tried to push Callie—then him—off the station platform.

They tackled him like pros, Shorty and Skinny grabbing Joe's arms. While he tried to pull loose, the third, a pimply faced wiry guy, grabbed him by the legs.

Writhing and kicking, Joe struggled madly. It did him no good. He had no leverage to fight off his attackers. They had no trouble lifting him up to the stone railing of the bridge. Below him was a sixty-foot drop.

And these guys were ready to send him down it.

Chapter

12

FRANK HARDY WAS FROWNING as he trudged along after Henri Berot. They hadn't gone two blocks, and already things were weird.

If Berot did work at the embassy, he was heading in the wrong direction. For another, Berot was using all the classic tactics to spot and lose a tail—hardly the actions of an innocent man.

The tail-spotting maneuvers began as soon as Berot reached a corner with a red light. The Frenchman darted across in front of the traffic. Not the kind of behavior you'd expect from him, Frank told himself. He refused to give himself away by darting across, too.

Frank did, however, cut the distance between himself and his quarry as they walked for several blocks. That wasn't difficult, since the morning crowds had become thicker and thicker, giving Frank lots of cover. Berot walked on and on, seemingly with no destination in mind. He headed north, then east, then south, wasting more than an hour in aimless wandering.

At long last the Frenchman checked his watch and nodded to himself. Then he started walking at a serious pace—south, and then west. They entered a shopping district, full of hurrying commuters. Frank used the mass of people to shield himself from Elementary Tailing Trick Number Two—using the plate-glass store display windows as mirrors to check behind you. Berot kept on stopping to "window-shop" at store after store.

Once, Frank let the crowd carry him past Berot. Sheltered behind two guys and a young woman, all of them carrying briefcases, he wasn't noticed. Then he just moved with the crowd, keeping Berot in sight with the same window-shopping trick the Frenchman was using.

As they moved through the neighborhood, the crowd of commuters grew. Then, finally, everyone swirled underground—into the local Metro station. Standing by a newsstand, Frank let Berot go down ahead of him.

As he followed on the escalator, Frank frantically dug through his pockets. He sighed happily when he came up with the fare card Joe had bought for him. At least he wouldn't lose Berot at the machines.

Frank slipped his fare card through the turnstile three gates over and six people behind Henri Berot. He crouched a little, hiding his height in the crowd. He let the moving mass of people take him over to the escalators and down to the train platforms. Now was not the time to call attention to himself by pushing closer to his quarry.

He kept a sharp eye on where Berot was heading, however. The Frenchman got on a blue line Metro train, heading downtown. Frank got on the same train, one car away. He had a bit of a struggle keeping a position near the doors against the press of the other commuters. But he had to stay there. At each stop he had to make sure Berot didn't get off.

Two stops after boarding the train, Berot got off at Metro Center. So did Frank, but Berot didn't leave the platform. Then Frank remembered that this was a transfer point. They were stuck on the platform together. If Berot glanced over and recognized Frank, the whole gig would be ruined. Frank was lucky. The French diplomat seemed more interested in checking his watch and looking down the tunnel where the train was expected. He didn't have any time to spare for his fellow commuters.

A red line train pulled in, and Berot got aboard. Then Berot pulled his antitail trick. He stepped onto the train, waited for a moment, then stepped off.

The tactic wasn't a new one for Frank. He was actually stepping off himself when a late commuter came racing through the doors, crashing into Frank and pushing him back inside.

Frank leaped for the doorway, throwing himself halfway through the closing doors. Then he struggled just as hard to pull himself back in. He'd just caught sight of Berot leaping into the next car. Apparently, after seeing nobody suspicious jumping onto the platform, the Frenchman had decided the train was safe and boarded it again.

Frank smiled for a moment in triumph, then frowned. There was a red line station much nearer to the Berots' building than the blue line station Berot had walked to. Every step of this journey had been designed to detect and discourage tails.

Two stops later, at Judiciary Square, Berot got off the train and stayed off. Frank followed the man up the escalator and onto the street, blinking for a moment as the morning sun reflected off an enormous building of brick and cream-colored stone ahead of him. For a second he nearly lost Berot in the rush-hour crowd.

Berot headed directly for the huge brick building, which had to be at least a hundred years old. Frank thought it might be some recently renovated office building. Instead, it turned out to be a museum of architecture—and the place was just opening.

Standing by the sign that identified the place, Frank hung back as Berot stepped briskly into the museum. Frank stood for a moment, trying to come to a decision. If he went charging in he could be spotted, and what if Berot was only using the place to shake anyone on his trail? He could be out a side door and lost forever in a couple of minutes.

Finally, taking a deep breath, Frank stepped into the dimly lit entryway. At the other end, he took a deeper breath, confronted with an enormous hall. The place was long enough to accommodate a couple of football fields and amazingly high. Enormous pillars supported the ceiling.

The worst thing from Frank's point of view, however, was that this vast place was empty of people. No way could he get near Berot. He did spot him off in the distance, glancing impatiently at his watch and gazing off at another entrance to the building.

He's waiting for someone, Frank realized. I need a better observation post.

That's when he noticed the series of arcades rising toward the ceiling. The place was built like the nineteenth-century version of a shopping mall, with a huge skylight and three floors of what—offices?—looking down on the central hall.

Frank decided if he could get up to the next floor, he'd be in the perfect place to observe Berot, without being seen.

He found his way to an elevator, which chugged its way slowly. As soon as he got off, Frank headed for the railing overlooking the vast hall below. A cement column even gave him cover.

Scanning the area below, Frank caught his breath. Someone was coming from the far end of the building, heading directly for Berot. The man wore a loud, European-cut sport coat and tight pants, and his head looked too small for his bull-like body. His skin was sallow, and even from his observation post, Frank could make out the pock-marks on the man's face. This was the guy who'd tried to knife Callie—and then tried to shoot her and Frank.

The two men surveyed the empty floor, then walked over to talk together.

Okay, Frank told himself. There is only one gang behind all of Callie's troubles.

As Berot and the ugly man spoke, however, Frank watched their gestures become shorter and more violent. He couldn't hear what they were saying, but from their expressions, they were having a disagreement. A serious disagreement.

Berot shook his head frantically. The big ugly

guy frowned, thumping Berot in the chest with a finger the size of a small cucumber. Frank had to admire Henri Berot for guts. He would hate to argue with a guy who could loom over him like that.

One gang, Frank decided. But if I'm not mistaken, there are two factions.

In spite of the way Berot argued, the other man apparently won the argument.

Berot seemed to deflate, then finally he shrugged his shoulders and shook his head. Even from his vantage point, Frank could see him saying, "Do what you want."

That was apparently all the big man had to hear. He abruptly turned and headed out of the museum.

Frank was caught off guard. Which one of them should he follow?

He decided on the big guy. Maybe he could find out where this man and his small army were heading out.

Frank dashed to the far end of the arcade and located a flight of stairs. He clattered down. With luck, he still might be able to catch up with the guy.

Hoping Berot wouldn't turn to see him, Frank ran for the far entrance. Just as he made it, the entranceway filled up with a mob of people. By the time Frank got through, the man was gone.

"First tour group of the day," a museum staffer told Frank.

Frank nodded grimly. His chance to link the attackers and the Berots had just disappeared into the city outside.

Chapter

13

IT'S MY LAST CHANCE, Joe Hardy thought as he struggled against his attackers. Twisting violently, he got one foot free and planted it in the chest of the man holding his legs. He kicked as hard as he could, and the pimply-faced thug went flying backward and fell flat across the sidewalk of the Buffalo Bridge.

Even without their friend's help, though, the two guys gripping his arms manhandled him so his feet were heaved over the concrete guardrail of the bridge. Joe grabbed frantically for the protruding lip of the concrete rail and held tight when the two strong arms let go of his arms. Rough concrete scraped against his fingers as the thugs kept pushing at him to make him fall.

Joe managed to pull himself up and lift one leg

over the rail to aim a glancing kick at the short, unshaven guy on his left. He flung his body up, trying to kick the other leg over, but in the process one hand lost its grip. The guy on his right tossed Joe's legs back over the rail. Now Joe was dangling by one hand fifty feet above an expressway and the rock-clogged waterway of a creek another ten feet below that and to the left.

"Ecoutez!" a high, shrill voice screamed. The arm pounding on Joe turned at the sound and forgot Joe. The voice now yelled, *"Les flics!"*

Joe didn't speak French, but he'd heard that phrase before. He also recognized the voice doing the screaming. It was Madeleine Berot!

The thugs looked at each other uncertainly for a moment, then dashed for their car, collecting the guy Joe had kicked.

Joe got a grip with his other hand and swung himself up and onto the bridge.

In seconds the thugs were all in the car, revving the motor and pulling away. Shorty, the guy with the unshaven face, leaned out a window. "Nadine," he yelled to Maddy, *"viens avec nous!"*

That sounded like, "Come with us!"

French words flew back and forth at lightning speed, a complete mystery to Joe.

As the siren came closer, Maddy frantically waved her arms. *"Allez! Allez!"*

Her gorilla friends pulled into a tight U-turn,

doubling back into Georgetown. Madeleine ran along the bridge back into Washington proper.

Joe scrambled to his feet and took off after Maddy. Before he'd gotten ten feet, however, he saw the source of the siren—it was an ambulance, blasting along on the expressway below him.

She'd have seen the ambulance from where she was standing, Joe thought as he started running again. She knew the cops weren't coming. That was a lie—a lie to save my life!

Maddy was far ahead of him now, tearing down the sidewalk as fast as she could. But Joe was the better runner, and he had strong motivation—curiosity. He had a lot of questions for this girl.

As he came up behind her, he called, "Hey, Nadine, why don't you just tell me the whole story?"

Maddy whirled, her eyes wide, bracing herself against the wall of a building. "I didn't know they were going to do that," she gasped out. "I called them when I realized you were following me, and they said for me to lead you to the bridge. I thought they would only try to scare you off—I didn't think they would try to kill you."

The flow of words slowed as the girl realized she had answered to the name *Nadine*. Her shoulders sagged and she slumped against the brick wall behind her.

"Come on," Joe said, taking her by the arm. "I'll introduce you to a new American custom."

He led Maddy back into Georgetown, to an ice-cream store they had passed. Sitting in a booth with ice-cream sodas in front of them, he suggested again that she talk. "And the whole truth this time, no stories. Let's start with your real name."

The girl took a deep breath. "It's Nadine—Nadine Rodier."

Joe nodded. "Cute. You used your own name for the girl who taught Madeleine Berot how to pick pockets." He studied her for a long moment. "I guess that's what you do for a living. So where's the real Maddy Berot?"

Nadine shook her head. "I don't know. We came over on the same plane. After her family left customs, they got into a car—driven by one of us. A few minutes later we came out and got into another car—one with their papers and luggage."

"I think I'm still missing a few steps," Joe said, shaking his head. "Maddy—I mean, Nadine—what's the whole idea?"

"You're right—I do pick pockets for a living." Nadine shrugged a little helplessly. "My parents left me with a gang when I was a little kid. The Old Man—that's what we called our boss—taught us to pick the pockets of the tourists. He got the money. If we didn't share, we got punished." She shivered a little. "About two months ago a man came to visit the Old Man. He showed him a

110

picture. The Old Man looked at it, then called me over.''

Nadine took a sip of her soda, then continued. ''I was scared that I'd done something wrong, but the Old Man said it would be all right. The man was renting me, to play a part in a scam. I was supposed to pretend to be his daughter.''

''So Henri Berot is a phony, too,'' Joe said.

''The whole family. The real Berots were picked up at the airport, and I haven't seen them since. Paul and Sylvie—those are their real names—just slipped into their identities. The real Monsieur Berot worked in Paris, and it seems no one in the embassy here knew him. Paul looked enough like Henri Berot to pass—just as I looked enough like the real Madeleine.''

''A whole family of fakes,'' Joe finally said. ''Unbelievable. So what's the scam?''

Nadine shrugged again. ''I don't know. I'm only here as window dressing. Paul—you met him as Monsieur Berot—is a professional thief, and he's supposed to steal something to do with the French embassy. I think Sylvie, the woman who's pretending to be my mother, is his assistant. I'm only here because they needed a teen-age girl who looked like Madeleine.''

''What about the rest of the gang?'' Joe asked.

''A strong-arm squad was sent to Washington ahead of us,'' Nadine said. ''They kidnapped the real Berots. The leader is a man called La Bête—

111

the Beast." She shuddered. "He's a very ugly man."

"I think I've met him," Joe said grimly.

"He's been arguing with Paul, trying to take over the operation," Nadine explained. "When we found letters from a pen pal in Madeleine's things, and then learned that Callie was coming to Washington, La Bête wanted to kill her."

"He's certainly been trying hard enough."

Nadine nodded. "Paul wanted to try scaring her away with the purse snatching." She looked down. "Then I was supposed to be so obnoxious, she'd want to leave."

"I'd say you did a pretty good job of that," Joe told her.

"I thought it would be sort of fun," Nadine said in a small voice. "Madeleine had such nice things—things I never had. But I was stuck in the apartment all day. I didn't have a chance to enjoy anything. So when you turned up, I argued with Paul to let me go out with you. Then I'd be able to go shopping, and dancing—"

"And make fun of us and get us into trouble," Joe added.

"I can't expect you to believe me, but I do feel bad about what happened in the store and the club," Nadine said. "I was doing my job. But"—she looked up at Joe almost shyly—"I found myself liking you all, even if you are—how do you say it? Straight-arrows?"

Joe had to smile at that.

"I hated watching Callie cry as we went to the police station," Nadine said. "And then we found out that La Bête wasn't following Paul's orders—his people were trying to kill Callie. They tried to push her, then you, under a train, and you mentioned something that happened in the Capitol—"

"I think that was La Bête himself, trying to knife Callie," Joe said. "He was the one with the gun in the car last night, you know, when you warned us."

Nadine nodded. "He's like a mad bull. Me—I don't mind stealing. But killing . . ."

She shook her head.

Joe decided to press his advantage. "Come on, Nadine. Tell me about the theft Paul's going to pull."

She threw out her arms. "I really don't know."

"Okay. I won't ask you to help me find out, but I want you to *let* me find out," Joe told her. "Take me back to your apartment. If I find something that gives me a clue, fine. If not, you're off the hook." He gave her a sidelong look. "It's the least you can do. You almost got us killed, too, you know. Remember Ansel and his car."

"All right, all right," Nadine said. "I'll let you in—but only for a fast look."

Time seemed to crawl on the half-mile walk from the ice-cream shop to the building where

Nadine and the others were living. At last, however, they were entering the Berots' apartment. "Sylvie?" Nadine called into the hallway. "Paul?"

She glanced back at Joe, standing in the doorway. "They're not here," she said. "Go on—look around. Don't expect me to help you."

They reached the far end of the living room, Nadine following Joe. Then they heard the sound of a key in the lock of the door.

Her eyes wide with terror, Nadine grabbed Joe's arm and threw open a closet door. Together, they jumped inside and swung the door shut just as the outside door opened.

They heard footsteps—probably a man's—on the polished wood floor. Moving toward them. Then the phone rang.

The man stepped into the kitchen to answer it, and Joe heard superfast French. Nadine whispered a translation in his ear, almost inaudible over the arguing voice in the next room.

"It's Paul—he's talking with La Bête—getting a report on how they failed with you."

Paul had now reached the shouting stage.

"Paul says La Bête is getting us too much attention. I think La Bête is saying too many people are suspicious already. Paul's telling him to stop the attempts on you three—"

She suddenly drew in her breath. "Now La

Bête wants to get rid of the real Berots!'' she whispered.

More French followed, and Nadine's fingers gripped Joe's arm so tight, it hurt him. "Paul says no—not until he finishes the job.''

Joe relaxed as the phony Mr. Berot finished his conversation, but Nadine maintained her painful grip on Joe's arm. Her voice was tight and strained when she spoke.

"The job,'' she whispered in a scared voice. "It's tomorrow night—after that, they're dead.''

Chapter

14

JOE TURNED TO NADINE, standing beside him in the darkness of the closet. "Do you mean—" he began, but she clamped a trembling hand over his mouth.

"*Not so loud!*" Her voice was a nervous hiss. "We don't want him to hear us."

They stood in silence for a moment, until Paul's footsteps receded into the distance. "He's in the rear bedroom now," Nadine said.

She eased the closet door open, peeking around it to check that the coast was clear. Silently, she beckoned Joe out of the closet. Then she shooed him out of the apartment.

"You've got to get out of here," Nadine told Joe outside in the hallway. "This whole situation is getting too dangerous for you." She dug in her bag.

"What are you doing?" Joe asked.

"Looking for the key," she explained. "In about two seconds I'll walk into the apartment, all innocence. I warned La Bête's people that the police were coming and ran away. I haven't seen you since, don't know anything about you, and don't *want* to know anything more."

Now it was Joe's turn to grab her arm. "And what about the people La Bête is holding? The real Berots?"

"Look, I don't want them to die," Nadine said. "But if the others find out I've been talking to you, *I'm* the one who'll get killed. Understand?"

"You hardly told me anything. What we've got to know is where the Berots are being kept." Joe's eyes bored into hers. "You said it yourself, Nadine. Stealing is one thing—killing is another. Are you going to let those people die?"

"I-I'll try to find out." Nadine glanced around, getting more and more nervous. "You can't stay here. If Sylvie turns up and sees you, I'm dead. Get it?"

She looked pleadingly at Joe's stubborn face. "How about this? I'll call you tonight—seven-thirty—with everything I've found out. Okay? But now you've got to go."

She pushed at his chest, and Joe finally left. As the door swung shut, his last view of Nadine showed her leaning beside her door, sighing in relief.

Joe sat by the phone that evening from seven-thirty until eight o'clock. Nadine never called.

Callie was sitting on the couch of the Hardys' hotel room. Frank paced the floor, looking at his brother every once in a while. "Okay, Joe, spill it. Why did you make us sit around here and stare at the phone with you. What's going on?"

"Time for a council of war," Joe finally said.

As Joe was sharing his information, Frank suddenly got up from the couch. "Okay, so the guy that Berot—"

"Paul," Joe corrected him.

"Whoever. The big ugly guy has to be La Whoozis—La Bête." Frank smiled grimly. "At least we have a name for the guy who's been trying to kill us. The question is, what sort of heist is his partner going to pull off tomorrow night?"

"I'm not sure what," Callie said abruptly, "but I think I know where it's going to go down. I followed Mrs. Berot, or Sylvie, to a costume shop today. Didn't one of those diplomatic brats mention a costume ball coming up this weekend?"

"That's right—something in honor of the Lafayette sword."

"Which Mr. Berot is supposed to be in charge of," Joe added.

"You don't think—" Callie said.

Joe shrugged. "There's only one way to find out."

The weather seemed a little cooler the next morning as Frank and Joe stepped into the chancery of the French embassy. The reception area of the office was a little disordered. A tall stack of gleaming white parchment envelopes leaned at a dangerous angle on the reception desk, where a young blond woman was slipping cards into them.

"Hey, she's cute," Joe said to his brother, loud enough to make the girl look up from her work.

Frank just took a deep breath. Was it hormones that made Joe act like an idiot sometimes? His younger brother was suddenly acting like the cool guy from situation comedies—the type who doesn't realize he's a real jerk.

"Seems a shame that a pretty girl like you has to work so hard on a Saturday morning," Joe said, resting both hands on the desk to lean over her.

The receptionist's green eyes inspected him for a moment as her hands continued to slip cards into envelopes, apparently working on autopilot. "These are last-minute invitations to a costume ball—"

"Right, right," Joe said, still looking into her

eyes. "Being held at the—the—" He snapped his fingers as if the answer were right on his tongue.

"The headquarters of the Continental Order. We are displaying the Sword of Lafayette at their museum."

"Sure—the Lafayette sword. Mr. Berot is in charge of that."

The blond girl nodded. "He's a member of the Continental Order. His great-great-great-great-great-grandfather was a navy officer who helped in your revolution. As the eldest son in his family, he belongs to the Continental Order. It shows how long the friendship between France and America has lasted."

"Of course," Joe said as if he were a member himself. "I guess this will be some party, huh? A chance to start all sorts of friendships."

"The ambassador will present the sword in a private ceremony, and then, on with the party." The girl frowned as she ran out of envelopes, and opened the desk drawer for more. She also glanced at the desk clock. "You're early, you know," she said.

Joe gave her a big smile and leaned closer. "Hey, I think I'm just in time. Tell me, have you got a date for this big hoedown?"

As he watched his brother grin expectantly, Frank suppressed an urge to throw up. If Joe pulled this one off, Frank knew he'd be hearing about it for years to come.

The girl behind the reception desk put her hand over her mouth. For a second Frank thought she was coughing. Then he caught the faintest sound of giggling. She was struggling not to laugh in Joe's face!

"I—I'm sorry," the girl finally managed to say, her cute little nose wrinkling as she fought to keep a straight face. "But you see, we have a rule here—we're not allowed to date the help."

Joe looked as if somebody had just socked him in the head with a hammer. "The—the help?" he stammered.

The girl stopped laughing now. "You're the messengers, yes? Here to pick up and hand-deliver the last-minute invitations?"

"Uh, no." Joe suddenly straightened up, mortified at being taken for a messenger boy. One arm knocked over the pile of envelopes stuffed with invitations.

Oh, great, Frank thought, having a hard time holding back his laughter, too. I'll never be able to tell this story, because Joe will die of embarrassment.

He held back, afraid to move as Joe scrambled to gather up the papers he'd knocked over. Joe picked some up, dropped them, then finally delivered a big, untidy bundle into the arms of the receptionist, who came around the desk to collect them.

Frank bit his lip, afraid he'd laugh out loud.

"No," the young woman said, looking into Joe's beet red face. "I guess you aren't a messenger."

"Actually," Joe said, looking at Frank for help or support or *anything*, "we hoped to see, um, Monsieur Berot—"

The young woman shook her head, checking a large appointment book on the desk. "I'm sorry, but I don't have an appointment listed for you. And on weekends—"

Her hand went to a phone, but then Joe started shaking his head. "No, no, that's okay. I'll, uh, talk with him early next week."

He slunk off toward the exit, with Frank trailing behind. As Joe opened the door, however, he stopped for a second, looking back. "Um, I hope you have a nice time at the party."

The girl looked back with a totally straight face. "Thank you."

Joe slouched out, with Frank in hot pursuit, shaking his head. "How could you make such a stupid spectacle—" he hissed.

His words were drowned out as soon as the door closed—by Joe's laughter.

Reaching into his jacket, Joe pulled out two gleaming white parchment envelopes.

"The spectacle worked, big brother. We've got our invitations to what may be the theft of the century."

"I FEEL LIKE AN IDIOT," Joe whispered. The cab he was riding in stopped short, and for about the fifteenth time that evening, he was jabbed in the ribs by his own sword.

It was supposed to hang beside his hip from a sash. It completed the outfit of his Continental Army officer's uniform. But in the cramped confines of the cab, it turned into a dangerous item every time they hit a bump.

Frank Hardy smoothed down the lace of his Virginia planter's outfit. "Calm down, Joe. You'll look fine when we get there."

"Right," Callie added, struggling with her own costume. "At least you don't have to worry about these stupid hoops sending your skirt flying up whenever you sit down."

"I'm just glad we get to wear masks," Joe complained. "Did you see the looks we were getting in the hotel?"

"That's just because we got into a cab instead of a limousine," Callie said. "It looks like everybody who's anybody knows about this costume ball."

"We should be glad we found costumes today," Frank said.

"Right," said Joe as the cab stopped and he got jabbed again. "Glad."

The cab left the expressway and began driving along the wandering roads that bounded Rock Creek Park.

"This is a nice neighborhood," Callie said, looking out the window at tree-covered estates hiding mansions.

"It ought to be," said Frank, who had spent the afternoon reading his guidebook. "The Vice President's house is around here—and so is the Russian Embassy."

"How fascinating," Joe told his brother. "How about the place we're heading?"

"It's an old mansion overlooking Rock Creek, which the last owner deeded to the Continental Order."

"And what's this order?" Callie wanted to know.

"It's sort of a veterans association, founded by the officers in the Continental Army," Frank said. "About two thousand four hundred men joined after the Revolutionary War. Membership passes down through each family to the oldest living son descended from the original officer."

"What about the house?" Joe prompted.

"There's a ballroom on the ground floor— that's where the party will take place," Frank went on. "The museum is on the second floor. It's full of paintings and memorabilia from the Revolution. That's where the sword will probably wind up." He looked at the other two. "You understand what our jobs are?"

Joe nodded. "I'll keep an eye on the Berots and try to keep them from getting near the sword." He gave his brother a hard look. "I mean, we are assuming this guy is here to steal the sword."

Frank shrugged. "It's something beyond price for a collector. And a mad collector is the only kind of person I can imagine paying the freight for the kind of operation we've stumbled onto."

"Anyway, you guys will be trying to get ahold of Maddy—I mean, Nadine," Joe went on, looking at Frank and Callie. "I hope you have better luck than I did, finding out where the real Berots are."

Callie smiled grimly. "Don't worry. After all she's pulled on me, I'll be happy to talk to her."

The cab passed an old-fashioned graveyard,

then pulled up to an iron gate. Security guards checked their invitations, then waved them in.

Frank paid the fare and adjusted his mask. "Well, we're in."

"I still feel stupid," Joe groused, setting his sash and his sword by his hip.

"Better smarten up quick," Callie advised, "before we start tangling with these thieves."

They stepped into the mansion and followed the sound of music to the ballroom. Spacious halls decorated with colonial flags and statues of Revolutionary War heroes led them into a vaulted room at least thirty feet high. A spectacular staircase led up to a musicians' gallery—that was where the music came from.

The ballroom looked like the set from an elaborate historical movie. Hundreds of people were standing around in colonial garb. Men in silks and satins, wearing powdered wigs, talked and danced with women in lace gowns, elaborate hairdos, and glittering jewels.

"We shouldn't feel stupid," Callie whispered, trying not to stare. "I think we should feel tacky."

"Forget about that," Joe said, adjusting his mask as they started circulating through the crowd. "We've got to find the Berots."

"There—by the entrance," Frank suddenly said.

Three people had just come in—a tall, thin,

hawk-faced man in a white uniform, a middle-aged woman in a dazzling gown, and a younger woman in a simple blue gown and a white-powdered wig with ringlets. All of them wore masks.

"We didn't plan on recognizing them in costumes," Callie said. "But I think those are the people we want. Look at the widow's peak on the man."

The woman scanned the growing crowd and rubbed her hands nervously.

"That's her little gesture. I saw her do that all the time I was following her yesterday. They're *definitely* the phony Berots," Callie said. "Now let's see if we can talk to Nadine."

Joe, Frank, and Callie started across the room, making their way around flouncing skirts and dress swords that stuck out at just the right height to trip them.

The swirling crowd hid them until they were almost on top of the false Berots. Then, as luck would have it, the glittering mob parted—and Nadine saw them coming.

Apparently, their costumes weren't as good as some of the others, because Nadine recognized them right away. Her face went pale as she turned to her supposed parents and excused herself. Then she dashed out the door.

The Hardys and Callie reached the double doors that led to the ballroom and saw Nadine trying to get down the now crowded hallway. It wasn't easy in the wide gown she wore. She glanced desperately over her shoulder as they came closer, then scuttled down a short flight of stairs. She ran down another hall, made for a door, went through, and slammed it in their faces.

Frank and Joe halted. " 'Ladies,' " Frank read. "We can't chase her in there."

Callie's hands balled into fists. "I can."

She burst through the door, giving the Hardys a momentary glimpse of a lavish pink and green interior. The door closed, and immediately after came some very unladylike shrieks—thankfully muffled by the thick walls. Then came a couple of loud thumps. Frank and Joe studied the ceiling, feeling very conspicuous.

The door opened to reveal a somewhat bedraggled Nadine. Her powdered wig was slanted at a strange angle, and two of the ringlets now hung in her face. Callie sailed along behind her, with a satisfied smile on her face. "Here we are, back again," she said as if nothing had happened.

"I was a little worried for you, Callie," Frank said, moving to make sure Nadine didn't try another run for it.

Callie's smile got bigger. "Let's just say Nadine was the one you should have worried about."

With her back to a marble wall and the three American kids surrounding her, Nadine wilted. "Okay, I found out what you wanted to know.

The real Berots are being held in a bad part of town.'' She rattled off an address. "The theft is supposed to happen tonight, but I still don't know what's supposed to be stolen." She bit her lip. "It's getting scary, guys. I think La Bête was talking to Paul about getting rid of me afterward— one less to worry about in the getaway. The guy is crazy."

Frank repeated the address to Nadine, who nodded. "Down in the southeast area. We'd better get going." He grabbed Nadine's hand and put it into Joe's. "You'll have to keep Nadine here—and keep an eye on the fake Mr. Berot," he said. "We're off on a rescue mission."

"But first," Callie said with a grin, "a moment for fashion." She took hold of the wig on Nadine's head and twisted it so it sat the way it should. "Much better," she said. Then she and Frank hustled for the exit.

They were lucky enough to hail a cab that was dropping off another couple. The driver gave them a surprised look when they gave him the address.

"You want to go there—looking like *that?*" the man said, staring at their costumes.

"We don't have a choice," Frank told the man. "It's a matter of life and death."

Looking very doubtful, the driver set off.

Frank could understand the guy's doubts when they reached their destination. It was a large,

129

dilapidated building that hadn't seen fresh paint or a clean-up crew in years.

"Only warehouses around here," the driver said. "You sure you got the right address?"

"I'm pretty sure," Frank said, looking around the deserted streets. "We're supposed to find some people here and bring them back to the party. Look, can I pay you something extra to ask you to stick around? I think it will be hard to get another cab in this neighborhood."

"Hard?" the driver said. "Try impossible." He shook his head. "This isn't a place where I'd like to hang out."

"Please?" Callie said. "What we're doing is very important—if it works out, we've got to get right back where we came from."

"All right." The driver shrugged. "I'll wait a couple of minutes."

Looking like ghosts from another era, Frank and Callie ran for the warehouse door. "Locked," Frank reported, looking at the rusted steel gate that blocked their entrance.

"What a surprise in this neighborhood," Callie said. "So how do we get in?"

Frank scanned the front of the building. "Wait a second. The gate on that loading dock isn't pulled down all the way."

They climbed to the top of the dock and examined the door. "I think I can slip through under there," Frank said.

"But there's no way I can fit under there," Callie said, shaking her huge skirt.

"I'll go in and check the place out—if there's no guard, I'll open the door."

Callie didn't look happy, but she didn't have a choice. "Okay," she finally said. "But be careful." She tried to smile at him. "Remember, we've got big deposits on these costumes."

"I'll try not to get mine dirty." Frank gave her a quick kiss. Then he slid through the opening under the door, blinking in the darkness of the warehouse interior. Slowly, he could make out enormous rows of shelves with empty alleys between them. He also realized that there was a very faint light off in one corner of the warehouse.

He was making his way to the source of the ghostly glow when he became aware of a sound behind him. Whipping around, he realized it was the sound of footsteps—heading away from him, back toward the loading bay door!

Apparently the thugs had left a guard, who was now making his rounds!

Silently the automatic door began to rise. Frank took off for the guard as fast as he could.

The guard was standing peering out at the dark loading dock, a pistol in one hand. He switched on the flashlight he held in the other.

Pinned in the beam of the guard's light, like a giant moth, was the white-gowned Callie Shaw.

Chapter
16

FOR A LONG MOMENT the guard with the light and Callie just stared at each other, each equally astonished.

That was all the time Frank Hardy needed.

He launched himself at the guard's back, crashing into him, bringing the man down before he could even raise his gun. The pistol the guy had been carrying clattered off somewhere in the darkness, while his flashlight skittered off in the opposite direction.

In spite of his surprise, the guard reacted quickly to Frank's attack. He squirmed out from under the attacking Hardy, rolled onto his back, and aimed a devastating kick at Frank's face.

The kick whipped right under Frank's nose as

he pulled back. It was so close, Frank could feel the wind from its passing.

They both got to their feet now, and the guard snapped a kick at Frank's stomach. Frank blocked it with his forearm and aimed one of his own at the guy's hip.

The guard nimbly stepped aside and swept Frank's legs from under him with a roundhouse kick. Frank got to his knees, but he was knocked flat on his back again when the guard's foot caught him on the chin.

Frank lay stunned as the man moved in for the kill.

The next thing he knew, the guy was crumpling to the floor.

"How—" Frank began. Then he saw Callie standing over him, the now-flickering flashlight in her hand.

"I hope this thing will still work," she said, jiggling the switch. "Maybe I broke it when I hit that guy over the head."

Frank unbuckled the guard's belt and used it to tie the man's wrists together. His tie was used on his feet. Then Frank and Callie explored the warehouse. There were no more guards, but in the corner of the place, they found an old sign that read Secure Storage Area.

The area didn't look all that secure. There was a simple cyclone fence blocking off one corner. But it was obviously secure enough to hold prisoners. Handcuffed to a set of metal shelves were three people—a tall, hawk-faced man, a pretty blond woman, and a cute teenage girl. The real Berots were not identical to the impostors, but they looked enough alike for Frank to feel an eerie chill.

Mr. Berot shouted at them in French, but it was Maddy whose eyes went wide. "C-Callie?" she said in disbelief.

"We found out what was going on, and now we've found you," Callie said, trying to open the lock on the gate in the fence. "We'll get you out."

The overhead lights suddenly flashed on, blinding them all temporarily, and a voice behind them said, "I do not think so."

Frank and Callie whirled around to find themselves staring down the muzzle of a 9mm pistol. Beyond that, they recognized the lumpy face of La Bête.

"That Georges, he is not a good guard," the big man said, shaking his head. "The others and I, we go to the cemetery to get ready for the getaway. But when I look from behind the gravestone, I see you two coming away. So I follow and find you here."

"You saw what went on with the guard? Why didn't you step in then?" Frank asked.

"I arrive just too late," La Bête said, coming a little closer, lining them both up under his gun.

"Then I decide it is better if I let you come deep inside, where things will be quiet."

He smiled at them, revealing stained teeth. "I have to kill these ones," he said, indicating the Berots. "And you make my job so much easier by coming here—"

His words cut off in a choke as Frank's hand shot up to release a cloud of orange powder in La Bête's face. Frank's other hand jarred into Callie, knocking her aside as the French thug, eyes streaming, triggered a blind shot into the area where they'd been standing.

Frank swung around La Bête, smashing karate blows into the thug's shoulders and neck. The man was strong—he took a lot of punishment—but finally Frank managed to floor him. The gun skittered away and Frank knocked him unconscious.

"What was that orange powder bit?" Callie said while Frank tied the thug up.

"Cayenne pepper," Frank answered with a smile. "I picked some up this afternoon while we were out costume hunting. Why not take a page from this guy's book and have a secret weapon on hand?"

"Well, it certainly worked," Callie said, watching La Bête blink in pain. "Hey, look what I found." She opened the desk drawer and came out with a ring of keys. "I think I know where these go."

Sure enough, the keys worked on the lock on the gate and on the handcuffs that held the Berots prisoner.

"We can put La Bête and Georges in here for safekeeping, then call the cops," Frank said. "I think their little scheme has just fallen apart." He quickly located a phone.

Through the glittering whirl of the costume party, Joe Hardy was moving across the ballroom floor, toward the stairway to the musicians' balcony. He tightened his grip on Nadine's wrist. "I think your pal is making his move," he whispered. "Why is he going up there?"

"What?" Nadine's head spun around from where she'd been eyeing somebody's jewelry. Joe was glad he'd kept at least one of her hands out of action.

"Paul is going up the stairs to the orchestra. The question is, why?"

High above them, the disguised thief handed some papers to the bandleader and chatted with him for a moment.

Instead of coming down from the music gallery, the Frenchman headed past the band. Reaching the door behind the musicians, he exited through it.

"Come on—we've got to catch up with him." Still holding on to Nadine's wrist, Joe led the way to the stairs. When she jerked to a stop behind him, he was almost pulled off his feet. "What?" he said.

Then he saw the reason Nadine had stopped. Standing at the foot of the stairway, guarding it, he decided, was the false Mrs. Berot—Paul's accomplice, Sylvie.

The woman looked from Nadine to Joe, and her face went cold.

Now Nadine was pulling Joe away. "I'm dead, I'm dead," she moaned. "She saw me with you, recognized you. They probably think I brought you here. They're going to kill me."

Joe swung the girl around to face him. "Look, this place is crawling with cops and security guards. We can go to them and stop this heist right now." She shook her head, cringing. "Then my only hope is to stop Paul from stealing that sword myself." He took charge now, heading for the ballroom entrance.

"I'm going upstairs to check out the museum."

Nadine stopped again. "Not me," she said decisively. "And I don't want to be left alone."

"How am I supposed—" Then Joe saw another familiar face. "Ansel, my man," he said brightly, grabbing the German kid's arm. "Glad you could make it."

Ansel's eyes went wide as he realized who was speaking to him.

"Hey, I want you to have a good time," Joe said. "Why don't you dance with Maddy here?"

He put Nadine's hand in Ansel's. "Rob him blind," he whispered in Nadine's ear.

Joe rushed from the ballroom and headed for the main staircase. He ran up the stairs and to the closed front door, but the door wasn't locked.

Pushing it open, Joe headed down a long hall lined with portraits of military and political leaders from the days of the Revolution. Glass display cases lined the walls as well, filled with medals, buttons, snuffboxes, and weapons from the War for Independence.

At the end of the hall Joe spotted a hint of movement—a shadow flitting around in the deeper darkness of the dimly lit museum.

Joe reached the end of the hall just as the white-clad figure lifted something from a display case.

"Paul," Joe called, "you can't get away with taking the Lafayette sword."

The thief whirled around, a jeweled sword and scabbard in his hands. "You!" he gasped. "What are you doing here?"

"I'm here to stop you from stealing that sword," Joe told him. "It's the least I can do to pay you and your pals back for trying to kill me." He gestured to the sword. "How do you expect to get that out of here, anyway?"

Paul gestured to the scabbard and sword he

was wearing with his costume. "I'll just make a substitution. My fake sword for this real one."

He slipped the Lafayette sword from the scabbard and stalked toward Joe, holding the blade at chest level.

"And believe me, this is a real sword."

Chapter

17

"I'LL GIVE YOU one final lesson in history," the thief said, moving on Joe like a bullfighter. "This is called a smallsword."

To Joe, the three-foot blade looked large enough.

"It's quite famous in the history of weapons," Paul went on, flicking the sword at Joe's eyes. "In its day, it killed more people than any other class of weapon. And it held the record until the invention of the machine gun."

"How endlessly fascinating," Joe said, backing down the hall. "And how did you find that out?"

"Research," Paul replied, matching Joe step for step. "In my business, you do quite a lot of research."

Keeping his eyes fixed on the point of the

blade, Joe tried to remember how many steps he'd taken to get from the door and staircase to where Paul was stealing the Lafayette sword.

Paul seemed to read his mind. "You're too far from the stairs to run or call for help," he said. "Besides, you'd have to turn your back on me to run." He flicked out the blade again, and Joe flinched back. "I don't think that would be a good idea."

A smile flitted over Paul's hatchet face, as if Joe amused him. "Besides, a fine, upstanding American like you would surely rather face death than take it in the back."

The smile disappeared—Paul was finished playing. He launched himself at Joe in an overhand thrust, aiming straight for Joe's heart.

Joe twisted aside, trying to pull the sword from his own scabbard to defend himself. No sword came out. The hilt and the scabbard were all one, a useless prop.

Paul's sword was far from useless. Although the thrust missed, the sharpened tip of the small sword sliced right through Joe's costume sash, releasing Joe's scabbard. The Lafayette sword may never have been used, but it had been kept razor-sharp.

At least Joe now had his phony sword free to parry Paul's thrusts. Two pieces of sash material flapped from it as he desperately warded off Paul's attacks.

Joe retreated down the hallway, managing to knock Paul's sword thrusts off-target. It wasn't easy, since the sword's point circled wickedly in front of him, threatening him from all possible angles.

Don't pay attention to the sword, Joe ordered himself. Pay attention to the guy's eyes. He managed to keep the plastic prop between him and death, but he didn't know how much longer the game could go on. The hallway restricted his field of action, and sooner or later Paul would send a thrust home.

Paul stopped stabbing with the sword and began slashing with it, taking nicks of plastic out of Joe's defense.

Joe just managed to leap back as the Lafayette blade sliced through the arm and half the front of his uniform coat. The coat gaped open, almost torn in two.

I'm going to have a tough time explaining this to the costume rental place, Joe thought. He ducked as the sword whistled over his head. That's the least of my problems right now, though.

Frank, Callie, and the Berots sat in tense silence as the cab driver roared straight for the mansion headquarters of the Continental Order. "Have the police arrived?" Frank asked the uniformed guard who stopped them to check their invitations.

A familiar figure stepped out of the shadows of the gate house—Lieutenant Grant. He wore another expensive suit and a dubious frown. "We've been here all night, Mr. Hardy. One of my people gave me a radio report that there was supposed to be a robbery going down. I decided to wait and check you out first. After all, you had some connection with the Berot girl's shoplifting attempt."

"That wasn't the real Madeleine Berot," Callie said, pointing to the people in the backseat of the cab. "*This* is the real Maddy—and this is her real mother and father."

"You've got a couple of impostors inside that headquarters building," Frank explained, "and a bunch of French thugs hiding next door in that graveyard."

Throughout this whole report, Grant's frown only deepened. "I think we'd better check out that museum upstairs," he said. "Then we'll worry about the graveyard."

Frank was with the first wave of plainclothes police to surge up the main stairway. When they reached the top, they all stopped in surprise, staring at a scene that looked like something out of an old movie.

Paul, in his gleaming white uniform, aimed slash after slash at Joe Hardy, whose costume now looked like a collection of tatters. The tip of his prop scabbard had been cut off, and it looked as if his ragged uniform coat were about to fall off, too.

As the police officers came charging up, Joe glanced back at his brother. "About time you guys showed up," he growled.

Joe had to give Paul credit for one thing—a lot of nerve. "I found this boy trying to break into the case to steal the Lafayette sword." He looked at the sea of police facing him and recognized Lieutenant Grant. "You know me, I'm Henri Berot, and the sword is my responsibility."

"Still trying to ruin people's reputations, are you?" Frank asked. "It won't wash this time, Paul. You see, the cops have already caught La Bête."

That jarred Paul badly, but he still kept up his act. "What is the word of a French criminal against that of an accredited diplomat? I still claim diplomatic immunity."

"No, you do not."

The real Henri Berot came out of the crowd. "That man is an impostor and a kidnapper. I demand that he be taken into custody, pending final proof of our identities from Paris."

"You cannot arrest me," Paul bluffed.

"Oh, we can," Lieutenant Grant assured him. "This isn't the French embassy, so we lowly D.C. police types have jurisdiction here. If you'll put down that piece of evidence you're holding—"

"No!" Paul suddenly brought the tip of his sword in contact with Joe's chest. "If you make a move toward me, I'll run him through."

Lots of pistols were aimed at Paul, but none went off. Joe realized that police regulations were as good as a bulletproof vest for the thief. As long as Joe was in the line of fire, none of the cops could shoot.

"Great," he said. "First this clown ruins my clothes. Now he's going to fill me with steel."

Joe shrugged, and his coat started falling off his shoulders. That's what he'd planned on. Dodging to one side, he flung the tattered costume into Paul's face.

Paul recovered quickly. He couldn't bring his entangled sword around, but when Joe tried to grapple with him, he straight-armed the younger Hardy.

Joe toppled back into the crowd of police, blocking their guns and their rush for a critical instant.

Paul took that instant to sprint down the hallway, sword still in hand, and smash through a closed window.

Burglar alarms began to clamor wildly, but the secret was out now. So was the priceless sword, still in Paul's grasp.

Lieutenant Grant led the police charge down

the hall and leaned out the window, checking out the ground below. "Where'd he go?" the lieutenant asked. "He's not down there."

Joe leaned out the window, a grim look on his face. "If he didn't go down, then he went up."

Digging his fingertips into the elaborate stone carvings around the windowsill, he began climbing up the face of the building. From the tip of the windowsill cornice, he discovered it was an easy stretch to reach the roof. "Come on, guys, you can climb right up," he called down to the others below.

He hesitated for a second at the low fence that surrounded the roof. He didn't want Paul to catch him half over the white stone railing—not when a well-placed kick could send him falling three stories.

Paul wasn't anywhere to be seen. Joe swung up and over. In the distance, he saw Paul legging it, taking a diagonal course across the graveled roof.

"Joe," a panting voice called from behind him. "Wait up for the reinforcements."

He glanced back to see Frank pull himself up. He'd gotten rid of his fancy jacket and shirt, wearing just a T-shirt and the costume pants.

Joe didn't even comment on how ridiculous his brother looked. He tore off in pursuit of the fleeing thief.

Paul was still carrying the Lafayette sword,

holding it over his head as he ran. He looked as if he were leading a charge. In this case, however, the troops were the police, who had just climbed the wall, and Frank and Joe Hardy.

A deep indentation—perhaps an air shaft—cut into the roof, separating one wing of the mansion from the rest of the building.

Hearing the noise behind him, Paul didn't even glance back. Increasing his speed, he thrust one foot to the top of the railing and jumped the empty space.

He almost made it.

Maybe if Paul had had both hands free, he'd have been able to grab the white stone railing. Instead, he landed, toppled, then slid down the face of the balustrade, frantically holding on with one hand to a small stone pillar.

"The guy's a goner," Joe heard one of the police officers say behind him.

He picked up his feet, taking the last few yards of the roof at top speed. *"Joe!"* He heard Frank's horrified yell behind him—Callie's, too. Somehow she'd also made it onto the roof.

Then he had no time to pay attention to anything. He was leaping into thin air.

The balustrade on the far roof came at Joe much faster than he expected. Still, he managed to grab it two-handed and swing himself over.

Joe moved along the railing until he reached

the spot where Paul was dangling, the Lafayette sword still clutched in his free hand.

"Don't be stupid, Paul. Pass up the sword, then I'll help you onto the roof."

Paul snarled, realizing his situation was hopeless. Finally he flung the sword at Joe. A moment later Joe returned the compliment, dragging Paul over the railing and flinging him to the roof. He had the thief in a half nelson by the time the police caught up with them.

While that little drama was being played out, the sound of sirens cut the air as police cruisers converged on the nearby graveyard. A fast car hidden behind a mausoleum threw up a shower of gravel as it tried to make an escape, but the road out of the cemetery was blocked.

Lieutenant Grant was smiling by the time Joe was back indoors again. "We caught three guys in the graveyard, yelling in French to one another," he said to Frank. "That's in addition to the two you left locked up in the warehouse—and the one *you* just tackled," he added, turning to Joe.

"Lieutenant," one of the plainclothes detectives called, coming up to make a report. "We've got the other two accomplices downstairs in the ballroom."

Police officers brought up a furious Sylvie, spitting French as she struggled against her handcuffs.

"What's she saying?" Joe asked Callie.

"I can guess," she told him with a smile, "but I wouldn't know the idioms."

The police also brought up a scared-looking Nadine.

"Something a little more serious than shoplifting this time," Lieutenant Grant told her grimly. "And this time there's no phony diplomatic immunity." He shook his head. "It's like I always say—petty infractions lead to worse crimes."

"Uh, Lieutenant," Joe said, stepping over to the police officer. "Don't be hard on her. Without her help, we'd never have been able to save the Berots."

Nadine's face was white, but her voice was calm as she spoke to Lieutenant Grant. "Sir, I will tell you everything I know about this plot."

Lieutenant Grant smiled at the girl and nodded. "In view of her cooperation, perhaps she could get off lightly," he said. "She just might."

"Well, it looks like we've tied everything up," Joe said to Callie and Frank. "The Lafayette sword is safe, Paul the thief is captured, his strong-arm man is in jail—"

"And the girl who got me in trouble with the cops is facing a lot worse than I ever got," Callie chimed in, grinning. "Even if you turned out to be soft on her."

"Me? Soft?" Joe protested. "She did help us, after all."

"Right. All we had to do was back her into a corner and threaten to punch her head in," Callie shot back.

Frank sighed. "The situation must be normal. You two are fighting like cats and dogs again."

He nudged Callie, nodding down the hallway. "Do you think you can knock it off for a couple of minutes, though? Your French friends are coming this way."

The real Berot family came up to Frank, Joe, and Callie, looking a little embarrassed. "We didn't have a chance to thank you properly for rescuing us," Mr. Berot said. Even in a torn suit and with unshaven stubble on his face, he was every inch the distinguished diplomat. "You saved our lives, and you saved the Lafayette sword. My family and I will always be in your debt."

He smiled and said, "If what I heard from the police is a sample, the impostors did not show you much hospitality. We, at least, hope to make up for that by showing you a good time for the rest of your visit."

"Yes, *indeed*," Madeleine said, stepping up to take Frank's arm. "Callie often wrote to me about the adventures of her friends the Hardys. But I never expected to see you in action. My hero," she said, flashing him a smile even brighter than Nadine's best efforts. "So brave—and so *handsome*. You never told me that, Callie."

"Well, Maddy," said Callie, taking Frank's other arm, "some things are best not shared."

They marched off with a very nervous-looking Frank between them.

Joe followed them, shaking his head. "Oh, boy," he muttered. "This is going to be some vacation."

FLESH AND BLOOD

Chapter

1

"THIS IS WORSE than a nightmare!"

Frank Hardy brushed back his wet brown hair and scanned the area. The scene looked more like a set for a war movie than downtown Bayport. Several buildings had been leveled, cars had been thrown about like toys, and traffic signs were twisted into pretzel shapes.

What stunned Frank even more was the fact that the destruction had been caused by a tornado.

Tornado? Frank thought with a shake of his head. He had seen pictures of tornadoes hitting places like Oklahoma but not in New York and especially not in a coastal city like Bayport. A hurricane would have been more natural.

A shout snapped Frank from his thoughts.

"Over here!" Joe Hardy was standing next to Chet Morton, waving for Frank to join them.

1

Frank rushed to his younger brother. If Joe could see himself in a mirror, Frank thought, he wouldn't believe it. Always particular about his appearance, Joe looked like a wet mop now. His water-drenched clothes hung on him like soggy rags, and his blond hair was matted flat on his scalp.

"I think I heard someone under this roof," Chet, the Hardys' best friend, explained as Frank joined them.

Frank scanned the red-shingled, fifteen-foot section of roof lying on the pavement. The roof had once covered the Bayport Pawn Shop. The tornado had ripped the roof off and thrown it to the ground.

"If anyone is trapped under there," Frank said, "he can't be alive."

The roof was made of thick plywood covered over with several layers of shingles. Bricks from the building had fallen onto the roof, adding to its crushing weight. Frank wasn't looking forward to seeing what was under the roof.

Frank knelt down and slid his hands under the plywood. "Lift on three," he told Joe and Chet.

Joe and Chet ran to the corners to distribute the weight of the roof evenly.

Frank counted three, and they lifted, grunting and straining. Slowly the roof cleared the ground with a creak and a groan. A bloody hand shot out from the side.

"Chet and I can hold it," Joe said quickly, his

voice straining from the weight. "You pull him out—but hurry."

Frank squatted and grabbed the hand.

"Help me," a man's desperate voice moaned. *"Please."*

Frank knew that moving the man might cause him further injury, but he also knew that Joe and Chet couldn't hold the roof for more than a few seconds longer. Their faces were already deep red from straining. He made a quick decision.

Frank pulled the man free just before the roof fell with a groaning crash.

"Good timing," Joe said, huffing. His face was still red, his breath coming in gasps. "Is he okay?"

Frank felt the man's pulse. "It's weak."

Frank turned toward Chet. "Chet. Call an ambulance."

Chet didn't answer. He was holding his left hand, grimacing as he looked at his index finger.

"What's wrong?" Joe asked.

"I smashed my finger when we dropped the roof," Chet said with a moan. "It feels like it's going to throb off." He started for the van. "I'll call the ambulance."

"Use the CB," Frank called after Chet. "The tornado knocked out the microwave tower, and the cellular phone is dead."

"Okay!" Chet shouted back, still cradling his left hand.

3

"Great job, guys. This ought to make the lead on tonight's news." Callie Shaw walked briskly up to Frank and Joe, her camcorder held firmly against her face, the red On light flashing. "I got the whole rescue on tape."

"Ever since you got that 'newshawk' job, you think you're a national newscaster," Joe quipped. Callie had recently been hired as a video newshawk —an amateur news reporter—for WBAY and was looking for her first story.

"This is the last time I make you a hero, Joe Hardy." Callie turned the camcorder directly on Joe and moved the camera up and down, capturing Joe's wet-cat appearance on videotape. "Wait until the girls get an exclusive look at you, Bayport's most eligible bachelor."

"Hey!" Joe yelled and made a move toward Callie, who dodged Joe's grasp.

Chet rejoined the group. "The ambulance is on its way. I thought he could use this." Chet handed Frank an army blanket from the van.

Frank spread the blanket over the man and reached for his pulse again. He glanced up at Joe and Callie. Callie's mocking smile and Joe's glare told Frank that things were slowly getting back to normal. Not even the presence of a freak early summer tornado could keep Joe and Callie from getting on each other's nerves.

Frank, Joe, Chet, and Callie had been on their way out of Bayport toward the beach when they

4

heard the tornado warning over the radio. At first, none of them believed it. Then, as they were heading back toward town, they watched in horror as the twister hit. Its angry twisting black funnel cloud snaked out of the sky, with furious winds striking a deadly swath one hundred yards wide and four miles long.

They had returned to Bayport and started helping the police and fire departments to search for people trapped in buildings. Callie picked up a camcorder at the TV studio and rejoined the boys in her car.

"Frank! Joe!" a girl yelled from behind them.

The group turned. Don West and Liz Webling trotted up. Liz was an old friend of the Hardys and had helped them on one of their cases, *See No Evil*. Joe had once thought of dating Liz. She was smart, athletic, and enjoyed sporting events, but what Joe liked best about Liz was her shiny short blond hair, large hazel eyes, and terrific figure.

The only thing stopping Joe was Don West. Don had lived in Bayport for three years and had been going steady with Liz for almost two. At six feet, Don was as tall as Joe, just as muscular, and every bit as good-looking. Callie often teased Joe that Don, with his steel gray eyes and long brown hair, was fast replacing Joe as Bayport's heartthrob.

Liz and Don had also been helping in the search for victims. They were working one block over from the Hardys.

"Did you reach your father?" Liz asked Joe.

"Not yet," Joe replied. "The phone lines are down."

"Use your CB," Don suggested. "You could reach a ham operator, and then he could call your dad."

"Good idea," Frank said. "Thanks, Don." He ran to the van.

"I was about to suggest that," Joe said.

"Sure you were," Callie teased.

Joe glared at Callie.

Frank and Joe's father, Fenton Hardy, was in Philadelphia testifying at a trial. The Hardys' mother, Laura Hardy, and their aunt Gertrude had gone with him.

"Find anything?" Callie asked Liz.

"No, thank goodness," Liz replied, looking at the man under the blanket. "Is he okay?"

"We think he will be," Joe replied. "We dragged him out from under that roof."

"Looks heavy," Liz said.

"Not really," Joe said with a shrug.

"Does my finger look blue to you guys?" Chet asked, holding up his swollen index finger.

"No," Joe said with a smirk. "It looks just as happy as the other nine."

Chet stared blankly at Joe for a second, then his face screwed into a frown. "Ha, ha," he said slowly. "You're a regular comedian."

"Whoever heard of a tornado hitting Bayport?"

Callie asked. It was a question that had been on all of their minds, but one for which nobody had an answer.

"Hey, look over there," Liz said, pointing down the street.

They all turned.

"Looks like Mangieri's using his five-finger discount credit card again," Joe said.

Martin Mangieri was just climbing out through the smashed front window of an expensive appliance store with a portable television in his arms.

Joe easily recognized the short, overweight teenager by his long hair, which had the texture and color of dirty yellow wall insulation and was pulled back into a ponytail. Even on a perfect summer day he was wearing his scuffed black leather jacket with the gory hand-drawn skull and crossbones on the back.

Mangieri had been a troublemaker at Bayport High and had been kicked out of school earlier in the year for breaking into the soft drink and candy machines in the student lounge.

"Let's cancel his credit card," Don suggested.

Joe was surprised at Don's suggestion. He had never known the quiet senior to be adventuresome.

"You're on," Joe replied with a wink. "Last one to the creep is a rotten egg." With that, Joe sprinted toward Mangieri.

"Hey!" Don shouted and then started after Joe. A moment later he was next to the younger Hardy.

Joe was surprised at Don's speed and wondered why Don hadn't played football or gone out for track.

They were ten yards from Mangieri when the small-time hood spun around. His face turned a ghostly shade of white, his jaw dropped, and his eyes widened into two large circles of fear. He threw the television at Joe and Don and then darted down the street.

In unison, Joe and Don hurdled the television as it smashed onto the concrete sidewalk.

Although short and fat, Mangieri was fast. He's probably had plenty of practice running from police, Joe thought.

Joe pumped his arms faster and began to gain on Mangieri. He glanced to the side and was pleased to see that Don was lagging behind.

Joe was an arm's length away when Mangieri suddenly stopped, twisted around, and planted a solid right into Joe's stomach. Joe gasped as the air was knocked out of him and he crashed to the ground.

Mangieri ran a half block farther and disappeared into an alley.

"I'll get him," Don announced, sprinting past Joe.

Joe jumped up and instantly wished he hadn't as his stomach muscles contracted from the pain of Mangieri's blow. He was embarrassed that a runt like Mangieri had outmaneuvered him. His embarrassment kindling his anger, he dashed up the street and into the alley down which Mangieri and Don had disappeared.

The alley was a dead end—and it was empty.

Joe moved slowly through the brick corridor, every nerve in his body tense. He listened for any movement.

The alley served as a back exit for several businesses and was lined with trash dumpsters. It ended at the back wall of another building.

Joe was halfway down the alley when he was grabbed and jerked to the side. Joe hit the wall, the breath nearly knocked out of him again. He clenched his fist.

"Not so fast, Joe," Don whispered.

"What?"

"Shhh." Don raised a finger to his lips.

"Where's Mangieri?" Joe angrily whispered.

Don nodded toward a dumpster directly across from them.

Joe peered at the dumpster. A bit of black leather jacket hung out between the dumpster and its lid.

"You want to do the honors, or shall I?" Don asked.

Joe rubbed his sore stomach. "I will," he growled.

Joe walked over to the dumpster and threw up the lid.

Mangieri popped up like a jack-in-the-box, swinging a piece of wood straight at Joe's head. Joe saw the blurred board in time and ducked. The force of Mangieri's swing and miss unbalanced the overweight thief, and he spun around and fell backward head over heels out of the dumpster.

Mangieri scrambled to his feet. Joe grabbed for the worm, but Mangieri wiggled free and planted a solid left to Joe's already sore gut.

Joe groaned and clamped his hands on Mangieri's black leather jacket. Twice Mangieri had outmoved him. Joe yanked Mangieri up until the punk was on his tiptoes.

"All right, *broom head*," he said. "Now I sweep up the alley with you."

Mangieri struggled to get free and staggered backward, dragging Joe with him. He tripped and slammed into the wall, Joe falling on top of him. Mangieri lay slumped against the wall. As Joe stood up he heard an ambulance siren stop wailing. The ambulance must have come to pick up the man injured in the tornado.

"He's out," Don said.

Joe rubbed his stomach. He fired an angry glare at Don. "Where were you? Why didn't you help?"

Don held up his hands in innocence. "Hey, man, you said you wanted to take care of this."

"You okay, Joe?" Frank shouted, running down the alley.

Mangieri groaned, and Frank looked down at the thug.

"Joe's just fine," Don answered. "But Mangieri's going to have a pretty bad headache for a while."

"Liz told me what happened while I was in the van," Frank explained. "I had Callie call the police."

"Were you able to reach a ham operator?" Joe asked, still holding his stomach.

"Yeah. Got one in Hoboken. He said he'd call Dad's hotel and tell him and Mom we're okay and so is the house."

"Let's get Mangieri to your van and wait for the cops," Don suggested.

Frank and Don helped Mangieri to stand. Mangieri wobbled and nearly fell over, and they had to hold him up as they walked back to the van.

Officer Con Riley and his partner were waiting when they returned to the Hardys' black van. Callie and Chet were gone.

"I see you didn't need any help catching the suspect," Officer Riley said with a smile, pushing his hat back on his head.

"Where are Callie and Chet?" Frank asked Liz.

"Callie wanted to get her tape to WBAY for editing in time for tonight's news," Liz answered. "Chet went with her after the ambulance left with that injured guy."

"You guys know Officer Stewart, don't you?" Officer Riley asked, pointing a thumb at the young policeman standing next to him.

"Sure," Frank said, recognizing the distinctive

white blond hair of Stewart. "You used to walk the beat at city hall, didn't you?"

"That's right," Stewart replied with a smile. "I'll read him his rights, Con."

Mangieri leaned against the police cruiser. "Do you understand these rights as I have read them to you?" Patrolman Stewart concluded moments later.

"Yeah," Mangieri answered weakly.

"He's probably got them memorized," Joe said sarcastically.

Mangieri's black eyes flared with anger. He stared at Joe and addressed Officer Riley. "Hey, Riley, how would you like to be a hero? Save somebody's life?"

"You referring to me, punk?" Joe took a step toward Mangieri.

Officer Riley put his hand on Joe's shoulder. Joe stopped. Stewart then spun Mangieri around to cuff his hands. "What are you talking about?"

"I got some information that could get you a promotion, Riley." Mangieri swiveled his head to face Riley. "Only you got to let me go first."

"You weasel," Joe blurted out.

"What kind of information?" Officer Riley asked.

"Someone's going to get killed." Mangieri was calm.

"Don't believe him, Con," Joe said.

"You're so smart, Hardy," Mangieri said with

a chuckle at Joe. He turned to Officer Riley. "Go ahead. Take me in. Why should I care if someone gets killed."

"Who?" Officer Riley asked.

Mangieri stared at Joe and said bluntly, "Fenton Hardy."

Chapter

2

"WHAT DID YOU SAY?" Joe lurched forward and grabbed Mangieri by the front of his jacket.

Mangieri's smirk quickly melted into fear. Joe held Mangieri up so that they stood nose to nose, the short Mangieri having to stand on tiptoe.

"Listen, you punk, you'd better explain that last remark."

"Easy, Joe." Con placed a strong hand on Joe's shoulder and squeezed.

Joe reluctantly let loose of Mangieri.

"Why do you want to kill our father?" Frank's brown eyes bore into Mangieri's like drill bits.

Mangieri, his voice high-pitched, said, "That's not what I meant, man. I didn't say I was going to kill your old man. I said that I heard someone was out to off him."

15

"Who?" Frank asked.

Mangieri's black eyes narrowed. "You want information, Hardy? Dial four-one-one."

"You slug!" Joe jumped at Mangieri again.

"All right, Joe!" Officer Stewart shouted and pulled Joe back.

Joe jerked free and stared at Mangieri.

"He's lying," Frank said.

Mangieri tried to avoid the cold, rock-hard stares of the Hardys. He slipped into the cruiser through the door Officer Riley was holding open. "Man, how do you know I'm lying?" he shouted from inside the car.

"Your lips are moving," Joe replied without missing a beat.

Mangieri looked like a caged animal. He pressed up against the door and stared straight ahead.

Suddenly he turned his head to Joe. "Forget it, man," he said with a laugh. "I don't say nothing until I see a lawyer. Then I see what kind of a deal I can cut."

Frank looked at Riley and started to ask, "Do you think—"

"Sorry, Frank," Riley interrupted. "This is out of my hands. He's asked for his lawyer. The only thing I can do is finish processing the arrest."

"Don't you believe him about someone out to kill Mr. Hardy?" Don asked.

"That's not the point," Riley said.

"What *is* the point?" Joe took a step toward

Officer Riley. "This creep made a threat against my dad."

Riley's face tightened into an angry expression. The police veteran straightened to his full height and returned Joe's steely stare.

"Your father's the best friend this police department has, and if someone's threatening his life, we'll take care of him." He took a deep breath, and his face relaxed. "Besides, Mangieri's been known to try to lie his way out of jail before. He's probably just bluffing." He looked at Frank. "You two take it easy until we get the truth out of him."

"Yes, sir," Frank said. He tapped Joe on the shoulder and nodded toward the van. Joe backed away from the cruiser, his eyes steady on Mangieri in the backseat.

Officer Riley slammed the back door shut, jumped into the front seat, waited for Stewart to get into the car, and pulled away from the group.

"What are you going to do?" Liz asked.

"Go to the police station to find out if Mangieri's telling the truth," Frank replied as he hopped into the van. Joe planted himself in the driver's seat.

"Call us if you need any help," Don said as he slipped an arm around Liz, and the two of them headed back to help with the tornado cleanup.

"Thanks," Joe said, his voice hard and distant.

Minutes later the boys walked into the officers' lounge of the Bayport Police Department. Frank threw himself into a chair and stared at his brother.

Con Riley was probably right, Mangieri's threat was only a lie, a diversion to get him out of jail. On the other hand, Joe had made sense: they couldn't take the chance that Mangieri was bluffing. All three Hardys— father and sons—had made plenty of enemies while investigating crimes.

"You think he's telling the truth?" They were the first words Joe had spoken since arriving at the station.

"I doubt it," Frank said with a shrug. "How would a greaseball like him get information about someone out to kill Dad?"

Joe stared straight ahead. Frank leaned back in the blue plastic chair and locked his hands behind his head. He knew Joe's anger had reached its combustion point and was now smoldering.

"We've got to let the police do their job," Frank said. Joe turned to meet his brother's hard stare with one of his own but said nothing. "Riley'll let us know if Mangieri is telling the truth or not," Frank added.

"They'd better find something out—and soon!" Joe crumpled the wrapper of the candy bar he'd been eating and tossed it into a corner wastebasket. He was tired and worried.

"Soon" stretched into a half-hour and then an hour. Joe tried several times to find out what Mangieri was telling Riley and the assistant district attorney, but all he got was a chilly warning from the desk sergeant that he and Frank would be thrown out of the police station if Joe didn't stop bothering him. He told the boys that the force was stretched thin due to the tornado. He said they should consider themselves lucky that Con was taking the time to question Mangieri then.

Frank mentally reviewed some of Fenton Hardy's most dangerous cases. Many crooks threatened the police officers who had arrested them or the district attorney who put them in jail or the private eye who tracked them down. Therefore, Frank knew that their father had received his share of threats.

"It's been two hours!" Joe all but shouted as he looked up at the clock on the wall. "You'd think they'd have found out something by now."

"We have."

Joe spun around. Officer Riley stood in the doorway, and he looked exhausted and worried. He motioned for the brothers to follow him. Frank and Joe were at his heels as he led them down the hallway past the interrogation room and into a viewing room.

"Where's Officer Stewart?" Frank asked.

"He asked for some time off," Riley said. "He's worked two straight shifts."

The viewing room looked into the interrogation room through a one-way mirror. The Hardys could see Mangieri sitting alone, smoking a cigarette, his hands uncuffed.

"What's going on?" Joe demanded. "Isn't he under arrest?"

"For now," Officer Riley replied. "How well do you two know Mangieri?" His voice sounded as exhausted as he looked.

"He was kicked out of school," Frank said. "Why?"

"Either of you ever hear of Leonard Mock?"

Frank and Joe glanced at each other and shrugged.

"Mangieri has." Riley turned and stared into the interrogation room.

"So?" Joe stepped up to the one-way mirror and stood next to Riley. "What's the big deal?"

Riley rubbed his eyes. "I was a rookie cop about the time your father resigned from the New York Police Department and started P.I. work here in Bayport. One of the first cases he helped the Bayport police solve involved a con man named Leonard Mock."

Frank's eyes suddenly lit up as he remembered why Mock's name sounded familiar. "He was selling shares in a dummy corporation that was supposed to build a theme park outside of Bayport."

"Correct," Riley said.

"But he's serving a life sentence for murder." Riley didn't reply. He only sighed. Frank shifted uncomfortably. "Isn't he?" he quietly demanded.

Riley locked eyes with Frank. "He was."

"Murder?" Joe spouted.

Riley moved to a table across the room and sat

on the edge. "When the police caught on to Mock's scam, Mock went into hiding. Your father was hired by a group of the investors, and he was able to locate Mock. When we started to arrest him, Mock tried to escape, shots were fired, and my partner was killed."

"Wait a minute," Frank said, his forehead wrinkled in confusion. "What do you mean 'was' serving a life sentence? He's been paroled?"

"I thought the mandatory sentence for a cop killer was life without parole," Joe said.

"It is. But Mock's attorney has somehow gotten the sentence commuted, and—"

"Mock's out of prison," Frank said, finishing Riley's sentence. The police veteran nodded silently.

"This Mock creep is on the streets after killing a cop? I can't believe it!" Joe thrust his hands into his pockets. "What's that got to do with Mangieri threatening Dad?"

Riley rubbed his eyes. "Mangieri says that Mock is trying to hire a gun, someone to kill your father."

"And Mangieri's been hired to—" Joe's voice rose in anger and he was unable to finish his sentence. He headed for the viewing room door. "That creep's not going anywhere."

"It's not Mangieri!" Riley shouted as Joe threw open the door.

Joe stopped in the doorway and slowly turned around. "Who?" he asked through clenched teeth.

For the first time since he could remember,

Frank thought he saw defeat on Riley's face. "We don't know."

Frank was quiet.

"What's your idea, Frank?" Riley asked, knowing Frank's silences meant he was thinking at computer speed.

"My dad's file on the case is full of letters from Mock threatening to kill him if he ever got out of prison."

"He threatened your father in open court while Fenton was testifying against him," Riley added.

"What if Mock is spreading a rumor about hiring a hit man to lead the police in the wrong direction? What if Mock is the killer himself?" Frank reasoned out loud.

"Why would Mangieri rat on Mock?" Joe asked.

"Mangieri would sell out his grandmother if he thought it would be to his advantage," Riley replied.

"Mangieri must know where Mock is hiding out," Frank said, almost to himself.

Riley cleared his throat. He hesitated, then said, "*We* know where Mock is." He paused again. "Mock checked in with a parole officer two days ago."

"And no one told you?" Joe asked, his voice angry.

"Paperwork takes awhile to get around, Joe. Besides, we've all been busy today with the tornado." Riley stood. "Where's your father now?"

"In Philadelphia," Frank answered.

"Good."

"Where's Mock?" Joe asked.

Riley's eyebrows lifted in a knowing glance. "Forget it, Joe. A squad car's been sent to pick up Mock. And Chief Collig has ordered me to tell you two to stay away from Mock. We've got things under control." Riley glanced at his watch.

Frank glanced at Joe and nodded at the door. Joe returned the silent signal.

"We'll try to call our dad in Philadelphia," Frank said, heading for the door.

"Good idea," Riley said behind them.

"Yeah," Joe added. "We'll stay around the house in case Dad decides to come back early."

Frank glanced back at Officer Riley just before he stepped through the doorway. It wouldn't be the first time that he and Joe had disobeyed police orders to stay out of a case.

"Where to?" Joe asked after they had hopped into the van and pulled away from the police station.

"If Mock's been released," Frank began, "then he'd have to check into a halfway house for felons until he can find a job and get settled."

"That rehabilitation place on Fulton Street?"

"Right."

"Suppose the police have already picked him up?"

"Then we'll just look around," Frank replied with a knowing smile.

23

Joe nodded and stomped on the accelerator. The van lurched forward.

Minutes later Joe's enthusiasm turned into a low groan as he pulled the van up in front of what was left of the Bayport Rehabilitation Center. The freak summer tornado had torn parts of the roof off the building and demolished the left wing.

"He's definitely not here now," Frank announced, just as disappointed as Joe.

They climbed out of the van and stared at the wrecked building.

"Let's see what we can find out, anyway," Frank suggested.

They took in the street with two quick glances before running into the building. Clothes and papers and books and debris had been chucked about by the unforgiving twister's violent winds. Puddles of water stood inches deep up and down the hallway and gave the place a musky, moldy stench already.

"Smells like chemistry class," Frank said, wrinkling his nose.

Although it was early afternoon outside, it was very cloudy and the inside of the building was dark. Frank and Joe pulled out their pocket flashlights and flicked them on.

Frank pointed to his right. "You take that room, and I'll search the office—see if I can find out where Mock's room was."

Joe's reply was a quick jog across the hall and

24

into the dark room. He moved his small flashlight around the room slowly, the shadows rising and falling like dark targets at a shooting gallery. The room was full of sheets, blankets, pillows, pillow-cases, and towels, all thrown about.

"Just a storage room!" Joe yelled across the hallway as he stepped out of the room. "I'm going to check the rooms down the hall." He started off, not waiting for Frank's answer.

Joe was halfway down the hall when he heard Frank yell out. Without hesitating, he spun around and darted back toward the office, splashing pools of water against the walls, his flash-light a tiny beacon bobbing and skipping in front of him.

He tried to stop as he reached the door, but slid on the wet floor and had to grab the door frame to keep himself upright. Joe stared into the coal black room. Frank's light should have been on.

"Frank!" Joe yelled into the room.

Joe heard a scuffling sound of people strug-gling. Then there was a fleshly slap and finally a low, deep moan.

"Frank!"

Joe adjusted the lens on the small flashlight so that it made a larger circle. Then he stepped into the room.

The office was as littered as the storage room. Joe swept the circle of light from his left to his right, slowly moving the telltale beam across overturned desks, chairs, file cabinets, and piles of wet and crumpled files.

Another deep moan caused him to jump, and he flipped the beam to his far right.

Frank lay on the floor holding his left side, his face twisted in pain.

A pale and gaunt man stood over Frank, a broken section of a board gripped in his hands like a club. Several rusted and twisted nails poked out of the end of the board.

"Time to die," the man wheezed. He brought the board down in a deadly arc toward Frank's head.

Chapter

3

FRANK'S EYES WIDENED in horror as he watched the board with the nails arcing down toward him. At the last possible second he rolled to his right, pain shooting through his left side like tiny needles. The board slammed down inches from his chest, the nails sinking into the floor.

"Aaargh!" the man screamed as the broken board splintered in his hands.

Joe dropped his flashlight and lunged at the gaunt figure. The two hurtled backward and crashed on top of a desk. A sickening gasp erupted from the stranger, and Joe knew that the breath had been knocked out of him. The room was as silent then as it was dark.

"Joe? You okay?" Frank asked in a forced, strained whisper.

27

"Yes." Joe stood. "I dropped my flashlight."

"I've got mine." A light flickered on. Frank stood and trained the beam on his attacker.

The man groaned and threw his arms over his face as the beam hit his eyes.

Joe reached down and pulled the man to his feet. He was surprised at how light the man was.

"Let's get him outside," Frank said.

Joe gave the man a slight nudge forward.

"Easy," the man said with a groan.

Guided by the beam of Frank's flashlight, Joe forced the man ahead of him.

Outside, he spun the man around. "All right, mister. Why did you attack—" Joe's sentence ended in a gasp. The man's appearance startled him, and he took a step backward.

The man was as tall as Joe, but he was too thin for his height. Can't be more than one hundred thirty-five pounds, Joe thought.

What stunned Joe the most was the man's face. His skin was tight against his skull and cheekbones, and small red sores stood out in contrast to the sickly yellow-white of his skin. The man's light blue eyes, which seemed to be covered with a milky substance, stared out at Joe from deep, dark sockets.

Joe had seen the look before, but only on dead men.

The man sucked in a deep breath through yellow clenched teeth.

"Ssssooo, Hardyssss," the man hissed. Then he coughed, deep hacking explosions that reminded Joe of metal being twisted and torn.

"Who are you?" Frank asked. "Why did you attack us?"

The man smiled, his thin blue lips pulling across his face in triumph. He opened his mouth to speak but doubled over in another coughing spasm. This time he fell to his knees. Frank reached down to help the man.

"Get—away—from—me," the man forced out through dry coughs.

"He was probably just looking for someplace to stay. Maybe he doesn't have a home," Joe said. "I'll call an ambulance on the CB." Joe ran to the van.

Why would a homeless person be hanging around the rehab center? Frank asked himself. Better yet, how would some stranger know our last name?

The man's coughing increased, and he fell flat on the ground.

Frank knelt beside him. "How can I help you?" he pleaded. "Joe, hurry!"

The man must have some ID, Frank thought. He reached into the man's front shirt pocket, but his hand was instantly smacked away.

"You—want—to—help—me?" the man wheezed. "Then—*die*, Frank Hardy!"

29

"What?" Frank wasn't sure he had heard the man correctly.

"An ambulance is on its way," Joe said, rejoining Frank. He stared down at the man. "How is he?"

"Delirious. I think he just told me to die."

"That'ssss—right." The man's coughing had stopped, and he was now breathing sporadically in screeching gasps.

Joe knelt on one knee. "Who are you?"

"Leonard Mock." The man swallowed hard.

"Mock?" Joe glanced at his brother and then back down at the pale figure of Leonard Mock. "What are you doing here? The police—"

"Came by the rehab center and went," Mock interrupted. "They couldn't find me, just like before."

"Before?" Frank was puzzled. "Before what?"

"Just like before. The first time. The first ti—" Again Mock succumbed to a fit of dry, hacking coughs.

"What are you doing here in Bayport?" Joe asked once Mock had stopped.

"Waiting for Fenton Hardy." Mock's hollow, dead eyes flicked from Frank to Joe. "But you two will do. You'll do just fine."

Frank knew they had very little time. Once the ambulance arrived, the police would take over and the Hardys would be forbidden to question Mock.

"You've come back to Bayport to kill Fenton Hardy," Frank stated.

The man attempted a laugh but only coughed. "No," he finally gasped.

"Then why?" Joe asked, anger replacing his impatience.

"I—came—to die," Mock announced.

"What?" Joe blasted back.

Mock swallowed and the grimace on his face and shudder of his body told Frank that the man's pain ran deep and hard.

"Cancer," Mock forced out.

"That's why they commuted your sentence," Frank said.

Mock turned to Frank and smiled. "You're the smart one, aren't you? The governor couldn't keep a dying man in prison. It's inhuman." Mock's head jerked back as he bellowed a laugh; the laugh was replaced by a deep, bone-jarring gasp that Frank thought would be the man's last breath.

"If you didn't plan on killing our father, why did you come back here? Why did you attack Frank?" Joe demanded.

"You startled me. I thought you were looters."

"How do you know who we are?" Joe continued.

"I know all about Fenton Hardy and his famous detective sons. Like father, like sons, huh?" Mock smacked his dry lips. "I subscribed to the local hometown paper. Couldn't miss an exciting issue.''

"Do you know Martin Mangieri?" Frank asked.

"No." Mock's voice was suddenly weak and soft.

"He's a two-bit crook who says he's got street news that you plan to kill our father."

"*Had* planned," Mock replied, his eyes widening. Then more softly he repeated, "Had planned. Your old man sent me to prison for life. I wanted him dead. Then I got cancer."

Mock closed his eyes and swallowed. Again his body shook, and he clenched his teeth against the pain.

Thunder rumbled low and deep in the distance. The faint shrill of the ambulance's siren could be heard several blocks away.

Frank knew they had little time left. "You mean that you don't blame our father for cracking the case against you?"

"Want to hear a little joke?" Mock replied. "The closer you get to death, the more you think about life. Real funny, huh? Well, I've made peace with my hate and anger."

"Good," Joe said with a sigh. He suddenly felt sorry for the man. "Can we help you? Can we do anything for you?"

Mock let out a screeching laugh that stunned the Hardys.

"You fools," Mock groaned. "I've only said

that I've made my peace with *myself*, not with your father. I may not kill him, but I still want him dead!''

Joe reached out to grab the man, but Frank knocked his younger brother's hand away.

"You want to hit me, don't you, Joe Hardy? You want to do something to hurt me. Now multiply that hatred by a lifetime sentence, and you'll have a little taste of the hatred that has eaten at me.''

"Why?" Frank fired back. "Why do you want our father dead?'' The ambulance was getting closer.

Mock's light blue eyes widened. "I rotted in that prison for years. Can you understand that? Fenton Hardy was free. Free to see his two sons grow up.'' Mock closed his eyes and swallowed. "To see his sons grow up. My son—my own son—''

Mock gasped and then choked, trying to suck in air.

The ambulance screamed to a stop. The thunder clapped closer and louder.

Mock inhaled. He opened his eyes and stared at the Hardys, a vision of death in his milky blue eyes. An evil smile spread across his yellow-white face.

"My own son," he began, softly, slowly, "will finish what *his* father could not. What goes around comes around.''

The ambulance attendants jumped from the vehicle. Mock sank back. Frank was afraid the dying man had lost consciousness. He grabbed Mock by his shirt lapels and pulled him up.

"What about your son?" Frank asked desperately.

"Everything comes full circle. Fenton Hardy put me in prison. *Killed me!* Now my son will kill Fenton Hardy!"

the HARDY BOY CASEFILES

Chapter

4

"YOU TWO WERE SUPPOSED to stay off this case, remember?" an angry Con Riley was saying through clenched teeth as the ambulance pulled away.

"We just wanted to look around, see if we could find anything that could help the police." Frank was trying to be tactful.

"Sure," shot back a doubtful Officer Riley. "What did you expect to find?"

"We didn't expect to find Leonard Mock," Joe answered quickly as his eyes followed the ambulance up the street.

Mock had barely spoken about his son killing Fenton Hardy when he had collapsed. Frank and Joe had watched as paramedics put the dying man on a respirator and then loaded him into the ambulance. Frank had asked about Mock recovering.

The paramedic in the back of the ambulance shrugged.

"What will happen to Mock?" Joe asked.

"He'll be in intensive care at Bayport General Hospital."

"Under guard," Frank added.

Riley's eyes were bloodshot and were staring past the Hardys. The police veteran said in a tired voice, "Yeah."

"It's not Mock I'm worried about," Frank said. "It's his son."

"Why?" Riley asked.

Joe explained about Mock's son, shaking his head.

Frank's forehead wrinkled in thought. He studied the devastated rehab center. "Why did Mock come back to the rehab center?"

"What are you driving at, Frank?" Officer Riley asked.

"Mock came back to the rehab center for something," Frank announced.

"In his room!" Joe shouted.

The Hardys started for the front door of the building.

"Wait a minute!"

Frank and Joe stopped and turned to face a tired and angry Con Riley.

"You two have been told more than once to stay off this case," the police veteran said firmly.

"We're not going to stand around while someone goes after our father," Joe responded just as firmly. "You don't understand—"

"I understand perfectly!"

Frank was stunned by the force and anger in Officer Riley's voice. He had known the police veteran since childhood but had never seen Con Riley shake with anger.

"Remember, Joe," Frank began softly, "Mock killed Officer Riley's partner."

Joe's face flushed with embarrassment. "I'm sorry."

Officer Riley shifted uncomfortably. "Forget it. The thing we've got to do is find out if Mock's son is in Bayport."

"Dad's old files might help," Frank suggested.

"That's a good place to start," Riley said. He headed for the building, stopped, and turned. "I understand why you two want to help. Chief Collig will probably have my badge for this, but if you promise to keep a low profile, I'll let you help."

Frank and Joe looked at each other, smiled, and followed Officer Riley into the building.

Mock's room was located in the one wing that had survived the tornado—even the roof was intact. Without electricity, they had to use flashlights, and the search was slow.

The sky rumbled, lightning flashed, and then a heavy rain fell.

Frank began searching in a chest of drawers. He

didn't like the rain or the slow pace of the search. He became angry as each drawer revealed nothing.

Mock had returned for something, but what? Obviously, Mock had kept in touch with someone in Bayport, or else how would he have known Frank and Joe well enough to recognize them on sight?

"Frank, look at this."

In the dim light from his flashlight Frank watched as Joe stood just outside the small closet, unwrapping a paper bundle. Inside were newsclippings about the Hardys and some of their cases, faded newspaper photos, and several photographs.

"He wasn't kidding when he said he kept tabs on us," Joe said.

"Not only us," Frank added, 'but our friends as well." Frank flipped through the photos: Frank, Joe, and Callie at the beach; Chet and Joe playing football; Frank and Joe eating at Mr. Pizza; Frank and Callie coming out of a movie theater.

"Surveillance photos," Joe said without emotion.

"Looks that way," Con said. "Someone's been watching you and keeping Mock informed."

"Who?" Joe asked.

"Mock's son," Frank replied. "But he hasn't been watching us for long."

"How can you tell?" Officer Riley asked.

"Look at the picture with Callie and me coming out of the theater. See the title of the movie?"

Joe nodded.

"The Majestic was showing that about eight months ago," Frank said.

Officer Riley took the photos from Frank and glanced through them. A smaller photo fell to the floor.

"What's that?" Joe asked.

Riley picked up the photo, studied it for a moment, then answered, "Looks like a school photo." He turned it over and read, " 'Bobby—Kindergarten.' The date's smudged, though." He handed the photo to Frank. "Recognize the boy?"

Frank looked at the photo. "He does look a little familiar, but I can't place him," he said after a moment. "The photo's old, though. Look at the shirt." He turned the photo so Joe could get a better look. "That style went out when we were kids."

Joe took the photo from Frank and stared. "He does look like somebody I know, but who I can't say."

"It's probably Mock's son, but why only a kindergarten photo? Why not other school pictures?" Frank took back the picture and flipped through the whole bundle one more time.

"Chief Collig will need to know about this," Officer Riley said. He cleared his throat and reached for the bundle. "I'll have to take those, Frank."

Frank hesitated, then palmed the kindergarten photo before handing the bundle to Officer Riley.

They walked out into the rain.

"I'll make sure our best detectives get on this," Officer Riley said as he opened the door of his police cruiser. "Try to contact your father and let him know what's going on."

"Right," Frank said, scrunching up his shoulders against the cold rain. "Our car phone's out, but we've got a CB that can reach a ham operator."

"Good." Officer Riley slid into his cruiser and fired up the engine. He stared straight ahead and said, "This kid of Mock's who's gunning for your father may also be looking for you two. I suggest you find a place to lay low for a while." He looked up at the Hardys, smiled slightly, then shut his door and sped away.

"What now?" Joe asked as he and Frank hopped into the van.

"First we need to figure out exactly who this is." Frank held up the kindergarten photo of Bobby Mock.

"Officer Riley's going to be upset with you," Joe said.

"It won't be the first time," Frank replied. "Or probably the last."

The Hardys' CB buzzed and clicked.

"Number One Girl calling Sherlock. Over," Callie said over the radio.

Frank sighed. Callie liked to use handles—trucker slang for nicknames. She had dubbed Frank "Sherlock," Joe "Bone Crusher," Chet "Pizza King," and herself "Number One Girl." It could have been worse, Frank thought.

Frank grabbed the handset. "What is it, Callie? Over."

"Number One Girl," Callie insisted.

"Okay, Number One Girl. What is it?" Frank glanced at Joe, who was laughing at Frank.

"Go to the *Times,* Sherlock. The Paper Girl's got something you ought to see."

"Paper Girl?"

"Liz!"

"Oh."

Joe laughed louder.

Frank ignored Joe. "Where are you, Callie?"

"I wish you'd use my handle, Sherlock." Callie paused, and Frank knew she was angry. "Pizza King and I are still at WBAY."

"How's Chet's finger?" Joe asked.

"Cal—I mean, Number One Girl, Joe wants to know about Pizza King's finger."

"He's got a splint on it, but it's really only bruised. Paper Girl is at the Bayport *Times* and has something she wants to show you."

"She say what it was?"

"No. She refused to say."

"Okay, Number One Girl," Frank said. "Will I see you later?"

"If you're lucky," Callie said. "Over."

"Over," Frank said. He hung up the handset and shot a glance at Joe. "What's so funny?"

Joe forced himself not to laugh while he said, "Ah, what fools we make out of ourselves for true love."

"Just drive, *Bone Crusher*."

Minutes later Frank and Joe were at the Bayport *Times*, listening to Liz Webling as she sat behind her desk. Don sat on one corner of the desk.

"I've been working as a stringer for some time," Liz was saying. Joe shot her a questioning glance.

"A part-time reporter," Don answered.

Joe locked eyes with Don. He had asked Liz not Don.

"That's why I have access to the morgue," Liz continued.

"The morgue?" Joe asked.

"It's what they call the file room where they keep the 'dead' issues," Don explained. "Get it?"

Joe locked eyes with Don again. Something about Don didn't sit right with Joe, but he couldn't put his finger on it—not yet, anyway.

"Another reporter heard about what Mangieri told the assistant district attorney and Riley. He managed to get his hands on the parole report on Leonard Mock."

"We've already found Mock, and it's not him we're worried about," Joe said impatiently.

"It's his son," Liz announced, leaning back in her chair and locking her hands behind her head.

"How did you know that?" Frank asked.

"I'm a reporter."

Liz leaned forward and stared intensely at Frank. Frank forced himself not to smile. He could tell Liz was enjoying playing the part of detective.

"Shortly after the trial," Liz began, "Mock lost custody of his son, and Bobby Mock was adopted by another family."

"What about Bobby's mother?" Frank asked.

"She died when Bobby was only three," Don answered.

Joe was about to ask Don how he knew that when Frank said, "If Bobby Mock was adopted, then his name would have been changed and that could be why we don't know anybody named Mock at school."

"That's right," Joe said, suddenly excited. "All we have to do now is find out who adopted Bobby Mock."

"Forget it," Don said.

"What?" Joe didn't like Don butting in, answering all the questions, and he didn't like Don's know-it-all tone.

"Adoption records are held by the vital records section of city hall," Don explained, sounding bored. "The only way vital records will let you look at adoption papers is through a court order. And trying to get a judge to unseal adoption records is like trying to get Joe to give out his book of phone numbers."

"How do you know so much about it?" Joe fired back, ignoring Don's jab at his numerous girlfriends.

"His dad is city manager," Liz reminded the Hardys.

"That's right," Don said smugly. "And while you two can't get to the records, I can."

"How?" Frank asked quickly. Frank could tell Joe was getting angrier by the moment. Joe didn't like interference, even helpful interference. Or was Joe jealous of Don because of Liz?

"I know everybody at city hall. Nobody's going to question my hanging around, especially during a crisis. I told you guys earlier I wanted in on this case."

"You're in," Frank said. Joe shot Frank an angry look. "And thanks."

"No problem." Don jumped up from the desk. "I'd better start now." He left the newsroom and disappeared down the hallway.

"We'd better start, too," Joe said, not wanting Don to get too far ahead of them.

"We owe you one," Frank said to Liz as they headed out of the newsroom.

"Forget it, Frank. On second thought, let me have the exclusive on this story, and we'll call it even."

"You've got it."

Once outside, Joe darted through the rain at a jog.

"Hey, what's your hurry?" Frank asked.

"You don't think I'm going to let Don solve this case before we do, do you?"

That confirms it, Frank thought, Joe *is* jealous of Don. With all the girls in Bayport Joe could impress, he had to decide to try to impress Liz Webling, the one girl who wouldn't have anything to do with him.

A roar split the air. It sounded like thunder, but Frank knew no thunder would crease his left temple with a searing hot wind. Shards of brick flew off the *Times* building where the bullet finally hit and exploded. A three-inch chunk of brick slammed into the back of Frank's head.

He fell to the wet pavement.

"Frank!" Joe shouted. He ran to his brother.

Blackness swam in front of Frank's eyes, slowly falling like a curtain over his brain. He tried to push himself up but couldn't. Time seemed to slow down. Frank raised his head and saw a man in a black raincoat and ski mask standing in the alley across the street. His hands were coiled around a .357 automatic, its deadly barrel trained on the Hardys.

The man fired again. Joe Hardy fell next to his brother.

Chapter
5

FRANK FOUGHT AGAINST the unconsciousness that sought to drown him. Through a red haze he watched as the black-clad man retreated into the darkness of the alley and disappeared.

He tried to push himself up again, but again he fell back to the wet pavement.

"Frank!" he heard someone yell in the distance.

His name echoed throughout his head, followed by a pounding that felt as though something were trying to push its way out through his temples.

He felt hands on his arm, turning him over. Once on his back, he looked up into the gray-black sky. Slowly the image of his brother came into focus.

"Joe," Frank said weakly. "I thought you were shot."

"Played possum," Joe said. "You okay?"

"Yeah, I guess." Frank sat up. "If you call an eighteen-wheel truck driving through your head okay." With Joe's help, Frank stood on wobbly legs. He had to lean against the brick building to steady himself.

"Not a truck," Joe said, fingering the three-inch hole the bullet had left in the brick wall.

"Automatic," Frank said, looking at the hole. "Three-fifty-seven."

"Frank! Joe! You okay?" Liz ran from the building, her face showing worry and fear. Several other employees were with her.

"Yeah," Frank said, trying to stand to his full height. He rocked back and forth as dizziness washed over him.

"What happened?" Liz asked.

"We don't know," Joe answered quickly. "I think I ought to treat that bump," he said to Frank. "And I think we have to get in out of the rain."

"Yeah," Frank replied.

"Everything's okay," Joe said to the small crowd that had formed around them. "Just a little accident." As the others headed back inside, Joe said to Liz, "I need to talk to you, Liz."

Once in the back of the van Joe got out the first-aid kit and began applying iodine to the back of Frank's head.

"Owww!" Frank shouted. He glared at Joe,

who only smiled. "You don't have to enjoy this."

"What happened?" Liz asked again.

"We were shot at," Joe began.

"Bobby Mock, we think," Frank interrupted.

"How can you be sure?" Liz asked. "According to my sources, Leonard Mock said that Bobby is supposed to kill *your father*. Not you."

"We're the next best targets," Frank said as Joe finished up and put the first-aid kit away.

"I think the police ought to know about this," Liz said as she started to open the door.

"Wait," Frank said. He made a grab for her but fell back. "Man, I'm going to have some headache."

Joe hopped out into the clean dry air. The rain had finally let up. Joe gently grabbed Liz's arm to turn her around.

He began softly. "Look, Liz, Chief Collig has already threatened to throw us in jail for interfering with the investigation. If he knows about this, he'll put us in protective custody, and we won't be able to help find this Bobby Mock before he tries to kill our father."

"I don't know," Liz said hesitantly.

"Please, Liz. For me." Joe flashed his best smile at Liz and tried to look slightly helpless to appeal to her sympathies.

Liz crossed her arms. "You don't have to try to charm me, Joe Hardy." She stared for a few moments into Joe's eyes. "Okay. If it'll help, I won't say anything."

"Trying to steal my girl again, Hardy?"

Joe and Liz turned as Don walked up to the trio, his hands in his pockets.

Joe flushed with anger and embarrassment. "No."

Don looked into the van. "Hey, Frank. What are you doing in there?"

"Just getting ready to leave," Frank replied, gently stepping down from the van. "Find out anything?"

"No," Don replied with a shrug. "The computers were down. I'll have to go through the files by hand. That's why I came back here. I need to know roughly when Bobby Mock was adopted."

"I'll get it," Liz said and dashed into the newspaper building.

Don turned back to the Hardys. "As soon as I locate the file, I'll copy it and give it to you."

"You'll get into a lot of trouble if your father finds out," Frank said.

"No problem. I'd hate to think what it would be like to lose my father." Don's voice was distant, distracted.

Frank looked at Joe. "We need to get home."

"Why are you going there?" Don's question was more demanding than curious.

"Just an idea," Frank replied, purposely being evasive. "Let's go, Joe."

"I'll drop by later with the file," Don said as the Hardys hopped into the van.

"What's this idea you have?" Joe asked minutes later.

"Turn here," Frank said in reply.

"Where are we going?"

"Bayport Electronics. To find out who this is." Frank held up the kindergarten photo of Bobby Mock.

"How?"

"I read an article a few months ago about a new computer program that can age the people in photos like this one. You get a computer-generated image of what the person should look like at any age."

"I saw that on the news. They use it to help find runaways or kids who have been kidnapped." They rode on in silence a few minutes. Then Joe finally asked, "So, how old do you think Bobby Mock is now?"

"Leonard Mock's only a couple years older than Dad." Frank stared at the photo. "And judging by Bobby's shirt, I'd say he's somewhere between fifteen and twenty."

"That's quite a spread."

"It's the best we have so far."

"How long will this take?"

"An hour, two at the most."

"I'm going to the hospital," Joe announced. He steered the van into the oval drive of Bayport

Electronics. "Bobby may get wind that his old man's there and try to visit him."

"I'll meet you there after the photo is done."

Joe waited until Frank entered the BE building and then drove away. He didn't really like the idea of splitting up, especially now that Mock's son had made his first move, but time was a luxury the Hardys could not afford.

"I'm sorry, Joe," said Officer Bill Murphy, "but Chief Collig will bust me back down to traffic control if I let you in there."

Joe and Officer Murphy stood at the nurses' station only a few yards away from the intensive care unit where Leonard Mock was clinging to life with the help of a life-support machine.

"I only want to talk to him," Joe pleaded.

"Nope." The young cop was unmoved. "The suspect is unconscious anyway. The doctors say he may not even make it through the night."

"Okay," Joe said. "But you can't keep me from waiting."

"No, I can't," Officer Murphy said, his thumbs tucked into his gun belt. "But I can tell you where to wait." He pointed behind Joe. "In the lobby."

"Humph!" Joe shook his head and headed back to the fifth-floor lobby. He was afraid that if he caused any trouble, Officer Murphy would have him escorted from the hospital.

Joe thrust his hands into his pockets and walked

slowly toward the lobby. He glanced over his shoulder. Officer Murphy was leaning against the nurses' station, talking to a young blond nurse. An idea flashed through Joe's mind: If Murphy could be distracted long enough, Joe could sneak into Mock's room.

Joe ducked into a closet. Green surgical shirts and pants, gloves, masks, and hair covers lined the shelves. Joe quickly put the hospital garb on over his clothes, finally covering his face with a surgical mask.

He opened the closet door and glanced down the corridor. Officer Murphy was still engaged in a lively conversation with the pretty blond nurse. Joe stepped into the hallway and walked casually toward the nurses' station.

He grabbed a clipboard from a nearby desk and pretended to be looking at it while he passed Officer Murphy and the nurse.

He held his breath as he neared the door to ICU. He glanced back quickly and saw that neither Officer Murphy nor the nurse had even given him a glance. He pushed the door open and entered the intensive care ward.

The ICU ward was a long hallway with several doors leading off it into individual rooms. Joe checked the names on the doors until he found the one marked "Leonard Mock."

He glanced back down the hallway, took a deep breath, and quietly opened the door.

The room was full of shadows produced by the blinking lights of the life-support equipment. A steady, persistent hum flowed from the machinery. Mock's wheezing breaths sent a chill through Joe. He shuddered and walked quietly over to the bed.

Leonard Mock looked worse than he had at the rehab center. His skin was stretched even tighter against his skull, and his lips were drawn back to reveal large, yellow teeth in a death's head smile. Even though Mock's eyelids were closed over his large, bulging eyes, Joe got the feeling that Leonard Mock was watching his every move. The life-support equipment hummed and beeped, keeping track of the last hours of Leonard Mock.

Joe suddenly thought he should leave and was about to go out into the hall when he heard footsteps moving toward him. He dashed into the bathroom and closed the door, leaving a slit through which he could see the entire room.

The door to the room opened, and Joe watched as a man walked over to Mock's bed and stood for several moments without saying a thing. The man was silhouetted against the lights of the machine, his black outline revealing a dark raincoat.

"Father," the man said, his voice low. He leaned over the bed.

Bobby Mock! Joe took a deep breath.

"The sons—Frank and Joe—are dead! Their friends are next. And when Hardy returns, he'll be dead, too."

Joe stepped from the bathroom. "Over my dead body," he said.

The man swung around. Through the eyeholes of the black ski mask, Joe could see the confused, questioning eyes of Bobby Mock but nothing else.

The man reached inside his raincoat. The gun! Joe thought.

Joe leapt at the man and threw a hard right punch to his left cheek. Then he shoved him against the wall. Joe grabbed the man's hand and held it inside the raincoat. Joe could feel the hard steel outline of the .357 magnum.

Bobby Mock backhanded Joe, knocking him against a life-support machine. A staccato buzzing filled the air. Leonard Mock twitched on his death bed.

Bobby Mock pulled the .357 automatic from beneath his raincoat and pointed it at Joe.

Joe kicked out and got Mock's hand with his toe. The gun flew across the room and hit the floor, exploding as it landed.

Joe lunged at Mock and caught him in the sternum with his shoulder. Pain exploded in Joe's shoulder, and he bounced off Mock. As Joe reached for his shoulder, Mock planted a crushing right on Joe's jaw. Joe staggered backward.

The room swam as Joe tried to regain his senses. He was dazed and breathless. Mock ran for his gun.

The door to the room burst open, and Officer

Murphy flew into the room. "What's going on in here?" he shouted.

Joe turned. He was distracted just long enough for Mock to grab his gun. Mock spun around, striking Joe across the cheek with an upward swing.

Joe crumpled to the floor.

Chapter

6

"IF YOU DON'T GET OUT of my hair and out of my office right now, I'm going to call security and have you thrown out!" yelled a haggard Bruce Smith.

What hair? Frank asked himself as he watched the overhead light bounce off the older man's bald head.

For the past fifteen minutes Frank had been arguing with Smith, trying to convince the president of BE to let him use a computer terminal and the photo aging program.

"I can be in and out of the program in an hour," Frank repeated for the umpteenth time.

"No! I don't have the time or the space for one of your hare-brained schemes, Hardy. The tornado caused our mainframe to dump just about every program we had, and we've got to get our systems back up or lose our government contracts.'' Smith rubbed his shiny scalp. With clenched teeth he said, ''Now, get out of my office and out of BE.''

Frank threw his hands up and left. A dead end. He'd have to think of another way to try to identify Mock's son. Perhaps a police artist could help. That would mean asking Chief Collig, and Frank knew the answer already.

He pulled the photo from his pocket and looked at the back. If only the date weren't smudged, then he could be more sure of Bobby Mock's age.

''Hey, Frank!'' someone called out just before Frank reached the front glass doors of BE.

Frank turned and saw David Simpson walking up to him. David was vice president of BE and had been out to Bayport High's computer club several times to teach new programing techniques. He had always been impressed with Frank's expertise.

''Hi, David. I hear your computers crunched all your programs.''

''Not all, thank goodness, but enough to make me wish I was driving a truck for a living.'' David pointed at Frank's bandage. ''Looks like that tornado just about wiped out your programming, too.''

''Yeah, I guess.''

''Say, if you're looking for a part-time job, we need temporary programmers until we're completely back on line.''

The thought struck Frank, and he almost said yes. What better way to get access to the computer program he needed. Then again, he would probably be assigned to punch in some boring government documentation. That could take hours—time he didn't have to spare.

"Sorry," Frank said with a shrug.

"Well, let me know if you need anything." David turned to leave.

"Wait, there is something." Frank looked at the photo in his hand. "I need to identify this kid."

David took the photo and looked at it. "Working on a case?"

"Yes. Missing person. It's important that I find him as soon as possible."

David looked at the photo again and then at Frank. "The problem is that I won't be able to get to you right away. I had to steal the break I'm on now."

"I understand, but this is a matter of life or death. I've already talked to Mr. Smith, and he—"

"Said no," David interrupted with a knowing smile.

"Right."

"Tell you what. Have you got a modem for your home computer?"

"Only the best," Frank replied, aware of what David was going to say next.

"I'll get to this as soon as I can and send the results via the modem. Let me make a laser print of this for our computer.'' David was gone and back in a matter of minutes. ''Here.'' He handed the small school photo back to Frank.

''Can you tell me about when I might expect it?'' Frank didn't want to sound too anxious, but the sooner they knew who Bobby Mock was, the sooner they could have him in jail.

''Sorry, Frank,'' David replied with a shake of his head.

'Thanks. I'll wait at home.''

''Take it easy, Frank. Say hello to your dad for me.''

''I'll be sure to do that.''

Frank left the Bayport Electronics building. He hoped that Joe had had better luck at the hospital. He flagged down a taxi and headed to Bayport General. He was tired. He sat back in the seat and had to force himself to stay awake. First the freak tornado had nearly torn apart Bayport, and now a killer was out to murder the Hardys. It had not been a good day.

''Ouch!'' Joe moaned as the doctor made sure Joe's shoulder wasn't dislocated. He was sitting on a bench in the emergency room, Chief Collig and Officer Riley hovering over him like angry parents.

''Serves you right for interfering with the police,'' Chief Collig growled. ''I ought to throw the book at you.''

''If I hadn't walked in when I did, you'd never

have known that Mock's son was in the hospital,'' Joe said.

"He's right, Chief," Officer Riley said in Joe's defense.

Chief Collig scowled at Officer Riley.

"I want Officer Murphy in my office tomorrow morning," Chief Collig ordered.

"Where *is* Officer Murphy?" Joe asked.

"Stationed in front of Mock's door, where he should have been in the first place," Officer Riley replied. "He's got a nasty bruise on his chin where Mock's son slugged him with that magnum, but he'll survive."

"Not when I'm through chewing him out," Chief Collig added.

"There," the doctor said. "You'll be okay, but you're sure you didn't run into the wall and not his chest?"

Joe looked into the young doctor's eyes. "I know the difference between a wall and some guy's chest." He turned to Officer Riley. "I'm telling you his chest was like steel."

"Joe!" Frank shouted as he entered the room.

"Please, don't shout," Joe said as he squeezed his eyelids shut.

"Good. You're both here." Chief Collig began buttoning up his raincoat. "I'm going to tell you two for the last time to keep your noses out of police business. Officer Riley, if you see these two working on this case, I want you to hold them until their parents return from Philadelphia.''

"Yes, sir," Officer Riley said.

Frank bristled at Chief Collig's order. "On what charge?"

"No charge," Chief Collig said as he put his hat on and buttoned up his raincoat. He smiled. "Protective custody." Then he stormed out.

Frank and Joe turned to Officer Riley.

Riley shrugged. "Sorry, boys. You heard the chief."

Joe was ready to tell Frank what had happened when a rapid, high-pitched beeping sounded in the hospital corridor.

Frank, Joe, and Officer Riley ran out into the hallway and followed the nurses to Mock's ICU room.

"What happened?" Officer Riley quickly asked Murphy.

"I—I—I don't know," the young officer stammered.

A tall thin doctor was leaning over Leonard Mock. He pulled the sheet over Mock's body and turned to the Hardys.

The doctor's face was grim, but his voice was matter-of-fact. "He's dead."

Frank and Joe returned home to find that electricity had been restored, but the phone lines were still down. Frank contacted the ham radio operator in Hoboken and relayed a message to his father that they were all okay. He didn't mention anything about Leonard or Bobby Mock.

Frank and Joe said little as they ate and got ready for bed. The one thought that kept crossing their minds was, How would Bobby Mock react to his father's death?

They decided to set the alarm system to the house after double-checking the windows and doors to make sure they were all locked.

Before going to sleep, Frank made up his mind to visit BE the first thing in the morning to check up on the aging progress of the kindergarten photo of Bobby Mock. With the phone lines still down, the modem was useless.

The next day dawned gray and wet. Frank had risen early to check his father's old files and was chewing on an English muffin when Joe walked into the kitchen.

"So, what's the plan for the day?" Joe asked as he took a mixing bowl down from a cabinet and grabbed a box of cereal.

"The phones are still out, so we'll have to go to BE for the photo of Bobby Mock."

Joe dumped the half-full box of cereal into the bowl and covered the flakes with milk. "Then what?" he asked as he crunched down on the cereal.

"Then we find Bobby Mock and turn him over to the police."

Joe reached behind himself for the orange juice sitting on the cabinet. Only a little juice remained in the bottom of the jug so Joe didn't bother to get a glass. He raised the edge to his lips and drank. The cold, tart juice felt good against his dry throat.

"You know what Aunt Gertrude would say if she saw you doing that?" Frank said with a sly smile.

"What she doesn't know won't hurt me," Joe quipped back.

The phone suddenly rang, and both Frank and Joe nearly jumped out of their chairs.

"I thought you said—" Joe began.

"Must have gotten fixed sometime in the night," Frank said. He was ready to answer the ringing phone when it suddenly stopped and he heard his computer blip on upstairs. He sat back down.

"Aren't you going to see who it is?" Joe asked, referring to the image that was printing right then of Bobby Mock.

"It'll take a few minutes to print." Frank bit down on the last of his muffin and washed it down with a glass of milk. He calmly dusted his hands and then headed for his computer.

Joe finished off his bowl of cereal and then scoured the cabinets for another box, but there was none. He imagined he knew what Old Mother Hubbard's dog felt like. Maybe, they could stop off at a convenience store and get some cinnamon rolls.

Joe walked from the kitchen to the living room and swung around the banister to head upstairs. He stopped short when he saw Frank sitting on the stairs.

"Whoa," Joe said with a smile, but his smile quickly vanished when he saw Frank's face.

Frank was holding the computer printout in his hands, his face was gray, and his eyes were fixed and staring.

"What is it?" Joe asked, his voice almost a whisper. Frank didn't answer. He only stared. "*Who* is it?"

Frank still didn't answer, but this time he slowly raised his hand to give Joe the color printout of eighteen-year-old Bobby Mock.

Joe gasped as he recognized the computer picture of their best friend—Chet Morton!

Chapter

7

"THAT'S IMPOSSIBLE!" Joe shouted.

"I think so, too," Frank said, his voice a whisper. "But that's why we thought he looked so familiar."

"Someone's trying to set Chet up," Joe said.

"And make fools of us. Mock had years to plan this."

"This sounds like something out of a spy novel." Joe sat down on the steps, still staring at the computerized Chet Morton.

"Before you got up this morning, I went down to the basement and got out Dad's oldest files, the stuff he didn't put on computer. Mock's file was full of letters threatening to kill Dad and destroy our family."

"How does this fit?"

"What better way to get even than lead us to believe that our friends are against us? Didn't you say that Bobby Mock promised his father that he would get our friends?"

"Yeah," Joe replied. "That's why he had those pictures of you, me, Callie, and Chet."

"Exactly."

"What now?"

"First, we find Chet and show him this." He pointed to the printout. "From what Bobby Mock said at the hospital last night, we can assume that Chet's life is in danger."

Joe stood up and walked back down to the living room. He put the printout on the coffee table and picked up the phone. He tried the Morton home first, but a telephone company tape recording told him that the phone was out of service. That would make sense. Not all the phones in Bayport would be fixed at the same time.

Frank called Callie to warn her that her life might be in danger. Mr. Shaw told Frank that Callie had gone to the television station. She had tried to call Frank, but their line was busy. Callie must have tried to call while the modem was working.

Frank tried WBAY. Callie had left with a tall, heavyset blond kid, the assignment editor said. The "heavyset blond kid" was probably Chet Morton. What was Chet doing at the television station? Frank asked himself.

The assignment editor went on to explain that Callie wanted to get some shots from the top of the old Farmers and Merchants Bank building in the downtown area. It had seen some of the worst damage.

"Looks like Newshawk Shaw is dragging Chet all over town," Joe said after Frank told him what the assignment editor said.

"We've got to find Chet and warn him—and Callie, too," Frank replied.

"You read my mind."

They were out the door when Don West pulled up in his red sports car. He jumped from his car and ran up to the Hardys.

"You're not going to believe this," he said, almost out of breath. He took a file from under his raincoat and handed it to Frank. "I had to wait until this morning before anybody arrived at work. These are only copies." He held up the folder. "Bobby Mock's adoption papers."

The three went into the house.

Frank opened the file and began reading.

"What happened to your cheek?" Joe asked, noticing a reddish bruise on Don's left cheek.

"Some boxes fell on me when I was trying to find those files," he replied with a shrug, avoiding Joe's eyes.

"I can't believe this!" Frank threw the file on the coffee table.

Joe picked up the file and opened it.

"I couldn't believe it, either," Don said.

"It looks like Chet Morton is Bobby Mock."

"He can't be!" Joe blurted out. "I've known him for years."

"What's that got to do with anything?" Don asked.

"Could anyone have planted this file in vital records?" Frank asked.

"I doubt it," Don replied. "I had to be sneaky just to get copies made without getting caught."

"These are fake," Joe said.

"What about the picture?" Don asked.

"What picture?" Frank eyed Don suspiciously.

"I went to the police station to look for you guys. Con Riley was all upset about a missing school picture. He said he thought you might have taken it."

"I don't know what he's talking about," Frank said. He glanced at Joe.

Don snapped his fingers. "I just remembered. When I went to city hall to look for that file, I saw Chet and Callie going to the old bank building across the street. Then I saw Chet come out by himself."

"So?" Joe asked.

"So he looked like he'd been in a fight. He jumped into his car and drove away."

"*What?* You didn't try to stop him or find out where Callie was?" Don's attitude was making Frank angry.

"I thought it was strange, but I knew you wanted this file right away, and I forgot about the whole incident until just now."

Frank studied Don for a minute before saying, "We've got to find Chet."

Frank and Joe headed for the door.

"What's wrong?" Don asked.

"We don't believe Chet is Bobby Mock," Joe answered. "But we do believe he is in danger."

"And so is Callie," Frank said, closing and locking the door.

"I'll help look," Don said as he headed for his car.

"Check out the television station," Frank suggested. He was hoping to keep Don as far from the bank building as possible.

"Sure." Don hopped into his car and drove away.

Joe had barely fastened his seat belt when Frank threw the van into reverse and peeled out on the wet pavement. Slamming the shift into first, he made the van lurch forward.

"Slow down, or we'll hydroplane," Joe said. Joe was just as anxious to find Chet and Callie, but he didn't want them to wreck. Traveling fast on a wet road could cause the van's tires to rise up and slide on a pocket of water. Frank would lose control, and the brakes would be useless.

"Why did you send Don to the television station?" Joe asked.

"To get him out of the way."

"That doesn't answer my question."

"It'll have to do for now."

They reached the old Farmers and Merchants Bank building in a matter of minutes. The building stood twenty stories high and was one of the oldest in Bayport. The redbrick bank was undergoing a facelift, and scaffolding framed its structure like braces on teeth. A large sign in front of the building announced that by fall the old Farmers and Merchants Bank building would be the new Farmers and Merchants Downtown Mall.

Frank jumped from the van and ran into the building.

Frank didn't know what to believe about Don's story. Perhaps Callie had gotten into trouble, and Chet had gone for help. Some floors of the building had been ripped up to make way for a new elevator system and an atrium, and maybe Callie had fallen.

Why wouldn't Chet have run across the street to city hall or down the block to the police station for help?

Then, too, Don only remembered seeing Chet and Callie *after* Frank doubted that the adoption file was genuine. Don seemed to have a good memory when it suited him.

"Frank! Wait up!" Joe shouted.

Frank stopped.

"Here. We'll need these upstairs," Joe handed

Frank one of two police-issue flashlights—both were eighteen inches long. Not only would the flashlights provide good light, but they would also be heavy enough to use as clubs in case of trouble.

Frank flicked the flashlight on and started across the lobby, which was littered with power tools, buckets of paint and plaster, wood, and mottled tarps. The whole place smelled from the odor of paint and thinner. There was no one working that day because there was no electricity in the building. Only vital buildings had been reconnected.

"Why would Callie come here?" Joe asked as they made their way carefully through the maze of buckets and lumber.

"The assignment editor said she wanted to get a bird's-eye view of the damage. This building is tall, and it's in the right part of town."

They found the stairs, and minutes later they were standing on the roof, blinded by the glare of a bright yellow sun. The clouds had broken, and the sun was shining for the first time since the tornado had hit Bayport twenty-four hours earlier.

Frank walked to the edge of the roof to look down. On the street, twenty stories below, lay city hall, the police station, and many of the buildings that had been hardest hit by the tornado.

"No sign of Callie or Chet," Joe said, joining Frank. Then he pointed. "There's Don!"

Frank and Joe watched from nearly two hundred and twenty-five feet up as Don's small red sports car pulled in behind their black van. Don got out, glanced around, and stood still, apparently unsure of what to do. Finally he went into the bank building.

"I'll tell him we didn't find anything up here, and then we can start searching the other floors." Frank nodded, and Joe left the roof.

Frank stood scanning the area and wondering where Chet and Callie could be. Chet was his best friend, and Callie—well, Callie *was* his Number One Girl.

Then the thought that had been nagging at the back of his mind hit him full force. Frank ran for the roof door and then down the stairs, calling Joe's name.

Frank burst through the ground floor doors, the circular beam of his flashlight leaping before him. He dashed across the lobby, dodging the saw horses and buckets of paint.

"Frank! Over here!" Don shouted.

"What happened?" Frank asked as he joined Don and Joe.

Joe was just getting up, rubbing his chin.

"Mangieri—" Don began.

"That's the second time that nerd got the jump on me!" Joe said.

"Are you so sure it was Mangieri?" Frank asked Joe.

Joe stared at his brother, a puzzled expression on his face.

"Actually I didn't see anyone," Joe said. "I was coming around the corner and got blindsided. The first thing I knew, Don was standing over me. He said he saw Mangieri hit me."

"Why didn't you help Joe?" Frank angrily asked Don.

"I was clear across the lobby," Don replied defensively. "I saw what happened and ran to help, but Mangieri went down the hall. I thought I should help Joe first."

"What are you doing here anyway?" Frank's question was more of an accusation. "You were supposed to go to the TV station."

"I tried my phone. They must have got the system back on line sometime last night. I called the studio, and they told me Callie wasn't there. I thought I could help you two here."

"What's wrong?" Joe asked Frank.

"Nothing," Frank said quickly. "We've got to find Chet."

All three went outside.

"How can I help?" Don asked.

"Uh, you find Liz and see if she's seen Callie," Frank replied.

"Right," Don replied and hopped into his car. Frank headed for the van after Don had left.

"Are you going to tell me what's going on?" Joe asked as Frank pulled the van away from the building.

"How long have we known Don?" Frank asked.

"About three years, when he moved here from New York City."

"He's lived here for three years, and we don't know anything about him. Why is it that he's suddenly such an integral part of our lives?" Frank didn't wait for Joe to answer. "Why is it that Don conveniently shows up all the time? When you chased down Mangieri, when we were shot at, finding the so-called adoption file on Chet, and just now?"

Joe shrugged. He knew that Frank wasn't really seeking answers, only thinking out loud.

"How did he know about that kindergarten photo?"

"He said Officer Riley was yelling about it being missing," Joe replied.

"Pretty convenient, don't you think?"

"Quit playing around, Frank, and get to the point."

"The point is," Frank said slowly, "Don West is Bobby Mock!"

Chapter

8

JOE DIDN'T REPLY but sat silently thinking. He digested the information Frank had just given him and came to the same conclusion.

"That may explain the bruise on his cheek," Joe finally said.

"What?"

"When I fought with Bobby Mock in the ICU ward, I hit him with a good right to his left cheek. It would have left a pretty decent bruise."

"And when we were talking to Liz at the paper yesterday, Don knew that Bobby's mother had died when Bobby was three. How could he have known that?"

"Unless he *is* Bobby Mock," Joe conceded.

"What bothers me is how your shoulder got hurt," Frank said as they neared the Hardy home.

Joe rubbed his sore shoulder. "I know. I still can't explain it. It was like hitting a brick wall."

"Yesterday you said it felt like steel or something metal."

"Yesterday I wouldn't have believed a tornado could hit Bayport," Joe said. "Why are we going back home?"

"I want to check Dad's files again. I must have missed something this morning. Perhaps a newspaper photo or something on young Bobby Mock. We can't go to the police with what we know now. Chief Collig would laugh us out of his office."

Having arrived home, Frank immediately headed downstairs for his dad's files.

"Hey, I thought you were going to check Dad's files," Joe said at the top of the stairs.

Frank turned around and looked up at his brother. "I've already done a thorough search of his computer files. What I'm looking for can't be found on a disk. I'm checking his paper files one more time. Much easier to overlook a piece of paper."

"Oh," Joe said, heading for the kitchen. "Let me know if you need any help."

Frank smiled and shook his head. They had eaten breakfast approximately an hour earlier, but Joe was like a great white shark on a feeding frenzy that day.

Mr. Hardy's paper files were located in one corner of the basement the Hardys used for storage. He found the Mock file and sat down to read it. Although a fast reader, Frank forced himself to slowly reread the yellowing papers his father had typed years earlier. He searched for any clue as to the identity of Bobby Mock. He found nothing.

Frank sat back in the chair and sighed. Fenton Hardy was as meticulous about keeping accurate accounts of his cases as he was about solving them. There had to be something identifying Bobby Mock. A photo. A newsclipping. Anything.

"That's it!" Frank shouted as he snapped his fingers. Frank jumped up and ran up the stairs. His dad's old scrapbook. Actually, it was a scrapbook that the boys' aunt Gertrude kept on all the cases Mr. Hardy had solved throughout the years.

Once upstairs Frank hesitated outside his aunt's bedroom door. She would be very upset if she found out Frank had been snooping around in her bedroom. Frank shrugged and opened the door.

Aunt Gertrude's room was neat and tidy and smelled of talcum powder, hair spray, and expensive perfume. Frank flipped on the light switch and walked over to his aunt's desk. He opened the bottom drawer and pulled out a large red scrapbook. He sat at the desk and began flipping through the pages. He found newspaper articles and photos of the Leonard Mock case about a third of the way through the book.

Again Frank read the articles slowly, then he scrutinized the pictures carefully. Only four newspaper pictures existed: one showing Mock as he was being led into the police station shortly after he had killed Con Riley's partner, and three others as he was being led from the courthouse during his trial. Mock was surrounded by a large crowd of people each time.

Frank carefully removed the photos from the scrapbook and headed downstairs. He wanted to examine them in better light and with a magnifying glass. Perhaps he could recognize someone in the crowd. Perhaps he could even find Bobby Mock.

Frank reached the bottom of the staircase as a sudden pounding filled the house. He ran to the door and flung it open.

"Chet!" Frank shouted.

Chet stumbled forward. Frank caught him and led him inside to a chair in the living room.

Chet looked at Frank, his eyes glassy and red. "I—tried—to—find you—earlier." Chet grimaced as he tried to catch a deep breath.

"Where have you been?" Joe asked, joining them.

"Callie—she and I—Mangieri." Chet slumped back and passed out. A black object slid out from under his windbreaker and hit the floor.

"What's that?" Joe asked.

Frank picked up the object. "Callie's camcorder," he replied, holding up the video camera.

"Why would he have Callie's video camera?" Joe asked.

"More important, why doesn't Callie have her camcorder?" A sudden uneasiness came over Frank. He punched the Eject button and pulled the video-cassette out. He walked over to the VCR, slid the tape in, and pressed Play. He grabbed the remote control and turned on the big-screen TV.

The first scenes of the videotape were from the day before and were of the damaged downtown area. Then the tape showed Frank, Joe, and Chet as they rescued the man from underneath the col-lapsed roof. Frank fast forwarded the tape until he recognized the outside of the abandoned Farmers and Merchants Bank building.

Callie and Chet had obviously gone to the top, and Callie had gotten her "bird's-eye view" of downtown Bayport. The scene flickered and then showed the lobby of the building looking out to the street.

"Hey!" the Hardys heard Chet shout on the video, and he suddenly ran across the picture.

Callie followed Chet with the camera.

Chet and a short man were grunting as they struggled and fought.

"Mangieri," Joe said.

Frank nodded.

"Chet!" Callie screamed.

The scene jumped again. This time the picture was turned sideways.

Callie must have dropped the camera, Frank thought, but it remained on.

Chet was overpowering the man, and Callie was helping when another figure entered the scene. Although the figure was silhouetted against the bank's picture window, Frank could tell that the second man was wearing a black raincoat and a ski mask.

Bobby Mock!

"You're dead, Morton!" Mock yelled.

Something about the voice sounded familiar to Frank, but he had to let the thought go for the moment—Mock brought a double fist down on Chet's back. Chet gasped and fell to the floor. Mangieri hit Chet twice, once across the left cheek and then a downward blow to the chin. A deep, sickening groan came from Chet as he tried to reach up and grab Mangieri. Chet missed and fell to the floor.

"Nooo!" Callie screamed.

Mock grabbed Callie in a throat lock.

"Callie!" Frank yelled and made a move for the television.

Joe pulled Frank back.

Frank was watching a recorded nightmare and was unable to do anything to help.

Callie screamed and struggled against Mock. Mock put his hand over Callie's mouth and yanked her head back. Callie reached back and tried hitting Mock in the eyes. Unsuccessful, she grabbed the ski mask and pulled it off.

Frank leaned closer to the big screen, hoping to

recognize the unmasked Bobby Mock. But the bright light from the outside created only silhouettes and shadows in the building.

Suddenly Callie gasped and stopped her struggling. Mock let loose, and Callie fell to the floor.

"Callie," Frank whispered, his mind whirling.

The scene jumped again. This time an unshaven, sweaty-looking Martin Mangieri stared into the camera, his face taking up the entire big screen.

"Want your girlfriend, Hardy? Come and get her before she becomes just another part of the big bang theory!" Mangieri laughed, his throaty cackle echoing throughout the house.

Then the big-screen television filled with static snow and hissed at the horrified Hardys.

Chapter

9

JOE TOOK THE REMOTE CONTROL from Frank and shut off the TV.

Frank sat staring at the blank screen, his eyes vacant.

Chet groaned.

The Hardys turned to see their friend sitting up in his chair.

"I'm sorry, Frank," Chet said, his voice weak.

"Did you get a look at the second man, at Bobby Mock?" Frank asked.

"No. Mangieri got in a couple of lucky shots, and all I saw were stars, Big Dipper and all." Chet rubbed his swollen jaw.

"I'll get some ice," Frank said.

"What happened? What took you so long to get here?" Joe asked.

85

"When I came to, Callie was gone, but her camcorder was still there. I played the tape back through the camera and saw what had happened. I had to find you, but I ran out of gas and walked the rest of the way."

Frank returned with a towel and ice. "Why didn't you go to the police?" he asked.

"Ow!" Chet groaned as he pressed the ice against his chin. "I knew Collig wouldn't let you look at the tape."

"Then you don't know what's going on?" Joe sat across from his old friend.

"What?" Chet's eyes darted between Frank and Joe.

Frank picked up the adoption file and handed it to Chet.

"Look at it."

Chet opened the file. "Hey! That's me," he said as he spotted the computerized image of himself. Then he read further.

A moment later he jumped up and flung the file at Frank.

"This is garbage!" he shouted.

"I agree," Frank replied. He reshuffled the file. "The copyright dates are all wrong."

"What?" Joe didn't like it when Frank kept clues from him.

"When we first looked at these," Frank began, holding up the file, "I noticed that the copyright date on the forms was from last year."

"So?" Chet asked, still pressing the ice against his chin.

"So, if your adoption had taken place years ago, the copyright on the forms would be from then or earlier." Frank let the file fall on the coffee table. "You've been set up."

Chet's eyes narrowed. Joe could tell his friend was thinking revenge. "Who did it?"

"Don West," Joe answered.

"We *think* it's Don West," Frank corrected.

Joe squinted at Frank in disbelief. He said in a low voice, "Who else? You were positive an hour ago."

Frank returned Joe's glare but remained silent.

"Don had access to the vital records department at city hall," Joe rattled off. "The pictures we found at Leonard Mock's apartment only go back three years—"

"About the same time Don West moved to Bayport," Chet finished.

Joe continued, "And this morning, when Don showed up here with the adoption file, he had a large bruise on his cheek on the same spot where I hit Bobby Mock last night." Joe paused. "So what's your problem, Frank?"

"It's too neat."

"You should talk about things being *too* neat, Mr. Clean."

"There's no such thing as the perfect crime *or* the perfect suspect," Frank replied calmly.

"Yeah, right. What's that from? Frank Hardy's Guide to Detective Work?" Joe spit out.

"I'm just saying we need to be cautious. First we have to find Callie."

"What did Mangieri mean about the big bang theory?" Chet asked.

"I don't know," Frank answered.

"Find Don West, and I bet we find Callie," Joe insisted.

"Maybe," Frank replied. "But if we go after West, and West isn't Mock, then we could be wasting time while Callie is—" Frank's voice broke off.

Joe and Chet exchanged a quick glance. There was no need for Frank to finish his sentence.

"One thing's for sure," Chet said. "We all know Mangieri's involved."

Frank's and Joe's heads jerked toward Chet.

"Leave it to Chet to point out the obvious," Joe said with a smile.

"Chet's right," Frank said. "We find Mangieri, and I bet we find Callie."

"And Bobby Mock," Joe added.

"Why is Mangieri even involved?" Chet asked.

"Money," Joe replied. "I'd still like to know how he got out of jail, what kind of deal he cut."

"That's a question Con Riley can answer," Frank answered.

"I say we find Mangieri and do a little knuckle

tap dance on his head.'' Chet stood to his full height. "I owe him a dance or two." He handed Frank the towel and ice and headed for the door. "Well?" he said as he stood with the door held open.

"Right with you, buddy," Joe said with a smile.

The trio jumped back into the black van. While Joe drove, Frank looked over the newspaper clippings. Besides being old and faded, they weren't very good photos. Frank pulled a small magnifying glass from the crime kit he kept under his portable laptop computer in the back of the van. He moved the glass slowly over the photos. After he had gone over each one carefully, he started over again.

"What are you looking for?" Chet asked over Frank's shoulder.

"A young kid."

"Why?"

"Mock was so attached to his son that it's possible he had him attend the trial. I'm trying to see if I can find a young kid in these newsclippings."

"Hey, you two going to help me look or what?"

They had reached the downtown area, and Joe was driving up and down streets where they shouldn't have been. The area was clearly posted as being off limits to keep looters away.

Chet joined Joe in the front while Frank stayed in the back.

"What's Frank doing back there?" Joe asked.

They were just about to turn onto Fifth Street when a siren pierced the air. Joe brought the van to a jarring halt as a police cruiser pulled up behind them.

A metallic voice boomed from the cruiser's speakers.

"All right. Step out of the van. With your hands in the open."

Frank, Joe, and Chet moved slowly from the van, their hands held open, palms out.

"Now stand against the van, legs spread. *And don't move.*"

"Officer—" Joe began.

He was jerked to one side and then slammed against the side of the van. He was ready to turn when he heard the click of a revolver and felt the cold steel of a barrel against his neck.

"Freeze!"

"All right, boys," began a second cop, "what are you doing here? This area is off limits."

"We were looking for a friend, Officer Stewart," Frank said, recognizing the slow drawl of the second policeman.

"Frank Hardy?" Officer Stewart turned Frank around. "Joe? Chet?"

"Yes," Frank said. "And we *are* looking for a friend."

"Tell your partner to ease up," Joe said.

"Cool it, Bud. I know these kids."

The first officer slowly let the hammer down on his .38, holstered it, and then walked back to the police cruiser.

Joe breathed for the first time in moments.

"Who you looking for?" Officer Stewart asked.

"Don West," Joe said quickly.

"We haven't seen him for a couple of hours, and we got worried," Frank added.

"The city manager's son?"

"Yes," Joe said.

"Haven't seen him," Officer Stewart said.

"Perhaps he made it home by now. We'll check there." Frank didn't want to hang around chatting with Officer Stewart while Callie was still in danger.

"I suggest all you boys head for home," Officer Stewart said. "The next cop who stops you may mistake you for looters, and you'll end up in jail."

"We'll be careful," Joe assured him.

"Hey, Stewart. Stop them. Chief Collig wants us to bring them in," Bud yelled from the cruiser, the mike of the police radio in his hand.

"Quick! In the van!" Frank shouted. He pushed Chet into the van, jumped in after him, and slammed the door shut.

Joe hopped into the driver's seat, threw the van into reverse, and peeled out. He made a hairpin turn in reverse, threw the van into first, and sped away.

"What's going on?" Chet demanded. He lost his balance in the turn and fell against the rear couch.

"Chief Collig threatened to put us into protective custody if he caught us working on this case," Frank explained.

"No one's behind us," Joe said as he checked the side-view mirror.

"We need a different set of wheels," Frank said. "You can bet Chief Collig will put out an all-points bulletin on this van."

"Aunt Gertrude's car," Joe suggested.

"No. I don't want to take a chance on the police being at our house looking for us."

"Hey! They won't be looking for my car," Chet said.

"Your car?" Joe didn't want to hurt his best friend's feelings, but Chet's car was little better than a junker. Joe had spent too many weekends under the hood of the sedan trying to keep it running. "But it's out of gas."

"No problem," Chet said. "We can siphon the gas from the van's reserve tank."

"Great idea," Joe said with a roll of his eyes.

Minutes later they pulled up behind Chet's car, which sat on a side road. At least, Joe thought, we won't be in traffic where a cop might see us.

Joe pulled a three-foot section of hose from the back of the van, unlocked the gas cap, shoved the hose down the tank, and took a deep breath. He didn't relish the thought of tasting gasoline.

"Here's the can." Frank placed a five-gallon gas can next to Joe.

"Thanks." But Joe didn't sound thankful. "Where's Chet?"

"He's rummaging around in his trunk for something," Frank replied.

"Yuck!" Joe spat gasoline as he put the hose into the gas can.

"Hey, Joe, I found it!" Chet dashed up to Joe.

"Found what?" Joe asked.

"The siphon hose." Chet held up a small hose that had a hand pump on one end—a pump that could manually create suction and drain the reserve tank.

"You mean I drank gasoline and you had a siphon pump all this time?" Joe's lips thinned, and his eyes narrowed.

"Well, sure. Dad bought this for me in case I needed gas from one of the other cars."

"Great," Joe mumbled.

The gas can filled, and Chet poured the gas into his car. He hopped in the front seat while Joe took off the air filter and primed the carburetor by pouring in a small amount of gasoline. He stepped back. After a couple of tries, Chet's car sputtered to life.

"Hop in, guys!"

Frank jumped in the back while Joe slid into the front.

"Where to?" Chet pulled the car away from the curb.

Frank sat silently. All the time Joe and Chet had been putting gas into the sedan, he was thinking about the videotape—Mangieri and Bobby Mock attacking Callie and Chet. Then Mangieri's face leering out at them, telling them that Callie would be a part of the big bang theory. Frank had always thought Mangieri was barely this side of crazy, but his last remark just didn't make sense.

"Frank!" Joe reached back and tapped Frank on the knee.

"Where to?" Chet repeated.

"What would Mangieri be doing with Bobby Mock?" Frank asked.

"Birds of a feather," Chet replied. "Creeps will hang around with creeps."

"You may be more right than you realize, Chet." Frank sat on the edge of the backseat. "Stop at the next convenience store."

"Why?" Joe asked.

"So we can do what we should have done in the first place," Frank replied. "Look up Mangieri's address in the phone book."

* * *

94

"Stop here," Frank said minutes later as Chet steered his sedan into a dead-end street in a run-down part of town.

"Why? I thought you said his house was in the middle of the block," Chet said as he slowed the car.

"I don't want them to see us pulling up," Frank replied.

Mangieri lived on the west side of Bayport in a low-rent area. All the houses on the dead end were semidetached. One wall was shared by two houses. Frank knew from the address that Mangieri's house would be in the middle of the block.

The trio got out of the car and silently shut their doors.

"Walk close to the other houses so they can't see us coming," Frank suggested.

Moments later they stood at the side of Mangieri's house.

"He's in the next half," Frank said. "Joe, you and Chet check the back in case they try to escape. I'll check the front door."

Frank moved silently and swiftly to Mangieri's front door. A screen door covered it. It was old, and the hinges were rusted. He knew he couldn't make a surprise entrance. He glanced in through the front window. Someone was sitting in a chair, his back to the door. In the dimness of the room, Frank couldn't tell if it was Mangieri or Mock.

"No back door," Chet announced as he walked up behind Frank.

Frank jumped back. His skin rippled with goose bumps. "Don't sneak up on me like that, Chet. And keep it down. Someone's inside." Then he noticed that Joe was missing. "Where's Joe?"

"He's checking out a back window. The glass was broken. He said he would enter through the back room and meet you inside."

"I wish he'd check with me first!" Frank had never liked Joe's impulsiveness. They should have worked out a plan of attack. Now he'd have to improvise and hope no one got hurt.

"I'm going to open this screen door real fast," Frank whispered to Chet. "You think you can kick the front door open?"

"No sweat." Chet stepped back and took a stance like a professional field goal kicker.

Frank would have laughed if the situation wasn't so serious. Instead, he only shook his head and peered back in through the window.

He saw Joe's head peek around the corner of an inner room. That was what Frank had been waiting for. He pulled open the screen door, and it creaked loudly.

"Now!" he barked to Chet.

Chet planted his foot next to the door knob, then kicked hard. The door groaned and snapped open, the knob and its lock falling to the ground.

Frank dashed in and confronted the figure sitting in the chair.

"Frank!" Joe shouted. "It's Callie."

Frank would have been relieved to find his girlfriend, but the digital timer on the bomb that was ticking at her feet showed that in thirty seconds they would all be dead.

Chapter

10

"DON'T TAKE ANOTHER STEP," Joe warned.

Joe pointed. Frank could see that the bomb was set to explode by any of three methods: the timer, a small, almost invisible trip wire, or if Callie moved.

Frank's eyes met Callie's, and he could see the terror that stared back at him.

He stepped over the trip wire.

"Don't move, Callie," he said calmly.

Twenty seconds.

"It's motion sensitive," Joe said.

"I saw it," Frank replied.

After dealing with terrorists, Frank knew enough about bombs to recognize the secondary fuse that hung in the center of a metal washer. If the fuse made contact, an electrical signal would surge through the mechanism, thus exploding the bomb.

Fifteen seconds.

"Okay, Callie," Frank began—he knew that talking to Callie would calm her—"I don't have time to untie you. I'm going to disconnect the primary wire going to the timer." Frank moved as he talked.

Ten seconds.

He tugged as gently as he could. The wire wouldn't budge.

"I think it's soldered together." Frank kept his voice calm.

Joe shoved his pocket knife between Frank and the bomb.

"No time." Frank had to keep his voice calm or Callie might panic.

Five seconds.

He clamped his fingers on the secondary fuse and lifted it through the metal washer—quickly but with a calm steadiness.

Three.

He tore the tape and the bomb from Callie's legs.

Two.

In one smooth motion he flung the bomb through the closed window in a perfect spiral, then covered Callie. The bomb shattered the glass as it flew outside.

Joe and Chet hit the floor.

First there was a bright burst of blinding white light, followed by a deafening explosion. Glass shards flew into the room, then dirt and dust.

A split second later the midafternoon day was calm once again.

"Callie!" Frank finished tearing the tape from around her legs. He gently pulled the tape from her mouth.

"Oh, Frank!" she cried.

Frank ripped off the tape that bound her wrists. Callie jumped up and threw her arms around his neck.

"Frank! I thought I was dead!" She continued to hug Frank.

"You're okay, Callie. You're okay." Frank put his arms around her. "Nothing's ever going to happen to my Number One Girl."

Before Frank had time to react, Callie kissed him hard.

"Enough already," Joe grumbled. "Let's get out of here before the cops arrive."

Frank attempted to move, but Callie hung on.

"Don't let go," she said, terror in her voice.

"We've got to go," Frank said gently. "I'll explain later."

Chet was already in the car, its engine revving. Several people from the neighborhood were gathering around, looking first at the small crater in the front yard, then at the blown-out window, and last at the four teenagers peeling away in the sedan.

Chet and Joe were in front. Callie sat close to Frank in back, her hand holding his in a firm grip.

"The police have orders to take us in," Frank explained.

"Arrest you?" Callie was still shaken, and there was a tremor in her voice.

"Not arrest us. Chief Collig doesn't want us on this case." Frank put his arm around Callie's shoulders. "Someone is out to kill Dad—and our friends."

"Wh-why?"

"To settle an old score. A blood law."

"A what?" Chet asked from the front seat.

Joe spoke up. "In Anglo-Saxon days they didn't have police or courts or jails. They relied on what they called 'blood law.' It's also known as 'an eye for eye.' Retribution."

"But wh-who—wh-what—" Callie held back a sob.

Frank quickly explained about Leonard and Bobby Mock, then about the videotape.

"Do you remember anything after Mock and Mangieri kidnapped you?"

Callie took a breath. She had to control her breathing while she spoke. "I—just remember seeing Chet fighting with Mangieri." She sobbed. "Then I tried to help. Someone grabbed me from behind—"

"Bobby Mock," Joe added.

"I guess."

"Did you get a good look at his face? Was it Don West?" Frank asked.

"*Don West?* I—I don't know. I was choking. I couldn't really see. I don't even remember tearing the mask off." Callie gasped. "You don't really think that Don is Bobby Mock."

"The evidence is pointing that way."

"Poor Liz," Callie said.

"What happened at Mangieri's?" Frank asked.

"When I came to, I was in that chair. Mangieri was standing in front of me with that bomb. He said Bobby had made it. Then he set the timer and left."

"What did he set the timer for?" Frank asked.

"Five minutes. Why?"

"That tells us how much of a head start he had," Joe answered.

"Why would he be foolish enough to kill Callie in his own apartment?" Chet asked.

"That's what's bothering me," Frank replied.

"Why not? It makes sense to me," Joe said with a knowing air.

"Explain it." Frank was skeptical.

"It makes sense if Mangieri is really Bobby Mock."

Frank was even more skeptical. "Why Mangieri and not Don West?"

"Mangieri has disliked us from the day he moved into Bayport over four years ago. Besides, before he got kicked out of school, he was a photographer for the yearbook," Joe answered.

"That's right," Chet blurted out. "I remember him taking pictures of us at the beach for some project he was working on."

"That project was us," Joe added.

"That sounds fine," Frank said with reservation. "However, who's the guy in the raincoat and ski mask who tried to shoot us and then helped kidnap Callie?"

Joe slumped in his seat. Hard as he had tried before, Joe rarely matched Frank's logic for looking at a problem from different angles. Joe liked to move straight through a problem. Frank liked to go over, under, or around a problem.

"What we need to do is find Mangieri and Don and get this thing settled before someone gets killed," Frank said.

"Like our father."

"Stop at that convenience store," Frank ordered Chet.

"Why?"

"I'll tell you in about five minutes."

Frank had the others wait in Chet's car. He shoved a quarter into the pay phone outside the convenience store and punched a familiar number.

"Hello," Con Riley said at the other end of the phone."

"Con," Frank said, then paused. He was glad that Officer Riley was at home.

"What is it, Frank?"

"I need a big favor."

Static hissed back at Frank. He knew that Con was thinking, considering what Chief Collig might say, what might happen to his career.

"First tell me what it is."

"Callie was almost killed a short while ago. A bomb at Mangieri's place."

"Why didn't you call that in, Frank?"

Con's tone was as authoritative as it was agitated. Like an adult's.

"I should have, Con." Frank tried to sound genuinely sorry. "But I was afraid Chief Collig would put Joe and me in jail."

"Do you blame him?"

"No."

"I'm listening. But don't be too sure I won't hunt you down and throw you in jail myself."

"Fair enough." Frank took a breath. He had to present this just right to Con or the police veteran would be true to his word. Then Frank and Joe would be helpless to stop Mock from killing their father.

"Dad and Mom and Aunt Gertrude were supposed to have left Philadelphia earlier today, but they haven't arrived."

"You think Mock has Fenton?" Con sounded concerned.

Frank was relieved at the change of tone in Con's voice.

"I don't know, but Mock isn't an amateur. That

bomb was professional, Con. What I need, what Joe and I need, is for someone with official jurisdiction to contact the highway patrol to see where Dad's car is."

"Then what, Frank?"

"I need to get into city hall tonight."

"And?"

"And I need access to the police computer."

"I don't have a problem with your first request, Frank, but let me see if I understand you about the other two. You want me to help you break into city hall in the middle of night and then sneak you into police headquarters to use our main computer?"

Frank didn't hesitate. "Yes."

"It would be easier to deliver the moon, Frank."

"I know, Con. But we're talking about my father's life. We're talking about one of your closest friends."

Again the line hissed static at Frank. The moments seemed like long minutes.

"Okay." Con sighed. "This is for Fenton. And for Stan Williams."

"Who?"

"My partner who was killed."

"I understand," Frank replied.

Frank then explained to Con that he intended to get into city hall through one of the basement windows in the rear of the old building and then make his way to the old file room in the basement.

He wanted to find the original adoption file for Bobby Mock.

He returned to the sedan and quickly explained his plan to the other three. They decided to meet back at the Hardy home at nine P.M., after dark. Then they took Callie home. Chet dropped Frank and Joe off at their van, and then he went home, also.

"Look who we have here," Joe said as he spotted Don West's red sports car sitting in their driveway. "He's been pretty smart up until now."

"We've still got to prove he really is Bobby Mock," Frank warned Joe.

"No problem." Joe stopped the van and hopped out. He checked Don's car.

"Where is he?" Joe asked as he followed Frank to the house.

"Right here," Don said as he stepped from behind a hedge, holding a hunting rifle aimed straight at Joe!

Chapter

11

"TAKE IT EASY, DON," Frank said, holding up his hands. "We don't want to hurt you."

"Hurt me?" Don laughed, but Frank could tell that it wasn't the type of laugh that results from something being funny. Don's laugh arose from nervousness and fear. "That's just like you Hardys. I have a thirty-thirty deer rifle aimed at Joe's heart, and you threaten me."

"We know who you are," Joe said bluntly.

"Yeah? Well, why don't you tell me who you think I am!" Don shouted.

Frank could see the tension in Don's eyes and the beads of sweat that had formed on his forehead. The finger squeezing the trigger of the deer rifle unfolded and then folded around the trigger again. Frank didn't know Don very well, but he knew enough about human nature to sense that Don was a fuse about to blow.

"You're Bobby Mock," Joe announced.

"I've been told that's what you believe," Don replied, his voice nearly cracking.

"Who told you?" Frank asked, suddenly aware that someone had betrayed them.

"Liz. She got a message from Callie and then called me."

Frank took a step to Don's left. "I don't believe you. Just like I don't believe the story about the box hitting you in the cheek. You got that bruise when Joe hit you at the hospital last night."

Watching Frank's move, Joe stepped to Don's right. They had to distract Don so one of them could jump him and take the gun away.

"Stay where you are, Joe!" Don ordered through clenched teeth. "You too, Frank. I'll use this if I have to." Don raised the barrel of the gun for emphasis.

"You going to kill us in cold blood in front of our house?" Joe asked.

"No," Don answered calmly. "I'm not going to kill you."

"We're not going to let you kill our father, either," Joe said.

"I don't want to kill your father," Don said.

"What?" Joe blurted out, confused. "But—"

"I don't want to kill anybody. I'm not Bobby Mock."

Frank saw the tension drain from Don, and the finger folded around the trigger of the rifle relaxed. Don lowered the rifle and held it down in front of him.

"I'm sorry," he said. "I didn't know what else to do." He handed the rifle to Joe.

Stunned, Joe stared at Don for a second, then slowly took the rifle from Don's hands. He looked at Frank, who only returned his questioning gaze.

"I've admired the two of you ever since I moved to Bayport. You've got a pretty mean reputation for bringing in the bad guys. When I heard you were after me, I was afraid I wouldn't be able to explain." Don paused and sighed.

"Explain what?" Frank asked.

"That I'm not Bobby Mock. That I didn't plant the bogus file on Chet. I really found it at city hall, and a box really did fall and hit me."

"How did you know when Bobby Mock's mother died?" Joe asked, gripping the rifle in his hands.

"I did the research for Liz before she called you two. It was in an old article about Leonard Mock's trial."

"He's right," Frank said with a nod of his head. "I read the same article this morning in Dad's file."

"That still doesn't explain why you've taken such an interest in us the past two days," Joe said, still skeptical.

"I told you—I admire you guys. Because of my

dad's occupation, I've had to move around a lot, and I never really made friends very easily, never joined any clubs or went out for sports. I was real lucky to find Liz. When I saw that I might be able to help you two, I leapt at the chance." Don smiled. "I guess I should have looked before I leapt, huh?"

Frank laughed. "I believe you," he said. He looked at his brother. "Joe?"

Joe stared at Don and then glanced over at Frank. He fingered the safety switch on the rifle and was surprised to find that it was locked. He looked at Don and smiled. "Yeah, I guess I believe you, too. But that leaves one question. Who told Liz we thought you were Bobby Mock?"

"I guess the *real* Bobby Mock set that one up," Don said, taking a deep breath. He held out his hand to Joe. "I'm sorry I pointed that rifle at you."

Joe grabbed Don's hand in a firm grip. "I understand. You still want to help us find Bobby Mock?"

"You mean it?" Don asked excitedly.

"How do you feel about back alleys and breaking into city hall?" Joe said as they headed into the house.

"What?" Don replied, a puzzled expression on his face.

The alley behind city hall was littered with garbage thrown about by the previous day's tornado.

Frank, Joe, Callie, Chet, and Don zigzagged their way through the mess to the rear of the building.

Don and Joe had gone in Don's sports car while Frank, Callie, and Chet had used Chet's sedan. They parked the cars several blocks away and made their way moving from shadow to shadow in the moonless night.

Joe had wanted Don to "borrow" his father's keys to city hall, but Frank had vetoed the idea on the grounds that, if caught, Mr. West could be implicated. Joe still liked his idea, especially after stubbing his toe several times on the garbage.

"Here," Frank said, and he put his arms out to halt the group.

"How can you see?" Chet said, frustrated.

"He's got the eyes of a cat," Joe answered.

Frank ignored both of them. He knelt down by the basement window and pushed against the glass. He didn't really expect it to be unlocked, but he was hoping it might have been broken by the storm.

He wrapped his hand in his handkerchief, broke the glass, and then unlocked the window.

He checked up and down the alley. He just hoped that Con was standing out in front of the police station to distract any other cops who might patrol the alley.

He slid in across the window and jumped to the floor. Callie followed, then Joe and Don. Chet was a tighter fit, but he did make it through.

Frank shut the window.

"Now you can turn your penlight on," Frank said to Joe. "But keep the beam on the floor."

"I've done this before," Joe reminded him pointedly.

"The old records section is in the subbasement," Don said. "I can show you where I found the bogus file on Chet."

Once downstairs, Joe tried a light switch. To their surprise, the overhead fluorescent lights flickered on.

"This might be easier than we thought," Joe said.

"Okay," Frank said as the others formed a semicircle in front of him. "Don, how did you find the file on Chet."

"Everything's on computer. I just waited until the computers came back on-line and then searched for the case file number."

"How did you do that?" Frank asked.

"I pulled up the file on Robert Edward Mock," Don explained.

"You didn't find the right file," Frank announced.

"How do you know?" Don asked.

Frank pulled the folded newspaper clippings from his shirt pocket. "Because of these," he announced. "Look." He laid the news photos on a desk. "In all four news photos, Mock is surrounded by a crowd of people."

"That makes sense," Callie said. "Mock's trial was the biggest sensation to hit Bayport in years."

114

Frank smiled at Callie. He returned his gaze to the photos. "I missed it the first few times I went over them, but then I spotted him."

"Who?" Chet asked.

"Bobby Mock. There." Frank pointed at a kid in the first photo who was half hidden by the crowd pressing around Leonard Mock. "And there." He pointed at the second photo, and again, the same kid was present. "And there, and there." In the third and fourth photos, the kid was more visible.

For the first time they all got a good look at a young Bobby Mock, his white blond hair uncombed, a halfmoon birthmark just above his upper lip.

"He's tall for six years old," Joe said.

"That's been our mistake from the beginning," Frank said. "We all assumed Bobby Mock was our age. He's not five in those photos. He's at least eleven or twelve."

"That means we're looking for someone who's twenty-three or twenty-four," Joe announced.

"I still don't understand how I picked up the wrong file," Don said.

"It's not your fault. You got the file you were meant to find," Frank replied. "Didn't they used to write all the case numbers in a big log?" Frank asked Don.

"They still do," Don answered. Then he snapped his fingers. "Bobby Mock's real case file could be found in the old handwritten log."

"Right," Frank replied with a smile.

Don darted down a row of shelves and disappeared. He returned moments later.

"Here it is," he announced, holding up a thick two- by three-foot book. "The old case log." He laid the book gently on the desk as though it were a valuable volume of literature.

Frank flipped through the yellowing pages. "Look at this." The others looked over Frank's shoulders. "Mock, Robert Edward, adoption granted."

"Does it say who adopted Mock?" Callie asked.

"No." Frank leaned up. "But it gives us the case number."

"Chet, I'll need your help getting the file box down from the shelf," Don said as he wrote down the case number. Then he and Chet disappeared toward the rear of the file room.

"That still doesn't explain why Mangieri's involved," Callie said.

"For money," Frank replied. "What bothers me is how he got out of jail," Frank added.

"Got it!" Don announced as he and Chet trotted back up to the desk. He handed the file to Frank, who placed it on the desk. He turned the cover back.

Staring back at them was a small photo of the same kid they had seen in the news photos, his eyes dark with fear and worry, his face a scowl, his hair mussed.

"Bobby Mock," Frank said.

"He looks so scared—and lonely," Callie whispered.

Frank flipped over the first page. The second page was a court order taking custody of Bobby away from Leonard Mock.

The third page was a request by a young couple to adopt Bobby Mock and legally change his name.

The fourth page granted the request.

Frank cleared his throat and said, "Robert Edward Mock then became—"

"Robert Edward Stewart," a deep voice said from behind them.

They all spun around. Officer Stewart stood at the base of the stairs, his .357 drawn and pointing at the group.

"Now, who'll be the first to die?" Stewart asked with a smile.

The fluorescent light bounced off Stewart's white blond hair and created a shimmering halo over his head like that of an angel of death.

Chapter

12

"I ALWAYS LIKED the meticulous way you thought, Frank," Stewart said. A sly grin spread across his face. "I made only one mistake—keeping that old file down here."

"That wasn't your only mistake," Frank said. "Officer Riley knows we're down here, and he'll—"

"Ah, yes. Officer Riley," Stewart interrupted. "My *partner*. Supposed to be watching the front, isn't he? He told me what you were up to, thought I would want to help, being a fellow cop and all. Quite a weird twist of fate, huh? I mean the son of the man who killed his partner now kills him."

"What?" Joe blurted.

"Don't get so excited, Joe," Stewart said. "He's not dead—yet. Let's just say he's resting. He's at the top of the stairs, unconscious. He's safe. For now.''

"How did you get the file changed?" Frank asked.

"My first job was working the night shift at city hall," Stewart answered without hesitation. "That's when we hit on the plan."

"Plan?" Callie asked.

"The plan to set Chet up to throw us off," Frank answered. Frank shifted and Stewart braced himself. "You're nervous, Officer Stewart."

"I'd be foolish not to be nervous."

"What now?" Callie asked.

"I say we rush him," Don growled.

"Yeah? You plan to be the first hero to die? I left a message with Liz that you were me." Stewart let out a bone-chilling laugh and waved the magnum among the five teenagers.

"How did you get Officer Riley in here?" Joe asked.

Stewart shrugged. "I suggested we check up on you kids, make sure you were okay. We told the cop on the night shift to take a break, that we would watch the place for a while."

"You're not getting away with this," Frank said.

"I've already gotten away with this," Stewart replied, smiling. "Riley doesn't know what hit him." Stewart held up his gun, and Frank could see a little blood on the butt end. "However, that's not the story Chief Collig will hear. No, what really happened is that Officer Riley and his partner, that's me, thought we heard looters breaking into city hall. When we investigated, gunfire erupted, and Officer Riley was killed, but not before he killed three of the looters." Stewart pulled a second gun from behind him. "This is Officer Riley's gun. I, of course, killed Frank and Joe Hardy."

"What about our guns?" Joe asked with a smirk.

Stewart put Officer Riley's gun down on the desk. He knelt down, keeping his dark eyes and the silver magnum trained on the group, and pulled a snub-nosed .38 from an ankle holster. "Here, catch!"

Stewart threw the gun at Joe, and Joe caught the gun and pointed it at the police officer.

"Don't insult my intelligence, Joe. It's empty. And now it has your fingerprints on it. Hand it back to me. Gently."

Joe looked at the pistol. He began to hand the gun to Stewart, then he threw it down one of the aisles, where it clanked to the concrete floor and slid under one of the shelves of files.

"That wasn't very smart, Joe." Stewart's triumphant grin twisted into an angry frown.

"You'll never find it under all those files," Joe said calmly. "How are you going to explain that one, wise guy?"

Stewart straightened himself and grabbed Riley's gun.

"Let's see, which of you gets killed by Officer Riley, and which of you is the lucky one that is killed by the hero, Officer Stewart?"

"You're not going to kill us?" Don said, a little cry in his voice.

Joe turned to Don. He was surprised to see Don cowering, backing up, frightened. He began to regret having Don along.

"Pl-please," Don stammered. "D-d-don't kill me. *Please.*"

"You coward." Joe sneered.

"I don't want to die!" Don blurted out and fell to his knees.

Joe was disgusted.

"Stand up, West," Stewart ordered.

"No, no, no," Don cried. Then he turned to Joe. "Don't let him kill me."

Joe was tempted to hit Don, to shut him up. Then he saw the slightest wink from Don's eye. Suddenly Joe knew that Don was only pretending to distract Stewart.

"I said stand up!" Stewart moved toward Don.

Don grabbed for Stewart's knees, and Joe kicked out at the magnum in Stewart's right hand. Stewart stepped back, and Don landed on the floor. Joe's kick connected with the magnum, and the gun flew from Stewart's hand and exploded.

"No!" Callie screamed and fell to the floor.

"Callie!" Frank rushed to Callie. The bullet had grazed her left temple.

"Don't move, punks," Stewart growled. He pulled back the hammer of Riley's gun and held it to Don's head.

Joe stopped and stepped back, his hands held up. "Okay, just take it easy."

"I'll take it easy, punk," Stewart spit out. He knelt and picked up his magnum. "Enough of this! Time to die."

"Stewart!" Officer Riley gasped from the top of the stairs.

He stumbled down, nearly falling. Frank saw a thin line of dried dark blood on the side of his forehead.

"Drop it, Stewart," Riley said with authority.

Stewart laughed and fired Riley's gun at Riley. Con flew backward and slid down the stairs.

"No!" Frank yelled and leapt for Stewart. Stewart swung around and caught Frank across the temple. Frank slumped to the floor.

"Frank!" Callie screamed and crawled over to him, cradling the unconscious Frank in her arms.

"Change of plans, folks." Stewart cackled. "Officer Riley was killed with his own gun by Frank Hardy." He pointed the .357 automatic magnum at Frank. "And I killed Frank Hardy!"

Chapter

13

CON RILEY KICKED out just as Stewart started to pull the trigger. The bullet hit the ceiling and bits of concrete and gray dust fell on Frank and Callie. Riley groaned and collapsed.

Joe sprang on Stewart and knocked him against a desk. He clamped his hands on both of the man's wrists to keep Stewart from pointing the .357 at him.

Don ran to Frank. "You okay?" he asked.

"Yeah," Frank groaned. Then he turned and saw that Joe was now struggling with Stewart. "Joe—"

Don ran to help Joe. The magnum exploded again, and Don yelled as he grabbed for his shoulder.

Joe turned. He was distracted just long enough

to give Stewart time to twist around. Joe's back was now against the desk.

Joe pushed Stewart away, and he flew backward, tripping over Riley and falling onto the stairs. He dropped Riley's gun. Joe kicked it away.

Stewart raised the magnum and fired. Joe dived behind the desk, the corner exploding in wooden splinters and chips.

Joe popped back up immediately, but Stewart was gone. Joe could hear the fleeing footsteps of the bad cop as he reached the top of the stairs.

Joe ran to Don. "You okay?"

"Yeah, it grazed my shoulder. It just burns a little." Don grimaced. "I'll be okay. Check Riley."

Joe dashed to Officer Riley. He checked the police veteran's chest and was shocked to find no blood. Joe ripped open Con's shirt to find a bulletproof vest.

"Is he okay?" Frank asked, joining Joe.

"Yes. How's Callie?"

"I'm fine," Callie said, holding Frank's handkerchief to her head.

"Look at this, Frank." Joe directed Frank's attention to the bulletproof vest.

"So?"

"So I thought I hit something hard, like metal, when I fought with Bobby Mock at the hotel room. Remember?"

"It wasn't metal," Frank said. "It was a bulletproof vest."

"Right."

"Is there a phone down here, Don?" Frank asked.

"Yeah," Don said.

"Good. Call the police station. Tell them we have an officer down and need assistance."

Frank and Joe walked into the darkened entryway of their home. Joe flipped on the living room light and threw himself in an overstuffed chair.

"I feel like I've been awake forever," Joe said, sighing.

"Me, too," Frank agreed as he yawned.

"You make sure the doors and windows are locked," Chief Collig ordered Officer Murphy. Murphy disappeared down the hallway as the police chief stood in front of Frank and Joe.

"What now?" Frank asked.

"Now you two go to bed and let real cops handle police business. You're lucky I don't throw you in jail for obstruction of justice." Frank didn't like the slight smile on the chief's face.

"What about Officer Riley?" Joe asked.

"He may be guarding a crosswalk for a while—"

"Is he all right?" Frank interrupted.

"The bulletproof vest saved his life. He's got a couple of cracked ribs, but he'll survive."

"Good." Frank sighed.

"Doors and windows locked," Officer Murphy reported as he entered the living room.

"Outside," Chief Collig said, pointing behind himself. He turned to Frank and Joe. "You two get a good night's sleep," Chief Collig said, his voice soft.

"What about Stewart?" Frank asked.

"We'll find him. Officer Murphy will be outside in his patrol car. You two *stay* home. Good night." Then he walked out the door.

"Now what?" Joe asked.

"Stewart's not going to try anything," Frank said, standing.

"How do you know?"

"He wants us too badly to risk getting caught at our house."

"You have a plan?"

"We'll take Chief Collig's advice and then sneak out in the morning," Frank said as he headed up the stairs.

Joe followed. He didn't know what Frank had planned, if anything, but he was too tired to care.

Frank and Joe rose at six A.M. Frank looked out his bedroom window. A patrol car sat at the curb. Frank smiled. Officer Murphy's head was back against the headrest, his eyes closed, his mouth open.

"He's asleep," Frank said.

"How do you plan to get the van out without waking him?" Joe asked.

"Put it in neutral and let it roll out into the

street, then start the engine and peel out. By the time Officer Murphy realizes what's happening, we'll be gone with the wind.''

"Solid," Joe replied.

They headed down the stairs.

"I want to call Callie and make sure she's okay," Frank said.

Frank picked up the receiver and punched in Callie's private number. Then he noticed the flashing red light on the answering machine. Someone had called. Frank put the receiver down and punched the Play button on the answering machine.

A moment later Laura Hardy's voice spoke from the machine, "Frank. Joe. We got your message, and your father wanted me to call to tell you he's renting a car and driving back after he sleeps a couple of hours. It's''—she paused—''eleven o'clock now. Your father said he should be in around seven or seven-thirty in the morning. He'll meet you at that truck stop. He said you'd know which one. Aunt Gertrude and I are driving back tomorrow. You two take care. 'Bye.''

Frank shut off the machine.

"What message?" Joe asked.

"We didn't leave a message," Frank said sternly.

"Stewart," Joe hissed.

"Right. Mom must have called before we got home last night. I knew I should have checked the answering machine." Frank picked up the phone and punched the number of the Philadelphia hotel where his parents were staying.

"What are you doing?" Joe asked.

"Calling Mom. Perhaps she knows what the message said."

"How are you going to ask her about that without alarming her about Stewart?"

"I'll think of something."

Mrs. Hardy and Aunt Gertrude had already checked out of the hotel, a desk clerk informed Frank.

"What now?" Joe asked.

"First we get past Officer Murphy," Frank replied and headed for the kitchen.

"We've got to find Stewart and fast," Joe said.

"If Stewart's the one who left that message for Dad, then he'll be waiting at the truck stop."

"Which one?" Joe asked as they stopped at the back door.

"We'll try the one on Highway Nine; that's where Dad would come in from Philadelphia."

They ran out the back door and sneaked around to the front. Using the van as cover, they opened the side door and hopped into the vehicle.

Joe put the van in neutral and silently rolled it out into the street. Then he flipped the ignition switch forward, fired the van to life, threw the shift into first, and stomped on the accelerator. The tires screamed as the van lurched forward and sped off.

Frank didn't know how Officer Murphy had reacted, and he didn't care. He could imagine Chief Collig's volcanic reaction when Murphy reported the incident, though.

Five minutes later Joe guided the van into the large parking lot of Trucker's Pit Stop, a truck stop just west of Bayport.

"Look for a rental car, something with Pennsylvania tags," Frank said.

Joe slowly snaked the van down and through the rows, but they found nothing.

"Maybe he's not here yet," Joe said after several frustrating passes.

"He should have been, if this is the truck stop Mom was referring to. Try around the back."

Joe turned and headed to the rear, back behind the large garage and oversize car washes.

"Look!" Joe said, pointing to a light blue sedan.

Martin Mangieri, his telltale black leather jacket and long dirty blond hair, was shutting the trunk of the sedan.

Joe pressed the accelerator, and the van lurched, moved, the tires squealing. Mangieri turned and horror filled his eyes as the black van sped toward him.

He ran to the front of the sedan and hopped into the driver's seat.

Joe hit the brakes, and Frank jumped from the van. He grabbed the door handle on the driver's side of the sedan and lifted it just as Mangieri locked the door. Then Joe saw his father's brief-case lying on the seat next to Mangieri.

"He's got Dad!" Frank yelled.

Mangieri smiled as he started up the car. He threw the car into reverse and shouted through the rolled-up window, "Your old man's dead, Hardy! *Dead!*"

Chapter
14

FRANK SLUGGED the driver's window but managed only to hurt his knuckles.

Mangieri laughed, and the blue sedan jetted away from the curb.

Frank hopped back into the van, and Joe turned it around.

"Dad's briefcase is in the front seat. I think Mangieri's got Dad in the trunk."

The Hardys always kept the engine and transmission finely tuned, and the hot-rodded van responded with a clean, even burst of speed and power. The van swooped down behind the blue sedan like a black bird of prey.

Mangieri glanced into the rearview mirror. Joe could see the fear in his eyes. Mangieri must have given the car more gas because it, too, suddenly burst forward. In a second he was putting some distance between it and the van.

"He's not going to slow down!" Frank yelled above the roar of the van's fireball engine.

"That sedan's faster than it looks."

The sedan jerked to the left, then back to the right.

Joe saw why a split second later. A large branch torn from a tree sat in the middle of the road. Joe didn't have time to turn the van. They slammed into the branch and flew into the air.

"Whoa!" Frank yelled and clutched his seat. The van smacked back down on the pavement, the shocks groaning and creaking against the sudden impact. Then the van began to swerve.

Joe fought to keep the van under control. He let up on the gas pedal and lightly pressed the brakes. The large vehicle responded to Joe's gentle touch and straightened out.

Mangieri had used the extra time to gain more distance. Joe again pressed the accelerator hard. The gap between the two vehicles slowly and steadily decreased.

Frank grabbed the CB and turned the channel button to nine, the emergency channel.

"I'm calling the cavalry," Frank announced as he pressed the button on the hand mike. "Mayday! Mayday! Any Bayport police. This is Frank Hardy. We are chasing a suspected kidnapper in a stolen car." Frank glanced at the corner street sign as the van zoomed past it. It was just a blur, but he was able to make out the letters well enough to say, "We're on Highway Nine headed west. The suspect's car is a light blue, late model sedan. Pennsylvania plates. A rental. I repeat, we are chasing a stolen car. The kidnap victim is inside, he may be hurt. Need assistance." He released the button. Frank was set to repeat the announcement when the CB buzzed.

"This is Bayport Police Department, please repeat your message. Over."

Frank began to repeat his message but was cut short.

"Frank Hardy!" boomed the angry voice of Chief Collig. "Where are—"

Frank shut off the CB.

"So much for that idea."

"Where's he headed?" Joe asked above the noise.

"Looks like away from Bayport," Frank replied.

Joe glanced at the speedometer. The digital speedometer flashed 70 MPH.

"C'mon, baby," Joe said under his breath to the van. He pressed the accelerator closer to the floor.

They inched closer to the sedan. The light blue digital speedometer flashed 75, then 80. Every nerve and muscle in Joe's body seemed to contract at once. One bad move—a quick swerve by Mangieri, another branch in the road, anything to cause Joe to lose control—and the black van would become their coffin.

When the van was a foot from the blue sedan's rear bumper, Mangieri's car responded with more speed.

Joe's eyes flashed. He couldn't safely go any faster.

Mangieri slowed a little. Joe pulled the van to the left and tried to edge up to Mangieri. He had to back off when he saw oncoming traffic headed toward him on the two-lane highway.

"Try to get on the other side of him!" Frank shouted.

Joe had been thinking the same thing. With traffic on his left and the van on the right, Mangieri would be trapped. Joe whipped the van to the right and was soon beside Mangieri.

"He's trapped!" Frank said.

Mangieri jerked his head from left to right.

Joe glanced at the car. He could see his father's leather briefcase lying on the passenger seat.

Just then Mangieri stomped the brake, sending the rear of the car into a violent fishtail. The sedan bounced off the van, and hot, white sparks shot out. The cars whipped back and made contact again. This time a high-pitched scream accompanied the crash as the sedan's fender was torn from its body.

Joe pushed his brake flat, and the van jerked, slowing.

Mangieri tried to speed up, but his car had lost its power.

"Now it's our turn," Joe announced.

"Careful," Frank warned. "Dad could be in the trunk."

"I'm just going to get in front of him," Joe said.

He pressed down on the accelerator and easily began to pull ahead of the sedan. He glanced over at Mangieri.

"Look out!" Frank yelled.

Joe jerked his eyes forward. The shoulder of the road had turned into an exit ramp, which curved sharply to the right. Joe's mind raced with decisions. Mangieri was on his left, the exit was on his right, and fifty feet straight ahead was a concrete pillar. He had to get in front of Mangieri before he hit the pillar or else he'd have to go off at the exit ramp.

Joe knew they didn't have enough time to give the van more speed to get all the way in front of Mangieri. They'd have to take the exit. He lightly pressed the brakes and felt the brake pads grab the wheel disks. They had to slow before taking the sharp right turn.

Just then Joe's foot and the brake pedal slammed to the floor as the brakes turned to mush.

"The brakes are gone!" Joe yelled. "I can't turn into the exit. We'll flip over."

Dead ahead the concrete pillar rose like a giant tombstone.

Chapter

15

JOE PRESSED ON the emergency brake pedal. He did it slowly or else the brakes would grip the wheels in a deadly lock that would send the van rolling like a large tin can.

The van jerked and then slowed. At the last possible second Joe spun the wheel and made the edge of the ramp. Mangieri had disappeared over the hill. The van coasted to a stop.

Frank brought his fist down on the dash. "What happened to the brakes?" His question was almost an accusation.

"I don't know!" Joe shouted back.

He hopped from the van and dived under the front end. He rose a moment later, a small, oil-drenched twig in his hands.

"What is it?" Frank asked.

139

"This must have broken off the branch we hit and stuck in the brake line," he explained, showing Frank the twig.

"Brake lines are metal," Frank replied.

"Not the brake lines going directly into the brake cylinder of the wheel. They're rubber."

"Can you patch it?"

"No." Joe got in and slammed the door shut. He snapped the twig with his fingers and tossed the broken pieces out the window. "We'll have to get a new one. But not right now." Joe turned the van in a hard right turn and hit the accelerator to go back onto the highway.

Frank knew that Joe was an expert enough driver to continue the chase using the emergency brake.

"Where is he?" Joe asked as they topped a Hill. The blue sedan had vanished.

"I'll keep an eye on the exits," Frank said.

They drove for another thirty minutes but still couldn't find the blue sedan. Mangieri could have taken any number of exits heading in any number of directions.

"Head back to Bayport," Frank said after another fifteen minutes.

"What?" Joe shouted.

"Mangieri would have headed back to Bayport as soon as possible."

"Give me one good reason why. We're not going to give up searching for Dad!"

"We're not giving up searching for Dad. Use

your head, Joe. Mangieri has only one place to go—Bayport!''

Joe let up on the accelerator and slowly eased the emergency brake down. The van slowed. He steered the van toward an exit. Frank made sense. Mangieri would have to head back to Bayport because that was where Stewart had to be—if Stewart was going to make good on his threat of killing all the Hardys and their friends.

''Where to now?'' Joe asked as they entered Bayport.

The sky had darkened as heavy, black rain clouds closed out the sun. A light drizzle was falling. Joe flipped on the headlights.

Frank had ridden in silence, forcing himself to shut out the image of his father in the hands of Stewart.

What would drive a man to such extremes to achieve murder? Revenge? Bobby must have kept in touch with his father over the years he was in prison. Mock's hatred for Fenton Hardy festered into a madness that had infected his son, Bobby. A blood law, Joe had called it.

''What did Leonard Mock say just before he collapsed?'' Frank asked, staring ahead through the water-spotted windshield.

Joe flipped on the windshield wipers. ''What are you talking about?''

''He said something about everything coming full circle. What do you think he meant?''

Joe glanced at Frank. ''He was talking about his son.''

''Maybe not just his son. The shoot-out with Leonard Mock took place at the old National Guard Armory,'' Frank stated matter-of-factly.

''You think that's where Stewart, I mean Bobby, has taken Dad.''

''That's exactly what I think!''

Bayport's old National Guard Armory was on the city's southeast edge. The Hardys were determined that it wouldn't become their father's place of execution.

They reached the large brick and stone building in under three minutes. From the outside, the armory looked like a medieval fortress, complete with towers and ramparts. Frank and Joe had often joked about the old-fashioned design of the building, but their jokes didn't seem funny right then.

Joe shut off the headlights a half mile from the armory. He turned off the engine and let the van coast in, parking it a hundred yards from the front of the building.

''If I remember right,'' Frank said, ''the fight with the police took place behind the armory at the old practice range.''

Frank and Joe trotted around to the side, then pressed themselves against the building as they neared the practice range.

Thunder rumbled. The drizzle turned into a

trickle. The sky darkened more, and it looked like dusk rather than late morning.

The ground was still muddy from the rain the tornado had dumped, and now it was becoming even more sodden and difficult to walk through.

"There's the sedan," Frank said as they turned a corner of the building.

The blue car sat with its trunk lid open. Frank checked the inside. He found a small smear of blood and a tie clip he recognized as his father's.

"They've got him," Frank said grimly.

They reached the end of the side of the armory. Frank moved his head slowly around the corner.

"Take a look," Frank said to Joe, and they exchanged places.

Joe peeked around the corner.

A little flame flared. Mangieri's face was cast in an orange and yellow glow. He was leaning against the wall ten yards down from them. He brought the lighter up to a cigarette that dangled from his mouth and lit it. He turned away and stared to his left.

"He's mine," Joe whispered to Frank.

"Be my guest," Frank replied.

Joe slid around the corner and crept up on the unsuspecting thug. Mangieri's attention was directed in the opposite direction.

Joe tapped Mangieri on the shoulder.

"Got the time?" Joe asked with venom.

Mangieri turned and gasped. A split second later

he fired a broad right fist into the center of Joe's stomach. Joe countered with a right of his own. Mangieri fell back against the wall and slid down into the mud, the lit cigarette still dangling from his lower lip.

Joe rubbed his knuckles. "He's not going anywhere for a while," he said with a smile as Frank joined him.

Frank patted Mangieri's leather jacket to check for a gun. "Empty," he told Joe.

"Too bad," Joe said.

They continued along the back of the building until they reached the far corner.

"The practice range," Frank announced. He peered around the corner, then gasped. "Dad!" Frank whispered, trying to suppress a shout.

Fenton Hardy was tied to a lamppost some fifty yards away, his hands tied over his head, the rope hanging from a hook. His head hung down, his feet slightly off the ground. The glare from the light and the drizzle of rain created an eerie halo about him, giving him a ghostlike appearance.

"I don't see Stewart," Frank told Joe.

They moved out slowly, hoping the darkness of the oncoming storm would hide them long enough to make a run for their father.

They were halfway to him when Stewart suddenly appeared, the deadly .357 magnum hanging at his side.

Frank and Joe froze.

"I've been waiting for you."

The boys moved slowly toward him, keeping their eyes on him and the magnum at his side. They stopped at the edge of the circle of light.

Fenton raised his head. "I'm okay," he said weakly to Frank and Joe.

"Shut up!" Stewart barked.

Fenton slumped forward again.

Frank and Joe moved a step closer to Stewart.

The magnum was up and fired instantly, mud splattering Frank and Joe.

"That was just a warning. The next shot drops one of you dead."

"Let—them—go," Fenton groaned.

"Say, 'please.' " Frank and Joe were stunned to hear Stewart's childlike voice.

Stewart laughed again. This time it was more hysterical and higher-pitched. Stewart reached into his raincoat pocket and pulled out the black ski mask, which he slipped over his head.

"You don't need the disguise anymore, Bobby," Frank said.

"I'm disappointed in you, Frank. You have such a brilliant, logical mind. This isn't a disguise. It's an executioner's hood."

"You're not going to get away with this," Joe said with great control.

Stewart's laugh was just as hysterical, just as high-pitched as before.

"An empty threat from an empty head. You

145

should have spent more time exercising the muscle between your ears, Joe Hardy.''

Frank reached out and grabbed Joe before the younger Hardy could make a move toward Stewart.

''You see,'' Stewart said gleefully, ''Frank is the smart one.''

''If you're wearing an executioner's hood, what are the charges, when was the trial and the sentencing?'' Frank glanced quickly at Joe and moved his eyes toward Stewart.

Play the game, Frank was telling Joe. Play the game.

''You want charges?'' Stewart shouted. ''I'll gave you charges.'' Stewart held up a finger. ''One: sticking his nose into other people's business.'' He held up a second finger. ''Two: causing a father and son to be separated for life.'' A third finger went up. ''Three: putting that father in prison until he rots and dies from cancer.''

Stewart began to pace in front of Fenton Hardy, all the time uncurling and curling his fingers around the pistol grip of the .357 magnum.

''This is the trial!'' Stewart bellowed, his voice more agitated. ''I, the jury, find Fenton Hardy guilty on all charges, the most serious of which is causing a son to be torn from his father.''

Stewart paced for a few seconds more, then suddenly stopped, his back to Fenton. He turned slowly, raised the magnum shoulder level, and aimed it at Fenton's head.

He spoke softly, almost in rhythm to the drizzle that fell about them.

"The sentence: death. Just as my father was sentenced to death. The sentence to be carried out immediately."

Stewart squeezed the trigger.

"No!" Joe shouted and lunged at Stewart, the gun exploding as Joe and Stewart fell into the mud.

Joe gagged and spit out a small amount of mud. He grabbed Stewart's gun hand and pressed it deeper into the mud. The magnum erupted again, and Joe felt the recoil and the heat of the explosion. Joe pushed himself up with his left hand and hit Stewart with a right cross. Stewart groaned once and relaxed.

Joe was trying to pull the gun from Stewart's grip when the man suddenly kicked up and caught Joe in the side with his knee. Joe groaned and almost fell over. He caught himself instead and planted another solid right to Stewart's cheek.

A gasp came from Stewart, and this time he lay still, the .357 sliding from his hand and into the mud. Joe scooped up the gun and stepped back from the unconscious man. He glanced over at Frank.

Frank was untying his father. He tugged at the last knot, and the rope slackened. Fenton began to fall, but Frank caught him and helped him to stand.

"You okay, Dad?" Joe asked.

"Yes," Fenton Hardy answered weakly but with a smile.

Joe took the rope that had bound his father and tied Stewart's hands together.

"Dad needs to get to the hospital," Frank said. "I'll bring the van around."

"I can make it," Mr. Hardy said. When Frank let go, though, Fenton fell back. Frank reached out to steady his father.

"I'll help him," Joe said. "Go get the van."

"I'll call the police," Frank said as he started for the van.

Lightning flashed across the sky, followed close by thunder, and then the rain began to fall in large, hard drops.

Fenton Hardy had only minor cuts and bruises and was treated and released from the hospital.

Three days later he was sitting in his favorite easy chair drinking a cup of coffee. Frank sat on the couch with Callie and Joe. Liz and Don were on the floor, and they were all watching the news on WBAY.

"And the judge refused to set bail for Robert Edward Stewart until the former Bayport police officer could undergo a psychiatric examination by a court-appointed physician."

Frank hit the Mute button on the remote control.

"Why?" Callie asked as she took the remote control away from Frank.

"Stewart's lawyer has made a motion to plead Stewart insane," Frank explained.

Chet entered from the kitchen, a large sub in his hands.

"Who's insane?" Chet asked as he chomped down on the sandwich.

"We are, for letting you eat us out of house and home," Joe replied when he saw the four-inch thick sandwich.

"I'm still amazed at the timing and the planning involved," Callie said.

Mr. Hardy stirred. "Leonard Mock was one of the most methodical crooks I've ever dealt with."

"Mangieri supplied Mock with the photos and news clippings," Frank added. "Mangieri turned state's evidence and signed a confession, but this time he didn't get any deal."

"Mock learned who had adopted his son and sent him letters over the years," Fenton said. "He blamed me for separating them." Mr. Hardy set his cup down and stood. "I'm going to pick up Con from the hospital and drive him home. You kids try to stay out of trouble while I'm gone," he said, raising one eyebrow before walking out of the room.

"The editor really liked my story," Liz said. "Thanks, Frank."

"No problem," Frank replied.

"What about me?" Joe asked, pretending to be hurt.

"You, too, Joe," Liz said with a laugh.

"Hey, look!" Chet mumbled, with a mouthful of sub, pointing with the half-eaten sandwich at the big-screen TV.

Joe Hardy appeared on the fifty-two-inch screen in living color, his blond hair plastered to his head like a wet mop, his clothes soaked and hanging on his body like rags.

Suddenly the sound blared from the stereo speakers.

"And now, news from the fashion world," the commentator was saying. "Joe Hardy, Bayport's most eligible teenage bachelor, was caught modeling the latest in tornado attire recently in downtown Bayport."

"Hey!" Joe shouted and turned his blue eyes on Callie.

Callie, the remote control in one hand, jumped up and hit the Eject button on the videotape player. She grabbed the tape that slid out and held it up.

"Looks like Newshawk Shaw captured another exclusive!" she said with a laugh.

"Give me that tape, Callie Shaw!" Joe demanded, jumping up and chasing her from the living room while the others rolled with laughter.

FRIGHT WAVE

Chapter

1

"WHAT WAS THAT?" Joe Hardy blurted out. Something had jolted him awake. He looked around quickly and saw his brother, Frank, sitting in the seat next to him.

"Just a little turbulence," Frank said. "Go back to sleep."

Joe started to do just that, but a second later he was sitting bolt upright, his blue eyes showing no sign of drowsiness. He remembered where they were headed. They had flown a long way from their hometown of Bayport, and now Joe was eager for a first glimpse of their destination.

Joe ran a hand through his blond hair and started to lean across Frank for a glimpse out the window. A sharp tug at his waist reminded him that he was still strapped into his seat.

1

"Whoa!" Frank exclaimed. "There's not much to see. From up here everything still looks pretty small." Just then Frank felt his ears pop as the plane dropped through the sparse cloud cover. He knew they'd soon be on the ground.

The wing outside Frank's window dipped down as the jet went into a tight turn, and the bright morning sun streamed into the cabin and directly into Frank's brown eyes. The bright light made his brown hair look lighter than it really was. He squinted and pulled down the shade.

"Please make sure your seat belts are securely fastened," a female voice crackled over the intercom, "and return your seats to the full upright position."

"Why?" Joe asked nobody in particular. "What difference does it make what position my seat is in?"

"Well, it might make a big difference to me," a voice from behind them answered. It was the voice of their father, Fenton Hardy. "The back of your seat's been in my lap for about two thousand miles—and my legs have been asleep for the last five hundred. How about giving an old guy a break?"

Joe shifted his muscular, six-foot frame. The movement made him realize that his whole body was stiff, and there was a dull pain in his neck and shoulders that he vainly tried to rub away. "Airplane seats are definitely *not* designed for comfort," he mumbled.

"Not if your flight is over thirty minutes long or you're over five feet tall," Frank added.

There was a soft bump as the wheels hit the runway, and a loud roar as the pilot threw the huge jet thrusters into reverse. They all strained forward in their seats as the three-story-tall jumbo jet rapidly slowed from 200 MPH to taxi speed.

When the plane finally came to a complete halt and the seat belt sign winked off, Frank and Joe jumped out of their seats. They were at the door before the flight attendant had a chance to pick up the intercom microphone and say, "Aloha—and welcome to Hawaii!"

It took almost an hour to claim their luggage, pick up their rental car, and drive to their hotel. "It took only eight hours to go five thousand miles," Joe commented as his father unlocked the door to their hotel room, "but it took sixty minutes to go the last ten miles."

Fenton Hardy fumbled with the key, and Joe rolled his eyes at his brother. They were both loaded down with luggage, most of which belonged to their father. The older you are, the more stuff you have to drag around, Joe thought.

Finally the key turned and the door swung open. Frank and Joe staggered into the room and dropped the bags in the middle of the floor. Joe let out a low whistle as he looked around. "You didn't say your client was *rich*, Dad."

They were standing in the middle of a large

living room furnished with a leather couch, several expensive-looking upholstered chairs, and an antique writing desk. On two of the sides of the room was a door leading into a bedroom and private bathroom. They turned slowly, taking it all in.

Joe looked over at his father. "Who is your mystery client, anyway?"

"You could say it's a large nationwide company," Fenton replied vaguely. "And just remember—it's *my* client. You're here on vacation. The only thing you have to do is sit on the beach, enjoy the scenery, and stay out of my hair."

Frank walked out on the balcony overlooking the Pacific Ocean. He looked down twenty-five floors to the waves lapping the shore of the world-famous Waikiki Beach.

Joe joined him and said, "What are we waiting for? It's time to hit the beach!"

"Right," Frank replied. "Let me just get out of these clothes and into my suit." He grabbed his suitcase and headed for a bedroom. "What about you?" he asked over his shoulder. "Don't you want to change first?"

"I'm one step ahead of you," Joe said, flashing a grin as he started to take off his pants.

Frank stifled a laugh when he saw what his brother was wearing under his clothes. "You're not seriously considering actually wearing those *outside,* are you?" he asked.

Joe glanced down at his bright, baggy Hawaiian

flower-print swim trunks and said, "You're just jealous because you don't have a pair."

A few minutes later Frank and Joe were on the beach, walking along the shore, letting the warm saltwater wash over their bare feet. High-rise buildings crowded right up to the edge of the long, thin stretch of sand known as Waikiki, on the Hawaiian island of Oahu.

"I was reading a guidebook on the plane," Frank said, scanning the skyline. "This beach is less than a mile long—"

"Lighten up!" Joe chided him. "We didn't come to Hawaii to study. We came to have fun in the sun!" He bent down, scooped up a hand-ful of water, and splashed the back of Frank's head.

Frank whirled to face him, and a movement behind his brother caught his eye. "Yeah," he said, nodding toward the ocean. "Maybe we could even learn to surf really well."

Joe turned and watched a couple of obvious beginners floundering in the shallow water. Their rented surfboards were stenciled with the name of a nearby hotel. Then beyond them—out in the serious waves—he saw something else. A lone surfer, racing down a cresting wave, then swiv-eling around and swerving back up the rushing wall of water.

The board was almost vertical to the water as the front end edged over the lip of the breaking wave. Then the surfer pivoted again, and the board flew out of the water, sending a spray back over the top of the wave. Joe thought the ride was going to end with the board and rider spinning off in different directions—but the surfer turned the board in midair, slammed back down into the water, and rode the dying wave all the way to shore.

Joe could hardly believe what he had just seen. As the surfer carried the board out of the water, he got an even bigger shock.

Frank noticed the look on his brother's face. "What's wrong?" he asked.

Joe kept staring and whispered, "It's a girl!"

She put down the surfboard and moved toward the Hardys, as if she had felt Joe's intense stare. Her hair was straight and black, glistening with saltwater. She looked faintly Asian, with brilliant green eyes. Even in her surfing bodysuit— a short-sleeved wet suit that covered her from her neck down to her knees—Joe thought she was beautiful.

"Aloha!" she called, smiling at Joe as she walked closer. "Do I know you from somewhere? I mean, the way you were looking—"

"No!" Joe blurted out. "I just . . . um . . . that is—"

"He just forgot that it's impolite to stare," Frank interrupted. "I'm Frank Hardy, and this is my brother, Joe."

"My name's Kris Roberts," she replied. "But all my friends call me Jade because—"

6

"Because of your eyes." Joe finished her sentence.

She looked at him more closely, a puzzled expression on her face. "That's right. How did you know?"

Joe shrugged. "Just a lucky guess." He wanted to say something else, but no words came.

There was a brief, awkward silence.

"Well, it was nice meeting you," Jade finally said. "Maybe I'll see you around," she added, looking right at Joe.

Then she was gone, walking down the beach toward a small group of surfers. All at once she stopped, turned back, and called out, "Hey! I don't suppose either of you malihinis knows how to surf, do you?"

"Mali-what?" Joe managed to get out.

Jade laughed. "Malihini. A newcomer, a visitor. I've lived here most of my life, and some islanders still call me a malihini."

"Really?" Joe responded, glad that his voice had finally returned. "You could have fooled me. I thought you were Hawaiian."

"With a name like Roberts? Not likely. My father still has relatives in Ireland, and my mother was Japanese. Almost everybody in Hawaii has come from somewhere else. There aren't too many native Hawaiians left.

"You didn't answer my question," she continued. "Do you know how to surf?"

"Not really," Joe admitted. "But I'll give it a try. How about you, Frank?" he asked.

"No thanks," Frank said. "I'll just sit here on the beach and admire your technique."

"Then I don't have to scrounge up another board," Jade replied. "We can use mine. Come on!"

The two of them waded out until the water was about waist-deep. It was fairly calm, with just a slow, rhythmic swell. Most of the big waves were breaking farther out. Every once in a while one did crash down around them, though, throwing Joe off balance.

Jade held the surfboard steady in the water. "The very first thing you need to do," she explained, "is play with the board."

"*Play* with it?" Joe asked doubtfully.

"That's right. Roll it around. Flip it over. Lean on it. Get the feel of it."

"Okay," Joe said. He took the board and flipped it over. It had three slight ridges running the length of the board, which ended in three sharp fins at the back. The front of the board tapered to a narrow point. He pushed one end underwater and felt the pressure as it popped back to the surface.

"That's good," Jade said just as Joe was concluding that surfing was a very boring sport. "Now it's time to learn how to paddle."

"That sounds easy enough," Joe remarked. "I bet you start by lying down on the thing, right?" He grabbed the edges of the floating board and tried to lie on top of it, his legs dangling off the end. But the back of the board sank under his weight, and the front angled up out of the water. Then the whole thing shot out from under him, flew into the air, and splashed down a few feet away.

Jade grinned and said, "Paddling *is* simple—staying on the board is the tricky part. Let me show you how."

As she started to wade toward the surfboard, Joe noticed a large wave rolling in. He realized it was going to break almost on top of him, and he started to duck and cover his head with his arms.

But as he did, he saw something else—a runaway surfboard tumbling through the rushing water, crashing straight down at Jade!

The roar of the surf made it impossible to shout a warning. There wasn't time to think, only time to react. Joe lunged through the water, desperate to reach Jade before the wild surfboard did. His arms strained forward, and he just managed to grab her shoulder with the tips of his fingers. He dug in and jerked her backward.

Jade barely got out a startled "Hey!" before Joe pushed her head under water, shielding her with his body.

Then the wave and the fiberglass missile slammed home, and Joe Hardy's world went black.

Chapter
2

FRANK WAS IN THE WATER in a flash, splashing through the foamy remains of the deadly wave. He had watched helplessly as the surfboard landed on his brother. He reached Joe's limp form as Jade came spluttering to the surface, gasping for air.

Frank grabbed Joe under his arms, lifting his head and shoulders out of the water. Jade quickly took one of Joe's arms, and together they started to haul him out of the water. Before they reached the shore, two other surfers joined them and helped carry Joe.

They laid him down gently in the sand. Joe was breathing, but that was his only sign of life.

Frank knelt down next to him and looked at the bruise on the side of his brother's head. It was too early to tell how bad it was.

"Ugh," Joe mumbled in a minute, squinting against the bright sunlight. "What a horrible dream."

Frank smiled with relief. "Yeah? Why don't you tell me about it?"

Joe struggled to a sitting position, propping himself up with one hand and rubbing his forehead with the other. "I dreamed I was on the beach in Hawaii. But every time I met a beautiful girl, my brother would come barging in and wake me up."

He glanced around, and his eyes found Jade. "This dream seems okay," he said softly, starting to grin but stopping almost immediately to wince in pain. "Except for the extra-strength aspirin commercial booming in my skull," he added.

"What happened out there?" someone asked.

Frank noticed that a small crowd had gathered around them. "That's what I'd like to know," he replied. He stood up, pushed through a couple of people, cupped his hands over his eyes, and scanned the shoreline.

He spotted the surfboard, lying half in the water and half on the wet sand. It seemed harmless enough now. But a few minutes earlier it had been inches away from doing very serious damage.

Frank waited a minute to see if anyone would claim the abandoned surfboard.

Joe got up slowly—a little wobbly, but otherwise all right—and joined his brother. "I don't know about you," he grumbled, "but I think I'll go over and kick the stupid thing a couple of times. It'll think twice before it tangles with me again."

Frank looked at him. "Doesn't it seem kind of strange that whoever owns that surfboard just left it there?" he suggested.

"Not really," came the reply, but it wasn't Joe's voice.

Frank turned to see a big Hawaiian guy standing off to one side. His black hair hung in wet curls over his forehead. Joe figured he must be at least six foot five and probably tipped the scales at around two-fifty. Frank recognized him as one of the surfers who had helped carry Joe out of the water.

Frank studied him carefully. "Why do you say that?"

"Crazy haoles don't know the first thing about surfing," the big guy said, and snorted. "They rent some cheap board like that from a hotel, and then they think they can go out and get vertical or shoot inside the tube the first time out. Some of them even think the wax goes on the *bottom* of the board."

"Hay-oh-lees?" Joe repeated slowly. "Could you translate that?"

"Anybody who's not Hawaiian," Jade explained, joining them. "It usually means a tourist from the mainland. But sometimes he calls me that when he thinks I'm cutting into his lane on a good wave.

"This is Al Kealoha," she continued. "Al's one of the few full-blooded Hawaiians you're ever likely to meet. So be nice to him. He really belongs here. The rest of us are just visitors. Al helped me pick out my first surfboard, and he taught me everything I know."

Al grinned broadly. "That's a good line—I think I'll use it after you take the Banzai. Then I'll start my own surf camp. Girls will come all the way from the mainland begging me to make them the next Jade Roberts. Yeah, I like it."

"The Banzai?" Frank asked. "What's that?"

"The Banzai Pipeline," Al replied. "It's one of the biggest surfing events of the year. Didn't Jade tell you? She's a top contender in the women's division."

Joe turned to Jade. "I knew you were good, but—"

"It's really not that big a deal," she insisted. Joe thought she looked a little embarrassed. "There are lots of girls who are just as good as I am—better, even."

Al gave a low chuckle. "I can think of only one who even comes close."

Frank didn't hear Al's last comment. His mind was on something else. "Is there any prize money in this competition?" he suddenly asked.

"Sure," Jade nodded. "A few thousand dollars. No big deal. Why?"

"Oh, no reason," Frank replied casually. "Just wondering. That's all." He happened to glance over at Joe and saw how pale his brother was. "I think one surfing lesson a day is just about all you can survive. You need to rest."

Joe rubbed his forehead again. "I don't need rest, but I think you're right about the surfing for the day. What else is there to do in Hawaii?"

"Have you been up to Nuuanu Pali yet?" Jade asked. "You haven't seen Oahu if you haven't been to Nuuanu."

"Well, in that case, we'd better get going!" Joe insisted.

A few minutes later Jade and the Hardys were sitting in an old army surplus, camouflage green jeep. Jade was driving, and Joe sat next to her. Frank had to share the backseat with a surfboard. The sun beat down on their heads. If the jeep had ever had a convertible top, it was long gone.

"What do you do if it rains?" Frank asked.

Jade shrugged. "I get wet."

The wind whipped through her hair as they rumbled down the road, and Joe realized he was staring at her.

He tried to think of something to say—again. He frowned slightly and cleared his throat. "There's something I need to know," he began.

Her green eyes sparkled. "Just ask," she responded.

"If this is Oahu—where's Hawaii?"

"Hawaii is the name of the state—and the biggest island in the chain," Jade explained. "But most of the population lives here on Oahu."

Joe noticed that they were headed inland, toward the lush, green mountains that shot up behind the city of Honolulu and hemmed it in. "You know," he said, "I have no idea where we are or where we're going. How about you, Frank?"

"Haven't a clue," Frank admitted.

"We're on the Pali Highway," Jade said. "It goes over the Koolau Mountains to Kailua on the other side of the island."

"You seem to know the island pretty well," Frank observed. "Have you lived here all your life?"

"Just about," she replied. "My father and I moved here when I was only two."

"Just the two of you?" Frank prodded.

Joe saw a troubled look pass over Jade's face. He put his hand on her shoulder. "Don't pay any attention to him," he told her. "He collects information like other guys collect comic books. He'll keep asking questions as long as you keep answering."

"It's all right," Jade replied. "I don't mind talking about it. We moved here from California right after my mother died." She paused for a moment. "I'm not sure how she died, and I don't know why we ended up in Hawaii.

15

"Not that I'm complaining," she continued, her smile slowly returning. "Not too many folks get to grow up in paradise!"

They had been moving steadily higher into the mountains. Jade pulled off onto an access road that didn't go very far before it dead-ended in a small parking lot.

"End of the line!" Jade shouted, bringing the jeep to an abrupt stop and jumping out.

Frank and Joe were right behind her. Frank stopped to look around. To the east and west rose the Koolaus, completely covered in a carpet of green growth. To the north and south blue ocean could be seen beyond the green.

Frank turned to say something to Joe but saw that his brother had followed Jade to a concrete platform. It was very out of place right there and more than a little ugly. Something obviously seemed to be holding their interest, and Frank jogged over to see what had captured their attention.

As he came up next to Joe, he said, "So what's the big—" He stopped in midsentence, sucked in his breath, and whispered, "Oh."

They were standing at the edge of a cliff that plunged almost a thousand feet straight down. The sheer side of the cliff was completely covered in green. Frank strained to make out the bottom.

"This is Nuuanu Pali," Jade said loudly. She had to raise her voice because of the wind gusting around them. "*Pali* is the Hawaiian word for 'cliff.' We're standing above the Nuuanu valley. Down there"—she gestured—"is Honolulu. And over there"—she pointed in the opposite direction—"is Kailua, on the other side of the island."

"Nice view," Joe shouted over the roar of the wind. "Maybe we should come back on a nice, calm day, though."

Jade laughed. "The trade winds rip through here from the Kailua side almost constantly, trying to find a way through the mountains."

"I think I can see Waikiki Beach," Frank ventured, "and the hotel where we're staying."

"Yeah, and this wind is probably strong enough to carry you all the way back there," Joe observed. "If you get a good running jump and then flap your arms real hard . . ."

Frank took another long look down the steep cliff. "You go first," he suggested.

"I've got a better idea," Jade said. "Let's *drive* back in my car. We can stop downtown and get something to eat. You may still be on mainland time, but around here it's lunchtime—and I'm starving."

Jade took them to a sidewalk lunch stand in downtown Honolulu. Joe thought it looked a lot like any other American city, except almost everybody wore Hawaiian shirts—and instead of hamburgers, fast food meant noodles in a Styrofoam cup with a plastic thing that wasn't quite a fork but wasn't exactly a spoon either.

They sat at a table near the curb and watched the cars buzz by while they ate. Finally Joe asked the question that had been following them around ever since they'd left the beach. "Do you really think that close call with the surfboard was an accident?"

"What do you mean?" Jade asked. "What else could it have been?"

"Maybe somebody doesn't want you to surf anymore," Frank suggested.

"Yeah." Jade nodded. "My father. But I don't think he'd throw a surfboard at me. What are you guys getting at?"

"Well, there is the prize money," Joe reminded her.

Jade shook her head. "I told you already. It's not a big deal. A few thousand dollars, that's all. Besides, the surfers around here are a pretty tight-knit group. We're like family. None of them would ever do anything to hurt me."

"Okay," Frank said. "So maybe it isn't anybody you know. But it could be—"

Frank didn't finish his sentence because that was when he heard a screech of tires. He watched mesmerized as a car swerved off the road, jumped the curb, and smashed into an empty table twenty feet from them.

It didn't stop there, though. It kept plowing ahead. And Joe and Jade were right in its path!

Chapter

3

"LOOK OUT!" Frank shouted, leaping from his chair at the same time. He would be in the clear, but what about his brother and the girl? Their backs were to the car. Joe, seated on the other side of the table, couldn't see the vehicle bulldozing a lane toward him.

Frank grabbed the table with both hands and pushed it as hard as he could—right into his brother.

Joe caught sight of the onrushing car when the edge of the table slammed into his stomach. He let out a startled "*Oof!*" as he toppled over backward. Instinctively, he grabbed Jade, yanking her out of her seat. She landed on top of him, knocking the wind out of him, but he managed to

19

wrap his arms around her and roll away from the path of destruction.

The next moment the wooden table was reduced to kindling and splinters, and a streak of blue metal and black rubber flashed by, inches from Joe's face.

The blue sedan didn't even slow down as it swerved back onto the road. Frank's heart was pounding, and the blood was rushing through his body at a furious rate. Without even thinking, he picked up a toppled chair and flung it at the car.

The flying chair smashed into the sedan's rear window and then rebounded, bouncing off the trunk and clattering to the pavement. The car kept moving—but Frank could see a spiderweb of cracks spreading across the shatterproof glass from the point of impact.

Frank watched as the blue sedan weaved frantically through the traffic and disappeared around a corner.

The people at the other tables were buzzing with excitement and concern. Frank heard someone behind him say, "What happened?" as another voice added, "Are you all right?"

It took a moment for Frank to realize they weren't talking to him. It was Joe and Jade they were asking about.

Joe was already on his feet, pulling Jade off the ground. "You know," she said, "my life was pretty normal until you guys showed up. Maybe you're bad luck or something."

"It's beginning to look that way," Joe agreed, brushing dust and splinters from his clothes.

"I don't think luck has much to do with it," Frank replied grimly.

"What do you mean?" Jade asked.

"I mean I might buy two accidents in one day," Frank said. "But this wasn't an accident. That guy was aiming at us. He never even tried to slow down."

"You don't know that for sure," Jade countered.

"No, we don't," Joe said. "But we will—once we find the driver of that car."

"What do you mean you didn't get the license number?" Joe demanded as they headed back to the hotel in Jade's jeep. "You're the one who's supposed to think of those things, remember?"

"I was kind of busy," Frank snapped. "Remember?"

"Oh, well," Joe said. "It's a small island. How many blue sedans can there be?"

"Lots," Jade said softly, as she pulled up to the front entrance. "There are almost a million people in Honolulu, and most of them have cars.

"But nobody I know owns a car like that one," she added, "and I know almost all the surfers in the islands. So let's just drop the jealous surfer theory, okay?"

The jeep rolled to a stop, and Frank climbed out the back. "Not jealous," he pointed out, "just greedy. Besides, it could have been a rented car—like the surfboard."

Joe started to get out, too. Then he turned to look at Jade. "Will I see you again?" he asked, trying to sound casual.

A smile passed over her lips. "Maybe," she murmured. "Now get out of here. My dad will start to worry if I don't get home soon."

That night Joe dreamed he was surfing with a beautiful woman. At first she was a stranger, then she turned into Jade. They were having a great time until a blue sedan—with cheap, rented surfboards lashed to its wheels—came rolling across the waves, its horn blaring angrily.

There was something wrong with the horn, though. It made a kind of ringing noise instead of honking. Joe thought it sounded just like a telephone. Slowly he realized that it *was* the telephone, and the dream slipped away as he drifted back to the waking world, groping for the receiver.

"H'lo," he mumbled into the phone. "Whozit?"

"It's Jade," the voice on the other end whispered hurriedly.

Suddenly Joe was wide awake. "Jade! What is it? Where are you? What's wrong?"

"I'm down in the lobby, but we've got to get out of here fast!"

Joe was already reaching for a pair of jeans with his free hand. He cradled the receiver between his ear and shoulder and used both hands to wrestle his pants on. "We're on our way!" he exclaimed. "Hang on!"

He dropped the phone and shook his brother awake. "Come on, Frank!" he shouted. "Jade's downstairs—and she's in trouble!"

"Wha—" Frank replied drowsily. "What's the problem?"

Joe threw some clothes in his brother's face and raced out the door. "I'm going to get the elevator," he called back. "I'll hold it for thirty seconds, and then I'm out of here!"

"I'm right behind you," Frank assured him, swinging his legs out of the bed and onto the floor. He pulled on a pair of shorts, grabbed the shirt Joe had tossed at him, and slipped his feet into his beat-up deck shoes. Then he was out the door. A second later, he was back, snatching up the shoes Joe had forgotten to put on.

Frank hit the hallway running, just in time to see the elevator doors start to slide shut. He put on a burst of speed, shoved his arm between the closing doors, and pried them open.

"Come on, come on!" Joe urged once both boys were on the elevator. He jabbed the button marked *L* over and over again.

Frank reached out and gently grabbed his brother's wrist. "Take it easy," he said. "Nothing's going to happen to her in the hotel lobby."

"Right." Joe nodded, relaxing a bit. When the elevator doors opened on the ground floor, he bolted out.

"It took you long enough!" Jade said, grabbing his hand and pulling him toward the door. "We've got to get going before it's too late."

They hurried out into the morning sunlight and climbed into the waiting jeep. Jade turned the key and the ancient engine coughed to life. Frank hopped into the backseat, which was occupied now by two surfboards. "Too late for what?" he asked, wedging himself in. "What time is it?"

"Oh, about eight-thirty, I guess," Jade responded. Her mood seemed to lift once they were on the road.

"You didn't answer my first question," Frank persisted.

"Yeah," Joe agreed. "What's up? Where are we going?"

Jade kept her eyes on the road and said, "We're going to Waimea, on the north shore of the island. That's where you get the really big waves this time of year."

Joe studied her carefully, his brain still a little sluggish from sleep. "You mean you rousted us out of bed because—"

Jade glanced at him and flashed a big smile. "That's right. Surf's up!"

If it had been any place other than Hawaii—and anyone other than Jade—Joe probably would have been furious. But the ride was beautiful, and so was she.

By the time they got to Waimea Bay, it looked

to Joe as if it were shaping up to be another great day in paradise.

Even though it was still early, there were already a lot of people on the beach. Jade found a place to park the jeep and hopped out. "Wait here," she said, "I've got to change. I'll be right back."

Frank and Joe got out, stretched, and took in the sights. Jade had been right about the surf—*up* was definitely the word for it. Some of the waves rose fifteen feet or more before curling over and crashing back down.

There were surfers everywhere, on the beach and in the water. Most of them wore the same kind of one-piece, short-sleeved wet suit that Jade had worn the day before. But Joe noticed the suits came in almost every possible color combination.

The suit that Jade came back wearing was subdued by the standards of Waimea. It was almost solid black, with a band of emerald green stripes running down each side. Joe thought she looked stunning, but he kept his cool. "Nice outfit," he said. "It matches your eyes and your car."

She gave him a curious look. Then she glanced over at the old jeep with its faded camouflage paint job and smiled. "I guess I just like green."

"Good thing, too," Frank commented. "Because this whole island is green."

Jade pulled one of the surfboards out of the

back of the jeep. "Come on," she said, tucking the board under her arm, "let's hit the beach."

Joe took one step out onto the sand and quickly backpedaled, yelling, "Yow! That's hot!"

Jade looked down at his bare feet. "You get used to it after a while. But maybe you should put on your shoes," she suggested. "I'll meet you down by the water."

Frank waited while Joe got his shoes. He watched the surfers slashing down the towering blue cliffs in the deep water. He didn't think there were any tourists or amateurs taking on those waves. Out there, you had to know what you were doing, or you wouldn't be doing it for very long. Or anything else for that matter, Frank thought.

Joe strolled up, wearing his battered high-tops. "Where's Jade?" he asked, his eyes making a quick search of the beach. "Oh, there she is."

He took off at a jog, coming up behind the girl and grabbing her arm. She turned to face him— but it wasn't Jade. Same height, same build, same hair, even the same suit, but most definitely not Jade.

Like Jade, she had oriental features. Hers were more Chinese than Japanese, though—and she didn't have Jade's piercing green eyes.

"Oops," he whispered. "Uh, sorry. I thought you were someone else."

She gave him the once-over, smiled, and said, "I'm sorry, too. But if you don't find whoever you thought I was, let me know. Maybe we can work something out."

"Well, I see you've already met Connie," a voice called out. It was Jade.

"Connie Lo, meet Joe Hardy," she said.

Connie grinned. "Wiped out by Jade Roberts again. This trophy's already yours, I take it."

Jade laughed. "You've already got a boyfriend, Connie. Besides, Joe doesn't really surf."

Connie frowned slightly, and her voice took on a serious tone. "I'm beginning to think that might be a real plus at this point."

Then she noticed what Jade was wearing and her grin was back. "Hey, cool suit, kiddo," she quipped, lifting her arms to reveal identical green stripes. "You've got great taste. And since I already have your suit," she continued, "how about letting me try out that new board of yours?"

"You've got it," Jade replied, holding out the surfboard for her. "What's mine is yours—any time. You know that."

"Thanks," Connie said. "I'll try not to get it wet." Then she turned to Joe. "You be good to her," she warned him, "or I'll break your legs."

Frank walked up in time to hear the last remark, before Connie sprinted off into the raging surf. "What was that all about?" he asked.

"Oh, that's just Connie's way," Jade said. "She's like a big sister. We surf together all the time. She's one of the best. Check her out."

Frank and Joe saw Connie as a black-suited

figure on a gleaming surfboard, starting to slide over the edge of a huge, breaking wave. Suddenly there was a muffled *pop pop!*

The board bucked violently, and the surfer started to pitch sideways into the raging surf, arms flung wide. The relentless wall of water slammed into the small dark figure and engulfed it.

Chapter

4

FRANK WHIRLED IN THE DIRECTION that the noise had come from. High on a cliff he saw another dark-clad figure. This one wasn't holding a surfboard—it was holding a high-powered rifle.

Frank squinted, tried to bring the figure into better focus, but it was too far away. He couldn't make out any details. He turned to tell his brother what he had seen, but Joe was gone.

Frank caught sight of him diving into the rough water and swimming toward something floating loose in the swells. It was Jade's new surfboard, the one Connie had been riding. Frank knew his brother was a strong swimmer, but he was wearing long pants. By now they would be totally soaked and very heavy.

Frank wouldn't have hesitated to follow his

brother even if he hadn't been wearing shorts. The fact that he was made him feel a little better as he kicked off his deck shoes and splashed into the rolling water. Not much, but a little.

He started to close the gap, stroking through the water strongly and evenly.

Joe had managed to power his way to the drifting board first. The nose was sticking out of the surf at a sharp angle, and the back was buried beneath the blue water as if it were tied to an anchor. Joe knew that the anchor must be Connie, dangling unconscious from the ankle tether that a lot of the surfers used so they wouldn't have to chase their boards after a wipeout.

He dove beneath the surface and easily spotted Connie's limp form swaying upside down in the deep current. A few strong kicks took him the short distance. He wrapped his arms around her chest and strained to turn her around and haul her up to the surface. But it felt as if there were lead weights on his feet, dragging him down. Then he remembered his jeans. They might as well be lead weights, he realized.

Joe started to wriggle out of his water-logged pants, and as soon as he let go of Connie, something pulled her up to the surface like a fish being reeled in. Joe followed her up and found his brother struggling to get Connie onto the surfboard.

"The next time someone tells you to keep

your pants on," Frank said, "don't listen to them."

Together they flopped the unconscious girl onto the board. Frank didn't know how much water she had taken in, but he knew they had to wait until they got back to shore to find out. The waves crashing around them were tremendous. He clambered onto the wobbly board, knelt over her, and paddled quickly to shore.

On dry land he pressed his palms firmly into her back. A small trickle of water dribbled out of her mouth, and then her body was wracked by a torrent of wet coughs.

Her eyes fluttered open. "Awesome wave," she groaned. "But I didn't see the shark coming."

"Shark?" Frank repeated.

Joe nodded to the front of the board, near where Connie's head still rested. "The one with the big teeth," he said.

Frank looked down and saw what his brother was talking about—two neat holes drilled clean through the fiberglass.

A crowd had gathered around them now, and Frank slipped away from them, motioning Joe to follow. "You know those bullets were meant for Jade," Frank stated flatly when they were alone.

Joe glanced back to see Jade kneeling next to her friend. "Same hair, same build, same suit, same surfboard," he noted grimly. "Yeah, I know. So let's find whoever fired the slugs and break his arms. I'd break his spine, but he probably doesn't have one."

31

"Good idea," another voice chimed in. "I'll help." It was Al Kealoha, the massive Hawaiian surfer.

Seeing Al reminded Joe of something. "Just the guy I wanted to see," he began, before his brother could say anything. "I think you said something the other day about only one other surfer being almost as good as Jade. I was just wondering who she is."

Al jerked his head back toward the small crowd. "You just hauled her out of the Pacific."

"You mean Connie?" Frank asked.

The surfer nodded. "Connie's got all the right moves. She can still beat just about anybody in the women's circuit."

"Anybody but Jade," Joe added.

"You're real *akamai* for a malihini," the Hawaiian said.

"A smart tourist," Frank translated.

Joe glanced at his brother. "Since when do you speak Hawaiian?"

Frank shrugged. "There's a lot of useful stuff in those guidebooks."

"Well, do the guidebooks say where to find suspects after you discover that your number-one choice is the victim's best friend and almost ended up as another victim?" Joe muttered under his breath.

Al shook his head slowly. "You guys are wasting your time if you think a surfer's behind this. We stick together. We don't stick knives in our friends' backs."

As Al started to walk away from the Hardys, a guy with shoulder-length blond hair stopped him by clutching his arm. He had the tan and muscular build of a surfer, but he wasn't dressed for the water. He was wearing a T-shirt and baggy shorts.

"Hey, Al. Wait up," Frank heard him say. "I just got here, and I heard that something happened to Jade. Is she all right?"

The big Hawaiian gripped the newcomer's shoulders. "Hang steady, Nick," he said calmly. "It wasn't Jade—it was Connie."

Frank saw the look of concern on Nick's face change to one of horror. "Connie," he croaked. "No . . . it couldn't be . . . I mean, I thought . . . Where is she? I've got to see her!" He broke away and pushed through the crowd.

There was a brief commotion, and then the Hardys saw him hustling Connie out of the circle of onlookers, his arm around her shoulder.

Frank and Joe looked at each other. "Are you thinking what I'm thinking?" Joe asked.

"I'm thinking we should find out more about this Nick character," Frank answered.

It took a while for the police to arrive on the scene. By the time they finished interviewing everyone and filling out their endless forms, it was late in the afternoon.

Joe could see that Jade was pretty badly shaken. It was finally starting to sink in that someone wanted her in the past tense, and Joe knew how hard that was to handle. So he decided to wait until she had calmed down a little before bringing up the subject of someone trying to eliminate her again.

Finally when they were in her jeep, driving back to Honolulu, he decided the time was right. "So who's Nick?" he asked casually.

"Nick?" Jade spoke distantly. Her mind was somewhere else—either on the road or replaying the events of the last two days. "Oh, Nick Hawk, Connie's boyfriend. Why?"

"His reaction seemed a little . . . strange," Frank suggested.

"Well, someone just took a couple of potshots at his girlfriend," Jade snapped. "How is he supposed to react? How am *I* supposed to react?"

"Hey, we're just trying to help," he assured her. "If you say the guy's all right, we'll just drop it. Okay?"

She nodded. They drove without speaking for a few minutes. Jade finally broke the silence and said, "Nick's a little edgy. He used to be a pretty hot surfer. But he shattered his knee a couple of years ago in a real serious wipeout.

"He can walk okay now," she continued. "He can even surf a little. But his competition days are over. So he channels all his energy into Connie's surfing. He's more like her trainer now than her boyfriend. I think winning means a lot more to him than it does to her."

"How badly do you think he wants Connie to win?" Frank prodded.

Jade shook her head. "Not enough to kill me. We may not all like each other, but we're still part of the same big family."

"Surfers are really important to you, aren't they?" Joe observed.

"Is your brother important to you?" she replied, not waiting for a reply. "Other than my dad, they're all I've got."

"You told us about your mother," Frank said. "But don't you have any other relatives?"

Jade shrugged. "None that I know of. I don't even know how my mom died. My dad doesn't like to talk about it. I think her death must have been very painful for him. I think we moved to the islands because he wanted to cut off the past."

A brief smile passed over her lips. "Sometimes I feel like we didn't exist before we came to Hawaii."

The sun was getting low in the sky by the time they got back to the hotel. Jade turned off the ignition and the engine shuddered and died. She shifted in her seat so she could take in both brothers. The tension on her face was evident, and Joe wanted to do something to make it disappear.

"Look," she began, "I'm sorry I yelled at you before. But this is all just a little too weird, you know? Who'd want to kill me? And why?"

"We'll find out," Joe promised. "But maybe

you'd be safer staying with us instead of going home. Our dad used to be a cop, and he still has some powerful connections.''

Jade reached out and took his hand. "Thanks, Joe. But I really should go home. Besides, even if Nick Hawk is behind this—and I'm sure he isn't—I don't think he'd try anything at my house. I'll be all right.''

"At least give us your address and phone number, in case we have to reach you,'' Frank urged.

She took a piece of paper out of the glove compartment, scribbled something on it, folded it once, and placed it in Joe's palm. Then she closed his fingers over it. "Keep it in a safe place,'' she said. "Our phone number is unlisted, and my father doesn't like my friends to come to the house. Not many people know where we live.''

Reluctantly they let her go and watched as she pulled the jeep out into traffic.

Frank's eye was caught by a blue sedan pulling away from the curb just then. It moved in right behind the old green jeep. At first he thought the rear window of the car was frosted. No, he decided, that wasn't right.

With a jolt, he recognized the spiderweb pattern of cracks, snaking out from where the chair he had thrown had smashed into the glass.

Chapter

5

"THAT'S THE CAR," Frank said, grabbing hold of his brother's arm.

"What?" Joe said.

"That's the car," Frank repeated. "The car from yesterday. Look at the rear window. That's where I hit it."

"And now it's following Jade," Joe cried out. "We've got to stop him!"

"We need a car," Frank said.

He jogged over to a man in a red coat who was standing next to a sign that announced Valet Parking. "Can I borrow your jacket for five minutes?" he asked.

The man eyed him warily. "How do I know you'll bring it back?"

Frank waved Joe over, turned back to the

parking attendant, and said, "I'll leave my brother as collateral. Okay?"

The man took one look at Joe's wide frame moving toward him and stripped off the jacket. "Here," he said, handing it to Frank. "Keep it as long as you want. No sweat."

Frank darted into the parking garage, thrusting his arms through the sleeves of the attendant's red jacket as he ran.

He slowed down as he neared a door next to a large window that looked into the garage. Through the glass, Frank could see rows of car keys hanging on hooks on the wall. He also saw a fat, bald man leaning back in a chair, his feet propped up against a desk.

Frank tugged on the sleeves of the red jacket. They were a little short, but they would do. He walked through the door. "The guy in twenty-five-fifteen wants his car," he announced.

The bald head turned slowly. "Yeah? Where's his ticket?"

Frank smiled. "He lost it. But he says he'll pay the lost-ticket charge." Frank stuck his hand in his pocket and pulled out a key attached to a small metal tag with a number engraved on it. "He gave me his room key to prove it was his car."

"You carhops come and go so fast, I don't even know your names. I don't think I've seen your face around before." Finally the fat man grunted and tossed something at Frank. "It's in stall thirty-eight. If anybody asks, you took it while I was in the john.''

Frank snatched the key ring out of the air and headed for the door.

Joe was keeping the nervous parking attendant busy. His muscular build could make him look threatening even if he was smiling, and sometimes that worked exactly to his advantage. Behind his smile Joe was wondering what his brother was up to.

About two minutes later a white, four-door sedan cruised up next to him. The driver rolled down the window and tossed something out. Joe ducked, and it sailed past him. It hit the attendant square in the chest. It was his red jacket.

Frank poked his head out the driver's-side window. ''Let's put this baby in gear and get out of here,'' he said.

Joe ran around to the other side and slid into the front seat next to his brother. The car was already moving as he slammed the door shut.

''I hope Dad wasn't planning on going out tonight,'' Frank said. ''This is the car we rented at the airport.''

At the end of the driveway, Frank turned in the direction the jeep had gone a few minutes earlier. ''There should be a map in there,'' he said, nodding toward the glove compartment. ''See if you can find the street Jade lives on.''

Joe found the map, unfolded it, and spread it

out in his lap. His eyes scanned it carefully, comparing street names to the one Jade had written down. It was slow going. All the Hawaiian names looked the same to him—mostly vowels with a few consonants thrown in here and there. "Got it!" he finally announced.

He glanced out the window, spotted a street sign, and then looked at the map again. "Turn right at the next intersection," he directed his brother.

Frank flicked the turn signal and moved over into the right lane. In the rearview mirror he could see a black van behind them do the same. Frank turned the corner, and the van followed.

He didn't say anything about it to Joe. He wasn't sure yet, and he needed his brother to navigate without any distractions.

Joe looked up from the map and peered out the window. They passed a few more streets. "Whoa!" he suddenly yelled. "Back up! I think we were supposed to take that street back there."

Frank made sure there was no traffic in the oncoming lane, cranked the wheel hard to the left, and came around in a tight U-turn. The black van held its course, moving off in the other direction. Frank let out a small sigh of relief, but then he noticed that their unwanted shadow was pulling into a driveway. Maybe he lives there, he told himself, but the van backed out into the road. Pretty soon it was close behind them again.

They rolled up to a stoplight. "This is it," Joe said. "Turn right here."

Frank didn't move. He checked the rearview mirror. The van was still there. He checked the traffic on the cross street. There were a few cars in the distance, but the intersection was clear for now.

"Come on," Joe urged. "You can turn right on a red light. It's legal."

Frank flicked on the turn signal, but he kept his foot on the brake. He glanced left and right. Cars from both directions were almost at the intersection. A few more seconds ticked by.

Joe reached out and shook his brother's shoulder. "Frank? What's wrong? Why are we just sitting—"

Frank slammed his foot down on the gas pedal, and the tires screamed. The car shot straight ahead. Horns on both sides blared a frantic warning. Frank ignored them, his hands gripping the wheel, his foot jamming the gas pedal into the floor.

They flashed across the intersection just before the cross traffic closed the gap.

"—here?" Joe finished his sentence on the other side.

Frank relaxed. He took his foot off the accelerator, and the car slowed down.

"What was *that* all about?" Joe demanded.

"We had company," Frank explained. "But I think we lost them."

There was a screech of rubber somewhere behind them. Joe snapped his head around to get a look out the back window. "Was it a black van? Sort of like ours back home?"

Frank's eyes darted to the rearview mirror and saw it, tires smoking and the back end fishtailing as the van imitated his stunt.

"Hang on," he muttered through clenched teeth. Then he punched the gas again, trying to put some distance between them and the black van. At the first street he came to he turned left, then right a block later, and another left at the next street.

Frank kept his eyes locked on the road in front of him, but still he had to know. "Is it still there?"

"Yeah," Joe said. "But we're pulling away. He probably can't corner too well in that thing. A few more sharp turns should do it."

A steep hill loomed in front of them. The road didn't go up it or around it—it went through it. "Turn where?" Frank shouted as they entered the tunnel.

On the other side, the road ended abruptly. They were surrounded by a towering wall of rock splattered with brownish green plants and vines. On a small sign were the words Diamond Head Park.

Joe searched for another exit. "There's got to be another way out of here," he insisted.

Frank slammed on the brakes, and the car skidded to a halt. "Yeah," he replied, "over the top. This is Diamond Head—an extinct volcano. We're sitting at the bottom of the crater."

They could hear the van coming through the tunnel, the rumble of the engine echoing off the walls. "I guess it's too late to go back the way we came," Joe said.

They got out of the car and looked up the side of the ancient volcano. The sun was beginning to set, and deep shadows filled the crater. Frank could just make out a lazy zigzag pattern near the top, and his eyes traced its downward path. "There's a trail over there," he said, pointing off to the left.

Behind them, they heard a car door open, then another. Joe whirled around and saw the black van. There were two unfriendly-looking men standing next to it. One of them was wearing a gray suit. A ragged scar slashed down the left side of his forehead.

The other one was wearing a windbreaker over his shirt. Joe knew that guys who wear coats on hot days are usually hiding something inside them.

"We want to have a little talk with you," the man in the suit called out.

"So start talking," Joe said as he backed around the rented car. He wanted to put a nice, thick steel barrier between himself and the concealed "conversation piece" he was sure the man's hand was resting on under the coat.

"What now?" he whispered to his brother.

"Don't worry," Frank said in a low voice. "I've got a plan."

"Great. What is it?"

"Run," he said. Then he turned and bolted toward the trail.

Joe was right on his heels. "I was afraid that was the plan!" he shouted in Frank's ear. He glanced back and saw the two men lumbering after them. Frank and Joe had a good head start, and they were in better shape than their pursuers. They could easily stay out of firing range—as long as they had someplace to run.

Joe wasn't worried about himself. He was thinking about Jade. If they didn't find a way out of the crater soon, they might not be able to stop the driver of the blue sedan—if it wasn't already too late.

"What do we do when we get to the top?" Joe huffed.

Frank looked up. He figured the volcano was about seven hundred feet high, but it would take a while to reach the top on the switchback trail. "I haven't figured that out yet."

"Terrific," Joe muttered.

They jogged past a dark opening in the side of the volcanic wall. It looked like a cave. But Frank thought it might be something else. He doubled back and peered inside. It was pitch black.

His brother joined him, poking his head into the gloom. "Great place to get trapped," Joe said.

"Not if this is what I think it is," Frank said, stepping inside. "Come on. This could be our ticket out of here."

44

Joe shrugged and followed him. They moved slowly through the darkness, stumbling over invisible debris. Frank felt his way around a corner and found himself in a chamber filled with long shadows and an eerie orange glow.

"What is this place?" Joe asked.

Frank pointed at the source of the light. It was the last rays of sunlight streaming in through a long, narrow opening carved into the far end of the volcanic wall.

"It's an old gun emplacement from World War Two. They turned Diamond Head into a kind of armored fortress. After the war they pulled out all the hardware but left the holes. The crater is honeycombed with these old pillboxes."

"So you were hoping maybe we'd find some old guns, too?" Joe asked.

"No," Frank said. "I was hoping we could lose those guys in the maze of tunnels. But it looks like this is a dead end."

Joe wiped the sweat off his forehead. "Well, maybe if we double back before—"

"Hey, Pete!" a muffled voice shouted from just outside the tunnel. "I thought I heard something over here in this cave. Maybe we should check it out."

"Yeah," came the reply. "Let's get it over with."

Chapter
6

JOE SCANNED THE CHAMBER for any kind of weapon. A rock, a brick, anything to give them a fighting chance. A shadow high up on the wall cast by the setting sun caught his eye. He looked up and saw a rusty metal rod hanging from the cement ceiling.

Frank saw it, too. "Steel-reinforced concrete," he whispered. "This place was built to take a lot of shelling."

Joe jumped up and grabbed the rod. It sagged under his weight and then snapped off. Joe dropped softly to the floor, holding a four-foot chunk of solid steel.

Frank saw another metal bar suspended above the narrow entrance to the room. He didn't think it would break off so easily—but he had an idea.

46

He leapt up and grasped it with both hands. He swung his legs up and planted his feet on the wall above the doorway. Then he pulled himself up until his head was touching the ceiling. Anyone walking into the room wouldn't be able to see him unless he looked straight up.

Joe knew what his brother had in mind. He flattened himself against the wall next to the entrance and held the steel rod ready to swing.

They could hear footsteps in the dark corridor, scuffling toward them. A figure appeared in the doorway, and Frank pounced. His full weight came down on the man's shoulders, toppling them both to the floor.

Joe didn't budge. He didn't want to reveal himself. He was waiting for the second man. Seconds ticked by. Nobody came through the passage. Joe glanced from the doorway to the two figures rolling and grappling on the dusty floor. First Frank was on top. Now he was on the bottom—and the man above him was raising a rock over his head, about to bring it down in a crushing blow.

Joe moved out in the open and swung the steel bar. The blow connected with the man's forearm. He screamed in pain and clutched at his arm with his other hand.

"Hold it right there!" a voice boomed from the darkness.

Joe lifted the metal rod and spun around. The man in the dark gray suit stepped into the dim chamber.

Joe could see the scar more clearly now. It cut through the man's eyebrow and continued on down his cheek. Whatever had made the mark had barely missed his left eye. Then Joe noticed that he was holding something in his hand.

Joe could see it wasn't a gun. It was a badge.

"FBI," the man said. "Assaulting a federal officer is a serious offense. I think you two have some explaining to do."

Frank got up off the floor and helped the injured man to his feet. "Who are you guys?" he asked. "Why are you following us?"

The man holding the badge turned to him. *"I'll* ask the questions. You'll give the answers. Clear?"

"That depends on the questions," Frank said.

"Okay, try this one. What happened to Fenton Hardy?"

"Something happened to Dad?" Joe blurted out.

"Fenton Hardy is your father?" The agent's eyes narrowed as he turned to his partner, who was still holding his bruised arm. "Next time get all the facts first. We've just blown half a day."

He looked back at the Hardys. "Sorry about all this. Come on, let's get out of here, and I'll explain."

As they walked down the trail the FBI agent talked. "I can't tell you very much. I don't know a whole lot myself. We're just watchdogs. Your father is working on a sensitive case for the

Bureau, and my partner and I are supposed to make sure nothing happens to him."

Frank nodded. "I see. You knew the car was rented to him. So you followed it, thinking he was in it. Then when we tried to give you the slip, you figured something must be wrong—like maybe we kidnapped him or something."

"Say, you'd make a pretty good detective yourself," the man said. "You've got all the answers."

"Not all the answers," Frank said coolly. "I still don't know who you are."

The agent smiled thinly. "Well, I see we're at the end of the trail, and there's your car. Drive safely now. We wouldn't want you to get hurt, would we?"

Joe didn't notice the icy exchange between his brother and the man in the suit. He was worried about Jade, and he wanted to get moving. "Give me the keys," he insisted. "I'm driving."

Frank didn't respond. He was studying the two FBI agents. He watched them walk back to the black van, get in, and drive away. Then he turned to his brother. "I think we'd better go back to the hotel and talk to Dad before we do anything else."

"Not before we check on Jade," Joe demanded.

"Our little detour took almost an hour," Frank replied. "If nothing happened to her while we were running around in here, she's probably safe—for now."

"At least let me call her," Joe persisted.

"It will only take a couple of minutes to get back to the hotel," Frank pointed out. "You can call her from there."

Fenton Hardy was waiting for his sons when they walked through the door of the luxury suite. He glanced at his watch. "I was starting to get worried," he began.

Joe braced himself for a lecture—something about responsibility, letting your parents know where you are, and not taking the car without permission. "Before you say anything," he cut in, "I can explain . . ."

His words trailed off when he saw the people sitting on the couch behind his father.

Fenton Hardy glanced back over his shoulder. "Yes." He nodded. "I'm sure you could, but I've already heard most of it. I'd like you to meet Kevin Roberts," he continued. "I think you already know the young lady sitting next to him."

Jade smiled at Joe. He thought she looked more exotic than ever.

"My daughter tells me some strange things have been happening since she met you," Kevin Roberts said.

"I spotted a car following me home today," Jade explained. "I think I shook him off, but it really spooked me. I told my father everything, and we decided to talk it out with you. I'm really sorry to drag you into this."

"You didn't drag us into anything," Frank assured her.

"That's right," Joe said. "We jumped in with both feet."

"I still don't understand why anyone would be after me," Jade said.

Frank exchanged a quick glance with his father and Joe. "I think I may have come up with something. There may not be much prize money in surfing, but what about illegal gambling? What if somebody has bet a bundle on another surfer in the Banzai?"

"It's a possibility," Fenton Hardy said. "There is organized crime in Hawaii, but not on the same scale as on the mainland."

Kevin Roberts nodded. "The big crime families from the mainland haven't been too successful in breaking the local mob," he said. "At least, that's what I've read in the papers," he added.

"Well, we all agree that there seems to be a definite threat to Jade's life," Fenton concluded. "What surprises me, Mr. Roberts, is why you came here instead of calling the police as soon as you found out."

Jade's father looked uncomfortable.

"We're talking about your daughter's life!" Joe snapped when Roberts didn't answer.

"I know," Kevin Roberts replied slowly. "That's why I think we shouldn't say anything to the police."

Joe was confused.

"If organized crime is behind this, there may be crooked cops on their payroll. I came to the same conclusion as Frank about heavy gambling involvement."

"So what do we do now?" Jade asked.

"You stay here tonight," Fenton replied. "Frank and Joe will sleep in one room, and you and your father can use the other."

Joe looked at his father. "What about you?"

"I have a hunch that I won't be getting much sleep," Fenton said. "I've got a lot of arrangements to make for you for tomorrow."

"While you're up," Frank said, "have one of your FBI friends run a check on a surfer named Nick Hawk."

At dawn Fenton Hardy hustled his sons and Jade onto an interisland commuter plane.

"Where are we going?" Joe asked.

"Maui," his father replied. "It's an island about ninety miles southeast of here. It's a little bigger than Oahu, but it's a lot less crowded."

"What do we do when we get there?" Jade wanted to know.

"Stay away from crowds," Fenton said. "There'll be a rental car waiting for you at the airport. Keep moving around until we can find out who's after you—and why."

He turned to his older son and handed him a slip of paper. "Frank, here's a number where I can be reached if I'm not at the hotel. Try to check in a couple times every day."

Just as Fenton Hardy had said, a car was waiting at the airport. Frank called his dad to let him know what their plans were. Joe got behind the wheel, and a few minutes later they were driving along a twisting, two-lane road. Jade was sitting next to him, and Frank directly behind him, looking out the window. On the left was a steep hillside, covered with tropical plants. On the right the ground fell away sharply, and the Pacific waited several hundred feet below.

"Jade should be safe," Frank said, "as long as we keep on the move."

"Well, we're moving right along," Joe observed, keeping his eyes on the curvy road ahead. "Although I'm not sure where we'll end up."

"This road follows the coastline south to the town of Hana," Jade explained. "But how long do we keep driving around?"

Frank shrugged. "A few days, maybe—maybe less."

"Do you really think your father can help?" Jade asked.

"With access to the FBI computers and the description of the blue sedan with the broken rear window," Joe said, "you'd be surprised what he might turn up."

Frank pounded the seat with his fist. "I knew I forgot something!"

53

"Your Bermuda shorts?" Joe ventured.

"No. I forgot to tell Dad about those two FBI agents."

"So what? We're all on the same side, aren't we?"

"I hope so," Frank muttered almost to himself.

Joe gestured out the window. "Relax. We're in paradise, remember? If that guy behind us would just stop tailgating, I could slow down and enjoy the view myself."

Then there was a loud, metallic *crump,* and the car lurched forward suddenly.

"Hey!" Joe yelled. "That guy just rear-ended us!"

There was another *crump,* and they surged forward once more.

"He did it again!" Joe shouted, struggling to keep the car on the road.

Frank spun around and got a good look at the other vehicle. It was a pickup truck, and this time he made sure to get the license plate number. But he didn't think it would do much good. The truck was larger and heavier than their car, and he guessed the driver wouldn't stop ramming them until he pushed them over the edge of the cliff.

Chapter
7

INSTINCTIVELY JOE SLAMMED ON the brakes, but when he did, the truck just rammed them harder. They skidded closer to the cliff edge. Then he switched tactics and hit the gas pedal.

But there were too many twists and turns in the road. He would barely pull away before he'd have to slow down for another curve. And then the pickup was right on top of them. *Crump!* The bumpers of the two vehicles smacked together.

"Is there any place up ahead where we can get off this road?" he shouted. *Crump!* His head snapped back and bounced off the headrest.

Jade shook her head. "How did they find us so fast?"

"I don't know! But I'm not going to stop and ask!"

Crump! Joe knew that sooner or later one of those blows would be more than he could handle, and the car would tumble over the side and plummet into the ocean below. Up ahead, the road climbed sharply, but it was a pretty straight shot, and Joe figured it was the only one he'd get.

"Hang on!" he screamed, and punched the gas pedal to the floor.

The car pulled away from the pickup and sped up the road. At the top of the rise, there was a sharp bend to the right, but Joe didn't plan on making the turn. He yanked his foot off the accelerator and smashed it down on the brake. At the same time, he cranked the steering wheel all the way to the left.

The front tires screeched and smoked. The rear end swung out to the right, and the car spun around in the middle of the road. It skidded backward a few feet and softly bumped into the guardrail on the outer edge of the curve.

Then Joe was jamming the gas again, and the car squealed back down the road. The pickup truck was plowing up the hill, hugging the inside lane, away from the cliff. Joe stayed on the same side and aimed straight for the truck, his foot glued to the gas pedal.

He was grinning wildly. "Up for a little game of chicken?"

Now they were close enough to see the terrified expression on the truck driver's and passenger's faces. He tried to pull off the road, but the shoulder was too narrow. The tires on the left side hit the steep incline and rolled up it. The whole truck tilted crazily to one side. Joe swerved back into the outer lane and zipped past just as the pickup rolled and fell over.

Frank twisted around to see the wreckage. "We've got to go back and get them out of there," he said.

"Are you crazy?" Joe burst out. "They were trying to kill us!"

"Frank's right," Jade said. "We can't just leave them there."

Reluctantly, Joe stopped the car, put it in reverse, and started to back up. He could see someone trying to climb out of the pickup truck. Then there was a sharp *crack*, and the rear window of their car shattered.

Frank dove for the floor. Joe ducked, pushing Jade's head down with his right hand at the same time. "I don't think they want our help," he said.

Frank was staring at a brand-new hole in the window over his head. "I think you're right," he replied. "Let's get out of here."

Joe slammed the gearshift lever and pressed down hard on the gas pedal. The car shot forward, and they left the overturned truck far behind.

They didn't stop until they came to a gas station with a pay phone. Frank hopped out and ran over to the phone. He punched in the number his father had given him.

After a few rings, a female voice came on the line. "Federal Bureau of Investigation, Honolulu office."

A few minutes later Frank hung up the phone and walked back to the car.

"Any news?" Joe asked.

"Well, there's good news and bad news," Frank said. "Which do you want first?"

"Let's start with the good," Joe suggested.

"Okay. The good news is those goons in the pickup truck were probably the last we'll run into."

"Did they find the owner of the blue sedan?" Jade asked.

"No," Frank said, turning to her. "But they didn't have to. That's where the bad news comes in. It looks like your friend Nick Hawk owes money to almost every bookie in town—and he's been putting down some heavy bets on Connie Lo to win the Banzai Pipeline. They arrested him about an hour ago."

"I can't believe it," Jade said. "Did he confess?"

"No," Frank admitted. "But the evidence is pretty strong. He was in deep. If he couldn't pay off his gambling debts soon, he was going to be shark bait. With you out of the way, Connie would be the top contender."

Joe looked at Jade. He could see that she was

fighting back tears. He reached out and touched her. Her arm felt stiff, and her fist was clenched tightly at her side. "I'm sure Connie didn't know anything about it," he said. "It's over. Try to put it behind you. You can go home now."

Jade looked at him. "I don't think I want to go back yet. I need some time to clear my head."

Joe smiled. "Hey, no problem. It's a sunny day, and we've got a full tank of gas. What do people do for fun on Maui?"

"I don't know," Jade said, perking up a little. "Play golf or hang out at the beach, I guess."

"Hmm, tough choice," Joe said, scratching his chin.

"Not really," Frank remarked. "We didn't bring any golf clubs."

"So that leaves the beach," Joe said.

"Okay," Jade nodded. "Just as long as we steer clear of surfboards. I don't even want to think about surfing today."

"No problem," Joe said, starting the engine and putting the car in gear.

"Yeah," Frank agreed. "Because we didn't bring any swimsuits either."

It was past noon by the time they rolled into Lahaina, a small town perched on the western coast of the island. A hundred years earlier it had been a major seaport for the islands, and it still had the look of an old-fashioned sailing port. Weathered clapboard buildings hung out over the bay, suspended a few feet above the water-line by sturdy wooden beams.

Frank noticed that instead of seedy dockside bars and musty tackle shops, the port was now home to expensive boutiques and custom T-shirt stores. Outside one of the stores, Frank spotted a public phone.

"Pull over for a minute," he said. "I'd better let Dad know where we are."

After he made the call, they drove along the coast. Beyond the small town on the bay, the beach took over again. Swimmers, surfers, and strollers dotted the shoreline.

"Just stop wherever it looks good," Jade said. "All the beaches in Hawaii are public."

Joe saw something floating in the air over the water. "Is that a guy in a parachute?"

Jade looked where he was pointing. "He's para-sailing. See that motorboat out there? The parachute is attached to the boat by a long line. It's the closest thing to a roller coaster you'll see in Hawaii. I've heard it's a lot of fun, but I've never tried it."

Joe steered the car onto the sandy shoulder. "Well, let's find out."

Frank studied the billowing, rainbow-colored shape being towed across the sky. "I think I'll sit this one out. Parachutes are great if you're in a burning airplane. I don't feel like putting one on when I'm already on the ground. You two go ahead and try if you want."

Joe and Jade walked across the sand to the water. They watched the motorboat make a wide turn, slowing down as it headed toward the beach. As its speed dropped, the parachute in the air behind it glided down. The boat turned again. Now it was barely coasting, just a few feet from the shoreline. The parachute swung over the beach as it dipped down, and the man strapped into it landed lightly on his feet.

Joe could see two men in the boat. They both looked like native Hawaiians—dark skin and thick black hair. The skipper was standing, holding the wheel with his left hand. He worked the throttle with his right hand, easing it back slowly. Without throwing out an anchor, it was tricky to hold the boat steady in one place. It looked like he had had a lot of practice at it, though.

The other man jumped overboard into the waist-deep water and waded ashore. He gathered up the flapping parachute and helped the rider out of the harness.

Joe grabbed Jade's hand. "Come on, here's your chance."

"*My* chance?" she said. "What about you? This was your idea!"

"Ladies first," Joe insisted. "Besides, you were the one who said it was fun."

The smiling Hawaiian from the boat held out the parachute harness. "You want to give it a try? Only ten bucks."

Joe shook his head. "Two for fifteen," he haggled. "First her, then me."

The man's grin widened. "Okay. You hold the chute while I get her strapped in."

Joe wrapped his arms around the bundle of multicolored nylon, making sure not to tangle the lines leading to the harness. Jade stepped into the harness and put her arms through the shoulder straps. The Hawaiian checked the straps that crisscrossed her hips and chest, making sure they were all snug and secure. He patted her on the back and flashed another big grin.

"All set," he called to Joe. "Just wait until I'm back in the boat, and then let go." He ran into the water and splashed his way back to the motorboat.

Jade tugged at the harness. "I'm not sure this is such a hot idea."

"It's too late now," Joe replied. "I already paid him—and I don't think I could get you out of that thing, anyway."

Joe saw the Hawaiian climb back in the boat, and he got ready to let go of the parachute. But then he saw another boat pull up next to it. This one was a flat, sleek white speedboat. Painted on the side was a red lightning bolt. On the stern, Joe could see the name *Big Deal*.

Two men were on the speedboat. They shouted something across to the other boat. Joe couldn't make out the words, but he could see that the newcomers were backing up their argument with a pistol. Then the long, thick line that ran between the boat and the parachute was untied and tossed over to the more powerful speedboat.

Jade glanced nervously at him. ''Joe? What's going on?''

Joe dropped the parachute and ran toward her. He heard the deep growl of the diesel engine as it roared away. He saw the slack go out of the line. The parachute billowed and rose upward.

Just as Jade was jerked off her feet and into the air, Joe leapt up and grabbed the harness. The parachute dipped slightly from the extra weight. Joe's feet brushed the sand.

''Let go!'' Jade screamed. ''You'll be killed!''

Joe clutched tighter. He didn't know what he was going to do, but he knew Jade was in danger and needed his help. Suddenly there was no ground beneath his feet. The parachute started to gain altitude rapidly.

After catching his breath, Joe looked down. The Pacific Ocean sparkled far below him already. How high had they soared? Fifty feet? A hundred? It was impossible to tell. Either way, it was too late to change his mind now.

He'd never survive the fall.

Chapter

8

THE SPEEDBOAT SKIMMED OVER the water, towing the parachute far from the shoreline. Joe's arms were starting to tire—the harness cut into his skin and burned the palms of his hands. He didn't know how long he could hold on, and he didn't want to find out the hard way.

"What do we do now?" Jade yelled.

With the wind rushing through his ears and the speedboat engine blaring below, Joe could barely hear her. "There's a Swiss army knife in my right front pocket," he shouted. "See if you can get it."

She reached around and managed to pull the knife out of his pocket. "Okay, I've got it. What next?"

"Cut the line!"

Jade opened the three-inch blade and stared at it. "It's going to take a while."

"I know," Joe responded. "But it's all we've got—unless you have a better idea."

Jade shook her head and started sawing at the thick nylon line. Joe twisted his head around and looked back at the island of Maui. He had his doubts that they could swim that far—and he had even bigger doubts that whoever was in the speedboat would give them a chance to find out.

He scanned the area for nearby ships. In the distance, he thought he saw a few navy battleships. They were too far away to take notice of a lone parachute, though.

The speedboat was headed in the direction of a small island. Maybe, if they got a little push from the wind, they could make it there. If they came down on dry land, Joe thought they might stand a chance of getting out of this alive.

They could run. They could hide. They could make weapons out of sticks and rocks. It wasn't much, but it was better than floundering in the water, waiting to get picked off.

"Got it!" Jade suddenly yelled.

The feeling of being dragged through the air abruptly fell away—along with the rope that splashed down into the blue water below.

The parachute started to drift downward, but the stiff trade winds were much stronger out in the open water, giving them a little extra lift and pushing them right where Joe wanted to go.

The speedboat circled underneath, like a hungry shark, waiting to see where the parachute would come down.

Frank had seen the speedboat pull up next to the Hawaiians' boat, but he was too far away to see what was going on. He didn't know anything was wrong until he saw Joe lunge at the parachute harness just as it lifted Jade into the air.

He ran down to the water, but the boat was already far out to sea. He watched the brightly colored parachute grow smaller in the distance. Just like that, Joe was gone as the rumble of the big diesel engine faded away. All Frank could hear then was the high-pitched whine of jet-skis, droning along the shoreline.

The two Hawaiians in the small motorboat watched in silence as the speedboat raced away. Frank waded out into the ocean, waving frantically to get their attention, but they didn't notice.

Frank swam out to the boat, grabbed hold of the gunwale, and hauled himself out of the water.

That got their attention. "What do you think you're doing?" the man clutching the wheel asked sharply, twisting to face him.

The other man moved toward Frank, fists clenched. "Crazy haoles. First you steal our parasail ride. Now you think you can steal our boat, too?"

Frank held out his hands. Both men were stocky and muscular. Although Frank was taller than they were, he doubted that he had a weight advantage over either of them. Even if he could take them out, he didn't want to start a fight.

"You've got it all wrong, guys," Frank quickly said. "When they stole your parachute, they kidnapped my brother and a friend of ours. So crank up the engine and let's get going."

"Go where?" the skipper replied. His anger had subsided, and now he looked at Frank with mild curiosity. "You can't take a boat like this into the interisland channel. It's too rough out there."

"Yeah," the other man agreed. "Besides, what would we do even if we *could* catch up with them? They had guns, man. *Big* guns."

"You can't just sit here and do nothing!" Frank yelled. "How about the coast guard—or the navy?"

"Good luck," the skipper said. "By the time you get to a phone and cut through all the red tape, that boat will be long gone."

"Terrific," Frank muttered.

He spun around to dive back in the water and saw something lashed to the side of the boat. He had climbed in from the other side, so he hadn't noticed it before. It looked like a cross between a motorcycle and a snowmobile—except it didn't have any wheels or treads.

Frank turned back to the two Hawaiians. He pulled a soggy wallet out of his soaking wet pants. "How much do you want for the jet-ski?" he asked.

"You'll never make it on that thing," the skipper said. "We just have it in case the engine breaks down and we have to ferry people back to shore. You can't take it out in the channel."

"That's my problem," Frank snapped. "How much do you want?"

The man shrugged. "Take it. Who knows? Maybe you'll get lucky and catch those jerks. If you do, just remember to bring back our parachute."

"I'll bring it back," Frank promised. "But how will I find you?"

"We'll be here," came the reply. "If we're not, just ask around for Freddie or Mike Ahina. All the locals know us."

Frank bent over the side and untied the lines that secured the jet-ski. He climbed down onto it, holding the side of the boat with one hand to keep steady. He pressed the starter and twisted the throttle on the end of the handlebar. The small engine sounded like an angry swarm of bees.

"Oh, well," Frank told himself. "It sure beats swimming in wet clothes."

Even though the engine wasn't very big, Frank discovered the jet-ski was pretty quick. It was made of lightweight materials and designed to skip across the surface of the water. That was exactly what it did. Every time Frank hit a small wave, the jet-ski flew into the air.

It took some getting used to. It was like waterskiing and motorcycle motocross racing jumbled together. Frank almost lost it a couple times, coming down hard and wobbly on the front ski. But after a while he started shifting his weight whenever the jet-ski took off, keeping the front end up and forcing the back end down.

The water started to get choppy farther out from shore, and it was harder to control the machine. Frank knew it would get a lot worse before it got any better. The volcanic mountains of the islands acted as giant windbreaks, keeping the ocean calm along the coastline. The winds whipped the water into whitecaps out in the interisland channel, though, and that was where the speedboat had gone. So that's where Frank was going, too.

A wave smacked the jet-ski broadside. Frank fought for control. Saltwater sprayed over his face and shoulders. He couldn't jump these waves as he had the smaller ones near shore. They were too big—and getting bigger.

He tried to weave between them. This is like running a marathon in a minefield, Frank thought. Except these mines are moving.

He began to think the Hawaiians had been right—he'd never make it across the channel on the jet-ski. Dodging one wave after another meant he had to swerve off in one direction, then cut back to get on course again, only to veer off again to skirt another whitecap. His chances of catching the speedboat had been slim when he was moving in a straight line. Threading a twisted path through the rolling hills of water didn't exactly improve the odds.

Frank knew he'd never catch them this way. He was about to give up and try to make it back to Maui when he saw a bright shape flashing across the waves. It was a white speedboat, with a ragged streak of crimson on the side.

Frank looked at the red lightning bolt. He couldn't believe his luck. They were almost headed right at him. But where was the parachute? Where was Joe?

Frank pushed those questions out of his mind. One thing at a time. And the first thing, he told himself, is to get on that boat.

He aimed the jet-ski at the oncoming speedboat. Frank held his breath, waiting for them to change course to avoid him, but the speedboat cut a straight line through the water. Frank closed the gap between them. Still no reaction.

Why don't they do something? Frank wondered. Can't they see me? He glanced down at the blue-and-white jet-ski and chuckled. He was wearing a white T-shirt and blue jeans. Perfect camouflage against the blue ocean and the white wave crests.

It suddenly occurred to Frank that he had no idea how he was going to get on the speedboat.

They sure weren't going to stop and offer him an invitation. "I'll just have to wing it," he muttered to himself.

A wave started to rise up between Frank and his target. Frank saw his chance. He twisted the knob on the handlebar and hit the swell at full throttle. The jet-ski soared over the crest and became airborne. It hurtled toward the speedboat, but Frank could tell it was going to fall short. The combined weight of Frank and the jet-ski was too much.

So he let go of the handlebars and kicked off with his feet. The jet-ski dropped away, and Frank sailed right above the boat and thudded onto the deck, landing on his side.

There was a sharp pain in his hip, but Frank ignored it. He jumped to his feet and whirled around to face two hulking brutes. Both were wearing dark suits and sunglasses. They definitely didn't look like sailors.

They definitely didn't look Hawaiian, either. The one holding the wheel had short, light brown hair with a small bald spot in the back. He turned and gave Frank a cold, hard stare. "Get rid of him," he growled to his partner.

The second man nodded and reached into his coat, but Frank slammed his foot into the man's stomach before the gun had cleared the shoulder holster. He doubled over from the blow, and Frank's hand came down on the back of his neck with blurring speed. The man slumped to the deck.

Frank didn't stop to admire his work. The thug behind the wheel was turning, starting to make his move. Frank spun around, swinging his left leg up for a roundhouse kick. The side of Frank's foot smashed into the man's jaw. The thug's sunglasses flew off, and his head smacked the steering wheel.

Frank didn't give him a chance to fall. He pushed him up against the side rail and reached inside the man's coat. He felt cold steel and leather and pulled out a .45 automatic pistol. Frank thumbed off the safety and shoved the gun in the man's face.

"Where's my brother?" Frank rasped.

The thug sneered. "You mean the jerk with the girl?"

Frank pressed the gun against the man's skin. "The only jerk I see is the one with the barrel of a forty-five up his nose. Now, where are they? I *won't* ask again."

The man shrugged. "It don't make no difference anyway. There's nothing you can do. They're on Kahoolawe."

"What's wrong?" Joe asked. He was standing on a rocky beach, the parachute bunched up in his arms. "Those guys aren't coming after us. As soon as they saw us land here, they took off. They probably would have ripped the bottom out of that boat if they tried to bring it in here."

Jade didn't respond. She had the harness half off and was staring at a signpost stuck in the sand. Danger! it warned in big red letters. Keep Off! Beneath that was a single Hawaiian word, *Kahoolawe*.

"Hey," Joe said when he saw the sign. "I thought you said all the beaches in Hawaii were public. Who's this Kahoolawe guy?"

Jade turned to him. There was fear in her eyes. "That's the name of the island," she said. "The whole thing belongs to the navy."

"So we'll get arrested for trespassing on government property," Joe replied. "It's better than wrestling with sharks."

Jade shook her head. "You don't understand. Nobody comes here—not even the navy.

"They use the island only for target practice."

Chapter

9

THE *BIG DEAL* raced toward Maui. Frank had the throttle wide open. Every time the boat hit a wave, the bow reared up out of the water and then crashed back down. Salt spray splashed the windshield.

Frank checked the fuel gauge. Almost empty. Barely enough to make it. If he had tried for Kahoolawe, he would have ended up stranded there with his brother and Jade. He glanced back at his two passengers, firmly tied up with the anchor line.

He pulled into the small marina in the harbor at Lahaina, ignoring the No Wake signs. He killed the engine and let the speedboat drift to the dock. He was already standing on the bow when it scraped against the pier. He jumped off and wrapped the bowline around a post.

"Hey, man!" a voice called out. "Where's our para-sail? You said you'd bring it back."

Frank turned and saw Mike Ahina, his brother Freddie behind him.

Frank nodded at the white speedboat with the red lightning bolt. "I got something almost as good," he replied. "The creeps that stole it."

Frank looked at the two hired thugs bound hand and foot on the deck of the boat. One of them was still out cold. The other was glaring back at him.

Frank turned back to the Hawaiian brothers. "Listen, could you keep an eye on those two until the cops get here? I'll call them right after I get through to Pearl Harbor."

"You know somebody at Pearl?" Freddie asked.

"No," Frank replied. "But my brother's stuck on Kahoolawe, and only the navy can get him off."

"Kahoolawe?" Freddie Ahina said. "You know what they use that island for?"

Frank nodded quickly. "Yeah, but I don't know when they plan to use it next. So I'm kind of in a hurry. Where's the nearest phone?"

Mike Ahina scowled. "You'd just be wasting your time, man. They won't call off a bombing run just because some kid calls them up and tells them to."

Frank looked at him. "You mean they're going to bomb it *today?*"

Freddie shrugged. "They bomb it all the time, but they've got some big exercise going on right now. Lots of battleships out there. Only thing you can know for sure—Kahoolawe's going to get a brutal pounding before it's over."

"Then I've got to get back there now!" Frank burst out.

"I know the fastest way to get you there," Freddie said. "Let me make a call and set it up."

While Freddie Ahina was gone, his brother jumped into the speedboat to check on the two thugs. "Hey, what's this?" he called to Frank. "Looks like a picture of the girl who was with your brother."

"Let me see that," Frank said. It looked like a photocopy of a page torn out of a magazine. It was a picture of Jade all right—but she looked a few years younger. She was holding a surfboard. Standing next to her was her father, Kevin Roberts.

"Where'd you get this?" Frank asked.

"I found it on the deck," the Hawaiian responded.

Ten minutes later a helicopter swooped down out of the sky, hovered for a moment, then settled down gently on the end of the pier. Frank was surprised that the dock could hold all that weight, but he didn't stop to analyze it.

The door of the cockpit swung open. Frank ducked and ran over to it, the rotors whirling just a few feet over his head. He started to climb in, grabbing the door frame with both hands and stepping on the front of the skid bar.

The helicopter wobbled slightly. Frank looked down. The machine wasn't resting on the pier at all. It was hovering just a few inches above it. Frank glanced across the seat at the pilot.

The man flashed a wide grin through his bushy beard. "Welcome to Doyle Island Tours. I'm your pilot, Hank Doyle. Hurry up and get in. I charge by the hour."

Frank clambered into the copilot's seat and strapped himself in. "Let's go," he shouted over the deafening howl of the engine.

Doyle tapped his headset and pointed to a similar unit on a hook on the side of the copilot's seat. Frank put it on. The headphones covered his ears, cutting out some of the noise. A small microphone was attached on one side.

"So you're a friend of Freddie Ahina's?" a voice crackled in Frank's ear.

"Actually I just met him today," Frank admitted.

The pilot turned to him. "You mean I'm supposed to take on the U.S. Navy for some lousy tourist? I owe Freddie a favor, but this is really pushing it. Who are you, anyway?"

Frank looked at him, trying to penetrate Doyle's aviator shades with his gaze. He chose his words carefully. "I'm a guy who needs your help. I can't make you help me—I can't even ask you. I wouldn't ask anybody to risk his life flying into a target area during a naval barrage."

Frank slapped the release button on the shoulder straps of the copilot's seat. "My brother's on Kahoolawe, and that's where I'm going. If you won't take me, I'll figure out some other way to get there."

He started to take off the headset. Doyle's voice came through the earphones. "Hold on a second. You didn't answer my question. Who are you?"

"What difference does it make?" Frank asked.

The pilot grinned. "If we're going to get killed together, we should be on a first-name basis, don't you think?" He took his right hand off the control stick and held it out. "My friends call me Skydog."

Frank grasped Doyle's hand. "Thanks," he sighed. "My name's Frank Hardy. Whatever it costs, I'll find some way to pay you."

Doyle pulled back on the control stick and the helicopter banked up and away from the pier. "Forget it." He laughed. "If I had a dollar for every grunt I pulled out of a fire zone, I'd be a rich man. Besides, I can't stand those armchair admirals and their pretend wars. Somebody should put some howitzers on that island and start shooting back. That'd give them something to put in their reports!"

Frank watched as Doyle worked the controls. It looked a lot like flying an airplane—except there seemed to be an extra lever by the left side of the seat. All of the pilot's controls were also duplicated on the copilot's side. Frank glanced over to his left and saw a lever next to his seat, too. He reached down and touched the handgrip.

"You know anything about flying?" Doyle suddenly asked.

Frank shrugged. "I took a few lessons back home. I could land a single-engine plane if I had to, but this looks a lot trickier."

That was an understatement. The dizzying array of dials, gauges, and switches were a total mystery to Frank.

Doyle nodded. "It takes a special breed to be a chopper jockey. Helicopters can do a lot of things airplanes can't—like hover, fly backward, and take off and land vertically. So they need more controls. It takes two hands and two feet all working together to fly this baby."

He patted the control stick in front of him. "This is the cyclic pitch control. Moving this changes the angle of the main rotor blades. You push it forward and you go forward. You pull it back, and you go backward. Simple, right?"

"So far," Frank replied. "But how do you turn?"

The pilot pointed at his feet. "See those pedals? They control the tail rotor. Press one and you increase the tail rotor thrust, and you turn one way." He pushed down on the left pedal and the helicopter banked to the left. "Press the other, and you decrease the tail thrust."

"And you turn right—right?" Frank said.

"You got it," Doyle replied. "Now all you need to know is how to make it go up and down."

Frank smiled. "I bet that lever next to the seat is the missing ingredient."

"Right again," Doyle said. "That's the collective pitch control. Pull it up, and up we go." He gripped the lever and pulled. The helicopter soared upward.

Then abruptly he pushed the lever down. The helicopter swooped in a steep dive. Frank's stomach felt as if it had just jumped into his throat. He clutched at the control stick in front of him. It was the closest thing he could hang onto.

The bearded pilot eased the lever up, and the helicopter pulled out of the dive just before they hit the water. "Yee-ha!" he yelled. "This is the only way to travel!" The waves rushed by just a few feet beneath them.

Frank realized a good-size swell could easily swamp them. "Shouldn't we pull up a little?" he suggested, trying to sound cool and casual. "Like maybe to an altitude where we might show up on the navy's radar?"

Doyle laughed. "Great idea, kid! Let's take

her up where we can get a real close look at some of those sixteen-inch shells that the sailors like to throw at Kahoolawe.''

"If they know we're here," Frank said, "they won't fire, right?"

"I wouldn't bet my life on it," the pilot answered. "Let's give them a call and see what happens." He thumbed a switch on the control panel and spoke into the microphone. "Mayday! Mayday! This is Victor Able one five niner. We have lost hydraulic pressure and are going down on Kahoolawe.''

There was a long pause. Static hissed through the headset. Then another voice crackled in Frank's ears. "Ah, say again, Victor Able one five niner. We didn't copy that.''

"Mayday!" Doyle barked. "We are making an emergency landing on Kahoolawe!''

There was another static-filled pause, and then, "Ah, negative on that, Victor Able. You are entering a restricted flight zone. There is a naval exercise in progress. Alter course immediately. Do not, repeat, do *not* land on Kahoolawe.''

The pilot looked at Frank and shrugged. He reached over to the control panel and flipped the radio switch on and off rapidly as he spoke into the microphone. "Signal breaking up. We did not copy last message. Repeat—we are going down on Kahoolawe. Mayday! Mayday!''

He shut off the radio and turned to Frank.

"Maybe that will confuse them long enough for us to get in and out."

Frank heard a hollow whistling sound, and something whizzed by overhead. He looked at the island ahead and saw a patch of ground erupt in a spray of dirt and smoke.

"I wouldn't bet my life on it," he replied grimly.

Chapter

10

JOE AND JADE huddled beside a small outcropping of rock. The ground shook every time one of the heavy shells exploded. Even though the action seemed to be focused on another part of the island, Joe didn't want to take any chances.

Jade put her hand on his arm. "Tell me again," she said, "about how somebody is going to find us."

Joe listened to the steady *krump krump krump* in the distance. He couldn't tell for sure, but he thought the noise was getting louder.

He patted Jade's hand and pointed to the beach. He had spread the rainbow-colored parachute on the ground, holding down the edges with football-size rocks. "From the air, anybody can see that. It's as good as a flare gun or a signal fire."

A shell exploded close by with a deafening roar that left Joe's ears ringing. Jade's fingernails dug into his arm.

"Tell me how we're going to survive until then!" she shouted.

"That was just a stray shot," Joe tried to reassure her. "They're concentrating all their firepower inland. All we have to do is sit tight."

There was another earsplitting blast nearby. Sand and pulverized rock showered down around them. The air was full of dark smoke and dust.

Frank spotted something down on the rocky beach. He heard the telltale whistling again, and then another chunk of the island was smashed into a rain of pebbles and dust. When the smoke cleared, whatever had been there was gone. Still, he thought it was worth a look.

He tapped the pilot's shoulder and pointed. "Take us down there! I thought I saw something."

Doyle nodded and moved the control stick. The helicopter turned and raced down the shoreline. Frank scanned the beach. Nothing but sand and boulders. A splash of color caught Frank's eye.

"Hold it!" he yelled. "Go back! There is something back there!"

Doyle's feet shifted on the pedals. The helicopter circled around and set down on the rocky beach.

Frank jumped out and picked up a strip of

yellow cloth. There were other scraps of material scattered in the sand. He recognized the rainbow colors of the parachute. There was nothing left but confetti. Frank shuddered. He prayed that Joe and Jade weren't anywhere near the parachute when the explosion ripped into it.

Somebody coughed. Frank whirled and saw a ghost—at least it looked like a ghost. The figure was grayish white from head to toe. It coughed again. "About time you got here," it rasped.

Another dusty figure crawled out from behind a small rock outcropping.

Frank stared at them. "Joe? Jade? Is that you?"

"Who else were you expecting?" Joe replied hoarsely. "The Ghost of Christmas past?"

"You look horrible," Frank gasped. "Are you all right?"

Joe looked down at himself. "Yeah, I think so." He tried to brush off some of the dust, and a small cloud puffed up around him. He coughed again. "I could use a bath, though."

"So where are we going?" Hank Doyle asked after Frank introduced Joe and Jade, and they had flown some distance away from the small, scorched island. "Back to Maui?"

Frank looked at Joe and Jade in the backseat of the helicopter. "We've got to figure out our next move."

"Let's fly back to Oahu," Joe suggested. "We'll go have a little talk with Nick Hawk."

He cracked his knuckles. "I'll give him five or ten good reasons to call off the dogs."

Frank shook his head. "Something tells me this goes way beyond Nick's gambling problems. They were double-teaming us back on Maui—first the guys in the car, and then the two goons in the speedboat."

Joe could see where his brother was leading. "That means somebody with heavy mob connections or a lot of money to burn on hired guns."

"Or both," Frank said.

"So what do we do now?" Jade asked. "We can't stay in this helicopter forever."

"We need to buy some time to come up with a plan," Frank said. "We need a place where nobody can find us for a while."

"I know just the place," the pilot said. He looked at the fuel gauge and tapped it with his finger. "We might just have enough fuel to make it."

"Might?" Joe responded. "What happens if we don't?"

Doyle chuckled. "Then we get wet!" He worked the foot pedals, and the helicopter banked hard to the left.

Frank glanced at the fuel gauge. The needle was still close to *F*. The tank was almost full. Frank smiled. Doyle had a weird sense of humor, but he was beginning to like him. "Cheer up, Joe," he said. "You said you needed a bath, anyway."

They were in the air for over an hour. Frank checked the position of the sun and guessed they were headed northwest. They flew over the small island of Lanai. They saw Molokai in the distance. Oahu passed by on the right. After that, there was nothing but blue for a while. Blue sky above them, and blue ocean below.

Finally a lush, green island loomed ahead.

Jade pointed out the window. "That's Kauai. They call it the garden island. That must be where we're going."

"What makes you think that?" Joe asked.

"Because if it isn't," Doyle answered, "it's an awfully long way to the next island big enough to land on." He turned to Frank and grinned. "Hang on—we're going in hard!"

The helicopter banked to the right and swooped down toward the island. As they got closer, Frank could see a vast, tropical jungle.

"Yee-hah!" the pilot whooped, skimming the tops of the trees. "I love this job! It's the most fun you can have without getting shot at."

Frank spotted a small cabin in a clearing in the jungle. Doyle pulled back on the stick, and the helicopter slowed down. It hovered over the clearing for a moment. Then he pushed down on the lever at his side, and the flying machine eased to the ground.

Doyle cut the engine power and unbuckled his safety harness. "One of the fringe benefits," he said, gesturing at the small cabin surrounded by forest, "is being able to live someplace where you never get uninvited visitors."

They all got out of the helicopter. Joe looked around. Something was missing. "Is there a road anywhere near here?" he asked.

"Depends on what you mean by near—and what you mean by road," Doyle replied. "There's an old dirt trail about a mile from here. I guess you could run a four-wheeler down it."

"So you can get here only by helicopter," Frank said.

"You got it," the pilot answered. He opened the cabin door. "Welcome to Chateau Doyle. Try to ignore the mess. It's been a while since any guests have been here."

They followed him inside. "Looks like it's been a while since *anybody* has been here," Jade said.

There were cobwebs everywhere, and a faint mildew smell filled the air. The sparse wood furniture looked handmade, Frank noticed. Probably carved from trees that grew in the area.

"Well, it has been a while since I was last here," Doyle admitted. "I don't really live here anymore. I just use it as a retreat—a place to chill out when the world gets too weird."

"Like now?" Joe ventured.

A grin spread across the pilot's bearded face.

"Are you kidding? I can't remember the last time I've had so much fun."

"Well, all this fun is making me hungry," Joe said. "I don't suppose you've got anything to eat in the refrigerator. That is, if you have a refrigerator."

Doyle laughed and slapped Joe on the back. "Let me show you the kitchen. We've got all the modern comforts. Refrigerator, stove, trash compactor—"

"Trash compactor?" Jade echoed.

"Sure," Doyle replied. "There's not a lot you can do with garbage. You can either bury it in the yard and end up living next to a dump, or—"

"Or you can haul it away," Frank cut in. "And if you have to carry it away in a helicopter that doesn't have a lot of extra space, a trash compactor makes a lot of sense."

"What do you do for power?" Joe asked. "I bet the electric company doesn't run any lines out here."

"If they did," Doyle answered, "I'd have neighbors pretty soon, and then I'd have to move. There's a diesel generator out back. It's not much, but it'll give us all the power we need. Come on, I'll show you."

He started to walk to the door and then stopped. He scratched his beard. "Of course, it isn't going to start without any fuel in it." He shrugged his shoulders. "Oh well, it doesn't matter. Any food in the refrigerator would be pretty rank by now, anyway. So I'll just have to jump in the old station wagon and drive down to the Food 'n' Fuel.''

"You want any company?" Frank asked.

The pilot waved him off as he headed out the door toward the helicopter. "Nah. You just hang loose for a while. I'll be back before you know it."

For the next few hours, while Joe and Jade sat in the cabin, talking, Frank stared out into the forest and reviewed the case. He glanced at his watch finally and started to get worried. Doyle hadn't returned and the sun was getting low in the sky. He doubted that even Skydog could find the cabin in the middle of the jungle in the dark.

Joe didn't notice the time go by—he was too busy talking to Jade. Eventually he did notice that something was bothering his brother. He walked up behind him and put his hand on Frank's shoulder. "What's up?" he asked.

"Doyle should have been back," Frank answered.

Joe shrugged. "Maybe he had too many items for the express check-out lane. Besides, it's given me a chance to find out some interesting things."

"Like what?" Frank replied. "Jade's favorite rock band? Her shoe size?"

Joe put his hand over his heart. "You wound me." He glanced over at the girl and then turned back to his brother. "Let's go outside and get some fresh air." He held the door open for Frank and then followed him out.

"So what'd you find out?" Frank asked.

"Do you know why Jade's father doesn't like her surfing?" Joe answered Frank with another question.

"Because it's dangerous?"

"No. Because of the publicity."

Frank frowned. "Replay that for me."

"When Jade first started to get known in competition, some dinky surfing magazine did a feature on her. She gave them this old picture of herself with her first surfboard. It was a present from her father—and he was in the picture, too. When her old man saw the article, he almost grounded her for life."

Frank pulled a piece of paper out of his pocket. "You mean this picture?"

Joe looked at it. "Where did you get that?"

"Off one of those thugs that took you and Jade for a joyride," Frank replied.

"It all starts to fit together, doesn't it?" Joe said.

"Yeah," Frank agreed. "No family, no past, no publicity—sounds like Kevin Roberts has been on the run for the past fifteen years."

"And whoever he was running from finally caught up with him," Joe added.

Frank looked at his brother. "There's something else bothering me."

"What's that?"

"How did those hoods back on Maui know where to find us?"

The *whup-whup-whup* of a helicopter cut through the air.

"Doyle's back," Joe said.

Frank looked up and spotted the helicopter close by. Something was wrong! It was weaving through the air, its tail swinging from side to side. Then it just dropped.

Chapter

11

FRANK COULD TELL the helicopter was coming down too fast. It hit the ground hard. The landing skid on the left side smashed down first. The struts groaned and buckled. Then the machine rocked the other way. The right skid smacked the ground, bounced up, and finally settled down.

The whine of the engine died down. Frank and Joe bolted toward the cockpit. Frank yanked open the door. Hank Doyle grinned out at him. "Sorry I'm late," he said. The smile wavered. "But the traffic was murder."

Frank poked his head into the cockpit. "Are you okay?" he asked the pilot.

Doyle nodded. "Yeah, but I think I've dodged enough artillery for one day."

Joe peered in over his brother's shoulder and

saw a single bullet hole in the windshield. "Something tells me this isn't the work of a disgruntled customer," he said. "So maybe you should tell us exactly what happened."

"I flew back to Maui to pick up some gear. A guy showed up at the hangar just as I was getting ready to head back here," Doyle replied. "He wanted to know where you were. I made a break for it, but he managed to shoot off a couple rounds before I got the chopper off the ground."

"Why'd you come all the way back here?" Frank asked. "Why not just head for the nearest police station?"

Doyle snorted. "Because he *was* the police. He flashed an FBI badge at me before he started asking questions."

"FBI?" Joe echoed. "What did he look like?"

The pilot shrugged his shoulders. "He looked like a fed."

"That's it?" Frank prodded. "No distinguishing marks?"

"Oh, yeah," Doyle said. "He had a scar over his left eye. Do you know him?"

"We ran into him once before," Joe replied.

"I have a bad feeling we'll tangle with him again before this is over," Frank said grimly.

He glanced around the inside of the helicopter. Other than the bullet hole in the windshield, there were no signs of damage. "Will this thing still fly?" he asked.

Doyle chuckled. "I got here, didn't I?"

"Just barely," Frank noted.

"The tail rotor controls are kind of stiff," Doyle admitted. "He must have hit one of the cables. But it's nothing I can't handle."

Frank turned to his brother. "Get Jade. We're leaving now. We've got to get back to Honolulu right away."

"Right," Joe said. "No wonder those goons were right behind us every step of the way. Every time you called Dad, that FBI agent tipped them off."

"If they knew where to find us," Frank added, "how long do you think it will take them to track down Jade's father?"

As the helicopter flew across the water, Joe told Jade what they had pieced together.

"Who was my father hiding from?" she asked. "What did he do?"

"We don't know," Joe said. "But a safe bet would be that it has something to do with the mob and the FBI—and it happened a long time ago."

"You mean before we moved to Hawaii," Jade said.

Joe nodded. "The government might even have relocated you as part of the witness protection program."

"It doesn't make any sense!" she protested. "Why now—after fifteen years? You can't tell me they've been looking for us all this time!"

"It does sound kind of farfetched, doesn't it?" Joe admitted. "But maybe they weren't looking at all. Maybe they just stumbled across you by accident."

Jade's shoulders slumped. "It's all my fault."

Joe reached out and took her hand. "You were only two when it happened—whatever it was. How could it be your fault?"

"The magazine article," she said. "No wonder my father was so upset."

"You had no way of knowing," Joe assured her.

She turned and looked at him. "What do we do now?"

"We fly to Waikiki," Joe explained, "and grab your father out of the hotel before anybody else finds out he's there."

"And then?" she asked.

Joe cleared his throat. "We're still working on that part."

"How do you know we're not already too late?" she pressed.

Joe didn't answer right away. He looked into her green eyes. "We don't," he finally said. "But we've got to try, right?"

The sun had set, and a full moon sparkled on the water. The only other source of light lay straight ahead. "That's Honolulu," Doyle announced. "I'll take her down over Waikiki Beach. But you're going to have to jump the last couple of feet—I can't risk landing more than once on that skid I busted back on Kauai."

"After we jump," Frank said, "you better get out of here. I don't know what we'll run into, and I don't want you to get stuck in the middle again."

The pilot grinned. "I like the fireworks. They make me feel alive, but I don't think I'll be much help in this crippled chopper. We're coming up on the beach now. Get ready to bail out."

The helicopter hovered a few feet above the sand. Joe pushed the back door open and jumped down. Jade stood in the opening. Joe reached out, and she jumped into his arms.

Frank watched to make sure they were all right. Then he turned to the pilot. "I don't know how to thank you for all you've done," he said.

"I'd send you a bill," Doyle replied, "but I don't have your address. Now, get out of here so I can go find some paying customers."

Frank opened the door and climbed out. The wind from the rotor blades whipped his hair around, and he had to shield his eyes from the blowing sand that pelted him. He flashed a thumbs-up gesture to the pilot, and the machine lifted off. Frank ran up the beach to join his brother.

Frank led the way back to the hotel through the beach entrance. When he walked into the hotel suite, the first thing he saw was his father sitting at the writing desk.

When Fenton Hardy saw his son standing in the doorway, he said, "I thought you were still on Maui. Why didn't you call and let me know you were coming back here?"

"It's a long story," Frank said.

"A very long story," Joe chimed in.

"Well, I dug up quite a story of my own," Fenton replied. He looked at Jade. "I got most of it from your father."

"Does it have anything to do with the witness protection program?" she asked.

Fenton looked surprised. "He told me you didn't know anything about it."

"She didn't," Joe said. "We just put it all together today."

"But we don't have any of the details," Frank added. "How about filling in the gaps for us?"

"Sixteen years ago," Fenton began, "an undercover FBI agent penetrated the heart of a West Coast mob bookmaking and loan-sharking operation. They took bets on anything and everything. They'd even lend you the money to bet with."

"Then break your legs if you couldn't pay them back," Joe said.

His father nodded. "Something like that. Anyway, this undercover agent broke the whole case wide open. His testimony sent the ringleader, Thomas Catlin, to prison. Catlin swore he'd get revenge.

"But criminals make threats like that all the

time," he continued. "Nobody took it seriously until a bomb demolished the agent's house. The agent was in a nearby park with his daughter when it happened. The only person in the house was his wife."

"My mother," Jade whispered.

"I'm afraid so," Fenton replied. "She was killed instantly. After that, you and your father got new identities and moved to Hawaii to start a new life. It should have ended there. But two years ago Catlin got out of prison and took up where he left off. About a year ago he started expanding his operation into the islands."

"Wait a minute," Frank cut in. "Jade's father couldn't have known that."

"He didn't," Fenton said. "Until I told him. That's why he came to me—the Bureau told him I was his contact. That's the real reason I'm in Hawaii. Catlin imported some heavy talent from New York. I've busted a couple of them before, and I know how they work. So I was brought in as an adviser."

He turned to his sons. "All this is strictly classified information. Top secret."

"I'm afraid it's not much of a secret anymore," Joe replied.

"What do you mean?" his father asked.

"He means somebody inside the FBI is working for Catlin," Frank said. "Every time I called to let you know where we were, a couple of trained gorillas homed in on us."

Fenton Hardy frowned. "The only person I told was Pete Gordon, the special agent I've been working with."

"I don't suppose this Gordon guy has a scar over his left eye," Joe said.

"Yes," Fenton replied. "How did you know?"

"Because a friend of ours saw him on Maui late this afternoon, trying to track Jade down," Frank explained.

All the color drained out of Fenton's face, and he slumped back in his chair. "Then it looks like we've got a very serious situation," he said gravely. "Gordon was supposed to be out setting up a safe house this afternoon—a place for Jade and her father to stay awhile."

"So we'll just get them out of here now," Joe said.

"Where *is* my father?" Jade asked. "He's all right, isn't he?"

Fenton Hardy raised his eyes slowly to meet hers. "I'm sorry," he said. "I didn't know. Gordon picked him up an hour ago."

Chapter

12

"WE'VE GOT TO GET Jade out of here," Frank said. "They could be back looking for her here. This is the most logical place for us to bring her."

Jade slumped down in a chair. "Why would they want me?" she asked glumly, staring at the floor. "They got what they wanted—my father."

"I'm not so sure about that," Frank answered. "They could have grabbed him anytime. Why now?"

Joe thought about it for a minute. "Because they couldn't get Jade."

Frank nodded. "All this time they've been trying to get her, not him."

Jade looked up. "But why?"

"I don't have the answer to that one," Frank

said. "But I think I may know someone who does."

He turned to his father. "Are the police still holding Nick Hawk?"

Fenton shook his head. "They didn't have any solid evidence. After we found out about Kevin Roberts's connection to Catlin, that shifted the attention away from Hawk."

Joe glanced at his brother. "I don't get it. Do you think Hawk is mixed up with Catlin?"

"Think about it," Frank said. "Catlin's a kingpin of bookies and loan sharks—and Nick Hawk has some heavy gambling debts."

"Let's go find out what he knows," Joe said, glancing over at Jade. "Do you know where Nick lives?"

She nodded slowly. "I'll take you there."

Joe put his hand on her shoulder. "No, it's too dangerous. We'll have to find a safe place for you to stay before we go after Hawk."

There was a knock at the door. Frank's eyes narrowed. He put a finger to his lips and stepped silently to the door. He peered through the tiny peephole. He wasn't surprised by what he saw. He could clearly see the scar over the man's left eye. He tiptoed back to the others.

"It's Gordon," he whispered.

There was another knock on the door, this time sounding harder, more insistent.

Joe's eyes darted around the room. They stopped at the balcony overlooking the ocean.

"There's only one other way out of here," he said in a low voice.

Fenton Hardy looked at the balcony. "Go for it," he said. "I'll try to buy you some time."

Joe glanced at Frank. His brother nodded. Joe took Jade's hand and led her out onto the balcony. He gripped the railing and looked over the edge. There was another balcony on the next floor down. But a misstep of a few inches would send him plummeting twenty-five floors to the ground. He took a deep breath and climbed over the railing.

He eased himself down until he was hanging from the bottom of the railing. His toes just barely touched the railing of the balcony below. But he couldn't get a solid footing.

The knock on the door changed to pounding. "Just a second!" Fenton Hardy called out. "I was in the shower! I'll be right there!" He had wet his hair in the sink and was now slicking it back.

Joe pumped his legs and started to sway back and forth. He let go of the railing as he swung in toward the lower balcony. Both his feet landed solidly on the cement floor.

Jade followed Joe. He grabbed her around the waist as she dangled from the railing, and pulled her safely in.

Above them, Frank glanced back at his father. "Go ahead," Fenton urged him. "As long as

Gordon doesn't think I suspect anything, I'll be all right.''

Frank grasped the railing with both hands and vaulted into the air. He swung over and down and dropped onto the balcony below.

There was no one else there. Joe and Jade were gone. The sliding glass door that led into the dark hotel room was open, but all the lights were out. Frank poked his head inside. "Joe?" he whispered. "Where are you?"

Someone grabbed his shirt collar and yanked him through the doorway. "Gotcha!" a voice said. It was Joe.

"What's the big idea?" Frank replied. He could barely make out his brother's features in the dim light.

Joe held something up. The moonlight filtering into the room glinted off the surface. It was a heavy, glass ashtray. "If anybody but you had come through that door, they would've gotten it."

"Well, let's get out of here," Frank said, moving toward the front door. He peered around in the gloom. "Where's Jade?"

"Right behind you," came the reply.

Frank whirled around. Jade was standing behind him, a table lamp in her hands.

Frank chuckled softly.

"What's so funny?" Jade asked.

"I was just thinking," Frank answered. "Most couples wait at least a week to start throwing furniture around."

Jade glanced at Joe. "Just ignore him," Joe said. "He was born with a crippling handicap—no sense of humor." He poked his brother in the ribs with the ashtray. "Come on. Let's get out of here."

They drove away from the hotel in Jade's faded green jeep. Joe tried to persuade her to give him the keys. He didn't want her to be there when they questioned Nick Hawk, but she wouldn't budge. She insisted on driving. "It's my car, and it's my life," she stated flatly. "You never would have found his house without me," she added as she pulled over to the curb.

"We'll take it from here," Frank said. "Which house is it?"

"The white bungalow with the palm tree in the yard," she replied.

Joe looked around. In the dark, all the houses looked like white bungalows with palm trees in the yard. But only one of them had a half-dozen surfboards lined up on the front porch.

Jade started to get out of the jeep. Joe pushed her back down gently but firmly. "No," he said. "This is as far as you go. If there's any trouble, you take off as fast as this bucket of bolts will go. Understand?"

She looked up at him. "Joe, I'm responsible. If anything happens to my father . . ." Her voice trailed off.

"Getting yourself hurt isn't going to help your father," Joe pointed out.

"And standing around talking isn't going to help much, either," Frank cut in. "Take a look over there."

In the harsh glow of the porch light, Joe saw a tanned figure with long blond hair. He had a suitcase in one hand and a backpack slung over his shoulder. It was Nick Hawk.

"Looks like Nick's going on a long trip," Frank noted. "And just before the big competition, too."

"Those bags look kind of heavy," Joe said. "Let's give him a hand." He walked quickly across the street, Frank following.

Frank put his hand on his brother's shoulder. "Slow down. Stay cool. He doesn't know who we are. We can take him by surprise."

Nick Hawk was throwing the suitcase and the backpack into the trunk of his car when Frank and Joe strolled up behind him. "Going on a trip?" Frank asked casually.

Hawk spun around. There was a switchblade in his hand. Frank could see that he was wound up tight. The blond surfer sized up the two brothers. "You guys don't work for Catlin," he said mostly to himself. "And you sure aren't cops. Who are you? What do you want?"

"We want some answers," Joe snapped. "And we don't have time to play around. So if you're going to use that blade, make your move now. I'd love an excuse to break your arm.''

Hawk's arm dropped to his side. ''I can't take much more of this,'' he said wearily. ''You're the two guys that have been hanging around with Jade, aren't you?''

Frank nodded.

''I saw you once and Connie told me about you,'' the blond surfer continued.

''You mentioned the name Catlin earlier,'' Frank said. ''Do you know Thomas Catlin?''

''Not personally,'' Hawk replied. ''He controls half the bookies on the island, and I owe money to most of them.''

''So that means you were in debt to Catlin,'' Joe said.

Hawk nodded. ''He sent one of his trained gorillas to tell me I could pay off the debt with one little job. All I had to do was make sure Jade didn't compete at the Banzai Pipeline.''

''So you tried to kill her just to pay off a gangster?'' Joe burst out.

The surfer shook his head. ''I just wanted to scare her off. I'd never kill her.''

''The runaway surfboard at Waikiki and the shooting at Waimea,'' Frank said. ''That was you, right?''

Nick Hawk stared at the ground. ''I was desperate. These guys play rough, and they play for keeps. But after I found out I almost shot Connie, I just couldn't go through with it. So I sent word to Catlin that I would find some other way to pay him back.''

"Now you're leaving town before his goons come knocking on your door,'' Joe said.

Hawk looked at him. "I got a phone call a little while ago. It was Thomas Catlin himself. He told me the debt wouldn't be paid until Jade was dead—or I was.''

"Did he say anything else?'' Frank prodded. "Anything about Kevin Roberts?''

"Jade's father?'' Hawk replied. He shook his head. "No, nothing about him. But he did say something weird.''

"What was that?'' Frank asked.

"Catlin said *his* daughter had been waiting a long time for this, but Catlin doesn't have any kids.''

Joe looked at the surfer. "So what are you going to do now? Run away?''

Nick Hawk shook his head slowly. "I was— but I guess I owe Jade more than that. Maybe it's time I told the police what really went down.''

"Not yet,'' Frank said. "Not until Jade and her father are safe.''

"What did Nick say?'' Jade asked when Frank and Joe got back to the jeep. "Anything that'll help?''

"We don't know yet,'' Joe answered vaguely. He didn't think it would help Jade to hear proof of Catlin's grisly intentions. "We still don't have all the pieces."

Frank yawned in the backseat. "We're not going to find any of them tonight. We need to find a place to get a few hours' sleep."

"We can go to Al Kealoha's house," Jade suggested. "I know we can trust him."

"Sounds good to me," Joe said. "Let's go."

"Stop at the gas station up ahead on the right," Frank said. "I want to call the hotel and make sure Dad's all right."

The telephone rang a few times before someone answered. "Hotel operator," a voice said.

"Give me room twenty-five-fifteen, please," Frank said.

"One moment," came the reply.

There was a strange clicking and humming on the line. Frank didn't know if it was a problem with the pay phone or the hotel switchboard. Finally, he heard his father's voice. "Hello?" Fenton said. "Who is this?"

"It's me," Frank said.

"Frank?" Fenton replied. "Are you all right?"

"Everybody's fine," Frank assured him. "We're going—"

"Don't tell me where you are or where you're going," his father cut in. "There may be a tap on this line."

As soon as Frank hung up, the pay phone rang. He stared at it for a moment. It kept ringing. He picked it up.

"I hope you get a good night's rest," a voice murmured in the receiver. It sounded like a man with ice water in his veins. It sounded like Pete Gordon. "Because tomorrow morning at eight o'clock sharp you're going to deliver the girl to me at Sand Island Park."

"What if we don't show?" Frank snapped. "What can you do about it?"

"We can kill Kevin Roberts," came the cold reply. "Very slowly—and *very* painfully."

Chapter

13

FRANK DIDN'T SAY ANYTHING about Gordon's threat when he got back in the jeep. He wanted to talk to Joe alone before telling Jade. He finally got his chance when they got to Al Kealoha's house.

"You guys don't mind waiting here a minute, do you?" Jade asked. "Let me just talk to Al alone first and make sure it's all right."

"No problem," Frank replied. "Take your time." After she was gone, he turned to his brother and said, "We've got a problem. We're running out of time."

"So what's our next move?" Joe asked after Frank told him about the phone call.

Frank looked at his watch. "I don't know—

but we've only got about eight hours to come up with something.''

Jade waved to Frank and Joe from the front porch of the house. They got out of the jeep and joined her.

Al Kealoha was standing in the doorway. The big Hawaiian surfer studied the Hardys for a moment. "Jade tells me you guys saved her life," he finally said. "I also saw what you did for Connie after that wipeout at Waimea. You can stay here as long as you want. Anything you need, just ask.''

They followed him inside. Joe looked around and saw electronic equipment everywhere. Televisions, radios, videocassette recorders, even a couple of microwave ovens.

"How about a stereo?" he asked.

Al Kealoha smiled. "Don't get the wrong idea. This stuff didn't fall off a truck. Most of them are broken. Like this TV here. I buy it cheap, fix it up, and sell it. Surfing's my life, but it doesn't pay the rent.''

Joe picked up a remote control for a garage door opener. "This isn't worth much all by itself.''

"You'd be surprised," Kealoha replied. "You can change the radio frequency so that it works with almost any garage door opener.''

Frank was inspecting a digital clock that showed the time as 88:88. He looked up at the Hawaiian. "What did you say?''

"I said you can change the radio frequency so—"

"That's what I thought you said," Frank cut in. "You wouldn't happen to have an old radar detector around here, would you?"

"I had a couple," Kealoha said. "But they go fast. Maybe there's still one around somewhere."

The Hawaiian poked around inside a few cardboard boxes. "Got one," he finally said, holding up a small, black object.

"What are you going to do with it?" Jade asked.

"I'll tell you in the morning," Frank said. "But right now, you should get some sleep. I have a feeling tomorrow's going to be a long day."

It was still pitch black out when Joe woke up. He hadn't meant to fall asleep at all. He had dozed off in a chair while his brother and Al Kealoha puttered around with the insides of the garage door remote control and the radar detector. He glanced at a clock on the table. He thought he must still be asleep. According to the clock, the time was 88:88.

"What time is it?" he asked groggily.

Frank looked at his watch. "A little after two."

"How much longer?" Joe wanted to know.

"Almost got it," Frank replied. He took the back-plate from the remote control and screwed it back in place. "Okay, Al—ready?"

"Go ahead," came the reply. "Hit the switch."

Frank aimed the remote control at the radar detector on the workbench across the room. He pressed the wide, rectangular button on the top. "Take that," he whispered.

The tiny red light on the radar detector winked on. Frank watched the numbers climb in the LED readout next to the indicator light: 2—3—4—5. The display held steady at 5. Frank moved the remote control slightly to one side. The numbers started to fall. He waved it back, and they rose again. He took his thumb off the button, and the red light on the radar detector winked off.

"It works!" he shouted.

Joe put a finger to his lips. "Shhh! You'll wake up Jade!"

"It works!" Frank whispered excitedly. "You know what this means?"

The big Hawaiian smiled sleepily. "Yeah, it means we can go to bed now."

Frank aimed the remote control and pushed the button again. The light on the radar detector glowed red. "It also means we now have a radio homing device."

The next time Joe woke up it was because the sun was shining in his eyes. He sat up and squinted out the window. It looked like it was going to be another perfect day in paradise. Then he remembered they had an appointment, and suddenly the sun didn't seem so warm and bright anymore.

Al Kealoha was fast asleep in another chair. Frank was curled up on the couch, eyes shut tight. Joe shook his brother's shoulder. "Come on," he said. He grabbed Frank's wrist and checked the watch strapped to it. "It's six-thirty. We've got to roll."

The bedroom door swung open, and Jade shuffled out. "What's going on?" she asked.

Joe looked over at her. He didn't have the heart to tell her, but he didn't have the stomach to lie either. "Just give us a few more hours," he said. "Then I'll explain everything. Okay?"

She frowned. "Do I have any choice?"

"Not really," Frank mumbled as he got up from the couch. He picked up the modified remote control and the radar detector and grabbed a roll of black electrical tape off the workbench.

"Just a few more hours," Joe repeated as they headed out the door.

"Where are you going without a car?" Jade called out.

Joe gave her a sheepish grin and held up a set of car keys.

"How'd you get those?" she demanded.

"I kind of borrowed them from your purse while you were sleeping," he told her.

As the Hardys drove away in the jeep, Joe watched Jade in the rearview mirror. She was standing in the doorway, hands on her hips. She looked beautiful. He hoped he'd get a chance to see her again. Reluctantly he shifted his gaze to the road ahead. They had a job to do, but first he had to make sure they got there in one piece.

He glanced at his brother sitting in the passenger seat next to him. "What do you think Gordon will do when he finds out we didn't bring Jade?"

"That's my problem," Frank said. He was busy wrapping electrical tape around the garage door remote control. "He's not even going to see you."

Frank wound the tape tightly over the wide button, making sure it was pressed down firmly. He kept the tape clear of the front end of the unit so it wouldn't interfere with the signal. After he was satisfied that the tape would prevent the button from popping up, he tore a few more long strips off the roll. He stuck them on the remote control unit, but he didn't wind them around it. Instead he left them dangling down like long, black spider legs.

"There's the entrance to the park," Joe said. "Are you ready?"

Frank switched on the radar detector and aimed the remote control unit at it. The red light glowed and the numbers crawled upward. He checked his watch. It was seven-fifteen. "Ready as I'll ever be," he answered grimly.

Joe drove into the empty parking lot. "There's only one thing wrong with this plan," he said.

Frank nodded. "We don't know where Gordon will park." He looked around the parking lot. On one side, it was bordered by a small, open field. On the other, there were bushes and trees crowding in close to the pavement.

Frank pointed toward the bushes. "Park over on that side."

Joe backed into a space, and they got out of the jeep. Joe walked over to the bushes. "These will give me plenty of cover—*if* Gordon parks on this side, too."

Frank shook his head. "Gordon won't park here. He's cautious. He'll suspect a trap." Frank gestured toward the field. "He'll pull in over there."

"But there's no place to hide over there," Joe protested.

"Sure there is," Frank replied. He pointed at a large garbage can, sitting alone in the clearing. "Right there."

Joe glanced at his brother. "Why do I always let *you* come up with the plans?" he muttered.

"You don't have to get *in* it," Frank said. "Just crouch down behind it. And don't forget this." He handed Joe the remote control wrapped in electrical tape.

Joe had barely gotten into position when a black van rolled into the parking lot. Frank checked his watch again. It was only seven-thirty. Gordon had shown up early, too.

Frank leaned against the hood of the jeep and

waited. The van paused in the entrance, and then slowly angled over to the far side of the lot, next to the clearing. A faint smile passed over Frank's lips.

Pete Gordon stepped out of the van. He glanced over at Frank. Then he turned around slowly, surveying the entire area. Finally his cold gaze returned to the jeep. He took a few steps forward to get a better look. "Where's your brother?" he asked.

Joe watched the rogue FBI agent step away from the van. It was time to make his move. He edged out from behind the garbage can and darted over to the van.

Frank kept his eyes on Gordon. "He couldn't make it," he said coolly. "He had other plans."

Gordon came closer. "Where's the girl?"

Frank shrugged. "She couldn't make it, either."

Joe slid under the side of the van and slapped the remote control unit onto its underside, using the long strips of tape to hold it in place. Then he quietly sneaked back to his hiding spot.

"You just signed Kevin Roberts's death warrant," Gordon growled.

Frank looked him right in the eye. "I don't think so. If you wanted to kill him, he'd be dead already."

The agent glared at him. "I'll give you two hours to change your mind. If you're not back here with the girl by then, the old man dies."

"I don't know if I could even *find* her in two

hours," Frank replied. "My brother took off with her. I don't know where they are."

"Six hours, then," Gordon hissed. "No more. Tell the girl. Let her decide."

He spun around and strode back to the van. He opened the door and paused. He was looking at the open field. Had he seen something? Frank couldn't tell.

Suddenly Gordon whirled around and pointed a gun right at Frank. There was a fat silencer on the end of the barrel. One side of Gordon's mouth curled up in a menacing sneer. "Sorry, kid," he called out. "I just can't trust you."

Chapter

14

THERE WAS A SOFT *thwump* and then a loud *blam*—right beside Frank's foot. The sudden noise made him jump. He spun around and saw the right front tire in shreds.

Gordon was laughing as he got back in the van. He pulled up next to Frank and leaned out the window. "Looks like you've got a flat tire," he said. "I hope you weren't planning on following me or anything like that." He laughed again and drove away.

As soon as the van was gone, Joe raced across the parking lot to inspect the damage. Frank was already unbolting the spare tire with a lug wrench. Joe grabbed the jack and stuck it under the front bumper. By the time Frank had the spare off its mounting, Joe already had the front end jacked up.

Two minutes later, they were ready to roll again. "We make a pretty good pit crew," Joe said as he cranked up the engine. "All we need now is a good race car."

Frank switched on the radar detector. He looked at the digital display and frowned. "Looks like we're going to need one if we want to catch Gordon. He's too far away. I'm not getting any signal."

"Hold on," Joe replied. "I'll get a signal." He slammed his foot down on the gas pedal and the jeep swerved out of the parking lot.

Joe peered up the road. There was no sign of the black van. "He must have turned off somewhere," he said.

"The only question is, where," Frank replied.

Joe shrugged his shoulders. "One street's as good as another." He turned the wheel suddenly, and the jeep veered off onto another street. There was still no sign of the van. Joe pressed down on the gas pedal, and the old jeep picked up speed.

Frank glanced over at the speedometer. It was edging past 50 MPH.

"Don't worry," Joe said. "You'll pick up any speed traps with the radar detector."

"We altered the frequency on both units," Frank replied. "This will only register the signal from the remote control."

"So are you getting anything yet?" Joe asked.

Frank shook his head. "Nothing."

Joe made another sharp turn.

"Where are you going now?" his brother asked.

"To the Pali Highway," Joe responded. "Gordon picked the opposite side of the parking lot, why not the other side of the island, too?"

Frank thought about it for a moment and nodded. "It's possible. Anyway, we'll cover more ground that way. If we get within a half mile of that garage door opener, this thing should light up like a Christmas tree."

The jeep chugged up the steep highway and over the mountain pass. Joe kept his eyes on the road ahead, and Frank kept his on the radar detector. There was no sign of the black van and no sign of life from the little black box in Frank's lap.

They drove down into the town of Kailua. Frank studied his brother. There was fierce determination in Joe's eyes, but Frank knew there was almost no hope of finding the renegade FBI agent now.

Frank turned away and gazed out at the town.

"What's that?" Joe asked excitedly.

"What's what?" Frank replied.

"The box!" Joe exclaimed. "The light's on!"

Frank picked up the radar detector. Sure enough, the red light was glowing. The digital readout registered 2—3—2—1. Then it was gone, and the light blinked off.

"Go back!" Frank shouted.

Joe slammed on the brakes and threw the jeep into reverse. He backed up to a side street they had just passed, and the red indicator light winked on again.

"Go down this way," Frank gestured.

They followed the winding road. As they slowly went downhill, the glowing numbers on the front of the black box climbed. The road ended at an ornate iron gate. Through the gate Joe could see a huge mansion at the end of a long driveway. Beyond that was the ocean.

Frank scanned the area. The compound appeared to be surrounded on three sides by a high brick wall. He nudged Joe and pointed to the top of the wall. Video surveillance cameras, silently rotating back and forth, cast a sleepless eye over the entire perimeter.

"This must be the place," Joe said.

Frank nodded. "Now all we have to do is figure out how to get in and out without being seen."

Joe shrugged. "I always wanted to be on television."

"How about on a game show where they shoot the losers?" Frank replied.

"Okay," Joe said. "Then we can approach it from the beach. It doesn't look like there are any cameras down there."

Frank shook his head. "They'd see us coming a mile away."

"Maybe," Joe said. "But maybe a few *surfers* wouldn't attract too much attention."

Back at Al Kealoha's house, Jade was sitting on the front steps, waiting for them. Her elbows were on her knees, her chin resting in her hands. Joe had hoped to keep her out of danger, but now they needed her help to save her father.

Joe got out of the jeep and walked up to her. He reached down, took her hand, and pulled her to her feet. "Come on," he said. "Let's go get your father."

Jade looked into his eyes. "Really?" she said hopefully. "You know where he is?"

Joe nodded silently.

"Let's talk about it inside," Frank said. "We're going to need Al's help, too—and anybody else's."

After Frank and Joe laid out their plan, Al got out a map of Kailua. "It's not going to be easy," he said, pointing to the cove where the mansion was located. "There's a small beach—but it's cut off by cliffs on both sides. We'll have to hit the water about a half mile away and paddle the rest of the way."

"Won't they see us coming?" Jade asked.

"That's why we need as many surfers as we can get," Frank answered.

Joe smiled. "We're just a bunch of surf punks looking for a good beach for a party."

The big Hawaiian ran his hand through his

dark, curly hair. "Kind of short notice. How much time do we have?"

Frank checked his watch. "Three hours at the outside."

Kealoha frowned. "Almost everybody's up on the north shore. That's a long drive. The only person in town today is Connie. This is one of the days she works as a waitress."

Jade shook her head. "I don't want to drag Connie into this."

"You don't have any choice," a voice called out.

Frank whirled and saw Connie Lo standing in the doorway. "How did you know we were here?" he asked.

Connie shrugged. "I didn't. Nick told me everything last night. I wanted to help, and I figured Al would, too. Looks like I figured right."

Joe didn't give Jade a chance to argue. "And you're just in time for a little surprise beach party," he said to Connie. "Come on in. We were just about to get out the paper hats and the noisemakers."

On a lonely stretch of windswept beach, they unloaded five surfboards from Jade's jeep and Connie's car. Joe glanced over at Frank and grinned.

Frank shot him a look. "What are you smirking about?"

"I was just thinking," Joe said, his grin widening. "None of those old beach movies was ever anything like this."

"Yeah," Frank replied. "The stars never did any real surfing."

"Just follow my lead," Jade said, "and don't try anything fancy."

"You mean I don't get to hang ten?" Joe said in mock disappointment.

"Get with the program," Connie said. "*Nobody* does that anymore."

They waded out into the water and paddled the surfboards out past a rocky point. On the other side of the point, Joe spotted the mansion nestled in the small cove. He let out a sigh of relief—the beach was deserted. There wasn't a guard or video camera in sight.

Jade paddled over next to him. "Ready to ride your first wave?" she asked.

"Sure," Joe said. "Do we get to shoot the tube?"

"*You* don't even get to do a bottom turn," she answered. "Just wait for the wave and ride it straight in. I'll be right next to you all the way."

Joe could see Frank between the other two surfers. He guessed his brother was probably getting the same instructions.

"Get ready," Jade said. She pointed the board toward the shore. Joe did the same. He glanced over at her. She was intently watching the ocean behind them. "When I give the word," she said, "start paddling like crazy."

Joe could feel the water swelling up under the surfboard.

"Now!" Jade shouted. Her hands splashed into the water, and she shot ahead of him.

Joe felt the building wave rolling in beneath him. He suddenly realized that it was going to roll right on by him unless he got moving. He put on a burst of speed, his arms windmilling through the water. He managed to catch up with Jade just as she stopped paddling.

The next moment she was on her feet. "Come on," she urged. "This is it!"

The wave was just starting to crest as Joe tried to stand. He almost lost his balance, his arms waving around crazily. But then he remembered what Jade had said on that first day. Get the *feel* of it, he reminded himself. He stopped trying to fight the surfboard. He loosened up and let his body flow with it. He was surfing.

His growing smile of satisfaction froze on his lips when he looked toward shore, though. A man ran out of the mansion toward the beach. In one hand he had what looked like a walkie-talkie.

If he had any doubts about what the guy held in his other hand, they were shattered by the sharp crack of gunfire.

Chapter

15

FRANK KNEW that they would run into some kind of reception committee, but he didn't expect them to just start shooting wildly. Luckily, there was only one guard, and he had only fired a warning shot.

Al Kealoha reached the shore first, Connie Lo a moment later. By the time Frank hit the beach, the guard already had the two surfers covered.

Frank could tell the man was nervous. He wasn't prepared for an invasion of surfers. He spotted Frank and started waving the gun around, not sure where to point it.

Frank approached him, smiling and holding his hands up. "What's the problem?"

The guard turned toward him. "Hold it, right there!" he barked.

"Hold what?" the big Hawaiian asked. "There's no law against surfing, is there?"

"And this is a public beach, right?" Connie Lo added.

The man eyed them nervously. "What are you doing here?" he asked sharply.

"Relax," a voice from behind him answered. "We're just here for a little beach party."

The guard whirled around to face the new threat. It was Joe.

"What's going on down there?" a voice crackled over the walkie-talkie in the guard's hand. He stared down at it blankly for a second.

A second was all Frank needed. He grabbed the guard's other arm from behind and yanked it back. He squeezed the wrist and twisted it sharply. The man cried out as he lost his grip on the gun.

The two-way radio squawked again. "What's going on?" it blared. Joe's fist smashed into the guard's face before he could respond. He fell to his knees. Frank let go of his arm, and the man pitched face first into the sand, out cold.

"What's the trouble?" the radio crackled.

Joe bent down and pried it out of the guard's hand. "No trouble," he answered. "Everything's under control."

Frank picked up the gun and handed it to Al Kealoha. Looking at the three surfers, he said, "You guys stay here. Joe and I will go in alone."

"Wait a minute," Jade said. "It's my father in there. I should go."

Joe shook his head. "Too risky." He looked deep into her green eyes. "If he's in there, we'll get him out. I promise."

They reached the house without running into anybody else. The back door was wide open. The guard hadn't bothered to close it in his rush to intercept the surfers. Frank and Joe glanced at each other.

"It could be a trap," Frank said.

Joe shrugged. "There's only one way to find out." He walked through the doorway, and his brother followed.

Joe moved quietly through the kitchen and a large formal dining room. He stopped suddenly when his shoes hit the marble floor of the front hall, and Frank almost bumped into him. The sound of their footsteps echoed in the large entranceway.

"Looks like crime pays pretty well for some guys," Joe said in a low voice.

The place seemed deserted. Joe cocked his head to one side. He thought he heard a faint noise upstairs. He motioned to a wide, curved stairway, and Frank nodded. He had heard it, too.

"Vinnie!" a voice suddenly blared out right next to Joe. "Where are you? What's going on?"

Joe looked down at the forgotten walkie-talkie he had been carrying the whole time. He held it

close to his mouth and pushed the talk button.
"Ah—I'm still down on the beach. You should
come down, too. The water's great!"

"What?" came the startled reply. Joe thought
it sounded like stereo. He heard it coming from
the two-way radio and from the second floor.

"Never mind," he muttered as he switched
off the unit and set it down on a table.

They climbed the stairs slowly, silently. At the
top was a long hallway. "This place has more
bedrooms than a cheap motel," Joe whispered.
"Where do we start?"

"At the beginning," Frank replied. He tried
the door to the first room on his right. It was
unlocked. He pushed it open and slipped into the
room.

Joe was about to follow him when a man suddenly burst out of a doorway down the hall. He
was clutching a short, ugly-looking submachine
gun, and it was leveled at Joe.

"You're not Vinnie," he growled.

Joe threw his hands up in the air. "I could
change my name if it would make you happy,"
he ventured as he moved away from the door.

"Shut up!" the man snapped. "Who are you?
And where's Vinnie?"

Joe started to back slowly toward the stairs.
"Come on, I'll show you where he is."

The man moved toward him warily, his eyes
riveted on Joe, watching his every move. He

didn't notice the partially open door as he passed it. "If you've done anything to Vinnie, I'll—"

He never finished the sentence because Frank had smashed a flowerpot over his head.

Joe whirled around to see his brother standing over the man's limp body, the shattered remains of the pot still clutched in Frank's hands.

He walked down the hall to the door the man had left open. Joe poked his head inside and found Jade's father gagged and tied up in a chair.

"Where's Jade?" Kevin Roberts blurted out as soon as Joe took off the gag. "Is she all right?"

"She's fine," Joe assured him. "She's down on the beach waiting for you."

"Where is everybody?" Frank asked. "We only ran into two of Catlin's goons. There must be more than that."

"Catlin and Gordon left with three or four men about two hours ago," Roberts said. "I think they were going to set up some kind of ambush."

Frank looked at his watch. "For us, I think."

"Gee, I'm sorry we had to spoil all their fun by not showing up," Joe said.

He looked at Jade's father. "What's going on here, anyway? If Thomas Catlin wanted you dead, how come you're still alive? And why are they after Jade? She didn't do anything."

"I didn't understand it myself until this morning," Kevin Roberts said. "That's when Catlin told me about his daughter. She was just a little older than Jade.''

"Was?" Frank said.

"She died in a car accident," Roberts explained, "just before Catlin was released from prison. She was only sixteen."

"So what's that got to do with you and Jade?" Joe asked. "It wasn't your fault."

"Try telling that to Thomas Catlin," Roberts replied grimly. "He thinks that if he hadn't been in jail while she was growing up, his daughter would still be alive."

"And since you put him behind bars," Frank said, "he wants your daughter's life for his."

Kevin Roberts nodded silently.

"We better get out of here," Frank said. "By now they should have figured out we're not playing the game by their rules. They could be back any minute."

They hurried down the stairs to the front hall. Through a window they saw a long, gray limousine barreling down the driveway, followed by the black van.

"Looks like we've got company," Joe observed.

They hustled Kevin Roberts through the dining room and kitchen and out the back door. "You guys go on ahead," Joe said. "There's something I've got to do first."

Frank stopped and turned around. "I'm not going anyplace without you," he said firmly.

"There's no time to argue about it," Joe replied.

"You're right," Frank agreed. He turned to Jade's father and pointed down to the beach. "Jade's waiting down there. Her friends will get you out of here."

"What about you?" Kevin Roberts asked.

"Don't worry," Frank answered. "We know what we're doing." After Roberts left, he turned to his brother. "What are we doing?"

"We've got to buy them some time to escape," Joe said. "We need to set up a diversion."

"Got any ideas?" Frank asked.

Joe grinned. "Ever take a ride in a limo?"

The two brothers sneaked around the side of the house. The limousine and the van had just pulled up in front. The limo driver got out and opened the back door.

A tall, slim man with silver-gray hair emerged. He was dressed casually in white shorts and a shirt. Pete Gordon jumped out of the van just then, and the man barked something at him. Joe couldn't make out the words, but it was clear the man in the white shorts was unhappy about something.

"That must be Catlin," Frank whispered.

"I wish I could see the look on his face when he finds out nobody's home," Joe said.

"I'd rather be a couple miles away," Frank replied.

They waited until Catlin and his men filed into the mansion. Then they dashed over to the empty limousine. The door was unlocked. Frank opened it and was greeted by a loud electronic *beeeeep*. He froze for a second, afraid that he had just set off a car alarm. Then he realized it was only the buzzer to alert the driver that the keys were still in the ignition. He slid behind the wheel and started the engine.

As Joe opened the door on the other side, he heard muffled shouting coming from inside the house. Then he clearly heard Pete Gordon's voice. "The back door's open!" he called out. "I think they headed for the water!"

Joe ran around the limousine and bounded up the stairs to the front door. "Hey!" he shouted. "Somebody's stealing the boss's limo!" Then he dashed back to the limo and jumped in.

Frank hit the gas, and the luxury car tore down the driveway. In the rearview mirror, he could see Gordon come running out the front door—with his gun already drawn. Frank turned the steering wheel left, then right, then left again, swerving the limo from one side of the pavement to the other. He heard a shot ring out, and then another. There was a loud *thunk* as one of the bullets thudded into the trunk of the limo.

Frank kept the gas pedal all the way down, and they sped out of range.

Up ahead loomed the iron gate. It was closed.

"Oops," Joe said. "I think we forgot one minor detail."

"What's this 'we' business?" Frank replied. "This was *your* plan, remember?" He spotted a small remote control unit—like the garage door opener he had turned into a homing device—stuck to the dashboard by a strip of Velcro. He grabbed it, pointed it at the gate, and pushed the button.

The gate began to swing open slowly. But it ground to a halt at about the halfway point. Frank punched the button again. Nothing. The opening was too narrow for the wide limousine.

They were trapped.

Chapter

16

"WHAT'S WRONG?" Joe asked. He could tell there wasn't enough room for the limo to get through the gate. "Why did it stop? Why won't it open?"

"They must have cut the power back at the house!"

"Then I guess it's time for plan B," Joe said.

"Plan B? What's plan B?"

Joe jammed his left foot down on his brother's right foot, pushing the gas pedal to the floor. "Go for it!" he yelled.

The car rocketed forward and smashed into the gate. The iron bars held, but the bolts sunk into the brick wall didn't. The force of the collision snapped rusty old bolts and ripped others out of the brick mortar. The gate crashed to the ground, and the limousine rolled over it and out onto the road.

"Great driving," Joe said, grinning wildly. "Reminds me of the first time we borrowed Dad's car. Remember?"

Frank shot him a look. "Yeah." He glanced in the rearview mirror. "Uh-oh, we've got company."

Joe twisted around to peer out the back window. The black van was closing in from behind. "Think we can lose him somehow?" he asked.

"Not on this road," Frank answered. "Too many twists and turns, and this limo is too long and wide. It doesn't have any maneuverability."

"Plenty of horsepower, though," Joe remarked. "Nice comfy seats, too." He glanced over at his brother. "I bet you could crank her wide open on the highway—and still have a real smooth ride."

"Let's find out," Frank said. He turned onto the Pali Highway, heading back toward Honolulu, the black van following. Frank punched the gas pedal. The limo shot ahead, widening the gap between them and the van.

Joe was right—it had a *very* powerful engine. Frank realized that Catlin probably had had it modified. He checked out the rear window again. The van couldn't keep up. It was dwindling in the distance.

Frank knew that the road would continue to climb upward until after they passed the Nuuanu

Pali. He breathed a little easier as the van grew steadily smaller in the mirror.

Suddenly the engine began to cough. The limo lurched and hesitated, then lurched again. Their speed started to drop. What was wrong?

Frank looked at the control panel. He smacked the steering wheel with his fist and swore silently to himself. "You're not going to believe this," he said. "We're out of gas."

Joe pointed out the window. "There's a turn-off up ahead. If we're lucky, Gordon won't realize we got off the highway until we're long gone."

"Long gone where?" Frank replied. "Off a thousand-foot cliff? That's the turnoff for Nuuanu Pali!"

"Okay, so it's not the greatest choice," Joe admitted. "But it's the only one we've got."

"And if Gordon finds us?" Frank persisted.

Joe shrugged. "I don't know—grow wings and fly away?"

"Terrific," Frank muttered, but he knew his brother was right. They didn't have any choice.

They barely made it to the scenic overlook before the engine sputtered and died. They weren't alone. There was a minivan parked near the concrete observation platform. Two guys were busy taking something out of the back of the van and assembling it on the platform.

"What is that?" Joe asked.

Frank studied the metal tubes and wires. He couldn't make out what it was until one of the guys unfolded a wide and roughly triangular sheet of brightly colored material. The colors reminded him of the para-sail that had snatched Joe and Jade off Maui. But the shape told him it was something else.

"You wanted wings," he said. "There they are."

Frank and Joe hurried over to the platform. One of the guys working on the contraption looked as if he was at least thirty-five years old, but in good shape. The other one was just a kid, not much older than twelve or thirteen.

Frank realized they must be father and son. "Nice hang glider you've got there," he said. "Interesting design, too. Looks like a two-man model."

The older man looked up from his work. "That's right," he said. "That's what happens when you refuse to grow old gracefully around your kids. Pretty soon, they want to play with all your toys."

A stiff wind whipped around them. The sail flapped wildly, and the man struggled to keep the hang glider on the ground.

"Let me help you with that," Frank offered. "Joe, go around and grab the other side."

"Thanks," the man said. "There's a good wind today. We could stay up for hours—sail all the way to Waikiki if we wanted."

"I sure hope so," Joe muttered under his breath.

"Dad!" the boy called from the back of the minivan. "I think we're going to have to repack the parachute."

"Parachute?" Joe asked.

"I've never needed it yet," the man said, "but why take chances?"

"I agree one hundred percent," Frank replied. "Go help your son. We'll take care of the hang glider."

"Thanks again," the man said. "This should only take a couple of minutes."

"Take your time," Joe said. "We're not going anywhere."

The man walked back to join his son. They had their backs to the Hardys, absorbed in the job of refolding the emergency parachute.

Frank quickly checked the hang glider's rigging. "She's ready to go," he told his brother. "Are you?"

Joe shrugged. "Why not? Sometimes you just have to take a chance."

Frank smiled. "I agree one hundred percent."

Joe held the sail steady while Frank slipped into one of the two harnesses. He glanced back over his shoulder. The father and son team hadn't noticed anything yet. But beyond them Joe saw something else—a black van was pulling into the small parking lot.

He ducked under the sail. Frank was still making a few final adjustments to the harness. A large triangular frame made of metal tubing hung down from the crossbar that supported the sail. Joe knew this framework controlled the flight of the hang glider. Suspended in the harness, the pilot made the giant kite go up and down by pushing and pulling the horizontal bar at the base of this control frame.

Joe grabbed the control bar and started running, pulling Frank along in the harness.

"What are you doing?" Frank yelled. "You've got to put on your harness first!"

Joe snagged one arm through the harness. "Hope this is good enough—because here we go!"

The hang glider sailed over the edge of the cliff, but then it nosed down sharply. Joe had one hand hooked in the harness while he clutched desperately at the control bar with the other.

"Let go of the bar!" Frank shouted at him. "You're putting us into a dive!"

Joe took his hand off the control bar and clutched at the harness. Frank shoved the bar forward, and the hang glider leveled out. They caught an updraft and started to climb.

Joe looked back and saw Pete Gordon standing on the observation platform, shaking his fist at the sky.

"Remind me never to complain about airplane seats again," Joe said as he tried to squirm into the harness. It wasn't an easy task. Every time he shifted his weight, the hang glider would pitch to one side. He could see that Frank was constantly fighting the control bar to keep their flight steady.

As they sailed along, Joe thought they probably could have made it all the way to Waikiki if they hadn't gotten off to such a shaky start. But they lost too much altitude while he struggled into position. Now they were too low to catch any more updrafts, and they were gliding steadily downward.

The carpet of trees below them gradually started to break up with the intrusion of occasional houses. "We're going to have to put her down soon," Frank said. "Look for a good clearing."

Joe pointed down. "How about that big lawn over there?"

They were getting dangerously close to the treetops. "It'll have to do," Frank said grimly.

They just managed to clear the trees at the edge of the yard. Ahead there was a sprawling ranch house. And between them and the house was a large swimming pool. They touched down on the grass. But their momentum dragged them forward—right into the shallow end of the pool.

As they splashed around and untangled themselves from the hang glider, Joe looked over at Frank and said, "At least we wore the right clothes."

Frank laughed. They were still wearing the swim trunks they had borrowed from Al Kealoha. "Let's just hope whoever lives here will let a couple of pool-hoppers use the phone. We've got to make a phone call.''

Joe nodded. ''And unless these folks want a slightly used and very wet hang glider, maybe they can help us get it back to its owners.''

Two hours later they were back in the hotel suite, dressed in their own clothes. Their father was there, and so were Jade and Kevin Roberts.

''As soon as you called and told me you were all safe and gave me the location of Catlin's headquarters,'' Fenton said, ''I called the police and the FBI. A combined task force hit the place. They nabbed Catlin and four of his men just as they were trying to make their escape.''

''Does that mean we're safe now?'' Jade asked.

''It looks that way. Catlin will be behind bars for years,'' Fenton replied.

Jade looked at her father. ''Then can I surf in the Banzai Pipeline competition tomorrow?''

''After what you've been through,'' Kevin Roberts answered, ''how could I say no?''

''What about Pete Gordon?'' Frank asked. ''Did they catch him yet?''

Fenton shook his head. ''No, but it's only a matter of time.''

The next day Frank and Joe drove up to the north shore with Jade to watch her in the competition. The beach was jammed with spectators, reporters, and surfers. Some of them spotted Jade and rushed over to her.

Joe took her surfboard out of the back of the jeep. "Looks like you'll be busy signing autographs and giving interviews," he said. "I'll carry this for you."

They walked down to the beach and people crowded in around them. Frank found himself swept up in a small human wave. He got separated from Joe and Jade and tried to work his way back.

He caught a glimpse of Joe farther up the beach, holding Jade's surfboard over his head. Even though Frank couldn't see Jade through the crowd, he figured she was probably right next to Joe.

Then Frank saw someone else he recognized—a man with a scar over his left eye. He also saw the blue-gray glint of metal in the man's hand.

"Joe!" he screamed. "Jade! Get down!"

It was too late. Pete Gordon had already pushed his way through the crowd—and his gun was leveled right at Jade Roberts.

Chapter

17

AT THE SOUND of his brother's voice, Joe whirled around and spotted Gordon.

"He's got a gun!" someone screamed. The crowd backed away from the renegade FBI agent, leaving him a clear shot at both Joe and Jade.

"I should have killed you back at Diamond Head," Gordon said.

Joe glared at him. "You should have *tried*," he growled.

He hurled the surfboard at Gordon. It slammed into his chest, knocking him over. Joe's foot stomped down on the agent's hand, grinding the gun into the sand. Then he was on top of Gordon, pinning him down.

"Had enough yet?" Joe screamed. "Your boss

is already in jail! It's over! You're just too stupid to figure it out!''

Frank shoved through the crowd. He scooped up Gordon's gun and pulled Joe off the hired killer.

Gordon struggled to a sitting position. "You're the one who hasn't figured it out yet. Prison never stopped Thomas Catlin from getting what he wants. He still calls the shots even from behind bars. Lots of guys took one-way rides while Catlin was locked up before. This isn't the end of it. It won't be over until—''

"Until I'm dead," Jade cut in.

Joe turned to her. "I told you I wouldn't let anything happen to you, and I always keep my word.''

She smiled weakly. "What can you do, Joe? Hover over me twenty-four hours a day for the rest of my life? They'd just kill you, too. I can't let that happen.''

Frank looked down at Pete Gordon. The man was a sleaze and a traitor. He had sold his FBI badge to a gangster. He would go to jail, but for how long? Not long enough, Frank thought. He might even finish off this job when he got out—if Jade survived that long.

He knew Gordon was right. Catlin's goons would keep coming until Jade was dead. That gave him an idea and he stared at his brother. "I guess we'll just have to let Gordon finish the job now.''

"Say *what?*" Joe replied in disbelief.

Frank turned to the FBI agent. "What do you suppose would happen if Catlin found out you botched the job and then rolled over on him to save your own skin?"

The look on Gordon's face brought a smile to Frank's lips. "That's what I thought."

"It seems like we just got here yesterday," Frank said as they walked through the Honolulu airport. "I don't know if I'm ready to go home yet—I never even got a chance to work on my tan."

Fenton Hardy stopped at the departure gate and put down his suitcase. "At least the last few days have been uneventful," he replied. "And Thomas Catlin won't be getting much sun for a long time."

"Neither will Pete Gordon," Frank added.

"Pete Gordon won't be getting much *sleep* for a long time, either," Fenton said.

Joe was pacing the floor. "Do you really think it'll work?" he asked his brother. "Do you think Catlin will buy the story that Gordon killed Jade?"

"He only has to believe it long enough for Jade and her father to disappear," Frank reminded him. "When Catlin finds out the truth, Gordon's life in prison is going to be pretty miserable."

Frank put his hand on his brother's shoulder.

"Jade will be safe from now on," he assured him. "Relax."

Joe stopped pacing. "I guess you're right, but I'll never get to see her again."

Frank smiled. "Oh, you never know who you'll run into."

Joe looked over his shoulder to see what his brother was smiling about. He saw a familiar face across the concourse. He walked over slowly and whispered her name. "Jade?"

She smiled softly and shook her head. "Not anymore. Jade's gone—I've got a new name now."

"Where will you and your father go now?" Joe asked.

"It's best if you don't know," she said. "I shouldn't even be here. I don't know if we'll ever really be safe."

Joe reached out and took her hand. "It's over. They won't find you again."

"How can you be sure?" she asked. "They found us once—and that was after fifteen years."

"That was just dumb luck," Joe said. "If Catlin hadn't expanded his operation to Hawaii and gotten involved in illegal gambling on surfing events, they never would have noticed you."

"I guess Nick Hawk didn't help the situation much either," she added.

Joe nodded. "That's right. He didn't know it—but all his betting on Connie focused a lot of attention on *you*. Catlin got greedy. He thought he could make even more money off surfing if he fixed the competition by taking you out of it. It was only later that he realized who you were."

"He saw the picture of me and my father in the surfing magazine," Jade said.

"Right," Joe said. "His goons were carrying around copies of it to identify you."

"Flight four-forty-four for New York now boarding at gate seventeen," a voice announced over the PA system.

Joe glanced over at the boarding area. Frank tapped his watch and pointed at the gate.

"That's my flight," he said. "I have to go."

"I guess this is goodbye, then," she said.

"I guess so," Joe said, but he didn't move.

She looked up into his eyes. "Jade asked me to give you something before you go."

"You don't have to give me anyth—" Joe started to say.

She leaned over and kissed him tenderly. "I'll never forget you, Joe Hardy," she whispered. There was the glimmer of a tear in her eye.

Then she turned and walked away, fading into the crowded airport.

Joe just stood in the middle of the corridor after she was gone.

Frank came up to his brother and waved his hand in front of his face. "Are you okay?" he asked.

Joe flashed his best smile. "Sure. She's a nice

girl, but it never would have worked out between us."

Frank arched his eyebrows. "Oh? You seemed to get along pretty well."

"Get real," Joe replied. "She's a surfer."

"So?"

"So the surfing is *lousy* in Bayport."

THE HARDY BOYS CASEFILES™